CLAY

by

Alan M Kent

Published in 1991 by

AMIGO BOOKS

18 Summerhill Road, Launceston

Cornwall PL15 7DU

Telephone 0566-773330

© Amigo Books and Alan M Kent 1991

All rights reserved. No part of this publication may be reproduced, stored in a retrieval system, or transmitted in any form or by any means, electronic, mechanical, photo-copying, recording or otherwise without the prior permission of Amigo Books.

ISBN: 1-872416-01-2

Printed in the West Country by

BPCC Wheatons Ltd, Exeter.

Jacket design: Ken Sheldon

To George Frances Stedman – the real Tom

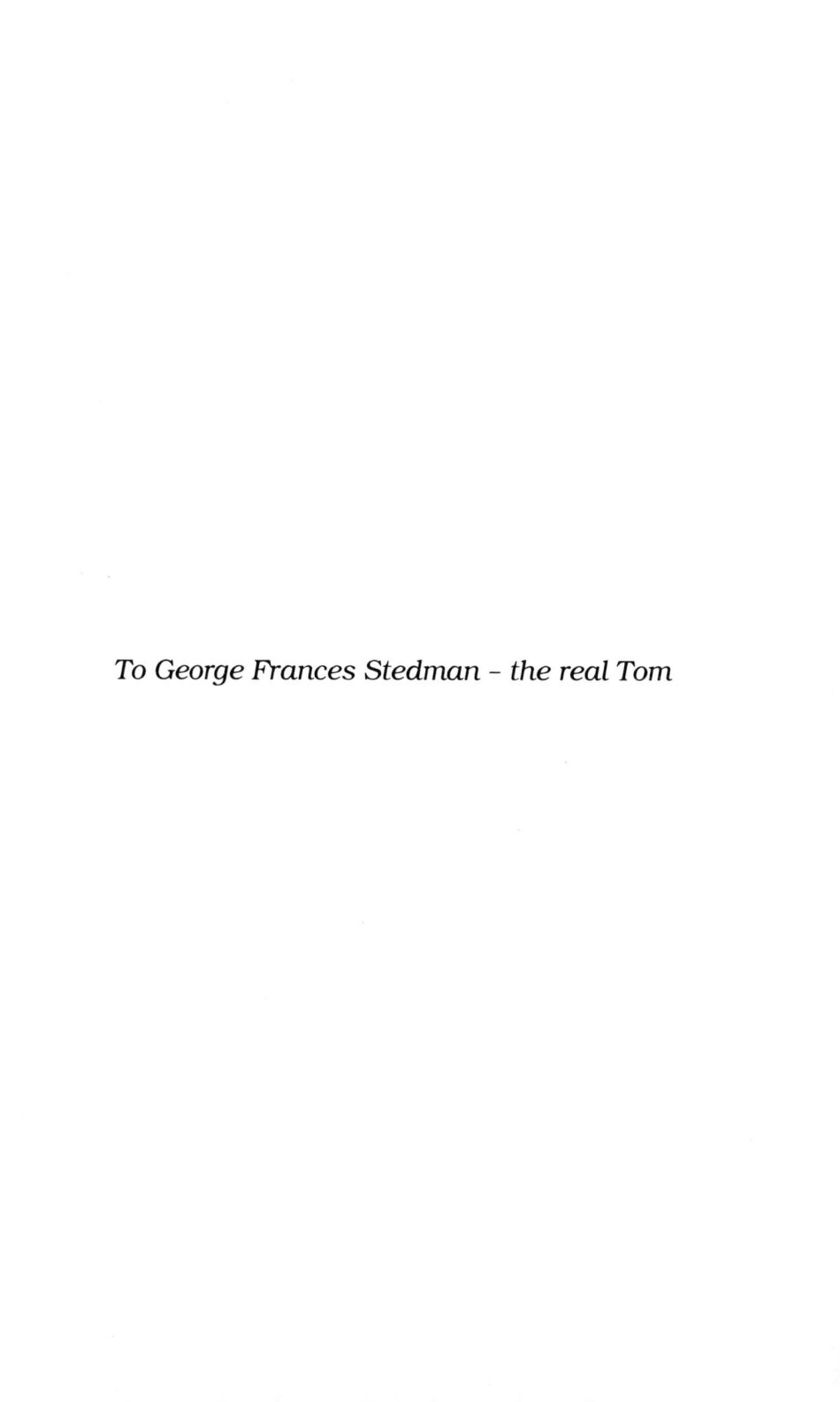

Note

The paper on which this novel is printed contains between 16 and 20 per cent china clay. The art paper used for the cover contains approximately 25 per cent.

*When we do not know the truth, we invent stories.
Stories last longer than lives. This is one of them.*

PART ONE

'As we entered St. Auste's, we were met by several carts loaded with barrels containing a white earthy substance; which on enqirey we understood to be the porcelain earth...'

Revd. Richard Warner, 1809.

OF LEGEND

BEFORE the clay – before any of it happened – there was once a Saint. Austell was his name. He lived in a bleak cell on Hensbarrow Downs, in the land they call Cornwall. One day, after performing many good deeds, baptisms and promoting the word of the Lord, he returned home, tired and weary, just as evening was falling.

Unknown to Saint Austell, the Devil was watching him, waiting to weave his evil over the moor. Until evening the day had been calm and clear, but now the Devil was summoning the powers of the earth to raise a storm.

The storm was a mighty one. The wind blew Saint Austell's hat off and carried it over the crimson, heather-clad downs. Not wanting to lose his hat, Saint Austell ran after it. But his heavy, wooden staff slowed him down, and so he pushed it upright into the peaty ground. Alas, no matter how hard he tried, he was unable to retrieve his hat. Sadly, he decided to collect his staff and return to his cell.

But by now night had fallen and the moon became obscured by dark clouds, so the poor Saint could not see where he was going while he negotiated his way over the moor. He had to abandon his search. He could regain neither the hat nor the staff.

That night, Saint Austell slept badly, wondering where his possessions might be. In the morning, when he resumed his hunt, he found that both staff and hat had turned to stone. And these stones were so large that later generations came to believe that they had in fact belonged to a giant.

One stone was given the name 'The Giant's Hat'. This stone is no longer to be found because, once upon a time – or so the story goes – some soldiers camped nearby on the downs and experienced bad weather during their stay. They remembered the legend and blamed the stone for the storms, and so the stone had to go. But Saint Austell's staff is still to be found, and it is called the Longstone.

Shortly after this happened began the time when the folk of the moor or downs – or 'Downsers' as they are more properly known – first wrote things down, and in good time a few secrets were explained. Then began the other time when those playing the dance of life on the moor became, whether they liked it or not, rainmakers...

See, Hensbarrow is a place of legend – not legends of King Arthur or any of those other airy fairy Cornish legends. Those legends are dead, but the legends on Hensbarrow live. They live in the present and can kill. They are as murderous as all those killers piled high in our crumbling prisons.

I know.

TWO years ago, around Easter time, I was on this humpback whale of a land, digging with bare hands in wet sand, wet clayey, bloody sand. It was still raining and the insides of my boots were full of grit.

They pulled her out from the sludge, quartz crystals gleaming on her hair, exquisite grains caught on the smooth downy hair above her lips, her fat belly ripe with a child, poking out from the grey purity. It was her eyelids that made me turn, though; open, staring, with grit scratching the conjunctiva. She wasn't breathing.

Legend had played its ace of spades and, as is the way with all deaths, it soon become absorbed into the greater legend...

Me – well, that's why I left; why I went the way of other Cornishmen, and escaped. Found a new dream time. And why I still keep a hold of an old toy lorry that some silly old bugger gave me.

There is another legend concerning Hensbarrow about a rain shower of blood, but let us leave that for now and think...

OF THE DIRTY BIT

THIS was the clay land. Somewhere else. This was no Cornwall. Cornwall was golden sands, azure seas and picture postcard harbours. Cornwall was a world away. A world away where things were done differently; prettier than this.

This was ugly, sad and barren. Too grim for most. Would you spend a holiday here? Someone was...

'They've spoilt it. What a shame. I didn't expect it to be so industrialised.'

'Wasted. Such a pity. Still, I suppose it's the only work people have down here...'

I heard these condescending voices as a youngster, outside the post office one summer. They knew no better. A newly-registered Ford Cortina pulled up outside the chapel and two pink-skinned men stepped out. They went inside the quaint post office with its wooden counter and stone floor to buy four choc-ices. The women inside the hot car chatted loudly.

'I don't think I could ever live here, do you Sandra? It's so dirty, dusty... and all those heaps everywhere.'

The men returned, their Fred Perry shirts escaping over their bellies.

'Choc-ices girls.'

'Thanks Don,' Sandra said, unwrapping the cold parcel.

'Mmmm... I needed that. Don...'

She wound her sun-chapped lips around the chocolate coated ice-cream.

'Yeah...'

'There's not much here.'

'I know love. You're right. It was a mistake to come out here. We'll go to Newquay this afternoon. You'll love it there. Real sand. Not the stuff they dump round here. I hear there's some good clubs just opening... We'll be able to hit the town.'

They were 'Up-Country' voices, voices that took Cornwall at a glance, like their Instamatic pictures of Polperro and Mevagissey, and all the other oh-so-pretty places that litter legendary Cornwall. They would never understand the clay. Never look under the stones; never feel the smoothness of the clay that causes this particular region to throw up its bowels so that all that had once been below is now conquered and overhead – the soil's virginity lost, its open-air status bewildering.

They sucked on ices in a world of clay.

The one word that described the clay land they had not even felt. That word was presence. No, maybe they had felt it but they had turned it around, metamorphosed presence into ugliness. I knew they were wrong, but then again the clay land had seen me acting out my fantasies of childhood upon it. It was my private world, a movie set adapted to my specific needs. It was something else to me. Something more. Something at the same time beautiful and bad, good and evil.

Old Walter, Watt they called him, wandered down the hill jackdaw-like. He knew the clay, poor bugger. Spent all his days mining it. But he knew its magic as well. Smiling, he crossed the road, admiring the visitors' car with a knowing grin on his face. He passed me by nodding. He had seen it all before.

'What, er em lost boy?' he whispered, showing his black teeth.

'No,' I answered.

They knew their way. Old Watt had never known his. Worked himself until he was bent over forwards. It was like a symbol of his toil. He carried the clay long after he stopped working. Watt was the one who was lost. A man like him was content, though, or so he would tell me. Why? A tricky one. Perhaps it was because the clay had carried him, bred him, nourished him, loved him. It would be with him when he passed away. That would not be long either.

I sat there on the gatepost of the chapel, mouthing it.

'Clay.'

'Cl-ay.'

Say it.

'Clay.'

You can only say it one way; a way which covers everything; covers your tongue in a sticky film, covers the ground with a powdery dust. Clay besieged Watt and everyone. They were trapped. Prisoners of the landscape. Slaves to an evil regime.

While I sat mouthing this, the tourists were ready to pull away. Don shoved the car into gear and revved the engine. They pulled away. I caught her last words:

'I'll be glad to get out of this dirty bit.'

'Dirty bit,' she had said. I thought I would hang on to that. And so it stayed with me...

FROM Hensbarrow you could see them all. All the dirty bits. The blots, the slurs and the slags. The pits; Dorothy, Gothers, Treviscoe, Virginia, Melbur – great blurs of sandy clay waste, almost pre-human, like shark fins or earlier, enormous triangular scales that ran down the back of the timeless dinosaur that was Hensbarrow.

This was the kind of sight that greeted you there. The land had been fossilised; and all the bones, the vertebrae, the ribs, the femurs and skulls of the earth, were flung up. They were on display like dead moths or butterflies preserved in a museum. Yet more was being discovered every minute. They were formed in piles of bones on the moor like some mass open grave.

Through them cut the road from Whitemoor – a true name if ever there was one - a sad little place, to Foxhole, another sad little place, where the holiday-makers had pulled in. The road ran chaotically across Hensbarrow Down, twisting every few yards, embroidered with tallish hedgerows laden with sleeping urt plants. Following it, you watched the road fall, as if off the edge of the world. This was because it ran steeply down to the centipede form of Foxhole, winding through the long yellow grasses and the just-purple heather, to the village that lay at the bottom.

Today, the hill was frosty and slippery, the cow-dung hardened on, the starlings sliding in their near hopeless pursuit of food.

On the upper stretches of the same road a cyclist of the old sturdy type could be observed, but was still some distance away. Behind him, or her – identification was difficult – the snow clouds from the Atlantic were creeping in. Great bagfulls of ice ready to be emptied on to Hensbarrow. White on white.

Hensbarrow Down, you should know, is an upland area of some considerable size north west of the town of St Austell. It is heavily riddled with the acne of the china clay industry. All the dirty bits lie within a rectangle eight miles from east to west and four miles from north to south, and it is in this rectangle that the clay is mined. The down's effect on the snow clouds was to force them upwards.

At Foxhole, in Hensbarrow's rain shadow, it was snowing heavily. Snow here, though, was never proper snow, like one sees on Christmas cards. It was more like a very cold and dry rain, falling like dandruff.

Every year Hensbarrow wishes it had hibernated. For thousands of years it never has. Perhaps one day...

THE cyclist was not moving very fast. Perhaps he had no urgency to arrive at the place he was going, though it was difficult to believe such a thing in this weather. Or maybe he was looking at the same things we all do sometimes. Or perhaps, and more likely, the wind and snow was so hellishly freezing that every turn of the pedals felt like torture. Ice was building up on his front mudguards. His dynamo was the only noise, humming slightly as the snow fell silently, as it always will.

He was whistling. On the breeze, the briefest of notes. His lips tightly pursed. The tune was an old one, from the early part of the century we are in now. An old mining ballad. He was cycling on the Old Pound to Whitemoor road. Old Pound was another sad little place, a hamlet of about ten characters, each of whom knew that the best policy was to stay indoors in these conditions.

Now, that road is gone.

It was swallowed up by Longstone's pit in an expansion programme. But in 1966 the road was there, and a cyclist was passing along it. It was three weeks into January, a Thursday to be exact; 'Guardian' day, as folk around St Austell say; the day when the local newspaper is delivered. The only contact with the outside world.

He was travelling slowly because his gear lever had jammed inexplicably and he was stuck in first gear, unable to build up any speed or momentum. He was dressed colourfully. Loudly you could say, but then these were his working clothes. He wore canary-like oilers with a beret, or as the Cornish say, a tam, rammed solidly on his head. Inside this he wore a woollen, scratchy, black donkey jacket. On his feet a pair of clay-smudged, slightly too large, steel toe-capped boots.

There was something strange however. At first it was difficult to ascertain the rider's sex because he was on a lady's bicycle, without the upper crossbar, so that there was an awkward tubular triangle below his groin. The bike was black also. With his yellow oilskins on, he looked vaguely bee-like, but then this was winter, and what would a bee be doing out here? Perhaps there really was honey to be found somewhere on the clay land.

Let's suck it and see...

IN THE basket in front of him sat a canvas bag smeared in oil, grease and pasty crumbs, holding his crib-tin and a flask – all consumed earlier in the morning. No-one could have guessed this man was angry, at least not from his whistling and manner. Yet he was. The weather was one reason for his anger. Another was the installation of automatic monitor hoses at Longstone's Pit that day. The technology had confused him. Yet a third reason was his gear levers. He played with them again but they were unresponsive.

The rider had left Longstone's, what, ten minutes ago maybe. That was all it took from there. A check of his leather-strapped watch under his gloves told him he was a little later than usual. He had finished morning shift until tomorrow. Then he would drag himself out of bed at half-past four to arrive at work at five. Forenoons were a real bastard this time of year. Hell, he hoped it would not be this cold tomorrow morning. It probably would be. His knuckles blue, even before he had shut the back door.

As bike and rider came nearer, entering the dip at Old Pound where two, or is it three, cottages stand, one could mark that he was an oldish man; one, however, who had not borne too many of the scars of life. As he continued, he turned left up a slight incline to confront Blackpool Pit.

The Blackpool of Cornwall was no seaside extravaganza. There was plenty of sand but no tower or piers. Its name was intrinsically grim, and grim it was. An enormous hole in the moor, so deep it became black where the light failed to reach its bottommost recesses. It was wide. In its expansion it had eaten villages – whole. The afternoon shift was just starting down there, squelching through the mud, more dangerous when frosty since you can never tell if all the ground is solid or not. Step in the wrong place and you are under. Soon it would be dark again. The night filtering downwards making a photographic negative of the pit. Black changed to white, and white turned to black.

There is no other place in the world like a clay pit. It radiates all kinds of pictures to its workers. Sometimes of extreme beauty, as the sun in early summer turns the walls orange-red and purple when it settles down for the night. Now it was an extreme place, full of violent and hostile encounters. A bastard to work in. And everywhere clay. Tacky, sticky, runny, over-powering, blinding. It felt like it was in your tea, in your crib, in the air, in your hair, in your pubes. No fun at all. And no arty-farty substance.

The snow was falling heavier, drifting in over Longstone's' tip. The cyclist could see it falling in sheets down Trewoon way, off the downs. No longer just finger-printing the road. Now it fell in lumps. White spittle collecting and coagulating. Ice freezing in the ridges of the tyres of the cycle. A good thing he was nearly home.

He pushed the pedals down once more, which carried him over the ridge and down the path to his granite stone cottage at Noppies. It stood on the very edge of the pit, where the worms found the chilly air and where the sponge layers of the embarrassed earth were exposed to the rain, the wind and now the snow.

The cottage was trapped between this and Blackpool's burrow – burrow is what the Cornish call a waste tip. Clay lay in front of him and behind him, below him and above him. After placing his cycle inside one of the numerous shanty town-like outhouses, he unlocked the back door, flung off his boots and changed into some clean clothes. Nothing like the smell of clean linen.

Some tea. Filling the kettle with water, he gazed out through the window just above the porcelain sink. There was a hairline crack in the sink where he had dropped a pan the other day. The sight outside made him shiver. He would bring some coal in soon. The land was white, becoming whiter still. It was impossible to stop it. The sky, pit, burrow and downs were all becoming one. He watched the kettle boil, wiped the condensation off the window and wished there were other colours to see. North Africa, a few years ago. Now, that was colourful...

Still, perhaps the spring. When the tea was well stewed he poured a cup, then sat down to rest and hibernate until four o'clock the next morning and dream...

FOR in the beginning, yes, the very beginning, before melting choc-ices and swarming tourists, before that innovative Quaker chemist, William Cookworthy, in his bombazine blazer and dusted wig, first took a shovel and pushed it with his right foot – or was it his left? - into the ground some two miles south of Tom's house.

For the old times talked of here are even before this, when the earth was still boiling, melting, burping into place. Rocks shaped by heat below. Unseen transformations beneath the surface. Then cooling, settling, re-heating, then cooling again. Elements forced together. Quartz, tourmaline and fluorite holding hands.

For all this happened long before Tom Cundy. For that was who the rider was. Long before Tom dreamt of it. Long before the dinosaurs walked over Hensbarrow – if indeed they ever did. Before the ice age. Before man was a twinkle in God's wistful eye. Before legend. Before Herodotus heard stories of Cornwall, and of men who mined there, and wrote of them in his histories. Before Phoenician traders ever visited. Long before Christ. Long before the brave saints from Wales and Ireland made the dangerous journey across the Celtic sea to label these places St Dennis and St Austell. Most of all, long before the Cornish dug.

For what is about to be told is older than time itself. Of when the earth was still hot and the only colours we can imagine are molten orange and raven black, when lightning zigzagged across the sky.

For there was no now, no then, no future. Time stood still. But at some point God must have said: 'Let there be clay'. And lo there was clay.

And from then, time on Hensbarrow began. Whether it began elsewhere is unsure. Yet from the moment a soft white rock could be dug from the ground, a past, present and future was found.

But geologists who have come to Cornwall with their hand-picks and rucksacks, and have left with samples, are inevitably atheists.

There is an adequate geological explanation of the formation of china clay or, as they prefer to call it, kaolin. The origin and mode of emplacement of granitic rocks, of which Hensbarrow is composed, is a subject of controversy between two major schools of thought; Magmatist and Transformist.

The work of God is generally not accepted as a theory. Though differing in their opinions, the majority consensus is that the granites of Hensbarrow, Bodmin Moor and Dartmoor were emplaced after the culmination of the Hercynian orogeny, at the end of the Carboniferous period, or possibly at the beginning of the Permian.

The clay itself is a result of kaolinisation, a post-joint process, although it is possible that it occurred in more than one stage. The clay is derived from the partial decomposition of feldspar, plagioclase in particular, in granite, which has become changed into a fine white powder, the other constituents, mica and quartz, remaining unaltered.

For all this happened before such a theory had been dreamt of.

Before the scholar, Richard Carew, had yomped across the moor. Before anyone had labelled Hensbarrow. And so while Bodmin Moor became famous for Jamaica Inn and Dozmary Pool, and Dartmoor sat resplendent in its mysteries and tors, and Carnmenellis and Land's End celebrated romantic tin mines and smuggler's haunts, Hensbarrow sat lonely through the ages until 1746, when Cookworthy arrived with a shovel and a pick.

The Dirty Bit came later.

WHEN Tom woke, he found the dream gone. Recalling it was impossible. It was lost to the night. So he went out to chop sticks and to try to remember it. But the rhythm of splitting the wood, the struggle, the aim, only reminded him...

OF YOUTH

I WAS remembering that January day in 1966. Then, I had been looking forward to it.

Now, it seems almost as far away as Tom's youth, and as innocent. I thought I could remember it all. I knew I had been kicking around a half-deflated football in the new back garden when it had begun to snow. My mother had called me in. She did not want me to catch a cold. So, reluctantly, I had gone inside to please her.

Inside it was all very new to me. The rooms. The windows. The floorboards. The way the ceiling was so crookedy. I had entered a fairy story somewhere along the line, but now I was unsure who I was. I had been unsure since leaving Essex a week earlier. Confused, I went upstairs, sat in the window in my new room and read from a book. Or did I draw? This was the sketch at least. Me in a window looking out.

I'll try to fill in the picture for you.

There were cases of unpacked clothes and a few cardboard boxes in the room containing some of my parents' junk. It was small but had a bay window at the bottom of my bed just long enough to sit in comfortably. Deliberately, I clouded the panes with my breath, drew some matchstick figures, then wiped them away. An easy death. The snow was building up on the window ledge. It was covering the windblown privet hedging at the front. It had already settled on the rusty shed roof.

Nothing moved.

But as I looked out, I had noticed that rider. I knew him to be old Tom cycling down to his cottage. Tom Cundy he was called and he was not really that old. It was just that old and him seemed to go together. He came to see my parents the day we moved in, just to check everything was all right and to tell us to give him a shout if we wanted anything.

'Old wispy bugger,' my father had said. 'Good as gold though.'

And there he was. The wispy bugger. Tom freewheeling down the lane, a bright light in the drabness. Good as gold. I watched Tom until the pane misted over again. The vision ended.

Downstairs, my mother was in the pantry covering some dripping and musing over our move. She shivered as she wrapped the greaseproof over the top of the bowl. She was still young,

young enough to be unsure of coming to Cornwall; more specifically to the clay mining area. My father played with Tessa, who was five and mentally handicapped. She had Down's Syndrome. She was innocent and young enough for the move not to bother her. My father, well, he was old enough; old enough to believe the move was the right one.

'He'll be all right Pat,' said my father, lifting Tessa off the slate floor. 'I mean, it's bound to be different. It's bound to be. Of course he misses his mates and everything, but it's no different here. He'll soon fit in and make new friends.'

'I know, but he's so quiet,' echoed my mother's voice in the pantry.

'I don't want him to be lonely. I'm worried for him. I mean, we're in the middle of nowhere... aren't we? ... up here. What the hell is he going to do after school? In the evenings? At the weekends? I didn't think it was quite like this.'

'Yes, it's a problem. But we'll sort it out. Please Pat, don't panic so...'

I heard their voices floating up through the spicy floorboards. I knew I was the topic of conversation. Looking out of the dusty window once more, those were the only voices I could hear. The place stank of silence. It oozed from the bracken, it flowered in the heather. It flowed in across the downs. It fell from the sky as snow.

The journey down had none of this kind of tranquillity. I had been excited. My father had gained employment in Cornwall in the clay industry, and they had decided to move down. With the new decade coming soon, and a new job, it seemed the right move.

The journey was the longest I had been on. All our possessions, furniture and junk, were being driven down, but we had come down on the train from Paddington. Travelling to Cornwall was like travelling to the ends of the earth. My father had shown me all the stations on the way, and I noticed how the names got stranger, almost magical, the nearer we got. They still lie on my tongue; Lostwithiel, Par, Bodmin, St Austell. Saint Austell was where we arrived.

The train was near empty. Not many tourists jammed into the seats in mid-January. I had been first out of the carriage on to the platform at St Austell. I noticed the old clock riddled with brown grime. The holiday posters to London. The Great Western Railway seats. The wooden ticket office and waiting room, almost of matchstick construction. The clock ticked on towards six o'clock. At least time was the same here.

We stepped outside and hired a cigarette-stinking taxi to take us up to Hensbarrow.

'Ben, you see up there. Look. See where all those white things are,' my father said, 'that's where we're going... up there.'

And so we travelled through the black to the white. The driver was from St Austell. He talked about the weather and where we were from. I sat quiet. By the time we reached our cottage at Noppies, near Old Pound, I had forgotten about the white. My mother made up a bed and I slept well.

In the morning, my room was cold. I had woken up in a dream. A dream time in which I was alone.

The picture I saw from the window blinded me. I had never seen a landscape so light that the sun in the east caused a reflection on the earth which hurt your eyes.

The sun rose across the brow of the hill, and its warmth fell on the massive hole in front of me. It reflected the rays like a vast organic radio dish. Here and there were touches of mist, smudges of ferns, brambles and heather, almost added as an afterthought by the artist to break the monotony. I could not make up my mind whether the landscape gave a Christian signal or a pagan one.

It was vast. I felt our cottage on the edge of the pit might fall in at any time, but the ground never moved. It was magical. Ethereal. Ugly. Another kingdom.

I looked at my watch and the bedside clock. The clock said nine-thirty. My watch read one a.m. Time had stopped in the night.My mother was calling me.

'Ben... come on now. Breakfast is ready. We've a lot to do today. Your father's got to sort out some things. He might need your help.'

I put on my clothes and ran downstairs to find the house empty. A new house. Suddenly it was not my home. It was someone else's.

'Who used to live here dad?'

'What... before we came?'

'Yes.'

'Well, I'm not sure because we went through an estate agent and the house was empty. But I think an old lady used to live out here... a hermit, or what's a female hermit called... yes, an old lady. Why did you ask?'

'Just wondered,' I replied, and thought of an old lady living here. Someone like my grandmother. Only older, more haggard.

The breakfast table was simple. My mother had remembered to bring a loaf, some butter and jam. The furniture and things were arriving today. All my things in the van, packed in tight and safe. I wished I could be like that. Outside it was so open. Nothing could pack you in. Hold you tight. Nothing. And so for much of the week I stayed in. I helped to unload the furniture into the cottage from the removal van, its tall sides rattling in the wind, its black square forming an absurdity on a white landscape.

The estate agent had said our house was a picturesque cottage set in rural Cornwall. Jokingly, my father said he would sue him for such a misleading description. He had not told us about the clay and how much it devastated the landscape.

Before any of the furniture could be brought in the place needed something of a clean because the old lady had died more than two years prior to our arrival and the cottage had not been inhabited since. Sand had blown in under the front door to form crunchy little piles over the floor, and where it had blown down the chimney it was blackened by soot.

The house was strangely built, like many Cornish cottages, with little steps in the strangest places, weird room configurations, and a steep narrow staircase. Additional parts of the house, like the back-kitchen, had been tacked on, as had the front porch, smelling of geraniums. The bathroom was stuck on the end of the kitchen and contained a very primitive bath. This room still smelt of warm linen.

My father planned to modernise it all. He went round the house, stopping every few steps, turning DIY problems over in his head. Now he would probably regret converting it. Everyone is looking for these sort of places now. Second homes for Yuppies. Real, multi-layered, ever-so-lovely places.

Not in clay land, however. Not in 1966. Not now even.

In the next few days we settled in and my mother made arrangements for me to start school the following Monday. I thought of this at the window, as well as the silence of the world into which I had been dropped. I was the changeling. I wished I was back in Essex. Things were all right there; ordered, cosy. I knew my place there. Cornwall scared me, and the clay already seemed to rattle its chains wherever I went.

On Friday, before dinner, I decided to take a look at the places I could see so clearly from my window. I rammed on my wellies, grabbed a coat and headed down the sand road to the pit. A sign warned not to trespass, but from what I had heard the chances of anyone seeing me were small.

My boots scrunched the snow, now quite deep and still falling. The road descended slightly at one of the side entrances to the pit, then went into a hairpin bend which took you down on to a larger plateau. I climbed on to the bank of the road and looked down. A set of Euclid dumper trucks were huddled together. I slid down the bank to cut off the bend, only finding I had to empty the sand out of my boots at the bottom. In the sand I noticed many tiny crystals of quartz and lumps of black granite. I picked up a few and threw them carelessly on to an iced pond. They skated across its surface. Bolero on frozen clay water.

This was still the outer periphery of the pit. The road was dissected by many dry gullies which made walking difficult. Between them lay rabbit droppings, some frozen hard, others squashed by heavy plant machinery. On the nearside lay a pile of rusty pipes, each about twenty foot long, their ends sealed with rubber. I looked for a stick to bang them with, but there was nothing. In the end I used a lump of granite.

The pipe had a spacious, reverberating sound. I tapped out a vague sort of tune. The melody did nothing for the area's inhabitants. Along the bench of the quarry were the dumpers. Enormous beasts, fantastical, and resplendent in lime green. You could smell them. They had their own scent. A mingling of diesel, oil, wet earth and clay. They smelt good.

I followed the lines of them, only just able to touch the top of their tyres. They were covered in a thin layer of white dust that made them feel used, real and splendid. In addition, a layer of snow covered every piece of steel it could possibly collect on. In their skips at the back ice had frozen, and at the grill of their filthy engines any water that had melted because of the heat had now re-frozen into icicles. I wanted to snap them but I didn't. They looked millions of years old, like the formations I had once seen at Cheddar caves.

The temptation to climb up the ladder and take a look in the driver's cab was, however, too much. I heaved myself off the ground. The gaps between the ladder rungs were as long as my legs, but I reached the platform and peered in. A steering wheel, some instruments, tools and a few levers. Fyffes banana stickers on the rear window. I swivelled around to go down the ladder.

'Hey! You ... Get off!' came a man's voice. 'Come on ...'

I could see a figure on top of the bank. He was dressed in black. At the bottom of the ladder, I brushed my clothes down while the man came around the bend. There was no option but to face him. Then I recognised Tom. He was walking with a stick, but only to steady and balance himself. He did not need it all the time. He reached the bottom, a tam on his head, with straggly white hair escaping at the sides and the back. He had a longish beard, albino white, which ran to the top of his donkey-jacket.

'What was you doing up there, you silly bugger?' he asked. 'Those machines are dangerous boy. You want to be careful. I'll tell 'ee that for nothing. Besides, old Cap'n Johns, he normally takes a look around here this time of day. You don't want to be caught by he do 'ee?'

'No,' I mumbled.

'Was 'ee having a look around Ben, was 'ee?'

'Yes... just seeing what was here.'

'I don't blame 'ee. 'Tis only natural. But make sure no-one sees you, that's all.'

I looked into his eyes. They were blue, as blue as the sky had been above us that day. And his face was rosy, the tiny capillaries just visible. Lay lines across his cheek and nose. The Cornish blood bursting out.

'How are 'ee getting on up there? Has father got everything going all right now?'

'Yeah,' I said. 'It's more homely now.'

'Well Ben, your father's a good sort of bloke. I'll tell 'ee that for nothing. Most of them people like you who are down from up country... well... some of them are a proper load of bigheads.'

I felt unsure of my position, and so changed the subject.

'I saw you cycling home yesterday...'

'Caw yeah, 'twas a heller be buggered. Could hardly see in front of me face. Twas the same this morning.'

Tom turned around and headed up the slope. I followed behind as best I could.

'See that down there boy. Well, that's all going tomorrow, or so Georgie Trebilcock tells me. They're blasting all that piece away over there. He reckons there's some good clay behind that. Good stuff. A good white wash in there.'

'What? They're going to blast it?'

'Yeah. Put charges in the top there. Explode them and break up the rock. I expect you'll hear it tomorrow. Then the 'ole rocks might come up and smash your windows.'

'They won't will they?'

'Might do. Never tell. Mind you 'tis a lot better than it used to be. Years ago you never knew which way the blast was going.'

'Have you always lived up here Tom?' I asked.

'Well... most of me life. All me working life that is. Before that... I come from Whitemoor way. I don't 'spect you know where that is though, not yet. Hell boy, you'me asking me some questions here.'

By now the sun was sagging over Longstone's and the two of us carried on back up the incline, our shadows stretching thin back to the edge of the pit.

'Have you always lived alone... by yourself?'

Tom paused.

'Not always,' he said, 'but nearly always...

A further pause.

'You know boy, you'me welcome to come around any time. You know where I live. I'm working afternoons for tomorrow, and the day after. You'me come in the morning if ye' like.'
I hoped that I could.
'Well boy, I'm goin' back for a bit of supper now...'
'Supper?. But I haven't had my tea yet.'
Tom looked slightly embarrassed.
'Well, now's when I have me supper...'
We were nearly back at Tom's cottage.
'What do 'ee think of it here then? Do 'ee like it?'
'It's different...'
'Eess, I 'spect 'tis. They should bloody well clean it up, shouldn't 'em... when they've finished.'
We parted.

Initially I felt like a worn rubber band, stretched between Southend-on-Sea and Hensbarrow. I still had friends back there. Deep down roots. Memories of crunching on the wet shingle on the beach, skimming stones out on the dreadnought sea. Once I had started school and met Tom the band pulled away from Southend. Soon it would be released altogether. I was always waiting for the sting of the rubber as it flicked to Cornwall. But it did not come. At least not then.

After a few weeks I could feel roots going down. Unstoppable. Almost as if I were someone else, and the dislocation began to go.

It was February. I still had chilblains and was scratching my toes. My mother was playing with Tessa. I was twelve, Tessa was a few years younger at five. It was sad. We were never properly together, not like real brother and sister.

Tessa had Down's Syndrome. That's what they call it now. They understand it better now; mental subnormality due to a chromosonal defect. In the original division, she had received three number twenty-one chromosomes instead of the usual two.

In Southend they called her a Mongol child. Always seemed to go with being a mongrel dog – sort of unwanted, a mess. It was only the people around her who were sad. They wished she had been normal. My mother accepted her better than my father. He treated her as not his own, more someone he was looking after. He never got over it really.

I could not remember the day on which they told them, but I remembered my mother taking her for the tests. It became better as I grew older. My father accepted her more. Time healing. She was better as a child. She would try to talk.

My father used to say: 'Take Tessa for a walk.'

I always caught the grief in my father's voice. But I liked taking her. We never went far. Only around the block. Climbed the tips.

She would love it up there. Come into her own. Like king of the castle. I would tell her stories. She liked that. Her greatest attribute was her affection. She was full of love, which in the main had come from our mother. When I finished a story, she would kiss me, and grin. Then she would grip my hand and drag me around the clay mountain tops with the agility of an Alpine goat.

Sometimes she went to school. Some days a man came and helped her. God, how she would scream at him, but he was a good teacher. He knew her needs. He used to say I was good for her. Once, he said Tessa had a special kind of intelligence, beyond our normal level. Said he couldn't explain it but it was there, lurking beneath the surface. It would come out one day.

My mother was a hairdresser. Her father had been a docker. I could not remember my grandfather, though I knew he was called Jack and was a good man. My mother was called Patricia but my father shortened it to Pat, which she preferred. She was the youngest of four children, the oldest a boy, the rest girls. She had been given love as well. She was her mother's favourite. I picked this up from aunts and uncles.

As a child she had been a ripe bud. Tessa was a weak little bud who my mother was trying to make ripe. I, too, had been a ripe bud. She let me go really. But I have no regrets. No chip on my shoulder. Her time with my sister was well spent. I suppose the time on my own might be one of the reasons why I began to draw. First of all, I could do it without anyone else and, secondly, for much of the time Hensbarrow was a lonely place.

School passed me by. I attended a good comprehensive in the village of St Stephen in the south. It was a china clay school full of china clay children, from the china clay villages, Treviscoe, Trethosa, Whitemoor, Foxhole, Roche, Nanpean and St Dennis. The ambitions of the pupils stretched to being Cap'ns in the clay pits, but no further. A few children looked beyond the horizon, but it seemed too far to go, and besides their root system was too deep.

I hated school apart from the art lessons, and couldn't wait to get home in the evenings, when I carried on with my discoveries on Hensbarrow, and with the mystic Tom Cundy.

Still, in geography they did teach us....

OF CHINA

Country, 3,700,000 square miles in area. Population – large. Land of bamboo forests and panda bears, laundry shops and chopsticks. Place of Cultural Revolution and green-coated workers, world of the terracotta army and paddy fields, bicycles and ornate temples. Now, land of Eastern culture rapidly becoming Westernised. Cliff Richard in Peking city. Going on a Summer Holiday in Shanghai. Levi Strauss 501 jeans in Nanchang. A new market for the multi-nationals of the West. So now, MacDonalds and the rice traders live next door to one another. Another revolution. They do say distances are getting shorter these days, though, don't they? But remember...

BEFORE the West had an influence on what occurred in the East, first the East had a say on what went on in the West. In 700AD a bright spark had the idea of using kaolin and ground china stone to produce the first delicate porcelain, which was also tough and durable.

The Chinese found kaolin some 5,000 years before the Cornish. The word kaolin comes from the mountain locality called 'Kauling' in Jiangxi province. The first samples of kaolin were brought to Europe in the eighteenth century. Suddenly there was a demand for a material to use to make this new Chinese China for the smart town houses of Bristol, Bath and Plymouth.

And where did they find kaolin? On a barren windswept Hell-on-Earth in mid-Cornwall, where they say a saint battled against the Devil; where, as legend would have it, Satan eventually claimed victory.

So, don't say that everything they teach you in school is useless.

OF A HISTORY

PARANOIA sat on my shoulder. Like I was being watched. It was a long time since I had been here. I am with Michael and Sarah. Michael is also a Downser and a friend from my days with Tom Cundy. Sarah is his wife. He met her while he was in the forces. We were all in Cornwall for a weekend break. I had a negative feeling about coming back, but Mike had wanted me to come down.

What could I say? Sarah and I hoped it would improve Mike's spirits after the 'accident' – or that's what he called it. Makes it sound better. A euphemism. People use them all the time, don't you know? But more of that later...

We arrived in Truro to spend a day shopping. I wanted to look around the men's clothes shops to buy a new sports jacket. I walked ahead of them, hacking my way through the people while Mike followed in his electric wheelchair.

We rounded the corner of Barclays Bank into Boscawan Street. Over near City Hall a brass band was playing. On the Georgian buildings of the city pigeons nodded in time with the sway of the music. People got on with their shopping. Cars rattled over the cobblestones. The drivers looked at us oddly as we crossed the zebra to the other side of the street.

Mike and Sarah knew I wanted to visit the museum. We decided to meet up, at three o'clock, for coffee. I watched them head towards the Flea Market. Mike tried too hard. They are normal, almost. Things are better for the disabled now. For a second, I visualised him in a flat cap selling boxes of matches for ha'pennies, propped up with a stick.

But he is all right. He is with his wife and she loves him.

I felt I was bound to meet someone, someone from the past. I looked up at the three spires of the cathedral, stalagmites of the city. In the haze of the afternoon they looked heavenly. I walked up Kenwyn Street, past the City Bookshop and the smelly fish shop, towards the County Museum. I wanted to read about Hensbarrow.

There was an abandoned brolly in the entrance hall of the museum. Inside, I knew there were the Egyptian remains, the Ethiopian skeletal remains of an Egyptian king. Skull like Yorick. Knobbly knees. And upstairs, on the right, the picture of

Anthony Payne, the Cornish giant who grew to the bizarre height of 7ft 8ins.

I asked the assistant if I could go upstairs to the Royal Institution library. She was young and helpful. I climbed the marble steps. They stank of disinfectant, and the passage held an air of mustiness. In the library itself I squeezed through a set of double doors. The readers glanced at me; I felt ill at ease. I hardly knew what to ask for. The woman at the desk rose.

'Can I help you?'

'Yes...' I stammered, 'Yes. I'm not a member of the institution. I'm trying to find out about a shower of blood that occurred on Hensbarrow Downs in 1664.'

'A shower of blood?'

'Yes... supposed to have fallen up there. They thought it was a warning.'

'Showers of wheat... we've had that... and it's rained fish...'

'Yeah. I know the sort of thing. Rained frogs as well, hasn't it?'

'But of blood... would you wait a minute please?'

'Sure.'

So, here was the history of Cornwall. Time bound and stored on the shelves. From one end of the room, the novelist Sir Arthur Quiller-Couch straddled the scene. Beneath him sat people reading; a student, an old man, and a woman trying to trace her family history. On the desk, a sign reading 'Pencils Only'. The librarian returned. She walked briskly. I felt she knew every word in the library.

'Try looking through here. It's a microfiche of the St Dennis parish register. But it only begins in 1668, so...'

'I'll try.'

She set up the file viewer and I ran through it. It was half-past two. Many names on there; Starkey, Crowle, Gilbert. I had half a hope that I might see one of Tom's family tree, but the hope faded as I waded through the material. I became restless.

'No good,' I said to the librarian, as if she was not trying hard enough.

This time, she returned carrying a book that looked as if it had been lucky to survive at all. The green cover was dusty, battered and mildewed. The corners of many of the pages had disintegrated over the years. She presented the book and turned over the pages.

'Be careful with this. It's due for preservation, but...'

'What is it?'

'Well, it dates from the early eighteenth century. It's something that was fashionable to produce then. A parochial history of Cornwall.

Everyone wrote histories of their counties, noting down all the interesting stories and anecdotes.'

She licked her fingers, carefully lifting each page over; the leaves were as delicate as a butterfly's wings.

'Now,' she said, 'this is what I wanted. This section here, look, on the parish of St Dennis. That might have something about it. Have a look through...'

'Who's it by?'

'Um... Kay, I think. Don't know. Have a look on the cover...'

I held back the book's cover. Yes. It was by Kay. William Kay. 'A History of Cornwall'.

I returned to the section about St Dennis. I skimmed through facts about sheep and parishioners. Then I found it. What Tom had told me about:

'Vpon these stones in the year 1664 at night rained for about an acre of ground of them, a shower of blood, which fell down in drops of the breadth of a sterling shilling which blood remained visible on these stones for many years after and on such as were carried thence and kept dry, the drops of blood were visible of a crimson colour twenty years later. After this shower of blood broke out the Great Plague, the Dutch and the French Wars, and the burning of the City of London.'

This was it. My eyes widened. I shut out the rest of the library and focused on the words. Wonderful. This was theory, about why it had happened. The reason. This land somehow was still run by the past, and its past was one of evil. In my mind I still had the story of the Saint losing. Then later, this blood shower. When it rained blood tragedies occurred. But I was convinced the tragedy could occur on two levels, the impersonal which was recorded here and the personal which was not. And that this story, this legend, like the one about the Saint and the Devil, was still somehow having an effect, as though the land were taking its revenge for the injury caused to it.

I would not have believed it myself, until... well... until, shall we say, they pulled her body out.

'Is it what you wanted?' the librarian asked.

'Yes... yes...'

'He was a bit of a scoundrel you know. Sort of had a reputation for falsifying things; making them up. Stories for the sake of stories...'

'Not this,' I said categorically, 'I know this happened.'

'How? How do you know?'

I did not want to tell her about Tom. It was his secret, so I answered: 'I just know.'

From here on, the librarian probably felt I was a bit strange.

But there had to be more. Kay had written this down in the eighteenth century, some sixty years after the actual shower. So where did he get his information? It was three o'clock when the librarian came back with an even older looking book bound in leather.

'This is slightly earlier,' she said. 'No-one has ever gone through it though... the language is so difficult. The author was only a boy, and his English was appalling. It seems he'd spoken Cornish for most of his life, and then took up the parish clerk job. The library rescued this from the remains of a fire which burnt down the church at St Dennis.'

I unclipped the cover and loosened my tie. Two initials were etched on the leather in a Gothic hand – T.T.

Mike and Sarah would have to wait. I would think up some excuse. When I opened the diary a Cornish smell grabbed me. For now, reading this was more important.

'*The Diarie of Tobias Trebilcock (Clerk to the Parishe of Saint Dennis), dated frome the Yeare of oure Lord 1662 till...*' and this was posthumously written... '*1717.*'

I scanned every page of the diary, flicking through, hoping some truth would hit me from the page. I was not really reading. This was more an admiring study of the handwriting, in a thick black ink that reeked of religion and some degree of learning. I knew that, for its time, the diary must have been a remarkable achievement, and the author an exceptional young man. I admired the long loops, the skill he must have had with the quill, places where the ink had run low, then heavier where he had re-dipped it in the well. The blotches of ink, cursed at the time, now gave the pages an authenticity and an uncanny prophecy, a story that both attracted and repelled me at the same time.

The paper was rough and textured, the sort I used to draw on as a boy, the sort schools I taught at advised should be used when lower ability kids did art. There was no clay in it. That process was a long way off. And it was not a proper diary. The pieces of paper had merely been stuck into the leather binding. They varied in size. Some felt like thin hymn-book paper. Yet within the text itself was a harmony. This boy, this sardonic wit, was talking to me through the centuries, almost addressing me personally. A diary written only for me. It was like talking to my own twin brother.

I began by reading every crafted page, but that proved too frustrating. There was just too much of other affairs, of his mother's poore health, and a lengthy recollection – seemingly almost copied down word for word – of his grandfather's mining days. There were also details of his previous parish. His training. The influence of one Cap'n Tredissick. Debris mainly. Of interest to the scholar but not me. I read on, more selectively, my heart beating wildly. The rhythm of discovery.

Then, the first entry of any significance. It was on a smaller piece of paper, Tobias's first move to Hensbarrow in the Parish of Saint Dennis, which lay adjacent to that of Saint Austell. I soaked up the words from the page. I wanted to sponge them up, pour them over my head. Drown in this old language.

It seemed a script that I knew. As if I could anticipate what would happen next. And I could make connections. The strands were there, and he was threading the needle. At first the line was tousled, and my hands were shaking. But then; they were there, the times, the days, the ages, the places, the fears and the coincidences. And so I steadied myself and pulled the thread through. Pieces of the seventeenth century were entering my mind, and these were wrestling with the more recent past. Childhood, youth and adulthood.

The text carried me away, and with it I was taking this century, my own life, and that of others. It was scary. Scary as hell. Possibilities shaping up into realities. The sickening feeling of knowing the very worst and not being able to do anything about it. I was, in those hours in the museum on that June day, a craftsman, a simple weaver, joining two pieces of cloth together from different times. And no matter how hard I tried to destroy it, de-construct it, challenge it or look for the gaps, there could no longer be any denying of it.

The pattern was identical.

TOBIAS

29th September 1664

My whole thoughts lately hath been concerned and perplexed withe a move I hath made from Camborne to the Parishe of Saint Dennis, whiche lies next to that of Saint Austelle, in mid-Cornwall. I have journeyed here to beginne vpon a position as Clerke of this Parishe from my 'Prenticeship in Camborne towne.

The Parishe of Saint Dennis is a great one, and it is with a whole hearte that I look forwarde to the infinite multiplicity of duties I shalle perform here. Indeed, for this Parishe is a farming one, albeit inconsistent and difficult for any crop to grow well here. Certainly, my hearte lifts to see a landscape not ruined by the displeasures of Tin-mining. I must be honest, and admitte to detesting all mine workings. How wonderful it is to stand and look vpon the horizon and not see some smoking stack or heap of vile waste.

However I am willing to admitte "was one mining man who did convince me to up my roots. Cap'n Tredissick first persuaded me to come here, when I saw him preach. The problem withe the Cap'n is his inconsistencies of preaching and womanising. But I am certaine that when the final grains of sand have dropped in his glasse, he wille be seen by the Lorde to be a good man. For 'Tobias,' says he, 'Go up Saint Dennis way. I knowe they do neede a Clerke up there. Tis your's, if you do want it, by the grace of God.'

I took his counsel, for I thought it but sound advice. Any perplexities I hadde are now gone, for all appears well. 'Besides,' he whispered later, 'the maids are nicer up there, they say.' And so I did beginne my position yesterday. The Reverende Brewer is a good man, though somewhat melancholy. However, he did smile this morning. And the good people here have accepted the church with open arms.

On the morrow I must go everywhither and examine new births in the Parishe. Reverende Brewer is also to show me a pagan stone vpon the moor, eastwards, for my consideration and, it appears, my abomination. It perplexes my superior somewhat; but devilish thoughts of suche stones appear to me most ill consid'red. For myself, I seek only clarity, not what many men of oure age do call superstition. My light burns low and my eyes tire. I close.

T.T.

OF PRY WYN

*Let me tell you the story, or the legend it might have become...
about identical patterns and the cycles of time.*

'GOING down Tom's,' as it came to be known within a few times of me going there, was like heading off into a different world. Tom did things differently at his place. It was a drop of magic on the edge of the pit, holding Tom the wizard, Tom the conjurer. It's difficult to explain... but he had a different kind of power.

The first time I decided to see Tom was a few days after he caught me playing on the dumpers. Tom was on night shift so I knew he would be at home. To reach Tom's cottage was not the easiest thing to do. You had to wind around a crazy labyrinth of wooden and stone sheds, still snow covered, all secured down, bricks placed on their galvanised roofs, wood in piles, frozen to death to be burnt later. In fact, there seemed to be so much wood, that Tom would never run out.

Some people collect stamps; Tom collected wood. It was propped against every possible wall, stacked in small piles next to where the chickens were kept. It tumbled over the back garden, behind the bantam coops, running in long lengths down to the pit. The wood was from elsewhere. There was no wood on Hensbarrow, and years ago it was a valuable commodity. It still was to Tom. Tom was a hoarder. He kept everything, but it was never littered, even though it might appear that way. He always knew where every bolt was, every grain of wood, right down to the number of knots in individual planks. It was as if he had a processing system inside his head. He would never have needed a Filofax. His faxing was older.

The back door was slightly open. On the worn doormat was a thin clayey dust. It seemed to be coming up through the floor, but then I saw Tom's boots tucked away around the corner; their laces carefully unpicked three holes down so he could put them on easily. The dust was from the boots. Tom was not about.

I called a few times and knocked hard on the door, but there was no reply. It was midday. He should be in. It was beginning to rain. Spots fell off the green-painted iron guttering, peppering my jacket. The clouds were coming up over Longstone's. Then I heard some movement inside. I shouted once more. Tom heard me this time and came into the back-kitchen. He invited me in.

'All right... you've come down...'

'Are you doing much?' I enquired.

'Well, not by rights. But I'm sure we'll find something to do. Always something to do... Though the old rain's coming in. I'm sorry I didn't hear 'ee. I was out the front checking me bottles...'

'Your bottles?'

'Es. Got quite a few of 'em. See...'

He led me through. In the porch were over a hundred bottles in various shapes and sizes. A wet patch was on the floor.

'That's where one of them burst open in the night.'

'What's in them?' I asked.

'Well. Sure enough 'tis wine, though 'cause I haven't labelled 'em this year, I can't tell 'ee what's in 'em to be honest.'

'You made it yourself then?'

'Awe 'es. Tis too expensive to buy these days. I love a drop of wine now and again see... but dunnee' tell any of them folk I see down chapel.'

I said I would not tell.

The strangest thing I noticed about Tom's house was how warm it was. It was much cosier than my own house. So warm, and with so many new experiences inside it. I was enthralled. We went back out to the kitchen through a modest living room with a large fire in the grate. The furniture was crammed in there. I narrowly missed banging into the sideboard. On it, in a silver ornate frame, was a picture of Tom; the hair shorter, the chin harder, the eyes brighter. He stood next to a woman. His hand was round her waist.

A few more steps and we were back in the kitchen. It smelt of potatoes – not an unpleasant smell – more a numbing out of any other smell; except for Tom. He smelt of soap and tobacco.

Tom was thinking what he could do with me. Having invited me down, Tom wanted to do something with me. But Tom never treated me as a child. Not ever, in all the time we knew one another. We talked for a while, but it was only about the new house. I asked him about the old lady who had lived up there.

'Aye,' Tom replied, 'a good woman she was...'

'Dad reckons she was a hermit.'

'Does he now? Up here we're all hermits you see. Hermit be buggered. I never thought of myself like that.'

He laughed. His wide mouth showing his yellow teeth.

'Well... I suppose you'd like to have a look around eh? See if we'en find something to do. I know what I was like at your age.'

Tom fumbled inside his pocket for a cigarette, then looked out through the kitchen window. It was not raining now; just some slight sleet coming in from the north west. He wandered out into the back kitchen. I watched him open the heavy door of the Rayburn and take out a pair of woollen socks. He put them on precisely, the corners of the sock meeting those of his foot. Then he put his boots and donkey jacket on.

We went out, Tom grabbing a bundle of keys on his way. I shivered in the open air. The landscape was greyer. The snow was stained with earth and grass.

Almost hidden among a network of sheds and outhouses running behind his cottage was one larger building right in the middle where he kept his bike. He pointed them all out.

'The tool shed's over there. Then there's the wood shed. My Homer's shed...'

'Homer's?'

'Es Homer's. Awe. I see what you mean. Well... that's bits n' pieces they don't want up work any more that I can make use of more than they can.'

He continued.

'Chicken shed... there look. Next to the tool shed is the nail shed. I know what we'en do now Ben... We'll go over to the nail shed, get some nails and put up a sign I've made for the house.'

I followed behind him, confused, our misty breath forcing itself out. Tom opened the shed door. It was a minute cavern with a galvanised steel roof, yet it was warm and dry. Upon rows and rows of shelves sat bottles and bottles of different nails, bolts, nuts and screws; specimens he had collected over the years entombed in jam-jar size bubbles. I shut the door. Now just the two of us in his nail shed. His exhibition.

The roof slanted at the other end of the shed, so we both had to crouch. Tom lent over and rummaged in a cabinet bespeckled with spiders' webs, its metal handles still shining like they had in someone's front room once. He took out six or seven nails, then put the jar back. It was marvellous in there. Bottled up. I wanted to fall asleep, spiders and all. The wood supported me and the nails held me there. I could have stayed there for ever.

But Tom ushered me out and we took the path up to his gate. It was silly. Tom had a gate and a hedge surrounding his land, marking off what was his and what was not. All his was in use. Broccoli, cabbages and potatoes were planted anywhere they could grow. Then there was the wood, which filled up everything else. The strange thing was that Tom never needed a gate or a hedge. He seemed to own all of it, the heather and the rabbits. But he would never admit to it.

The sign had been hand carved by Tom with a wood chisel. The wording was bold and forceful, the grooves painted black. I did not understand it. It was another language.

'What does it mean?' I asked.

'Tell me what you think it means,' he said, hammering the first nail through the sign and into the gatepost, the noise resounding across the quarry.

'I've no idea.'

'Well. Pry Wyn... it means white clay. I thought it would be a good name for the house. It's never had a name before see...'

It was the correct name for the house. Clay was all you could see from every window.

'It's Cornish then?'

'Yeah. Cornish. There was a chap up work talkin' 'bout how he'd learnt it, so I asked 'un.'

A second nail went in, closely followed by a third. Then he put the other nails in his pocket, took a last long drag on his cigarette, then threw the butt away. The wind carried it down through the garden, over the ridge and into the pit. We followed it, replacing the nails Tom did not use. Then we returned to the house.

'Aren't you ever afraid the house is going to fall in? It's so close to the edge...'

Tom looked at the cottage. It fitted him precisely.

'Well... it's never bothered me much. They says they ain't coming this way no more, so I think I'll be all right. If they do want to come this way, I won't mind, but they'll have to find me somewhere else. I don't want to move from here now, though. Not at my time of life.'

Both of us stood in silence for a while. I felt so young next to Tom. On the horizon you could see the white triangle of Greensplat tip, brighter than the grey clouds passing overhead. Beside it stood a stack and engine house; not that long ago since they were used, dark, black even, its stack a phallus on a breast and navel landscape.

The next moment Tom was not there. He had gone around the side of the cottage to use the outside toilet. It was sleeting heavier now. I rubbed my hands. They tingled. I felt the chilblains in my feet. To ease them I stood on my toes. Still they burned. A warm body on what seemed to be a landscape of death.

OF BLASTING

...which is an essential process in the mining of china clay, or kaolin, or as some used to say – probably around the same time as the Saint and the Devil had a tiff – Pry Wyn.

TOM came back, doing up the buttons of his working jeans. He suggested going inside for a cup of tea. I agreed. Though just as he opened the door, a dull whirring siren could be heard; the sound filtering up through the pit and across the downs. I had only related this sound to an air raid before. The noise made me shiver, but it didn't have the high pitched scream of an air raid siren. This was more of a low pitch hum. Tom recognised it instantly.

'Ah... They'm blasting that piece off today. You want to stay and watch this...'

'Okay... It'll be the first blast I'll see.'

'That's right. Now if you look over there. See everyone is making their way back up the pit. That steel thing there is the blasting hut. Three-inch steel that's made of. That's where the blasters sit and make the charge work. They'll blast at one. What's the time now?'

'Nearly one,' I answered.

The siren continued.

'By rights,' Tom said, 'we shouldn't be here. They say rocks and stones fly miles. Bloke up Dorothy was injured a few years back. Stone caught him. He was about half a mile away...'

When you are waiting for a blast it is a strange sensation. You think it is going to hurt, and so you hardly look; unless you are Tom, and then you watch without blinking. He had seen many blasts. It was past one.

'They're late,' I said.

'Yeah. Tis a bit late.'

'Has anything gone wrong?'

'Something must've. Look, there's the blasting gang. They're getting out of the shelter... That's Bert Davies's gang. I'm sure...'

I turned around, thinking the blast was going to be a non-event. A cup of warm tea was now uppermost in my mind. Then, from the pit, came silence, but I knew the blast had happened. Rocks were tumbling down the ridge, exposing the clay. I turned to watch again. Then in that half, no, more like a quarter of a second, came the sound. It ripped through the air, cracking it in two. The rest of the stone landed. The dust hung in the air.

'Bloody hell,' said Tom, 'there's two blokes under that lot...'

He scrambled down over the bank, his tam falling off as he did. I stood on the bank unbelieving. A crack had appeared in Tom's house. I felt it snapping my body also.

And let that be a lesson to 'ee, for the clay pit, as Tom so often said, is no place for a woman or chield...

The dust from the blast never seemed to settle. It hung in the air for hours afterwards; a sandstorm hovering over the pit, a black cloud over Blackpool. The spectroscopic sun had dropped. The rain had stopped.

I stood on the ridge all afternoon, observing the aftermath of the accident. It had scared me. I would dream about it for years afterwards. A man had been killed, pulped by a piece of granite. There would be an enquiry. The other, Bert Davies, had his leg smashed. He had been flung several feet by the force of the blast.

It was then I first realised I lived on a landscape of death.

After it happened, Tom was one of the first on the scene. It had scared him, but he knew he had to be down there. I watched him dig into the wormed earth with his hands. It was like bailing out a sinking dinghy with a teaspoon, but then Tom would not give up. He came up later, his hands cut, blood and clay mingling on his forefinger. The ambulance crew had praised him.

The cause of the accident was uncertain. Something about the timing of the charge. The two unfortunates thought the charge had failed. They momentarily forgot procedure. Bert was lucky. He had survived. Bill Brewer was not so fortunate. They watched the captain head up to the office. That phone call would have to be made. A sweaty hand and a lowered voice.

I surveyed the activity in the pit. All work had stopped. Everyone knew Bill. As his bloody body was unearthed using the loader, the clay workers bent their heads. Four figures carried the stretcher from up the pit benches to the waiting ambulance. All heard its siren. Tom rejoined me, after picking his way down the slope to rescue his tam.

'I'm sorry boy. Tin a very good day for Blackpool. Bill... you know. He was one of the best. Worked with 'un plenty of times years ago. Twill be a hellish shock for his missus, what with him having only a few months to go before he retired.'

Tom looked again down to the pit bottom,

'Tis a heller. That bit they've blasted. Best lot of clay behind it they've found in years. You'd best go home now boy, before I starts to cry.'

I knew Tom was serious. He headed up the garden path, then kicked off his boots and went inside to wash. I told him that I would see him next week. He took one last look at the blast's remnants, then watched the sun finally collapse; its redness collecting on the English Channel below Hensbarrow. I went home and cried in a nightmare of clay.

I was caught in a dream world. A strange world. A world of...

OF DIGGING

HOLD an ear trumpet to Cornwall and the sound you are most likely to hear is that of digging. Throughout time, someone in Cornwall has been digging for something. Surely the end of the world will come when the Cornish stop digging.

And the digging does not stop at the River Tamar, for wherever the Cornish have emigrated in the world; once having settled down, they dig. Dig in America. Dig in Australia. They call them 'Cousin Jacks' there. Dig in Africa. The Cornish are the very moles of the human race, digging as often as possible, wherever possible.

But there is a reason for this. Remember Cornwall, at the start of time, had nothing. One day someone must have scraped at the earth with bare hands and found something. Perhaps a crystal to delight the ancient Cornish tribal leaders. A few more people dug at the earth to see what it held. Then, instead of hands, they used shovels and axes, as the earth became harder and rockier. They dug down, and then dug down some more. And in time they found it all; gold, copper, tin, zinc and uranium. Yes, it's all been found in Cornwall.

So, the Cornish have always dug, and now digging is like instinct. It is natural for a Cornishman to dig, more natural even than a child on a beach digging the soft sand. It is to discover what lies beneath you.

There's more, you see. The only way for the Cornish to leave Cornwall by land is to cross the Tamar or head seaward on dangerous waters. So, in a sense, they are stuck on this elephant's trunk of a land. That's why they dig deeper. Little wonder then that the Cornish, an isolated race, resolved to dig deeper into their land to see what could be obtained from it.

And do you know some of my first memories, the changeling's memories, are of digging. Digging in the back garden with toy spades and Tonka toys. Di-gg-ing. Digging... digging down.

But the sad thing about digging is that it is almost inevitably self-destructive, both as an instinct and an industry. All right, so things dig okay for a while, but soon the cost of raising the mineral exceeds its value. That is why Cornwall's most famous diggers have died. That is why all over Cornwall you see little places where people have had a go at digging and failed. Little dig holes.

Places where people just had to dig. A compulsion to tear at the earth.

And so the Cornish have been digging through the centuries. They were digging when the Phoenicians visited Cornwall. This is mentioned by Herodotus, who ludicrously called Cornwall the Cassiterides, 'the islands of tin'. Poor scholar; he knew no better. The Cornish have dug on through thick and thin. So, even when the Cornishman digs the garden on a Sunday afternoon, he is doing something age old; something his body was meant to do. Anything else is unnatural.

Digging, though, inevitably causes enormous mole hills over the county; the waste of digging, the waste of mining for a valuable commodity.

And now people dig on Hensbarrow, where the waste from the clay covers the landscape, and where men still dig. The bones of Cornwall dug by the Cornish to be sent away. Pieces of Cornwall in toothpaste, pills, paper and pottery. Pieces of Cornwall all over the globe. Dug out. Never to return. And the clay pits stand as the wounds, great symbols of the Cornish penchant for digging. But without the digging Cornwall would die, for there is little else in this land. Dig or die is the option open to the Cornish. Environmentalists have no chance of correcting the ecological balance in Cornwall. Digging is everything, my friends.

All right, so they don't dig with shovels and spades now but use high pressure hoses and mechanical shovels and dumper trucks, yet the Cornish are still there, ready to take the next bite of soil. To go down deeper and wider, to find more deposits, to keep the old instinct alive, to find the inner depths of the Earth. Without digging, this land would die.

It's that kind of race, and the Cornish must win.

TOBIAS

1st October 1664.

I finde it difficult indeed to alter my language in the Parishe of St Dennis, for in this part of Cornwall the population do not speak the native language, but choose a variation of English. As we had in Camborne, they have their owne words for suche items as tools in the farmyarde and types of hedges. My duties today, outlined by the Reverende, have been in the main most tiring, he suggesting I woulde do well in sorting out the Parishe records of the last one hundred years. This being an uneventful and repetitive task I founde myself completing, I must confess to drawing o'er my papers and by purpose making inke blotches.

I contemplated today the future of this Parishe that I am nowe at once part of, for I see here now no use for it. It is the most bleake place to live, and I worrie for the people here of what worke will come in the future. The Downs, though bearing some semblance to those around Camborne, are not generously stocked withe tin or those other minerals that men find valuable, though I notice that some souls bearing the correct notion towards gain in that field have tried digging, I must say to little success, the soil in fact being most clayey and of little use to man nor beaste. I pray to God that some windfalle comes to these people.

For myself, today I went to market in the village of St Dennis, buying meat of doubtful origins, vegetables and, for the Parishe, inke and paper. Indeed I have noticed that prices in St Dennis for suche commodities are not so deare as in West Cornwall. Thus today, having some change, I treated myself to a stick of sugar that I did eat whilst carrying the provisions o'er the moist moore. By night I read the Bible, for, as the Reverende says, it is good for the soul and I have a hope my soul may become a good one. Though I write here that I read Christian words, my mind wanders to the maid who supplied yonder food to me today. She hath the face of an angel and, deare God, I finde myself thinking most unchristian thoughts. My deare mother recommends cold baths for suche thoughts to my brother – he who is a farmer at Helston – but having contemplated this and not having one bath at hand, I chose instead to read my Bible in peace. Amen.

T.T.

OF A WORD OR TWO WITH YOU

...about China clay and the industry my father had stepped into.

ARTHUR Sexton, my father, chose to leave the suburban ease of Essex and move to Cornwall. When he came to Cornwall the Cornish called him 'Art', so it seemed that he had left something of himself behind. He had been there as a boy on holiday, but that was to the nice bit; not the dirty bit that he found himself in now.

He was a tall, drooping man, who never really aged. Ever since I can remember he has hardly changed. Still slightly balding, hair swept over to cover his bald spot. Still the smell of Old Spice and Juicy Fruit chewing gum. But in 1966 he was young enough – and old enough – to take his family to the edge of the universe, bring them to Hensbarrow; and he was brave enough to start in an industry he knew nothing about. And I loved him, and still do, and so, a word or two...

It was fairly easy to find a job with the china clay company then. You applied and were taken on. As simple as that. In the pit you were either a hoseman, pumpman or beltman. Above that you could be a chargehand, which is the clay word for foreman. And above that is the captain or cap'n, the production supervisor.

Arthur was taken on as a pumpman up at Littlejohns Pit to begin with, and he did well considering he is a Cockney, and in the clay mines they don't like Cockneys – or anyone else come to that – taking their industry. But he got on all right. See, clay mining is more than a job. It is a life attitude. Some of the boys up with him are third generation clay miners. They are a proud and solid people, but never troublesome.

Clay people like people who are easy going, and they like people to say what they mean. Be honest. My father found this out from Tom, and it served him well. He became a naturalised Cornishman. Is that possible? He came close. I think I may have come closer...

It's like the tin mines, like 'Poldark', but it is more magical than that. It is a fairy tale and a horror story. It's both. It's an industry of ambivalences. It is an industry of men with granite for bones and clay for blood.

To begin mining clay you take off the overburden, the earthy soil on top of the granite. This is done by great excavators and dumpers whose roar can constantly be heard. The clay is found in layers, called stopes, set up on benches around or in the bottom of the quarry. A stream of water is guided at high pressure over the stope. The water then runs back over the inclined plane of the bench, down into the pit, carrying the clay with it.

Sometimes, in sunny weather, the stream is so hellishly white it hurts your eyes to look at it. It runs back to the pumphouse; here it is pumped to the top of the pit, where the coarser residues, such as sand and mica, are separated from the clay. It then goes to be processed and refined. And that, friends, is a simplistic overview of the china clay mining process.

Think of the people employed by the industry. Over five thousand hosemen, pumpmen, cap'ns, chargehands, tankmen, slurrymen, storemen, sweepers, baggers, drivers, technicians, fitters, electricians, carpenters, refiners and every other job that can be found anywhere happens here.

And in the clay works, everything revolves around shifts, so that Hensbarrow can be mined twenty four hours a day, three hundred and sixty five days a year. When you are sleeping, someone else is mining. And when you have finished sleeping, you go and mine.

Before the late 1970s, the clay industry worked a pattern of shifts which called for one week of seven mornings on the trot, one after the other, then a couple of rest days, then afternoons for a week, then rest days, then nights. Then it started all over again. That was Arthur for Tom's working routine.

But you want to know what it looks like, this place so frightening. The prevailing colour is white, though the rock itself may vary from yellow to brown to black. You sit in a hose hut, like the cab of a digger, and operate the monitor. The monitor is basically a curled piece of pipe which spurts out the water on to the rock face. It is operated by two levers, inevitably greasy with tellus oil, the hose lubricant. You sit in the hut for hours at a time.

The hut smells of people, of urine and fags, but it is homely when outside it is cold and raining. And you sit there, like some kind of demented chimpanzee, playing with the levers, jerking them in the direction you want the hose to go. All over the pit, the rusty red pipelines of water are connected. Every so often you see a valve, which turns on the jet. And then you wash... and wash... and wash.

Sometimes, a friend helps you in a loader, sort of gingerly prodding around the stope for pieces of loose rock and sand already mined. At night it turns surreal. Sometimes you close your eyes so that you can open them and find it gone. But the pit is still there, like a ghoul. And it's hard. You're on night shift, and it's the graffiti man's 'bog-eyed hour', one o'clock, and your head feels heavy and your eyelids flicker. But you must not let your torch go out. That's what you're being paid for. But they do it you know; the worse thing of all, sleeping on the job.

'It's the shifts you see, Cap'n. They muck up your biorhythms.'

Back in the pumphouse, you watch the pump. Babysit it. Watch it like a hawk. Watch for stones which could damage the propeller. Turn the motor back a little if the pool is getting low. And, if things run smoothly, you can boil the kettle and drool over the porno mags. Milk mingling.

It's all changed now though. The pumphouse was a good place to go deaf. Tom's friend Woody was a pumpman all his life. When he retired he was, as the saying goes, 'as deaf as a post'. Now they wear ear protectors. Build little soundproof cabins. Because those pumps, even my normally no-swearing father shouted, were 'bleddy noisy'.

And in the late 1960s, they replaced all the skips with conveyor belts. The hoses became better, some computerised, and the loaders got bigger. And the industry is safer – if mining can ever be safe.

And I thought of my father, riding back in the Land Rover, head hitting the roof as the four wheel-drive bounced over the channels and rivulets. He is scratching his head where the safety helmet has made his temple feel sweaty, and he is talking to the cap'n about the pontoon game at crib time, and he is smelling of Old Spice and chewing gum. The cap'n is looking forward to going home to bed with Mrs Cap'n, and my father looks forward to seeing my mother. And I know that after night shift, you are riding up out of the pit, tired as a dog, feeling like you have just come out of a war zone. And you enjoy watching the morning shift gang go down, knowing all too well that tomorrow you'll have to come in and do it all over again.

Some things have changed and some things have stayed the same. You'll find the porno mags behind the isolating cabinet in the pumphouse.

AT Longstone's, the shift cap'n wanted a word.

'You're up on the hose again Tom. Sorry mate...'

Tom trudged up the quarry, following the milky stream that

flowed ceaselessly to the pumphouse. He lit a fag and tipped his helmet backwards. Ahead lay the monitor, a great red beastie, half-buried in sediment and kaolin. The hose was a fourteen inch-thick thing that was not noisy in the conventional sense; but every time it hit the rock it would crack like a whip and hit the higher levels of hearing sensitivity.

Working it at first was like a pub football table; you know, spinning the players so they kick the ball. But soon it becomes more powerful than that. It becomes sexual. The water shoots out in spurts on to the virgin soil. Tom could hear the roars of pleasure as he ran the hose across again.

And the clay runs so milky you want to drink it. Lap it up. Put your hands in it and wash. Back at the pumphouse the water swirls in such a way that Cleopatra might have used it as a Jacuzzi.

If you place your hands in a clay solution at first they feel dirty; but when they are dry, little pieces of clay collect in the folds of your skin with a softening pleasure, softer even than talcum powder. It was with these hands that you worked.

And you washed all shift, pointing the hose at an overhang, undermining it until it released its wealth, finally splitting the piece in two so that it tumbled down, breaking into hundreds of fragments that were then washed to release their precious milk. That's what it was like. It was milking the soil, and here she rarely ran out. Tom was suckling at the teats of the earth.

It was a relief when the shift ended. Billy and Eric were up belts to do some work, so there had been no-one to play cards with at crib time. He wrapped up himself in layers underneath his donkey jacket in the boot house, then went home.

The wind was blowing sand crystals across the unhappy down, sprawled out like a stripped carcass; its insides gored out. It could have been the Antarctic, but in fact it was home. The moor mist, shuffling in from the shore, lowered shyly, silhouetting those shark-fin tips in the distance, and hovering above the peasoup water of the unused quarries.

Tom was walking down to the old engine house, his steps noisy, small globules of mica adhering to his boots. The evening was silent except for the drone of a distant generator and the hoses. Riot control of kaolin.

Only the heather and a few lonely trees broke the grey, though remnants of yellow gorse managed to poke through the crust, only losing their flowers to the wasteful wind. Tom was thinking. He caught one of the flowers in his hand for a second. With the next gust it was gone, blown down into one of the gullies. They both came to rest on the same trickle of mica, stone cold.

The place was sacred to Tom. The tips stood as his pyramids, the ruins of mine-workings, his relic-crammed tombs. He stood in a desert. He was the nomad in there somewhere. Across the gullies, an old heap looked like an Aztec temple, turning Mexican green and jutting sacrificially into the sky. No rituals here, though, Tom thought, forgetting his own ritualistic existence.

He let his mind wander. Some Cornish giant must have been here, gathering up the earth and stuffing it into his mouth. The soil had been digested, assimilated, absorbed, only to be excreted on to the moor, suffocating the heather and squashing the weeds. Perhaps the same giant who owned the hat. The only thing left edible the giant did not eat was the occasional dust-covered, hardly ripe blackberry.

Strange to have something so sweet in the middle of something so sour.

At Gunheath, the belt summoned him, its two fingers beckoning him to go to that higher place. But he could not. Below, a solitary seagull shrieked and flew from telegraph pole to pole, a message from production to shift gang passing below. The earth-moving machinery was stomping about its lair, loading the dumpers with soil, re-filling their buckets, then loading again and again. All covered in exhaust fumes. There was a smell of diesel fumes, but a hint of something else; a delicate fragrance, maybe from the clump of heather beside the blasting warning notice. On them, Tom could nearly hear the frog-spit chuckling.

Traversing through three hundred and sixty degrees, his view turned from white to purple, white, then green, then back to white once more. It could have starred as a miniature mountain range. It could have been glaciated, if it were seventy million years old, but that scar down there at his feet was only excavated last week. Still, a scar in a sea of pain amounts to little.

There was a fascinating forty five degree angle that cut the pit and tip in two. In times before, skips ran up vertical tracks, supplying the volcanos with their lava. Tom could remember them crossing overhead, like enormous worker bees taking nectar to their cells. They clattered loud and strong. Now the pit was quiet. The track was still there, rust eaten into every bolt and joint, except where the ragwort grew.

The mist reached the bottom of the pit at twilight. The few rabbits there hoped Tom would soon be gone so they could begin their evening meal. They skipped past rusting valves, through the slurry to join their companions, where a circle of green still grew. When the lights came on the place looked warmer. The volcanos received their last lava from the depths, while the light fittings slung in convoy patrolled the pit like battleships. Scapa

Flow left. Jutland right.

As the moon began to rise the landscape did not turn black. It never has. Its light was captured and held on the pallid surface, turning telegraph poles into petrified figures standing quite, quite still. A mock Avalon lamented its loss. The mica testing boat tied to the landing stage held no king. A rock involuntarily, or perhaps purposely, fell into the pool, giving radio wave ripples which moistened the dry levee. Beyond the levee you could get lost in the maze of levels and intricate steps running down into the pit; an enormous amphitheatre, revealing a stage of lunar blandness.

Tom could feel life passing him by. It was creeping up on the upturned cones like a scavenger, until they teemed with throttling brambles and weeds, like maggots boring into their flesh. He felt it leaving without him. He felt their bite. He dangled his legs out, and sat on the over-burden. Down there, they were eating at this apple called the Earth, taking huge chunks out of it.

'Go on. Go on,' Tom muttered. 'Dig.'

'Dig,' he said. 'Dig down... and around. Down. Dig down. More, more...'

Tom wished they would find the pip. He spat. It dropped into the pit. He only wished he had the guts enough to follow.

And this, all because...

OF A QUAKER'S FIND

Because of a Quaker's find – a very fortunate find – you hear them, at half past eleven, shouting, peeing on the pavement, dreading the alarm's wicked ring when, at four in the morning, the clay workers must rise to go to the morning shift.

'PISSED again, Shaun?'
'Es. Ten pints, and that's before breakfast...'
'Up in the morning?'
'A heller, I tell 'ee.'
And the clay workers spend their pay in 'The William Cookworthy', drinking it down, and splashing it up against the porcelain wall, never dreaming the clay will run out and that one day no-one is going to be getting up for a morning shift up at Rocks Pit. So for now, they carry on... and on. Drinking the white clay away. Turning the clay psychedelic. Acid clay. Outside, a man stands puking over a drain, writhing in the chill. Inside the music beats ceaselessly, the sweat and cigarette smoke extracted through fans to drift up over Hensbarrow. Voices just heard at the brow of the hill, where the old Linhay squats. Staggering bodies fall down Tregonissey Lane End. And it's all because of a Quaker's find.

What must he be thinking; the spirit of this man who watches these hard drinking people. To have a public house named after him – The William Cookworthy. That Quaker lad must be crying in his grave. Those fattish cheeks, half-rimmed spectacles and wig have all turned to dust, returned to the ground from which he gave these people life. And so the discoverer now becomes the clay itself.

A smart man, the Quaker who first took the clay from the ground. Try to imagine what Hensbarrow looked like in 1746, before he started to dig. The Quaker patented his process, and in 1768 he started a pottery in Plymouth, where the first true hard-paste porcelain in England was to be made.

And then came the others, the names of those who are found in all the grand houses of England; Wedgwood, Minton and Spode. And they followed because of a Quaker's find, clay workers can get pissed on Friday nights and Hensbarrow can puke up its belly's contents and writhe like the man who stands over the drain telling dirty jokes...

AND, have you heard this one?
Well, it's about the 'porcelain earth'... so maybe you should listen...
For years and years it was thought that the fine white clay of which the porcelain was made was found only in the Celestial Empire, and specimens that arrived in this land sold for a high price. It was discovered in Saxony in a peculiar way. A merchant called Schnerr, being struck with the whiteness of some clay near Schneeburg, collected some of it and used it for powdering his wig. This new powder made the wigs very heavy. An apothecary named Botcher analysed the powder and discovered it was identical to Chinese kaolin...
And from that point onwards Cookworthy and Cornwall never looked back.

OF THE MOIST MOORS

Mist on the hill
Brings water to the mill
Mist on the moor
Brings sunshine to your door.

(Cornish weather rhyme)

WHEN I returned to Hensbarrow as an adult, with one of the women I have loved in my life, we would often walk on the old road, past Longstone's Pit. For old times sake...

This was the road I would cycle along to go to Michael's, past old Janey Gummow's house and out towards Cocksbarrow Clayworks. Michael lived at Karslake. Yes, the Michael I now push through the streets of Truro.

Karslake no longer exists. It is like Blackberry Row and Halviggan. They are gone. Swallowed up by the clay industry.

But Karslake used to be there. A row of houses, slightly incongruous on the middle of the moor. You had to be hard to live up there, they used to say. Had to be hard to be a Karslaker, for the hamlet was situated a thousand feet above sea level and was the most prominent place in central Cornwall. When Michael lived at Karslake only a few families were left. Most of the houses were just shells. Empty buildings with the windows knocked out, black eyes looking towards Whitemoor and over the Longstone like the empty sockets of bleached skulls. Behind the houses was a disused mine.

Michael's grandfather said there used to be a tin stream works there but most of it had been stripped away by Longstone's Clayworks. Michael would always be looking out for me from his top floor window. His bike stood against the front of the house. He would be inside shoving on his anorak so we could go out and explore the moor. The door would open.

'Out in a bit, Ben,' he would say, stuffing bread into his mouth.

Then I heard Michael's mother's voice.

'Back by nine mind, Michael. I want you to fetch some furse for the fire drekkly.'

'All right,' Michael would shout.

'And dunnee clunk down that bread so.'

'All right mother... stop fussing,' he said under his breath, and banged the door shut. Then, in one movement, he would clamber on to his bike, spin it round and head down the path to where I waited.

'Where us going tonight then?' he said.

'Dunno,' I replied. 'How 'bout down Roche?'

'No. Too far tonight init?'

'Wouldn't mind goin' up Cocksbarrow. My grandfather was telling me about a Spitfire that crashed up there in the war.'

'Sounds all right to me,' I said.

It was May now and the nights were opening out. Summertime had touched us both. Over the moor the skylarks were singing. You could always hear them on Hensbarrow. We rode two abreast, tiny pieces of hot tar sticking to the tyres of our cycles.

Michael was a real friend then. A soul mate. Both our ambitions then were to drive the Euclid trucks up and down the tips all day. We spent hours looking through glossy magazines about trucks, and both knew the horsepower and cubic capacities of all the vehicles that worked in the pits.

Michael Stevens had no father. At least he'd had a father somewhere along the way but all he would ever say was that 'he went off one night.' I could see him in the window behind the red curtains, watching his father's lonely steps down the path. But it was never a problem. His mother looked after him well, and his grandfather lived with them. So Michael and I cycled on Hensbarrow. The road was ours, the moor was ours and the stones were ours.

Up at Karslake crossroads we had to let pass a tractor pulling a trailer of hay, then we headed up to Cocksbarrow. Michael reckoned the Spitfire had crashed a few yards away from the drying shed up there. We cycled around the back of the ruined dry to find a fern infested dip.

'That's where it crashed,' Michael stated emphatically.

'How can you tell?' I asked.

'Got to be it,' Michael said, jumping into the dip and trampling down the vearns. He was about to begin a search for any wartime memorabilia in the dip.

'There'll be nothing down there. You're wasting your time,' I said.

Michael continued his search.

'Mondy,' he said.

'What?'

'Mondy. That's what he was called. Pilot Officer Mondy. Southern Rhodesia...' He said Rhodesia like a tribal elder.

'Who?'

'The pilot – the bloke who crashed here. That's what he was called.'

'Who told you that?'

'My grandfather. He helped to move the Spitfire. A lorry came to collect it.'

'Tom would remember that wouldn't he?'

'Spect so.'

After the dip had been flattened, Michael stopped searching.

'Nothing here,' he said.

'Told you there wouldn't be.'

'Give us a hand up.'

I stretched out and pulled Michael's heavy body out of the dip.

When we were on the same level, Michael began marching over the moor.

'Where are you going?'

No answer.

I followed. Then I saw Michael fall to the ground in a deliberate fashion. I ran over the moor, squashing the heather as I trampled along. Michael lay with his back on the heather, several plants supporting him like a bed. Before I had a chance to lay beside him he spoke. His voice was philosophical,

'I wanted to lie down up here. I want to remember this because they're taking it away soon.'

'Who?' I asked, nestling my head between two clumps of heather.

'The clay company.'

It was then I realised Michael had an undiscovered poetic bent, but it was to be several years before this stretch of Cocksbarrow went.

Returning now, I could not even remember where we had lain. The ground has gone, and in its place a white hole. But it's worse than that my friends because, as the place goes, the memory tends to go as well.

We lay there for about half an hour. Then Michael leapt up.

'My ass is wet,' he stated.

Mine was as well. The moor was still wet from a shower earlier in the day. Two moist bums cycled home.

It was too dark to fetch the furse for the fire now. The door of Michael's house closed, and I pictured his mother clipping his ear. If he were a few years younger it would have been early to bed without a mother's goodnight kiss. And a reading...

45

OF A STORY

One day, when the nightmare becomes the dream, story-tellers will relate this tale to children to make them sleep.

THERE was once a young warrior who lived in the land of Hensbarrow, and he loved a beautiful princess. The princess's father, the King of Hensbarrow, said to the young warrior that if he wished to marry his daughter he must complete three difficult tasks.

The first, he declared, was that he must scour Hensbarrow for the purest lump of clay he could find.

The young warrior set off, searching wherever he could for such a pure clay. Upon chance he met an old woman and he asked her if she knew where he could find such a clay. The old woman told him to dig beneath his feet. And sure enough, beneath him was a lump of the purest clay he had ever seen. The young warrior thanked the old woman and made his way back to the king's castle. The king was pleased to see that the warrior had completed the first task.

Next, he set a second task. This time, the young warrior was to find a potter who could mould the clay into the most perfect image of the princess.

The warrior went off across the moor and again he met the old woman. He asked her if she knew of such a potter. She told him to see an old blind man who lived near the coast. The young warrior found the old blind man busy at work in his cottage near the sea, and asked him to make the clay into an image of the princess. The blind man asked him to return later and, sure enough, when the warrior returned, he had created the most perfect miniature of the princess. The warrior thanked the potter and ran as quickly as possible back to the castle, where the king was impressed with the figurine. The princess was also delighted. She hoped the brave warrior could complete her father's final task, for secretly she was deeply in love with him.

Her father's final task was a difficult one. To gain the princess's hand, he must tell the king how many grains of sand had been mined from Hensbarrow. The young warrior set on his journey again, but when he asked the old woman how many grains of sand there were on the moor she looked at him, and a tear rolled down her cheek. She told him he must count them himself. Alas, not all fairy tales end happily, and the young warrior was never seen again.

Some say he is still counting. Some believe he gave up long since. Some say his ghost still haunts the moor.

And so the dream becomes the nightmare. A voice reading numbers... the voice of...

THE Reverend Matthew Trevenna, slightly lispy, reading the hymn number to the congregation. Number three hundred and th'ixty four he repeats. 'O, for a thousand tongues to th'ing.'

He tells the congregation the hymn was written by Charles Wesley, in memory of brother John, the preacher, who liked to have a thousand people at his prayer meetings. In Old Pound Chapel there stood maybe twenty people. O, how the Wesleys would have cried.

I was with Tom in the pews. He was here because it was Easter and, like many Cornishmen, he was on the first of his three visits to the chapel each year. Once at Easter, once for the Harvest Festival and once at Christmas. He was trying to sing, but the words came out gargled, a sort of low religious hum. A Downser's chant. He had forgotten his spectacles. I tried to sing, but my voice never reached the high notes of the ladies in the pews opposite. The chapel was cold, my breath freezing, and I thought of all the other people over Hensbarrow trying to sing hymns in chapel for Easter.

Religion on Hensbarrow is of one kind only. Methodism. No-one contemplates being anything else. Methodism is in the blood, in the tools, in the clay, and where there is clay there are chapels. And they are always simple, inexpensive buildings, all built at the end of the nineteenth century, when people went to chapel. They are tall and oblong, with windows like children would draw for churches, long, thin and anaemic. And always the cream-painted walls, the plastered ceiling, the wooden floorboards, a slight trace of clay on them. All built at the same time, the chapels with their small organs, the Sunday Schools at the rear smelling of worn crayons and Brylcreem. Rude words and drawings in the hymn books.

And I was in a chapel that was dying. All those dirty places, the dirty bits have them, at Foxhole and Lanjeth, Greensplat and Whitemoor, St Dennis and Stenalees. They all have chapels, wedged in between places of insignificance and other places of insignificance, between clayworkers' cottages and grains of sand. And you know it is sad because they are dying. The founder's names on the plaque could be anyone's. No-one can remember them. Though they must have been good Christian people to begin it all, musn't they? And they must have had higher attendances once, or was it all just a dream ? Like the story of the young warrior and the princess, and how it all went wrong somewhere along the line.

When the service was over the two of us headed back to Noppies. I looked back at the chapel, a grey, stone monolith standing before the newly formed sandtip of Old Pound Pit. It was like a scene from the Bible, but instead of yellows and reds I saw whites and greys. A drizzle began to fall. Overhead the vague form of a Shackleton aeroplane crossed our path; an absurd black crucifix above a Hellish landscape.

Fairy stories were never much fun anyway.

HANDS up. Who remembers childhood?

So far away now it could be where time began. Right there when God created the clay. That's the way it seemed to me. To Tom as well. Like a medieval story-teller Tom gently swayed to and fro on a Victorian rocking chair, churning time over and over. He would tell me of Cap'n Pascoe, and I would imagine a sour-faced, middle-aged Cornishman with a drooping jet black moustache and obligatory bowler hat, black waistcoat white with clay, gaiters strapped around his hobnailers. Perhaps being over-imaginative if you believe he had a gold watch and chain, company issue of course, forever checking if the time was too fast, and saying to those below him:

'Still marking time?... Mind the time in your own time.'

And Tom would tell of Cap'n Pascoe and men like him, men he admired from when he had started as a kettleboy in his fresh-faced innocence and slightly too big cap. Stories as many as hairs on his chin, grey but still strong. As a kettleboy you began work at around thirteen, maybe earlier. It was the traditional way of entering into the claywork; boiling great urns of weak tea, warming pasties, cleaning, doing all the 'ing' words no-one else wants to do.

And I had never known a childhood like this, for that is what Tom was then, still in essence a child. But Tom could go back further with me. He would tell me of when he was younger, when the Great War was on, when electricity on Hensbarrow was still a long way from coming. And here we would meet. Tom told me how he used to go down to the claywork and build dams in the clay water channels. When a large enough pool had collected, he would smash the dam and let a tidal wave of white water run down to the tanks, confusing the tankman who for the last couple of hours had only received a trickle of water.

We met here because I had done similar things in the old works at Mid-Cornwall pit. Tom had smelt the same smells, the same feeling as the dam burst over fifty years ago, as I had done this year. It was at this point that our childhoods met. Time no longer mattered.

And then Tom would go urt-picking, as I had done, on the downs. But he did it in the very early morning, almost at dawn, when the mist lay in the waterlogged depressions of the moor which he called 'sladdys'.

This was not for any real reason, but perhaps it might have been because the urt berries were fresher covered with the night's dew, or more probably because the picking was more magical; stooping down into a layer of mist to pick the purple fruit. As Tom told me, I saw the cold berries burst on his tongue. And he licked his lips.

He would tell me of the times he went swimming in some abandoned pits near Carloggas. Naked, he said, especially around midsummer. There, he would dive into the now flooded pits, their waters a Mediterranean vivid blue, caused by the suspended particles of clay. He said he swam there for ages, a humanoid form in the motionless, never-swum-in-before water of Carloggas. And I imagined the young Tom, the athlete, the Tom before his beard and swollen hip, the Tom someone must have loved once, the virile Tom, climbing out of the blue-green water, skin teeming with tiny mica crystals, putting on his shorts behind a yellow flowered and sharp needled gorse bush. It was like swimming in a dream, and Tom had done it. I could feel the gorse flowering in his fingers; the needles of time puncturing this old man before me.

I looked out of the window for a while, the window carved out of the galvanised walls of this part of the house. Immediately outside was the chicken shed. Beyond that, the twin tips of Halviggan pit. A few birds in the sky. A slight drizzle. Returning my scan to where Tom sat, I found he had gone out into the kitchen. He was rummaging about in a cupboard. On the side of the armchair his pipe had fallen over, scattering ash on the carpet. When Tom came back into the room he was clutching a toy tightly. After returning his pipe to his mouth he held up the toy, now identifiable as a lorry, to eye level. Tom closed one eye and seemed to measure its proportions. Then, without warning, he blew hard, the dust falling off the lorry in my direction.

'For you,' he said.

'Me?'

'Yes. Used to be mine years ago. All this talk of when I was younger reminded me of it... Tis a model, see, of a steam wagon.

My granfer made it for me when I was a youngster... but it ain't right that it isn't looked after any more. I'd like for you to have it, Ben.'

Tom handed me the model. It was weighty, made of steel and tin and hand-crafted, resembling a latter-day Tonka toy. The wheels turned and were bolted on tightly. Winding a lever at the back made the bucket of the lorry tip up. Like many things on Tom's holding it was painted in a dull orange galvanising paint to prevent it from rusting. The cab was open and highly detailed. Tom's granfer was a true craftsman. On the side was painted 'Carclaze Clay Company' in tiny lettering.

When Tom gave me the toy it was like any other, only not quite so good. Being hand made it never seemed to me as a youth to have quite the look of more regular toys. That toy is one of the few things I have kept, and its value to me has increased. And so the toy passed from Tom's granfer, name unknown, to Tom, and then to me, Ben Sexton, and now it shall pass from me to...?

When the rain came down, and Tom became sentimental about his youth, I became philosophical. Picture it.

Somewhere a war is being fought. Take any section of the globe, any piece. Go on, pick a war. You choose.

Not that long ago, before the coalition and the Middle East, Britain was in a war on its own, an us and them war in the South Atlantic. And when it was all over Cornwall breathed a sigh of relief. After all, Cornwall is closer to Argentina. And then we carried on again, so these figures on Hensbarrow are just dots, and the shells go off somewhere else. Beirut. Kuwait. Iraq. Northern Ireland. And all the time the clay is still being dug. There's still someone washing at the bottom of the pit. Still Hensbarrow is being milked.

It was the same in 1940, Tom told me. Though production slumped while the men went away to fight, the clay still flowed out of the ground. The war never really touched Hensbarrow. That sea of tranquillity. Except that is for a few evacuees from London and Manchester and places like that. Children like me, who must have thought Hensbarrow a very strange place compared to that of the city. Children who had arrived in St Austell, just as I had done, to see the great cones, slightly smaller then, on the moor; to begin to wonder if they would have been safer in London. Children with labels, children for Hensbarrow. Children crying, the sand blowing in their eyes. So these people on the moor must be used to strange accents like mine, and the Cockney offspring got used to these people who ate pasties for crib, who called their lunch 'dinner', and rolled their rrr's.

The war hit in other ways. One night, Tom believed it to be the winter of either '41 or '42, a squadron of German bombers flew across the Channel to attack the dockyard at Plymouth. The attack being unsuccessful, it was decided to off-load the bombs on the south coast of Cornwall. Several bombs hit Hensbarrow. Of all the places, why Hensbarrow? If it had been daylight they would have seen that there was nothing to bomb, only sand and clay. Was the moor not cratered enough already? And so the Longstone saw them fly overhead, and they passed all the places bleeding white, Goonbarrow and Rosemellyn, Bluebarrow and Rostowrack, Wheal Martyn and Carclaze, and they dropped their bombs. Some fell on Hensbarrow, some on Foxhole, some on Nanpean. In Foxhole and Nanpean, two houses were blown to pieces. On Hensbarrow, there was no damage. Tom says the bombs lie unexploded up there somewhere.

Tom did a couple of years war service.

'Where?' I asked him.

'Guess?' he said.

'Burma?'

'Some hope... nah, served in bleddy North Africa didn't I and 'twas bleddy full of sand out there as well.'

His face became contorted as he thought of the irony, and then we both laughed. He spoke again.

'And then there were prisoners...'

'Prisoners?'

'Es. Prisoners of war. Italians they were. The clay people used to use them, see boy, used to use 'em for labour, down Spicers and Carpalla Pit.'

And my mind wandered. To think what the Italians thought of this place. That hellhole they were being held and forced to work in.

Perhaps those prisoners saw what I first saw, that the people of Hensbarrow were the real prisoners. They were the ones who really needed to escape, and they are the ones now who go to 'The Cookworthy' on Friday nights to drink their china clay blues away.

When Tom went out of the room to make himself another cup of tea, the rain tapped on the window and prodded me back to reality. He laid a ragged towel on the window ledge to stop the rain coming through. There would be no repairs done today.

I believed Tom thought of the war when he saw the 'Shacks' go over. It would make his day to see a pair of them come up over Longstone's tip, the droning bug-like planes, black against the white. The Avro Shackleton, later made by Hawker Siddeley. Four 2,450hp Rolls Royce Griffon 57A piston engines. Maximum speed 260mph. Wing span 120 feet. Length 92 feet 6 inches.

'Beautiful planes in' 'em boy?' he would say to me.

And they were. The things to see Hensbarrow in. Sure, you could climb to the top of Longstone's' skytip and see way down west or north towards Brown Willy, and Tom would do this. But in a plane it would be so much better to see them all, to see behind the crib hut where the brambles muddled, all the dirty places like Burgotha and Melbur, and Kernick and Parkandillick, and come in low over them, so low as to catch the hose's spray of Gothers and Littlejohns, Dubbers and Dorothy, take it up high and see them as a massive white blur, all these strange sounding places; Blackpool, Bluebarrow, Ninestones, Gunheath and Greensplat, all the places I went to see with Tom, all the places he loved so much.

'Pity we're earthbound isn't it Tom?'

'Yes,' he said, his eyes still watching them.

'Earthbound,' I said it under my breath.

Again, earthbound.

Earthbound.

'Es. Folk like me bin' earthbound all their life. Folk like me n' Watt over there.'

I turned to see Walter struggling along the track. He raised his walking stick to greet us.

'Ah,' said Tom, stooping to the old man's level and spinning around to face him.

'But, a man's reach...'

He paused a little; then re-thought.

'A man's reach should exceed his grasp, or what's a Heaven for.'

I looked at him in amazement.

'Some poet said that boy. Dunnee' go asking me who now...'

And as Watt and Tom greeted one another I began to look just how far I could reach. Moonbeams came out of the night and I was wishing I could touch them.

A few years later, and all the Shackletons were scrapped from RAF St Mawgan. Now they fly Nimrods, and still do... until they decide to scrap the Nimrod. And then I might find myself saying, as Tom did: 'There's no character to them boy...'

Not like the 'Shacks' who flew over the land so low they caught the spray from the hose.

But now, listen to this tall tale...

OF BOYS AND MAIDS

'A'RIGHT boy?' Watt asked Tom. And the way he said it, this one old man to another, sounded as though they were still boys at Whitemoor, still kicking a football across the sand slurs.

It is something you see in the Cornish. No-one ever wants to grow up in this land. No-one ever wants to find out they have lost all innocence. No-one wants to know about age and, by the words these people use, they are able to scrape the years away and pretend their lives are just beginning; and so you will hear them, old women in shops calling their brothers of fifty... sixty... seventy... eighty, 'boy', and they in turn telling them not to be women. To them they are still 'maids'.

This is where it becomes absurd. On Derby and Joan coach trips from the clay villages, old men say: 'Maid, you can't remember that. That was before the war!'

And deep down the women like it. It makes them feel innocent again. It makes them young. So no matter what life has thrown up at her, some droll Cornishman will always call her a 'maid'. It seems sexist but it's not. It is like a call for childhood again. A call for a time when there was no worry. No pain. No regret.

On Hensbarrow the elders use these terms all the time. Just listen to the moor on a still night. Hear the wind carrying away the years. Hear the lives being stripped away. Hear the re-birth. See the old couple dressed in black walking briskly to chapel. See his white longjohns just peeping out of his trouser bottoms. See her nylon stockings. Does she wear suspenders any more? Bet he still calls her 'maid'. They enter chapel in silence.

It is on Hensbarrow, where they use terms like 'bal-maidens' and 'kettleboys'; all these tribal initiations to take the child to the adult, all these labels attached to people born on a lump of granite in a peninsula jutting into the sea. And now... well now... this land of innocence is dying. The few old people still say 'boy' and 'maid', but they use it less frequently, afraid to sound Cornish, afraid someone might want to stop them reeling in the years, fishing for a childhood. Now, some children of Hensbarrow call each other 'maid' and 'boy', but it only lasts for a while. They learn that it appears quaint, and so the old customs die and the land of 'boys' and 'maids' now contains more 'men' and 'women', still crying, still wanting youthful folly, but finding it so difficult to achieve.

But why? Because they have it all; the television, then the video, then the compact disc player, and then the satellite television, and soon there will be no 'boys' and 'maids' left, and no childhood to remember. Soon friends, the baby shall be born the adult.

Then who shall remember thoughts...

OF FOXGLOVES AND FLYING MACHINES

It is so strange isn't it? The silly things you remember from childhood. The things you know you will remember when you are sat in your favourite chair, looking for your glasses to read stories with...

WHEN summer trickled in and the days grew longer, very often I would cycle up to the top of Hensbarrow. Then I used to take the old road round the rear of Longstone's Pit. I would leave quite early in the morning to spend the day up there, so I would take a packet of biscuits and shove them into my anorak pocket. The sultry air was not that windy so it was reasonably easy to cycle. I passed under black telegraph poles on the road that wound through the sandheaps. Somehow, they always reminded me of the mesa and butte formations in the Wild West of America. I wanted to meet a stagecoach. I wanted to see Cherokee Indians thundering across the moor on white stallions.

They never came.

Longstone's was a deep pit. Long and full of stones. The road cut just above it. A sheer drop to the right. To see the bottom of the pit you had to stand on the pedals of the bike and bunny-hop along the road, trying to move as slowly as possible. I wondered if Tom was down there. The pit never looked as bad in sunshine. Sometimes it would look holy, Christian even. The colours so clean and virginal, as if it were the earth's reincarnation of Mary.

A Land Rover turned out from the entrance to the pit. I rode properly. I could not recognise the sun-tanned driver. The Land Rover had come from a small plot of land on which was perched a building. It was fairly new, housing pumping equipment or something, but it looked strange, especially at this time of the morning, a rectangular silhouette; its lime and cement walls already turning red. It seemed to burn on the moor. Buildings looked out of place on Hensbarrow.

There was only one thing that should be there, and that was the long grass and heather just stirring in the breeze.

Anything else should be an infringement. But now the moor

seemed but an infringement on the clay. It was always silent up there. Not a sound could be heard. Always you felt it by hearing nothing. Nature had only done half its work. Either that or it had left, betrayed... I always heard the silence.

At the top of Hensbarrow, or the place I had designated the top, I dumped my bike down and gazed out. And that's all I would do normally... just watch the downs. I felt the granite's energy charge through my feet. I could feel every blade of grass around me, as though I were touching them all. I would lie on the grass making pictures out of the clouds. Pictures of dreams. Pictures of things I knew. The tips, the pits, the moor, the flowers, the stones. Then they would disappear and I let the sun burn me.

Sometimes I would take some felt pens and paper up there and draw all that could be seen. They are still in the attic I believe, those sketches; to the north, Roche – its mystic rock forcing its way above the village. Farther away, Brown Willy and Rough Tor, higher points on Bodmin Moor. In the haze they could have been clay tips, but I knew them to be real mountains, not the false ones we had. Southwards lay Gunheath Pit, a hole scooped out of one side of Hensbarrow like a painful wound. But she never cried a bit. Not this moor. She was above tears.

Even then, while I sketched, I knew I would bring her up here. The her I would fall in love with. It would be one of the first things we would do; walk up to Hensbarrow to show her all this. Most times I would close my eyes, my fingers teasing the velvet flower of a Foxglove. I drifted into a partial sleep, a fantasy that reached beyond the clay and back to Hensbarrow, before the clay was here.

'We will come here,' I dreamt.

'We will come here,' I told myself.

'We will come here and make love; make love on a moor of clay mines.'

I knew we would.

In dreaming this I never really took any notice of what the dream held. It was now that I felt it, after it had all happened, like negative deja vu. And I didn't need convincing I felt it. I had felt the smoothness of the foxglove's petals, their smooth hairs and tender stamen. I shook the pollen and pulled the flower apart.

She loves me
She loves me not
She loves...

THE petals blew across the downs. There was no knowing

where they might end up. There was no knowing how far they would travel. I saw them carried by the breeze northwards. The Atlantic would carry them away. Foxgloves from the land above Foxhole washed on to a foreign shore. They were travelling in style, and all the whiteness had gone.

When I knew it would happen, I woke. It was mid-day. A few flies had gathered around me. I sat up and shifted my form. They followed, so I swung at them with a cumbersome hand, the flies dodging me at every blow. In the end I let them go. I scratched my chin. It was hairy. Well, not so much hairy but rather a down was beginning to appear. I ran my fingers over it again and again. It felt horrible. I would need to shave soon. I turned red. I felt the flies were watching.

The two drawings I had completed that morning had been screwed up into two balls and I had thrown them behind my shoulder. I stood up and, as usual, walked along the track. This was where people used to come to learn to drive when they first started. So much had begun here – my own artistic journey and travels being among them.

I was heading to Gunheath Tip, a flatter pile of sand than any of the others on Hensbarrow. From there you could look further to the south east, down through Ruddlemoor into Gover Valley and finally out into St Austell Bay. There you could see the ships, six thousand tonners or more carrying clay from Charlestown, Par and Fowey across to Europe.

Steam from Par Rotary Refinery could be observed as well, a haze over St Austell. In this weather the town seemed to melt; like the ice-creams the tourists licked. Through the relative tranquillity of Ruddlemoor were a number of trees hiding a few cottages and an old water mill.

There was never any activity on this burrow. This part of the tip was not to be extended any further. I stood there while it was going through a transition from a white tit to a gorse-woollened mound, like a baggy jumper.

Now it is just a green hillock; few even knowing the whiteness that lies beneath. Few even bothering to think.

Resting on a large lump of rock, I ate some biscuits and wished I had brought a drink. I threw some rocks down the edge and crunched through the crust with my shoes to create a small avalanche.

By the end of the activity I had to sit down to empty my shoes of sand. There were thousands of particles of sand in it. I considered how many there were on the moor, then the whole of the clay mining area. The figure went into space. It was enough. Possibly enough to swap with all the beaches in Cornwall, and still have enough spare.

As I was banging my shoe, to get the last few grains out, I heard an aeroplane overhead. I felt it from behind me. It was low, coming in from the north east. You could tell it was a bulky thing, the engines were droning, its dark shadow cast over the pit's edge.

The plane was a Shackleton. They were ugly beasts, like flying black lizards. There were bubbles of glass all over them like blisters, and they were really black, except for a few yellow, red, white, and blue lines of insignia.

The Shackleton was no surprise. They regularly flew over Hensbarrow and the clay district. Their function was anti-submarine warfare and maritime defence. It had flown from St Mawgan aerodrome to the north, near Newquay. You could almost see the aerodrome today. I knew that from the aerodrome you could see the clay.

The Shackleton had an easy sound to it. Easy because you could imitate it with your finger on your nose. It felt good to make the noise, homely even.

The planes flew over often. I loved them. Loved their humming. Loved their blackness. I loved them. I loved them not. I loved...

The downs seemed to offer sacrifice to the aeroplane. It was almost regal. The Shack circled a number of times. It seemed to be carrying out a figure of eight manoeuvre out over Wheal Bunney and Carclaze, then around again over Whitemoor and Roche. She was black, but an angel, and as long as she was there I would watch her.

My treat did not last long, though. After the fourth circle I saw her bank over Longstone's and disappear heading westwards. The moor fell silent again.

When the Shack had gone, as a present for my mother I thought I would gather some flowers from the downs to brighten up the house. I scrambled over the edge of the tip up a couple of sandbanks to find a nest of foxgloves resplendent in purple and gently swaying in the breeze.

Foxgloves are difficult to pick. Pick at the bottom and the whole plant comes up, roots and all. Pick at the top and you inevitably lose some of the flowers and end up with a twisted, untidy stalk. In the end I elected for the latter, hoping my mother could tidy up the stalks once I was home.

The flowers smelt sweet and bees hummed around me as I cycled back to Noppies. I kicked off my wellingtons at the back door and ran in with the find, with socks like jester's shoes without the bells. I entered the kitchen.

'I got these for you, mum.'

'Don't bring them in here...'

'Why?'

'Because it's unlucky to have foxgloves in the house,' she said with a great urgency, as if I had committed a mortal sin.

'Take them outside! Throw them over the edge of the pit.'

Wiping the tears from my eyes, I scrunched up the foxgloves and ran angrily down the path to the pit. I watched the purples, pinks and greens tumble down the white sides of the quarry.

I loved them not.

TOBIAS

3rd October 1664.

I do finde today that Cap'n Tredissick's words are but true, and this gives me some satisfaction, though coupled with at least some perspiration. Yon maid at the market and I, yea I, are tomorrow to go walking upon the downs together. This cheers me wonderously, though I do not know the Reverende's position upon this. Knowing him as I already do, he wilt tell me that the temptation of the flesh is evil, and should be avoided. I willt tell yon Minister 'tis not the flesh I am after, to calm his blood. The maid I do thynk of a quantity ist named Susanna. She dost tell me I am cute, at whiche I redden cons'derably and do shy like a fright'ned deer!

This after', I hast been working in the garden at the rear of my newe lodgings, tealing potatoes and cabbage plants for the spring, and turning the o'ergrown black sod. Folk here do chatter wonderously. Several times, some fellow dost call me to the hedge and lean on the stones and tell me some tale whilst chewing lengths of grass. One suche fellow, of a very droll and exceedingly witty nature, dost tell me allt legends of yon downs. 'Now,' says he, 'hear this one... about Saint Auste and the Devil.' He do tell me some fiction concern'd with a battle twixt the Devil himself and yon Saint. And even more strange, he do say that yonder tall stone upon the downs is none but the Saint's staff. That ist all that remaineth Christian here, the moor being an eville place. The other stone nearby, says he, is his 'hat'. I do face him seriously, but I know not whether to believe suche tales. People do say so much in these modern days, I am uncertain what to believe. The droll fellow then dost wander on and leaves me to my gardening.

The Reverende, aye, he withe the big ears and, I should say, big nose as well, seems to me most concerned with the downs. He willt not venture upon them alone for, says he, they still carry on Pagan practices upon it. He do tell me of Witches who do live up there. 'No,' says I, 'they are but little wizened shrews who know no better.' The man remains unconvinc'd. I think this is no way for a man of the cloth to behave. Yea, he should be on the Downs dealing withe people, telling suche souls the word of the Lorde, not backing away.

Tonight by candlelight I read the 'Ordinalia', a most lively mummer whiche all soules in Cornwall should see or read. I have no proper copy of yon play. 'Tis only notes I do take from a performance each year. No doubt the Reverende has great dislike of suche occasions, as he has of me. I close. I am tired.

T.T.

OF BLACKBERRIES AND MICA

...which to the Chinese, now listening to Cliff Richard on their Sony Walkmans, might be the sweet and sour of Hensbarrow.

THE fruits of the land are never gathered now. Food comes in plastic packages and cardboard. The current fashion is for foods with no additives, no preservatives and no colouring. Green food. This, we must all agree with, but nevertheless the food we buy is still processed. Never again will folk harvest the earth with their own hands. Not like the moor people – the Hensbarrow Downsers.

In the clayland of my youth, more people gathered food from the earth than they do now. It was a seasonal occurrence – in July the urts, September the blackberries. And they could be seen, patches of families out in the fields, on the moor, on every scratch of ground, picking, squeezing, pulling off blackberries. Girls in long lace dresses getting hooked by the barbs, and boys stuffing the ripe sweetness into their faces so that they drew a ring of purple juice around their lips, and handed their mother a half-full jug.

Tom never had a freezer. Yet he was out there every September. He knew the best places; the unreachable places, and how to get to them. He knew when most berries would be ripe, and sometimes, when Michael and I went up there, he would be on Old Pound tip, a pink-skinned old man among the brambles, searching under every leaf to find the perfect berry. And Tom would cook the most delicious pies with them. I have never tasted anything as sweet as Tom's pies.

Once Michael and I decided to have a competition with Tom. We believed we could find more blackberries than Tom. We had found a new spot near Mid-Cornwall pit. You could only reach it if you were small enough to crawl through the pipe over which the brambles scrambled. Tom accepted our challenge. It was the last week of the school holidays. We were both convinced we could beat him. The spot was near the Drinnick end of the

Blackpool Refiner railway line, which ran parallel to the village. We headed along Beaconside and climbed down the edge of the bridge. The soil was dry and our clothes became dusty. At the bottom we brushed one another off.

The line ran straight for about a mile, always on a pink ballast. Towards Carpalla, at the southern end of Foxhole, the lines seemed to converge, where a heat haze was rising. But after that it swung around to the right, next to the chasm-like drop into Carpalla pit. Mike bent down, pushing his head to the greasy track, appearing to listen to the ground. I began to pick the berries. He was still there.

'What are you doing?'
'Listening.'
'What for?'
'Trains.'
'Trains?'
'Yeh. If you put your ear to the track you can hear the train miles away.'

This seemed too much like a Cornish superstition, but I put my head to the track.

'I can't hear anything,' I said.
'You can't?'
'No.'
'Well, I can't either. We're okay then. There'll be no trains for a while.'

We both knew the dangers of the line, but no-one in the village took any notice of any railway regulations. The line seemed public property. Even more so when the cutting hosted a large number of blackberries. Michael took one side and I the other. We worked hard, pinching off the berries and placing them into jugs. When the jugs were full we emptied them into a huge bread tin we had stood on a signal mounting. After an hour or so we had collected a quantity of berries and had made our way quite a distance along the cutting.

However, the berries here were hardly perfect. Each had a white coating that resembled icing sugar. It was not sugar, though. It was dust that had blown from the railway wagons as they tumbled through the cutting. Most vegetation here was covered with the same dust.

Every quarter of an hour Mike bent down and placed his ear to the track. Then he would resume picking. A Shack flew over a couple of times and we were kept company by the numerous flies and gnats in the bracken. The blackberries tasted good. They seemed to taste better the nearer we got to the pit at Mid-Cornwall, where the cutting descended and the track ran over a small brick bridge. Here there had been a leakage of clayey water on to the plants. I ate a few more – I had never tasted blackberries before I had come to Cornwall. I had barely tasted any urts or berries fresh from the plants that bore them. I had never drunk water from a spring.

Blackberries, somehow, seem the right fruit for the clayland. They have such a wonderful colour – a deep purpley black. When you drop a berry in the white mica they set each other off well, the mica like skimmed cream. The blackberries also matched the Foxgloves. It was as if a purple colour was pushing up beneath the whiteness, demanding a richness where there was a blandness. While I was thinking this, Michael shouted.

'Look. There's men working down there...'

He was right. Beyond a small hillock a group of men were working on the construction of some kind of dam at the southern end of Carpalla pit.

'We'd better get to that good place before they see us,' Michael said.

I followed him down the embankment, dragging the bread bin half-full of berries. Michael nipped over a pipe with great adroitness, balancing himself like an acrobat. I shimmied across, holding the bin on my knees. Below us bubbled a mess of mica overflow. A few yards from this pipe was another large enough to crawl through, into the spot where we knew there were many blackberries. Michael came out as quickly as he went in.

'Bleddy hell... there's an adder in there.'

'An adder?'

'A big bugger,' Michael said, as he grabbed a stick and began to poke the reptile from a safe distance.

'Don't,' I said. 'You're getting him annoyed.'

'Yeh, I want to.'

'No. We want to get him out. The more you poke him, the more he'll stay in there.'

'Okay smartass. You have a go.'

Taking a larger, thicker fern, I tried to move the adder. It was difficult. The snake wanted to stay where he was, and every time I forced him to move the two of us jumped back. Eventually, I dragged it to the end of the pipe, then held it there. Mike used his stick to push it out of the pipe and into a ditch. The snake tumbled down. It was certainly a large adder. The piping was warm and had been a useful place for him to raise the temperature of his body. We were both apprehensive at going back into the pipe, but there were no more snakes. Inside, it was a blackberry paradise and we picked until the bin was full.

We made our way out through the pipe and back to the bridge.

Mike put his ear to the steel once more. He pushed me back after placing a ballast stone on the track.

'What are you doing?'

'Get back. Get down. There look...'

He pointed to a hollow next to the bridge.

'It's a train. I'm certain.'

I scrambled down, trying to handle the blackberries carefully. Somehow, we both expected the train to come from the Drinnick direction, to the east. It was a surprise then that it came up from Blackpool, a 108 class engine pulling fifty or so empty clay wagons, their sheetings folded down.

'What's the rock for Mike?'

'You watch... just watch the train crush it.'

Our eyes were level with the train's wheels. Our noses became clogged with the stench of diesel smoke. Fumes landed on our hair and the blackberries. The train had instantly crushed the stone. My whole body shuddered as it did so. I saw the driver inside the cab. I looked up a little to see the wagons go by. Mike pushed my head down. Musically they passed, their buffers and chains clinking. After the train had passed we stood up and climbed up on to the line again. It was single tracked.

'Can you balance?' I asked.

Mike did not answer. He just climbed on to the track and carefully held out his arms like a ballerina, daintily putting one foot before the other and making a good deal of progress. I tried but I was still carrying the now heavy blackberry bin.

'Give us a hand...'

Mike waited, then grabbed the other handle of the bin. The move should have stopped there. We walked on regardless for some distance. Then my shoe encountered a leak of engine oil on the track. In a moment I lost balance and the handle of the berries. With the cantilever broken Mike fell as well, taking the berries with him. The bin clinked on the ballast and toppled over; the day's work tumbled into a clayey trough between the ballast and the embankment. I reached over to try to save some. The rest were covered in residual mica and clay. Mike looked at me hard.

'You bloody fool,' he said.

'You as well,' I said, then we laughed and threw lumps of mica on to an overflow pipe. When it grew dark we took a large stone and flung it into Carpalla pit. It is still down there, that stone, submerged and alone, under a cover of mica.

Mica is a horrible substance. Everyone knows about it on Hensbarrow. It is the waste residue from the processing of raw clay. The clay people dump it in disused pits so that any further clay may settle, and so may be dredged up once more and processed. There are lakes of mica in the clayland – lakes of sloppy whiteness, as if some giant being has sucked out all the colour. Smell mica and it smells of the earth – damp, years old, sort of rich, but a don't-know-what-to-do-with substance.

And gallons of it are pumped up from the pits when the clay is separated, and then it is piped distances through pipes, around which the sweet blackberry grows, through ferns and lupins, to plop into a white death pit where no water boatmen swim and where you find no fish. The only thing that lives is the mica.

When it has been stationary for a time the mica develops a crust like cold custard – the school teachers used to tell it that way – and so even though it appears hard it is soft underneath. It is everywhere over Hensbarrow, in ditches where it has leaked from pipes, little lumps coagulated along the railway line, great tracts of it in the disused pits. And mica is to children like honey is to bears. Mica is evil, yet it also has something resolutely playful about it – the way it squidges, the way it squirts, the way the crust breaks when you stamp on it. And so if you look hard enough you will see little discarded wellingtons where some unfortunate mite has had to leave a boot behind and hobble sock-footed home. Because once the mica grabs hold of you it is a tough battle to make it release you. Like flies in spiders' webs.

If you want to see mica residues then go to Kernick or Terras, or Mid-Cornwall, or Carpalla – for that is where Michael and I used to go. 'Come, let me take you down, because we're going to Carpalla pit... Nothing is real...'

Carpalla is a lovely clay pit my friends. A silly thing to say, but it really is, or rather was, for the only thing that remains of it now is the fragile shell of the engine house, a tacky comparison to the tin mines of Penwith; and the remains of a lengthy dry, where the railway used to pass loaded with shipments for Par docks and Fowey. But even after it had closed, and even when the water rose high, it still remained my favourite place. All the workings, the buildings, the pumps, the settling pits, the tanks, the screens are all in their positions still, and it is at Carpalla where time has stopped. Peering into the cap'n's office, see a pin-up, now probably drawing her pension, see the coal-tar soap still wet from the last hands to use it, the kettle still plugged in... and yet the men have gone. Now this place belongs to the spirits and children.

Though the plants have sprung up from the mica drags, and the oblong clay tanks bustle with reeds and bulrushes and frog spawn, nature's own sago pudding nestles in the corners where the clay once flowed. It still seems that tomorrow someone will come in, clock-on and light the fire in the kilns. There is still coal there, black – energy yet to be released. However, even these things must end and a time must come for them to go, to disappear and to crumble. And that came with the news that Carpalla was to be made into a vast mica pit, for residual clay coming along the railway line from Goverseth Refinery.

Unknown to the workmen, Michael and I would go down to Carpalla, climb the tip and laze all day long in the lupins, watching the earthmovers and scrapes constructing a dam in the south to stop the mica running down the valley. The construction of the dam was an immense undertaking with tonnes of overburden and sand brought in, the trucks dumping the earth over places which would never see light again. And when the beaver-like activity of the diesel creatures ceased, in the evenings, Michael and I would stand on the dam and throw larger stones down the bank towards the Coombe Valley, green and luscious. Then we would turn, look north and see the village of Carpalla, itself tagged on the end of Foxhole, a snake of houses running along a contour of Hensbarrow. Above that, Watch Hill, and above Watch Hill the ever-increasing tip of Blackpool pushing its way skywards and northwards.

The actual flooding of the pit, and the area created by the dam, came a few weeks later, after environmentalists had entered the woodland above which the dam had been constructed. Watt said they had rescued a pair of foxes and a sett of badgers, but they were sure there was another sett down there they had been unable to flush out. They wanted the mica to enter the pit with great speed, but instead it was a mere trickle, gently plopping out of the pipe into the main lake up over a sluice gate and into the additional area created by the dam. But they did see the twigs, white with the ooze, and the grasses, mosses, ferns and leaf-litter gradually covered with mica. It looked a beautiful way to go. That's how I felt I wanted to go, consumed in a sea of whiteness. But when the mica reached higher, I saw that it was no sea – just a thick smelly white mud, settling over all in its path. A white plague...

By the time it became dark, and the arc lights around the pit were on, the area was still only half full. We had wanted an avalanche of mica, a great swirl of solution. Instead, it came as a slow killer. At least the badgers had gone with dignity.

I saw Watt tap at the mica half way down the dam with his walking stick. The mica was still runny. He swore. He could not find a place to wipe the stick off without covering it in grains of sand. Nor was he able to climb up the bank again without our help. And so the dam was flooded. By the next day it had filled up completely and we saw men with yellow helmets looking at documents and blueprints of the operation. It had gone to plan.

Three weeks later we went down to inspect the new lake. Just as we were gathering a collection of small stones from the track that led there, in baskets created from our shirts, I saw Michael stand bolt upright, dropping all his stones.

'Look,' he said.

I turned around, still holding the stones close to my belly.

'The cows.'

I could see nothing.

'What?'

'Come here. Look. See the cows. They've got down over the embankment and walked out on to the mica dam.'

I moved to where Michael was standing. On the edge of the dam three hefty Jerseys were knee deep in the mica. They had broken the crust and now, with their legs dangling helplessly in the slop, were struggling and frightened, though one of them still strained her neck for that lush grass which had first attracted them on to the dam.

A fourth cow was still roaming on the bank of the dam, oblivious to the danger her companions were in. It was strange to see them there, wallowing in the white. Trapped in a milky sea. Their dung-splattered legs were coated with a clay residue. The cows belonged to Mr Mellow. If he lost them that would be the end of his smallholding.

But before I thought any of this Michael had legged it up the track. I urged him to get as many men down to the pit as possible and call for a fire engine and a vet. In the meantime, I slid down the bank, ripping a hole in my ass pocket and filling my shoes with sand. How did the stupid buggers get down here? And after that the cows had to climb over the railway line and up the walls of the dam itself. This was no easy thing for a human, let alone a cow, great hulking beasts that they are. When I reached the top of the bank, out of breath, the fourth cow became scared and hung nervously on the levee, from where the other cows had gone on to the dam. How do you calm a cow? How do you tell it that mica is dangerous? The smell of bovine yellow, of milk wet fingers. The eyes – those eyes, dark and timeless. Never is black so beautiful as in the eyes of a cow.

'Don't go in there cow. Come on. Follow me...' I said, treating this cow as a person.

But she stayed there, glancing over at her friends. She could not let them go. Her udders shivered as the wind blew across the lake. She swung her tail to kill the last flies of summer. So gentle, so pensive...

I ripped out a gorse bush, walked around behind the cow and gave a hefty whack. It made a move. I hit her again and she let out an almost inaudible cry. These cows were not mooing – not now.

In this time, I realised the best thing to do was to let her go down on to the railway embankment. At least there she would be away from the mica and I knew no trains ran in the evening.

Now, when I return to Mid-Cornwall, I wonder how the hell they went through the crust, because now the lake looks like a field. It is covered in grasses, bulrushes and water boatmen. And the mica, well, the mica you can hardly see. It is stained purple and brown and has red ants crawling over it. But then, as the cows went into the soup, the red ants did not dip their toes.

Two of the cows were fairly close to the bank, but the lighter cow had been able to walk out further, merely to find that sweeter mouthful of grass. It seemed like a surrealist winter scene that had happened before, except that on Hensbarrow cows fall through industrial custard. I edged down to the lake and could almost touch the first cow, which was about half submerged by now with small traces of mica globules on her whiskers, warm juices from her mouth dripping into the pudding. There was nothing I could do. Certainly, you do not step on broken mica. That would be like stepping on quicksand. And so all I could do was say comforting words and make sympathetic noises. And pray to God for somebody to get down here with ropes and boards. And the cows watched me, and I watched the cows. And they could not understand why I did not help them.

Some twenty minutes after Michael had left I heard voices running down the rough track and up over the embankment. He had found some men – Georgie Allen, Eric Julian and a few boys with ropes and ladders. They had got in touch with Mr Mellow, and he was on his way. As they reviewed the dilemma the sound of a fire engine was heard coming through the village from St Dennis. Within minutes the tender had halted along the trackside and a group of firemen were scrambling up the bank the same way I had – all of them getting thorns somewhere in their hands.

Rescuing the first of the cows, the one nearest to the bank, was relatively easy, with the men laying boards down around the animal, then attaching ropes to her, which ran back to a winch in the fire engine. She came out with a plop, as the mica fell in on the space created by her bulky frame. A couple of boards were lost as well. The cow was milky, her udders weighty – dribbles seeping from her teats.

'Two more to go,' Georgie said. 'Do 'ee think we'en do 'un boy?'

I said that I hoped so.

Mr Mellow arrived with the veterinary surgeon. Mr Mellow, in his threadbare jumper, a few day's growth on his chin, his left cheek stained yellow where a cigarette always hung. The vet – smart, serious and smelling of soap – spoke with a Welsh accent. Mr Mellow, as the Cornish say, 'sized up' the situation.

'You've saved two of them then, be buggered.'

All nodded their heads cautiously. He spoke again. This time to Michael and myself.

'Can you go down the embankment an' try an' stop them cows going any further up the line.'

I clambered down, stopping myself sliding too fast by grasping at lupin plants. Michael elected to stay up top. I prevented the cows from roaming up the line any further, then sat and listened and watched the blue lights flashing on the fire appliance – each revolution turning the landscape azure. Above, a sickle moon winked at the scene between puffs of cloud. The smell of Mr Mellow's tobacco, rich and decadent, filtered through the bushes. Then came a thunder of four feet down the bank, and a white cow stood before me, eyes impenetrable, hairy coat painted in clay. So, this manatee had risen out of the waters. I watched her as she lifted her tail and excreted the anxiety of the last few hours.

The moon went into hiding for a few minutes and the railway line became very dark. I heard the hum of activity above and the rush of men's voices. I closed my eyes and wallowed in an armchair of dock leaves. And then the cows stopped mooing as a crack from a pistol reverberated across the filled pit. At least they had managed to rescue three.

Michael was first down the bank. He looked at me with eyes as dark as the cows'.

'Come on. It's time we got back up Karslake...'

I stood up and followed him, his trousers wet with mica.

'Lads...' came a voice, 'Thanks for what you did... good thing you was down here...'

It was Mr Mellow. 'Lads,' he had said strongly, but after that his voice faltered. We decided to walk on quickly, neither of us wanting to see him cry, for just as we got to the railway bridge Michael said:

'The one they shot... you know... she was calving soon.'

The fire engine's light had been switched off now. We walked up the hill in silence. And I could not keep my mind off a mother and child who had drowned in a sea of milk, but I would never have known then what was to happen to my own loved ones. Not ever. Not in a million years...

TOBIAS

4th October 1664.

Oure Age, I believe, is one of transition. My mind has not the capacity to contemplate all suche changes, yet I have enough learning to note that man's worlde is changing. I do not know if it is for the better. I merely know that it changes. Thynkers, philosophers and men of the like sway me to this opinion. The King's minister, the good Earl of Clarendon, ist oft old-fashion'd. He shalt soon fall. I finde we must change withe the times we do live in. Each week I hear of new discoveries in Physick, and of conquering of new lands ne'er thought of before on this earth, where they find all manner of strange creatures and vegetables. In the near future we shalt travel into the Heavens, by God. Of course, yon stable Brewer, like Clarendon, ist not in favour of suche motions.

I do discuss these motions withe dearest Susanna whilst we walke vpon the downs today.

Before we do meet, I do shake enormously and have thoughts that suche a meeting may be ill-cons'dered. These thoughts disappear once she dost rest her arm ont' mine, whilst we do tramp through the heather.

We do walk across from that part of the downs known as Whitemoor to where the good Longstone stands. The day ist cold and crisp, though wonderously sunny.

Susanna, being polite and brought up well, listens intently to my spoutings about the future. She, being a more realistic soul than I, believes thyngs wilt be slow to change. Fortune comes to us, however, as when we do rest in a sladdy our bodies do come sweetly together.

At first, I did kiss her squarely on the cheek. After this, and "is a terrible thyng I knowe, we do kiss on the lips by Heaven; and this, alack, vpon oure first walke together.

My father, God rest his soule, I knowe did court my mother some thirty times before he wast allowed a kiss. Me'thinks some of London's bawdiness ist in this maid. However, it suits her, and me, wonderously well.

We do returne, however, since in yon sladdy it is damp and wet. 'Tis the dew,' says I, but Susanna correcteth me. 'No,' says she, 'tis the clay. Tis always wet.'

We walk home with white clothes, embarrassed in the extreme. I pray that the Reverende didst not catch sight of me. If the man did, then I would receive a lecturing vpon my sins. For myself, however, I do not care. The age is reckless and I finde myself slipping. What humours alack! Tonight, I must sweep the church. Thyngs bode so well for me now that I do not notice the dust.

Lorde, thou art in my hearte forever. Amen.

T.T.

PART TWO

'The position with regard to the resources of china clay in Cornwall and Devon may be best summarised by saying that, at a rate of production of about one million tonnes per year, there are in these two counties sufficient resources which, if effectively developed, would last at least for 100 years, and this is excluding possible future discoveries remote from those already known.'

Board of Trade Working Party Report on China Clay, 1948.

OF PAGAN DESIRES

During the Bronze Age someone – an earlier digger – erected a single standing stone on the western edge of Hensbarrow to the north east of Watch Hill near the hamlet of Karslake. It had stood there for thousands of years, and now a boy called Ben Sexton goes to see it almost every week.

I LOVED the stone more than anything else at that stage of my life. It was one of the few natural, vertical things on Hensbarrow, standing twice my height and perfectly upright. You saw it long before actually arriving beneath it, and I marvelled at its shape. Each time I went up there I hugged it, the grey-green lichen staining my clothes. It felt like touching time itself.

The stone was one of the few Menhirs remaining intact in Cornwall. The site had been excavated by archaeologists. They had found that a timber post stood there once; then this was replaced by the stone. Curious isn't it? It was 3.2 metres high. From ground level, it towered above the heather like a Dark Ages skyscraper. Tom said his father had told him the stone was a lunar or solar setting point for a stone circle close by, but the circle had been obliterated by the clay workings.

'It had astronomical significance, then Tom?'

'That as well,' he would say, playing upon his scientific confusion.

'That as well...' Sometimes it was as if he knew something more, something beyond what we chose to call 'science'.

'Father used to say to me twas Saint Austell's staff.'

'Saint Austell?'

'Es. He used to live on the moor here once, or so they say. Devil changed his staff to stone. Land belongs to the Devil now. Our only protector is that staff.'

I could not milk any more information out of Tom. This was either all he knew, or all he was telling.

In actual fact, the monolithic stone was a lump of common granite with some beautiful quartz crystals visible. But the most interesting thing of all was its shape. Firstly, of course, its length, giving the stone and the section of moor around it its name. More than that, though, it resembled a canine tooth, sharp and pointed, indented on one side. I always felt its roots, like human teeth, must go down deep into the soil of the moor. Fang-like, it stayed in the summer, when the grasses grew long around it, and in winter, when ice collected and cracked the stone's surface. Yet it never seemed to change, and while man bit into the earth all around it, this tooth was the only thing that never changed. When the sun set in the west, if you caught it just right, the stone became a black shadow; the rays of the sun permeating around it. A Bronze Age aurora still alive.

There are many standing stones in Cornwall which have stood waiting for thousands of years; simply waiting. Perhaps that's all they were meant to do, wait for the moment. This stone, however, was more special to me. I really believed it to be the tallest stone, the longstone. I loved the way the Cornish said it – 'Looooongstooooone', emphasising its very quality. But there was something else about it, something pagan, something phallic. The things wet dreams are made of.

And something diabolic; that put many Cornish off it. The Cornish Methodism has now almost replaced any remnants of pre-Methodist Celtic power. But I did not care, neither then nor now. In Essex, they had none of these, and if the Cornish no longer wanted to embrace the stone, then I would. I called it my stone, and though it was everyone's, I felt it was to me it belonged. As if I had met it before. When I stood next to it I felt the rays of a saintly past home in on the stone.

As well as this, we used to have adolescent fantasies. In our late teens, Mike and I used to go to the stone and confess what we would do if we had a girl there alone. Pubescent fantasy? Perhaps. Or rather it was more Mike talking frankly and me listening. He told me how he would like to take a 'maid' up here, and get her gear off. It would have to be a sunny day he said. Perfect conditions. Then he would shout out what he would do with her. Loud, so that everyone on the moor could hear. But there was really no need. It was inevitably drowned out by the roar of the hoses in the pit below. I would be more subtle, I believe, explaining how I would like to have a picnic there, sitting with our backs to the stone, then falling asleep together, and then...

'Give her a good...' Mike said slowly.

But there was to be no sex on Longstone's Down, next to the stone, since our contact with girls was small. And in 1969 Longstone's Pit was expanded beneath the site of the stone, which had to be removed. The stone never witnessed our sexual antics, only our adolescent dreams.

It now stands out of context, surrounded by dwarf trees and shrubs before an old people's estate in Roche. On it is a plaque.

'This stone, erected during the Bronze Age on the Longstone's

Down, was removed to this site in August 1970.'

'Thousands of years it's stood up there, and now they move it just because they want more clay. Bastards,' said Mike, on our way home from cycling to see the stone in its new site.

And so that is the story of the stone my friends. One of many, you might say. Will it stay at Harmony Close for the next thousand years; safe and sound?' We shall see...

OF GOOD, AND BAD MEDICINE

'There are some plants which are disallowed or neglected by botanists, but whose qualities brought into action by some church-town crony will sometimes cure a disease which has been given up by her betters as irremediable.'

(Polwhele, 1826)

'LOOK love. They're not getting any better, are they? Are you still putting on that stuff the doctor gave you?' said my mother, grasping my arm about the wrist and holding my hand close to her face.

'That one's really terrible...'

'Yeh. I keep putting the stuff on,' I said nonchalantly.

'Well, I don't like the look of them. I was speaking to Mrs Grose today, you know Julian's mother, and she says you should go and see Mary who lives up in Greensplat, up at Carroncarrow there...'

'But...'

'She reckons Mary can cure anything like that. It's where Mrs Grose goes for all her ailments.'

'But...'

'But what?'

'But they say... she's a witch or something.'

'Don't be silly,' said my father gruffly.

'Go on Ben; it's only twenty five to six. You'll be over there by six.'

'Who told you she's a witch anyway?' asked my father.

'Oh... a few people. Mike reckons she is.'

'Jesus boy, don't you take any notice of him. He's only trying to put the willies up you. Go on. If she can get rid of your warts then you're all the better for knowing her.'

So I left home on my bicycle and headed across the purple moor, past the Longstone – the spider's home – and up around Karslake. Rounding a corner, I rang my bell, the warts on my hand seeming great lumps. I put my hand into my pocket, not wanting the world to see me as a leper or someone with a plague. And then, not really wanting to see this woman Mary. Didn't she have a last name? Mary. Mary. It seemed she was still a small girl. Why wasn't she called Mrs something or other, or Aunty thingy?

And as the clouds rattled in over the moor all I could think of was fairy stories, a hooked nose and a black cat. Of cauldrons and lizards. Tales to scare children. And that name, Mary. Mary, the partner to my Joseph once in the school play. Mary in a blue dress with a babe in swaddling. Mary. Mary.

'Mary, Mary, quite contrary, how does your garden grow? With silver bells and cockleshells, and pretty maids all in a row...'

Unknown to me then a figure watched me cycle, just as I had watched him cycle once on a lady's bike down to Noppies. And he was sitting with the sun behind him, his stick pushed into the sand, and he was twirling the years of his beard. And I never noticed him, though he sat on Lower Ninestones Tip, an isosceles triangle thrusting up from the moor.

Tom sat on its very tip with his legs crossed, like he used to sit when we went rabbiting; he resembled an Aztec god. And the sun set, making a rich mosaic of the quarry floor, and when he told me of this, I somehow knew he had been watching me hard, both eyes eagle-sure. I knew his head had then swivelled like an aged owl, and he would blink, then watch me disappear over the brow of Cocksbarrow Hill. Then Tom climbed down.

By which time, I had stopped outside Mary's cottage. I took my hand out of my pocket, to steady myself, then got off the bike. I dumped it in the hedgerow and peered into Mary's. Her cottage was rather more a shack, made of black, galvanised steel, hammered and twisted into shape, hellishly hot in the summer and bitterly cold in winter. But then it occurred to me that the structure had a recognisable shape, and that in fact the shack was composed largely of an old railway carriage, which had been converted into this sombre looking dwelling.

Any cockleshells and silver bells were hidden by the profuse growth of brambles and other strange plants about the cottage, though a clear path wound through them up to the front door. The picture was still, save for a wisp of woodsmoke running skywards. This was how fairy stories began, I told myself as I walked ill at ease up the path and rapped hard on the door. There was no answer. I tried again. This time knocking with my warty hand. On the third try, a figure approached me from around the back of the house. She held a sickle and wore a lace shawl. Death and birth in one body.

'Yes?' I thought I heard her say.

'I'm looking for Mary.'
'Mary?'
'Yes. Mary. I'm told she can rid me of these warts on my hand. Look...'
I showed her.
'What's your name?'
'Ben. Ben Sexton.'
'Ah then, Ben. Come inside with me, and I'll see what I can do for you.'
She walked past me, dropping the bright sickle on the path. She took off her scarf and shawl, displaying her odd blonde hair. Odd because no woman I had seen before had hair that shiny at her age. Age appeared not to have touched her. Her smile was beautiful, alluring even. Finally, she spoke.
'I'm Mary.'
'Nice to meet you, Mrs... Mrs... Mary,' I replied.
So this was my witch, my cackling hag. This woman who stood before me, who I felt was in her forties and yet she had preserved her looks so well. Her hair was almost like that of a twenty year old, and it fell down her neck in tiny curls. Perhaps this box she lived in had preserved her. Perhaps, because time had left her alone, jealous women called her a witch.
'You're not from Hensbarrow are you Ben?'
'I was born in Essex. We've only lived here a while,' I said, as she took my hand and carefully felt the warts.
'We live down Noppies, down Halviggan way.' And when I said this I put on a more local accent.
'I live down that way, near Tom, old Tom Cundy. He works up Longstone's. He probably knows you.'
'Yes,' Mary said. 'Tom and I used to do a lot together... once. Your warts, how long have you had them?'
I felt her hand grow cold, and eventually she let my hand drop unexpectedly from her clasp.
'About three months.' I said.
'I see,' she said, distractingly, with the confidence of a lifetime doctor. 'I have to fetch something.'
When Mary went out of the room I knew this woman was no witch, though she was certainly different from many people on Hensbarrow. For one thing her house was wildly decorated with dried flowers, twigs and berries, which hung from the thick rafters of the cottage, giving a sleep-inducing aroma. A strange smell of nettles came from the kitchen. The room was also oddly decorated with soft water-colour pictures of Hensbarrow. I recognised the view from just outside the house, before Greensplat pit had recently expanded, and on them, in the neatest writing, was

written 'Mary' in the bottom right-hand corner. On a table were several hand-bound books, and next to them a thick fountain pen.

There was something else strange about Mary, and that was her clothes. The clothes she wore were the fashion, I guessed, from quite a few years back, and the outer garments she wore when I had greeted her resembled that of the old clay bal-maidens, who used to scrape the clay blocks ready to be sold so that at least they looked clean, even if they weren't. I had seen photographs of them at Tom's place, and this scared me because I really did begin to think time had stopped here. She had no radio or television.

Mary came back from the kitchen. For a moment, I drew back in my chair. She carried a porcelain bowl, and in it was a murky, green solution, the colour of the clay pit pools.

'Dip your hand in this Ben. Don't worry. It won't sting. Tis only one of Mary's remedies m'andsome. Hedgerow medicine, that's what I call it...'

I stayed there, with my hand dipped in the bowl for some time, Mary occasionally taking a cloth and putting the solution over the rest of my hand, which remained uncovered. As I prayed that the warts would disappear after this, I thought carefully; for though I knew Mary to be no witch, I found her both disturbing and strange.

Now, in these green times when we have almost pushed superstition and stories out of the window, we would probably like to know Mary, to ask her to set down all her herbal medicines and natural methods of curing.

In the late twentieth century, homeopathy is no longer witchcraft. It is fashionable. Natural. Body and environment friendly. It is something we all must consider. Except, where do we find the plants now? They are all gone... But Mary had them all. I saw shelves in the kitchen packed with glass bottles of solutions and leaves, roots and stems.

Later, Mary would list them all for me. Angelica leaves and elder flower for colds, ivy for wounds and cuts, groundsel for ague, mallow leaves for bruises, crowfoot for eye ulcers, coltsfoot as a precaution against lung disease, the small section of ash wood she carried in her pocket... for her rheumatism. But there was no eye of newt or wing of bat. Was this what kept Mary young, those natural ways, those old ways? The ways 'The Body Shop' makes millions from. I wondered if she dug the clay to make a face pack with. I still believe she kept some in the larder...

'That's enough now,' Mary said, and she wiped my hand with a piece of linen. 'They should drop off soon and you won't know you had them.'

While I waited to thank her, as she threw the solution away in the dairy, I noticed in the corner, on a roughly made chair, a china-faced doll in a grand christening dress.

'That's a nice doll,' I commented when Mary returned.

'Yes,' she said awkwardly.

I recognised my cue to leave.

'Thank you for the stuff you put on my... warts. Thank you... Mary.'

She smiled and opened the door for me. The last thing I saw her do was pick up the sickle and walk into the twilight around the back of the house.

'I escaped,' I muttered to myself half jokingly, half fearfully. 'I escaped the witch...'

Cycling towards the very top of Hensbarrow, I viewed another cyclist in the distance, one who had obviously just pushed her bike up Gunheath Hill. At the top she had switched on her dynamo, as the twilight was turning to darkness. And yet I could see her hair trailing out behind, her face red from the tough push up the hill.

'Good evening,' I said, but she passed without a word, like the moths of the night who flickered before her front cycle lamp.

AT the bottom of Lower Longstones tip, Tom emptied his boots of sand and was now carefully picking his way over an area of broken stone.

Another ley-line was about to furrow his forehead. His beard was soon to turn a shade whiter. Thoughts that he believed he had buried years ago had been churned up by this boy, this changeling, this saintly soul whom he loved, this strange boy new to Hensbarrow.

It set Tom thinking, going over it all – everything that happened so long ago that it seemed in the year one, when the clay was still burping into place. It set him thinking of why it all happened, and how, and where, and how he had failed, and how he felt so sick about it all. He had not spoken to a soul about it for years. Would the rumours start again he wondered? Would the clay people's tongues wag as he walked through Foxhole or went to chapel. Yes, chapel. See, Mary never went to chapel. None of her family ever did. People knew they were strange.

Bad blood in that family. Tom, well, he was different. He was everyone's idea of a 'strong chap'. They never liked her for that...

Tom thought of the time when he believed the fiction, believed the stories, and took little notice of what she said. And it all ended so bitterly – her running across the moor, taking, taking everything from him, and by Ben's visit he felt the sinews of his heart dusted down, ready to be twisted and distorted again. And how he restrained himself when they had called her names. He pictured her face when they pulled her hair, and kicked her in the solar plexus. Her face streaming with tears, bloody tears. And she wasn't the only one to be kicked. Tom had his share of 'sense' instilled in him as well.

In the seventeenth century she would have been tied to a stake and burnt... 'A Most, Certain and True Discovery of a Witch.'

Then he was brushing through the lupins with her. He pictured times before that when even the clay felt good, when he could forget the evil and go down to Carne Tor, and they could chase one another around the stones, to rest in a bed of ferns, the fronds catching them in their youthful madness. And that is what he used to tell himself, that it was all youthful madness. Some kind of midsummer night's dream he had been a part of. Maybe one of the lovers... and yet at times he would stand at his window at Noppies and look up to Carroncarrow, below Greensplat, and wonder how she was. That was where he would begin to dream of things that might have been. So near, and yet so far.

So this old man, limping down over the moor heard his heart talking to him, and yes, he did feel a twinge of hardness in his groin when he thought of her body, soft as it was, when they had time together alone in the fifties on the moor, making love beneath a cloudless azure sky. Perhaps he was being over-imaginative here, but it did not rain. And it was, shall we say, before the clay, before it really started to fall out of the earth...

Tom watched a pair of foxes stalk down to Blackpool, tongues wet, tails warm, and he thought of all the time, all this time, the thing we look at our wrists for, thought that he should have tasted her wetness, felt how warm she was. Except now he was shivering and it is hard to imagine on Hensbarrow. Shivering in the wind with a head full of fantasies that he never even got to tell her about. When the foxes spied him they darted across the field, their tails bobbing above the long grass. As darkness came down, Tom caught a last glimpse of their yellow eyes – as frightened as he was.

At home, he kicked off his boots in the kitchen, making a mess over the lino, and went into the sitting room where the embers of the fire were just dying. He had forgotten to add some coal to the fire before he went out.

Tom took the silver-framed picture from the dresser and studied it hard. How did she look now Tom? Her body as old as yours. Her teeth as rotten as yours. He replaced the picture on the dresser, setting it face down, and went into the porch and brought in a bottle of wine, plonking it on the dresser so that the picture bounced. Tom knew it to be a good one, an urt wine of ten, possibly fifteen, years old. He uncorked the brown bottle and raised it to his mouth. This was the only medicine he needed now. The medicine of forgetting. The wine burnt its way down into his gut, and he remembered the azure haze again.

Seven hours later his alarm went off, for Tom was on forenoons, but this morning he slept on.

WHEN I reached home it was pitch black, though I could see Tom's light on. I dumped the bike in the outhouse and entered the kitchen.

'Ah Ben,' said my mother. 'You should have taken your lights with you...'

'I got back okay, didn't I?'

'Did you see Mary? I see she didn't turn you into a frog or anything...' she joked.

'No,' I replied, 'she's not a witch, but she is a bit strange. Her house has a funny...'

'Funny what?'

'Funny atmosphere or something. I can't explain it. She dipped my hand in some green stuff and told me not to wash my hands today.'

Later, when I retired to bed, I noticed Tom's light was still on, and I thought this unusual since he was never late to bed for a morning shift. As I tossed and turned, first I thought of Mary's beauty and tried hard to think where I had seen it before, but I soon became tired of this and so, as my awakening thoughts shifted to my sleeping ones, I had a fixation of the moth girl, and how she had fluttered past me, past the place...

OF THE SKYTIP

CLAY quarries can never sleep. Each day they are hammered, drilled, washed, exploded, blasted, dug, scooped and exposed, and then, when the day ends, it all starts again in the night. So, moon or sun, on Hensbarrow the clay is being raised.

For the workers the clay world is one turned upside-down; at night, when all is dark elsewhere, the pit is lit up by hundreds of powerful arc lights, and working by day the clay is so glaring it is necessary to wear sunglasses to prevent damaging the eyes. From a distance, it all looks silly.

The men, for it is a men's world in the pits, sit in little huts of steel working hoses which look so frail from above but which rap on the quarry's gnarled face.

But go in close, trek up the quarry floor, and you will find Tom, or people like Tom, painting pictures with the hoses.

Tom has done this for the last thirty years, but he never lets his concentration lapse, he never needs a radio, and still the roar of the hose thrills him, a beast that he can master – making it work.

But Tom is not painting tonight. Tonight he is up on the skytip – that is after he has carried out Cap'n Martin's instructions. Another timeless task, turning on a hose. It was ten to nine. The night shift has just come in, Cap'n Martin's gang. The men in the boothouse were talking about the European football on tele last night, and who is collecting the Pools money this week – their one chance of escape. But Tom had other things on his mind. He was down the pit before the rest of the gang.

'What Tom!' a rugged voice shouted from behind the gravel pump. Tom raised his arm, not really noticing Freddie John taking a leak before his shift ended. Tom began to walk up the stope where he had to turn on the hose. The hose valves were enormous things. To open them, you had to use your whole body weight on a bar that was attached to the valve spindle, and then push it around. So around each valve there was a little circle of footprints which had stamped the soil firm. And when you had pushed just far enough, you felt the ground rattle and vibrations come up through your arm as the water went rushing through the network of pipes, up to the hose at the end of the stope, like some kind of man-made geyser. There, it shot out and told the clay it was time to leave its age-old site.

Around him, the pit hummed. The humming of generators, the humming of arc lights, the humming of mechanical loaders. In summer, in addition, there were the whispers of the dusty dragonflies which congregated around the lights and pools. Tom tasted the air. It was warm, so he knew this would be an all right shift tonight. It was a bastard to work up at the Skytip in rain.

The skytip was found at the top of all the clay tips. You rarely see them now, but you might say they were all the rage. Basically Tom's job as a skytip worker was to clear away excess sand from the tracks of a pulley-pulled wagon which ran from the bottom of the pit to the top of the sand tip. Years ago, the eight tons of waste for every one ton of clay were spread out across the moor, but to avoid covering future reserves of clay, conical tipping became the in-thing, keeping the tipping area small. Down at the 'dog's hole', the clay was loaded in. Tom believed Charlie to be down there tonight.

He got to the top at about nine-thirty, and worked contentedly for three hours. To work at the skytip required a degree of concentration, for one had to be reasonably alert to avoid being hit by one of the wagons, and to remove the inevitable spillage of sand each time the wagon tipped. Then Cap'n Martin drove up to the tip in his Land Rover.

Tom heard the engine of the vehicle shudder to a halt, but he continued shovelling. Cap'n Martin was the same age as Tom. They had played together once. Cap'n Martin, yes, he had got on in the clayworks. Never put a foot out of line.

'Ow's it goin' Tom?'

'All right Cap'n.'

Cap'n Martin paused, watched Tom for a while, then spoke again.

'No Tom. I mean how's it really goin'?'

'Eh?'

'Well, talking 'bout yesterday's forenoons. You'm all right be 'ee? Nothing wrong is there? I've never known you to miss a shift all these years boy...'

'Nothing wrong Cap'n,' Tom replied. 'Bleddy new alarm didn' go off. That's all twas. I was a bit tired yes'day as well...'

Cap'n Martin believed him.

'Well. I'll leave 'ee to 'un Tom. You know we'm having conveyer belts put in here soon dunnee' know?'

'I heard Billy and Charlie talkin' about it...'

The Cap'n put his hand in his pocket and jangled his change. Then he spoke: 'Es, next month I hear, the belt gang's coming out to put 'em in.

'Tis all going Tom, all going. The next thing 'twill be in the claywork, is they won't be needing no men!'

'I reckon you're right there.'

But Cap'n Martin felt awkward. Tom clearly did not want to take the bite for a chat with him as they had always done up here, Tom always sharing a cup of strong tea with him. They both pushed back their hair, which was blowing in the wind. The Cap'n looked out towards St Mawgan. Was that a Shackleton he could hear? Was this picture they had painted together about to end? The Cap'n noticed a difference in his companion, if not a difference then at least a distance. For a second the Cap'n toyed with the words pit and tip in his mind, thinking how they were opposites in a way; then he turned his mind back to Tom, thinking how far apart they had grown recently.

'I'll pick 'ee up around quarter to five, Tom. See 'ee then...'

'A'right Cap'n,' said Tom softly.

The rest of the shift went slowly, as anyone can tell you who has worked shifts; anticipate a shift to pass quickly and it inevitably drags. Expect a shift never to end and it very often races along without you noticing. Tom's shift that night went slowly, but when the spirits of the clay artists had returned again, and their eyes grew tired, and they dreamt of their soft beds at home, the skytip wagon jammed.

'Bleddy Tom up there. Bugger's fallen asleep...'

And the gang all laughed. But when Freddie and Cap'n Martin took the Land Rover up to the top of the tip, they could see Tom nowhere. That was until Cap'n Martin looked over the edge of the tip, down the forty-five degree angle that divided the tip from the pit.

'Over here Freddie,' Captain Martin said.

'Tom?' said Freddie.

'Fraid so...'

Tom now in another place, drifting, a... part...

OF A DREAM TIME

ON the other side of the world, where the Cornish went to dig as 'Cousin Jacks', the Aborigines have an expression which explains the way things are. Why, for example, the kangaroo has such large feet, and they call it the 'dream time'.

It is the explanation of the first two chapters of Genesis. Hensbarrow has a dream time, also, or maybe we should call it a 'time for dreaming', and for Hensbarrow the dream time has never changed. It was the dream time then, it is the dream time now, it will be the dream time tomorrow.

For on Hensbarrow, though small things change, like when they moved the Longstone, Hensbarrow still stays the same; nothing changes, certainly not the people – these people who dig the clay but are too reserved to paint it on their faces in grotesque designs, unlike their dream time cousins in Australia or the Ancient Britons who smeared themselves in woad.

And it makes you wonder; what if you could dig a hole through the earth, right through, right through those bits in the middle still burping into place, and out the other side into a Southern Hemisphere desert, instead of a Northern Hemisphere moor.

Perhaps then dream times might merge into one, and somewhere, perhaps under a rock, in that one insignificant place where cockroaches and millipedes once used to feed, the dream might become the truth and everything might be good again.

See, the dream time was the best time of all. But then maybe we are only dreaming. Yet you know what they say; keep your head in the clouds, your feet on the ground, and keep looking at them stars...

On Hensbarrow, few dreamed of an Aborigine's face. Instead, I dream of the moth girl and believe I am flying with her above the moor, and that I am brushing her hair. But we are trapped by a spider's web spun on the Longstone, with a damp pillow tight to my belly. Then I wake, wondering what has happened, then fall back to sleep believing I am wearing a large hat and pointing a staff in a 'hold thy peace' position towards the clay.

Watt dreams in his mahogany bed with Mrs Watt of their honeymoon in Bournemouth, and of his pink toes upon the sandy beach. He dreams of candy floss and a donkey ride. Then, and because she had a stutter, that Mrs Watt was n-n-nuzzling into him. He must chop sticks tomorrow for her.

Mary dreams children's dreams of monsters beneath a bed of heather and healing plants. She dreams motherly dreams of pram-pushing in a park – where the hell do you push a pram on Hensbarrow? – and hatred dreams of those who left her unhappy. When she wakes in the early morning she finds her armpits are more sweaty than normal.

The moth girl dreams of the film she saw at the cinema all night, except at five past two when she turns over and dreams, only for a second, that she will not wake tomorrow to look out of the window at the side of her bed and see Halviggan tip.

Then she turns over once more, and dreams of the film again. Her breasts make it uncomfortable for her to sleep too long on her front.

Tom dreams of nothing, though Cap'n Martin swears he heard him say 'Mary' when they carried him into the ambulance. And the young gang laughed, having never known the true Mary of Tom's life; they thought he might be turning devout Catholic.

WHEN Cap'n Martin and Freddie climbed down the tip side to where Tom lay they thought he was dead. But it transpired he had suffered a massive heart attack, paralysing his body instantly and causing him to topple over the edge. When they reached him, Freddie watched the tears trail out over Cap'n Martin's cheeks.

'Tom... Tom. Tom, you bugger...'

In their anxiety to get to him, they caused Tom to be carried further down the tip by the small avalanche of sand they created. Fortunately, the Cap'n had some elementary first aid knowledge, and he put his lips over Tom's and blew hard, tipping Tom's neck back.

'Ambulance...' the Cap'n said to Freddie.

Freddie scrambled down the tip while Cap'n Martin tried his hardest to resuscitate Tom. Between exhaling into Tom's mouth, the Cap'n also tried to kick start Tom's heart with one hand upon the other.

'Come on boy... Come on.'

His own lungs heaving. His ribcage rattling. He exhaled again. More steadily now. Each time he put his face down on Tom's, he felt the body sink into the wet sand until he could no longer see the bottom half of it. This panicked the Cap'n more, like the earth was trying to consume Tom's body. He tried again. It was only on the fifth attempt that he felt Tom breath back some air, and he saw his ribcage rise, letting some sand fall behind his back. Tom opened his eyes.

'Hang on Tom boy. 'Tis gonna' be a'right. You'm a'right now. Don't worry...'

Tom felt for himself but could not move. When he did manage to lift his fingers he felt a numbness, a feeling of not really being there, an incredible lightness, as if his spirit was half out of his body but could not decide on the next move.

'Cap'n Martin,' Tom mouthed. He always addressed the Cap'n properly.

'What Tom? Don't worry now...'

'I've just had the most wonderful dream...'

But Cap'n Martin cared little for the dream of Tom. And when the ambulance crew came awkwardly up the side of the tip and laid Tom on the stretcher, the Cap'n lay back in the wet sand and pulled away the hairs he had in his mouth from Tom's beard. He chewed his teeth, then looked to the skytip and saw the night running away.

He turned and saw Tom being lifted into the back of the ambulance surrounded by drips and an oxygen mask. And he thought of them kicking a football together. And his heart felt as cold as the newly mined wet sand that he lay in.

Yet of all the dreams on Hensbarrow that night, of all the dreams that Hensbarrow had ever dreamed, the one that Tom had was a true one.

Tom was dreaming of a memory, of a day when he forgot the clay, of a day before the dream he had mixed feelings about, of a day after the dream that he knew was right, a momentary impulse, but one that he now felt good about, and that he hated himself for exiling himself from happiness and the rest of the world for so long.

When he thought about it in the ambulance it made him smile, and so the crew considered him to be a very strange character. Nobody had thought to explain that this was indeed true.

In the dream time Tom looked so different. In the dream time, Tom courted a woman. In the dream time they kissed in gorse bushes – a place to lie together and not be seen. How Tom loved something so soft in the middle of something so prickly. In the dream time they swam together in the false lakes. In the dream time they let themselves go. In the dream time Tom tasted a woman. In the dream time they made love. Back then, Tom thought, they loved each other silly. Then they woke up... and Mary was pregnant.

Now, think hard. Put on your cap (or tam) and think...

OF REAL TIME

MY father told me about Tom in the evening. The radio was on. I was humming along to a record, balanced on a chair re-arranging the magazines I had collected over the years and deciding whether to throw the old ones away. I knew my father had something bad to say. I had heard the whispering in the kitchen earlier on.

'Ben. I've... turn down the radio a minute,' he said.

I switched it off.

'I've got a bit of bad news. Tom's had a heart attack. Had it this morning – night shift up Longstone's. He's all right though. He's down Truro hospital. We'll go down soon n' see him. When he's better.'

'I don't want to see him down there,' I said.

'Why not? He's asked for you they say.'

'Because... because...' I mumbled.

'Anyway,' my father said uneasily, 'you know now. See you later.'

And the reason was because Tom belonged up here, and if I could not have him here, and go down Tom's no more... Well, it was best, I felt, that I never saw him at all.

As a child I always thought I would cry in a situation like this, but you don't. Instead, you take it, as they say, like a man of the world and believe that first there is life and then there is death; and there is either one or the other, the same way there is either evil or good, and that is the way things are.

So I told myself not to let Tom affect me too much. After all, I was getting on, and that tobacco he smoked could never have done him much good. But I knew as I turned on the radio again, trying half-heartedly to blot out the bad thoughts, that my friend was leaving me, and that we would never sit popping the hardhead plants again, backs to the Longstone, swearing like schoolkids; the schoolkid I still was, and the old man he might not be any more.

Later, I could not sleep, and took a magazine from the pile I had put in the bin to read. But it was a science fiction story and I flung it across the room, not wanting that now. Then, with feet clinging to the bed, I pulled over the bin, dragging the rug with it. This time my lucky dip prize was a comic. Sophisticated teenage reading. I read all my magazines until dawn, scattering them across the room until they coated every surface. And in the morning I was dog-tired and my mother had a job waking me for school.

TOM was awake. He coughed. A green one came up, tasting of medicine, which he swallowed again. He was in bed, his back propped up by several thick pillows. He breathed in the hospital smell.

Tom was aware of what had happened, and he found that he could barely move a limb. A nurse had advised him to rest, so he lay there – face staring forward, his dull eyes following a fly's course around a yellow fluorescent tube on the ceiling.

He prayed – the first time he had mumbled to God for quite some time – that soon all this resting must end, but in his ill-at-ease heart he knew the prayer would probably be fruitless.

His thoughts drifted, as all our thoughts do when there is nothing else for them to engage. His thoughts turned from his heart attack to a broken heart, and he let the fragments drift around the room. Old fragments these. Mildew, dust, thick cobwebs encased them, along with regret, fear, bitterness and sentimentality.

Their love was no normal love. It began and ended on Hensbarrow, all within a year. Once it was over it was almost as if it had never begun.

Their story was a short one; Tom met Mary when he did some work for her father down in Gover valley. That was old Wally Stephens, and Tom had helped him to put a new roof on one of his cowsheds. Mary used to watch them as they worked. She helped on the farm and nursed her mother, believed to be a very wise woman who was going blind in her old age.

She had started it. She had asked him to come for a walk with her. So they became involved with one another, but problems were inevitable.

For a start, Tom was approaching middle age and still a bachelor, while Mary was in her early twenties. And then there was the rest of the Stephens family who were, according to the rest of the moor, a 'crowd' not to have much to do with.

There was evil in that family, they said. Evil as strong as the Devil. There were rumours, legends, ghosts operating beyond their control. Old Wally himself was supposed to have been born out of an incestuous relationship, and questions were asked about his daughter. None of them went to church, and though the rest of the hypocrites of the moor didn't, Wally made it explicit.

'I don't see nothing in the Bible. Never have done, never will...'

So perhaps Wally still had some of the Celt in him, some of the pagan. We'll never know.

But Tom... Well, Tom was considered a good man, and she tempted him. Tom had no control. She had cast a spell over him – a real spell. No-one of Tom's type would normally want to go with a maid like that. But there is more. For though Mary was no Christian, she was also the most beautiful maid on the moor. Men stopped work when she walked by.

The women shouted at the men for looking, and gossiped, and the hatred began, looming out of these granite people. If there were rules of relationships in this land, then they had broken them, side-stepped the story and all of Hensbarrow gossiped.

In the beginning, they coped, even when the claws began to flex and the back-stabbing began. Tom and Mary lived the dream time, and Tom wore his youthful grin and danced with her on the mica. Her skin was soft like foxglove flowers, her lips as rich as the urts they picked. And her legs, they went on forever.

But because of jealousies and because people didn't want to see Tom corrupted by this evil, they made up stories, fairy stories and wicked tales, which hit both of them hard. And they left them presents. Like the dead cat Tom found in his locker.

So Tom and Mary met at night, and caressed one another as they felt was right, and when they did this the dead cats and jibes became the fiction. They went to town one day and had a photograph taken. The photographer had asked him to put his arm around her slim waist.

When they touched they melted. Ice-cream on a hot summer's day. And night after night the two of them met by torchlight at a secret place, where there was a spring by the name of Chutney Well. Tom was always the guilty one.

'We have to end things... They're right. We've no future together. They'll always... Always...'

And always she would say: 'Then we must move away. Get away from Hensbarrow. Leave the clay people. They don't understand...'

Mary was always exclaiming their paralysis. Her frustrated sexuality was now gloriously exposed.

'Tom... We couldn't yesterday. Come please,' she used to say, kissing him, her tongue against his. 'Love me...'

'So I'm evil eh?'

'No.'

And she placed his hand to her breast and made him rub it hard. She pulled him on to her and Tom let his instincts go. The wind blew lupin flowers over their bodies, and only the sound of the spring and their love could be heard on the moor.

When Mary became pregnant, it happened at the wrong time. Her mother died a few days before she knew about the baby, and the taunts had been particularly awful. And a baby born out of wedlock... In the fifties on Hensbarrow, it did not happen.

Violence had resulted one day when Tom went to chapel. Tom punched a man who told him his girl was evil and spoke of her incestuous ancestry. Others called him a cradle snatcher or a dirty old man. They wouldn't leave him alone.

Tom became cold and would not let Mary near him. She tried hard, but Tom was softer and they worked on him more, finally breaking him. She last saw him crying softly on Halviggan tip, a relic of the man he had been to her. Their secrets never shared. Once again there was a call to escape.

'Tom... let's go from here. Get away from this bastard place. Come with me please.'

But Tom did not hear her any more. He knew it was over. How she pleaded though. Still the cutting edge of her words inside his head.

'So, you're going to let these people, these animals who call me a witch for snaring you, you're going to let them beat us, jealous as they are. Don't let them Tom... Don't let them break us...'

'Break us,' Tom was saying when the sister came in to ask him if he needed anything. 'Break us.'

'BREAKFAST, Mr Cundy?' Or so she thought Tom had said.

Tom understood her mistake.

'No, nothing thank you.'

Then he remembered the last thing he gave to Mary, the china doll he had bought in Truro.

'For our daughter...'

'Daughter? How do you know?'

'I know.'

That was the last Tom saw of Mary. A fortnight later he heard she had been seen with Ronnie Parsons, a man nearer her own age – a farmer's son – and that there was to be a shotgun wedding. Ronnie had been in trouble with the law enough times. A stolen car down Treviscoe pit, a brawl in a pub in which he'd smashed a bottle over someone's head. He'd been sacked from the clayworks and was therefore also a social outcast.

They'd be well suited, folk said. And Tom, well Tom, knowing Tom, he'd be sure to find a decent woman. That was scandal enough, and for the time being it was possible to believe the clay people had forgotten.

OF CLOUDS AND A CARNIVAL

YOU have to travel a long way in Cornwall to be out of sight of the clay mines. And once you have seen them you can never quite forget them.

From the Roseland and Truro, looking north east, you see Melbur and Treviscoe, and then higher, on top of the moor, Blackpool and Littlejohns. From Newquay you see them – a white ridge running parallel to the A30 across the flatness of Goss Moor. And from the south you see them still, the wasteland shark-fins beneath the clouds.

Between a sandwich of clay at the southern extremities of Hensbarrow, where it falls steeply to the sea, there lies a town, a Saint's town, named after Saint Austell. It is found at the bottom of two valleys which cut through Hensbarrow; the first Gover, the second Ruddle. Over both of them run two magnificent viaducts which carry the mainline railway to Penzance on the edge of Hensbarrow.

Always in the winter this town seems to sleep. Then in June they come, waking her, chattering in Alymer Square, laughing in Vicarage Place. The tourist arrives.

Let's consult the guide book:

'St Austell is a leading market town, and the centre of the china clay industry; also a good place from which to tour Mid-Cornwall. The best looking buildings are the plain Georgian Quaker Meeting House (1829), the Italianate Town Hall (1844), and the eighteenth century White Hart Hotel. Holy Trinity Church has some interesting carved figure work on the outside walls. On Hensbarrow Downs, north of the town, huge white mounds of sand and quartz, the mock mountains of the china clay mines, add a weird touch to the landscape.'

No surprises.

What the guide book fails to say is that everything in Austell's town – everything – is made from clay. Not literally clay, but all this town's wealth, its prosperity, its founding, its thisness, is made of clay. Without it, St Austell would die.

So the money in banks, the money spent in shops, the money

taken at the cinema, is all founded on clay. Clay money. It is real enough, but it is made of clay. And even in the shops you can see clay. You can almost smell it. In W H Smith, in Woolworths, in the Co-op. Little clues of it; the clay company design on trousers, the splash of mica on the wheels of cars, the clay words being spoken. And the slight, very slight white dust on all the people's clothes.

One day in St Austell is much like any other day in St Austell, except that more clay has been mined and more money has been spent.

I'd often sit above the town cloud watching. Cumulus, cirrus, cirrostratus, cirrocumulus, altocumulus. Shapes that have lasted from time's infant wobbly steps. Shapes which have seen it all. Shapes which will see more than you or I ever will. Poor shapes... Shapes which saw paradise. Shapes which will see the dark. Giraffes, cigars, hands, heaven, candy floss. Let the dream form when you cloud watch. Cloud watching is like riding a bike, you never forget it.

I may not have cloud watched for months at a time, but then an opportunity presented itself and I was straight into it, absorbed by the patches of white and grey and black. Cloud watching contrasts with clay. The one high, the other low. The one an escapism, the other reality. The one soft, the other harsh. The one air, the other earth.

Hensbarrow must be a near perfect environment to watch the clouds since there are no distractions, no buildings, no people, no noise. You just lie back on the heather or baked sand, open your eyes wide and watch.

I read once that what you saw in the clouds was a prediction of your life ahead. Make what you will then of the giraffes I saw when I was young. I went by things like that. I read my stars in my father's newspaper. But now things like that were of little use. I look at them now and can only see myself looking back. I see the hour glass, not so much half full but more half empty. A few years back it may still have been half full but... things change. Though sometimes, on the very warmest days when I come back to lie on Hensbarrow, I can still see the giraffes.

But I've got out now. Escaped the past. Allowed the dream time to return. You'll see.

Cloud watching is all about forgetting where you belong. Forgetting you live on some bleak Cornish moor, where the sand grows taller every day, where the shadow over the cottage grows larger every day. It is about pretending you are something else, once in a while, loving the clay and knowing its worth, but now and then hating it a little, perhaps a lot.

Letting go... In the early summer the clay people let go with carnivals, and instead of turning the land inside out they turn Hensbarrow upside down. So that floats of decorated wagons, and screaming toddlers dressed as spacemen, drift through the dirty bits. Bunting rips in the breeze, stretched from telegraph pole to chapel. The clay community forgets, and while the parade passes by they jump on to the float in their minds and join the cowboys and indians, the circus, the Alice-in-Wonderland float. A moment to let go as Bill and Ben, Laurel and Hardy pass by, for clay workers to dress as dames in chiffon dresses with balloon boobs, laddered tights and clay company wellingtons. A chance to laugh. Nanpean Carnival. Everyone is watching. Even the ones who said they were not interested are watching from behind net curtains upstairs. Even those with petty jealousies, daughters who never became carnival queen, still glance down to the street.

My mother and father were watching. My sister walks with Mrs Grose, who leads a trail of children and wears a sign around her bust which reads 'The Old Woman who lived in a Shoe'. And Tessa waves and her mother and father wave back, and for once she does not cry.

Michael and I were on the cowboy and indian float, entered by the Old Pound Youth Club. The entire float shouting 'yee haw' loudly, and holding cans of baked beans around a papier mache fire. But they laughed and when I pointed my pistol at a man in the crowd he pretended to be shot. The youth club were judged runners-up in the float category – the first prize going to the St John Ambulance girls from St Dennis, just behind us in the procession, with the Mad Hatter and the Dormouse.

Watching. Escaping. Fantasising.

The youths in the crowd really want to push forward when the carnival queen rides past in her shimmering cart, pulled by a well-groomed horse, but stay in the back-row, straining their necks. This year the queen was a well-developed Catherine Fay, a girl who attended my school still but who, on the cart, with her hair's first perming, is not a maid but a woman.

'Cathy,' the boys say, without opening their lips. The bravest wolf whistle, but today she does not blush.

I did not watch Cathy on the float behind. My gaze was upon a figure alone, standing in the shadow of the Grenville Arms public house. It was a female figure, and when she noticed my stare she turned and glanced at the carnival queen and ignored me. The youth club cart rounded the corner up to Currian Vale. I thought it strange, for this time the moth girl had shied away from the light. When the carnival went back down the hill to the playing fields she was no longer there, as if the painter of the scene had rubbed her out. I looked at all the faces in the crowd and could not see her. But I knew moths rarely came out in daylight.

Neither did the moth girl come out to dance that night after the carnival. I had desperately wanted her to be at the dance, just so I might speak to her, find out who she was, where she lived, though obviously she lived on the moor somewhere.

I thought about her all evening at the carnival dance, and barely moved out of my seat. Mike had finally managed to wrap his clumsy arms around Cathy for the last dance. The rest of my friends went home when they realised Cathy was taken. When the lights came up in Nanpean Church rooms, and everyone was asked to make their way home, her image cluttered my mind completely. I hung on for Mike outside Drinnick Stores while he was saying good night to Cathy.

'Cathy then, eh?' I said.

'Yeh boy. She's hot,' Mike said, extending the 't' of hot as long as he could. 'We're going out tomorrow.'

'Yeh?'

'Yeah. I just got a feeling it's going to be good.'

'Great.'

Our speech died for a while, then Mike began again.

'Christ, you were quiet tonight. Hardly got out of your seat. That girl from Whitemoor, Cathy's friend, she really fancied you.'

'What? The one with the earrings?'

Yeah... that's her.'

'Well, I didn't feel like it tonight. Had a few things on me mind.'

'Tom?'

'Yeah, Tom I suppose,' I lied. I had not thought of Tom all evening. I had only one thing on my mind.

We talked of trivialities, football and music until Old Pound Church when Mike, leaning on the postbox, asked:

'You do want to go out with girls don't you?'

My pride was hurt. Mike had caught me off guard.

'Yeh... of course... I'm not a homo you know. It's just...'

'Just?'

'Just, there aren't any I like around here really.'

'I got you Ben. Waiting for the right one to come along eh?'

'You got it mate,' I said. 'Waiting for the right one.'

My heart was pounding, telling me the right one was the girl who came out at night. We parted and made our individual ways home at Old Pound crossroads. Me to Noppies with thoughts of the moth girl, Mike to Karslake with dreams of Cathy.

Thoughts now...

OF HOME

...which is where, they say, the heart lies. And my heart these days – if I still have a heart – tends to lie on that bleak Hell-on-Earth where the clay was first dug...

THERE are days on Hensbarrow when the fog is so thick it is easy to believe the moor has risen several hundred feet into the air like a flying citadel and become shrouded by clouds.

On the day Tom was to be come home from hospital the fog was no worse than usual. I could only see the bottom slopes of Blackpool pit, and when I took the scraps out to the bin in the morning it was almost impossible to see the bottom of the pit and the old Lower Halviggan pump house.

The fog swirled in over the cottage – another grey colour making pit, tip, sky and moor indistinguishable, and it could stay like that for days in the winter months. It was there when you went to bed; it was there when you got up. It never used to scare me. It was more of a reassuring presence; if you could not see off the moor, then below they could not see you. But the worst thing about the fog is the dampness; not the kind of dampness that leaves your hair wet and you armpits sweaty, but a longer lasting dampness that seems to soak through your body day after day, and even through your hair. You were soaked under the skin, soaked by this cunning mist.

Sometimes, instead of falling on you, it caressed you... The fog would only lift for a few hours in the early afternoon, while the animals found their bearings, and my mother tried drying some washing, but almost as soon as the final pair of socks went on the washing line, in the fog would roll to cover us again, though I did like the way the top of the Longstone could be seen while the heavier fog hid the bottom-most half of it.

My father, Mike and I picked up Tom from hospital. The month was November. We left the moor in the morning before the fog had cleared. Tom was thinner. His hair shorter. His beard trimmer. He was older. It had aged him badly, this heart attack. But he still spoke in his old tone:

'A'right boy,' he said to my father, as we drew up to pick him up from the hospital. He had been waiting for us:

'Let's go back home, back to Noppies.'

Though apart from some niceties, as to how he felt and if he was looking forward to going home, he remained silent for much of the journey, until we turned right at Foxhole, up over Watch Hill to Hensbarrow. And I saw him in the front seat; how his cheeks swelled upon seeing Blackpool laid out in front of him.

'Foggy today in'a Cap'n?'

Tom called everyone in charge Cap'n, and today he presumed my father to be in control, though I knew Tom had seen foggier days. He was trying hard to divert our attention, even though the three of us had seen Longstone's tip, the site of his accident. Tom saw it as well, but he was unsure whether he would walk up there for some time. When we all arrived at Noppies, Tom suddenly leapt out of the car and bounded across the yard, leaving his walking stick in the car. When we caught up with him beside the chicken shed, he was distressed and I saw a tear in his eye. The straw that broke the camel's back, or something like it.

'Bastards,' he mumbled.

'What's on Tom?' father asked.

'Some bastard's been down here while I've been gone. They've nicked me wood. Could see it, coming down the lane. Had a bleddy great pile of it here for the winter...'

We tried to console him, though for the first time in many weeks Tom had forgotten about his heart attack and was thinking of something else.

'Ought to be strung up... the buggers who nicked me wood. The buggers...' he said as we helped him into the cottage. He was home again.

'Must've been raining red while I been gone,' Tom mumbled as he began to catch up on jobs around the house.

'Red rain?' father asked.

'Es. Made of blood. Things happen boy. No good for any of us.'

Tom stopped his work and turned wide-eyed to face us, silent. He realised he had let out a downser's secret. Back home, I laughed – blood falling out of the sky causing bad things to happen. What rubbish. Another legend. Yes, at this time I admit to sniggering. I admit to not believing.

If I had only listened...

TOBIAS

9th October 1664.

TODAY, being the day of Rest, I rose early in order to help the Reverende with preparation for the morning service. Tis well that he is in a good mood this morn, since later he has to performe a Christening of one William Webb, aged one month and a half. I helped the Reverende to clean the pews in the churche, and o'ersaw the pronunciation and grammar of his sermon. He is most good at writing, though I may well comment that his letter 'h's are not how I would ascribe mine. The morning sermon was indeed a copious one, concerned with the Good Samaritan. The congregation do staye, so I presume they are enthralled with the Reverende's oracy. I for one find the lesson moving, and spirit-wise most enlightening. We sing several hymns. The Hensbarrow people are most goodly singers, being loude and cheery, as if there were no morrow. For myself, I opened my mouth, but I know that I am poore as far as singing ist concerned. Before me the Reverende's mouth is open wide, and sound does exude in great quantity from him. The message herewith in this sermon I do note down here:

'Do as to others as ye would have do unto you.'

From the Reverende this seems sorely good advice. I hope the congregation have taken notice of his wordes.

The Christening goes well since the child does not scream and cry. I must recorde this event: Mr and Mrs Webb putting their cross on the document for the records of the Parishe. I also recorde the Reverende's signature, for it is he who certifies suche acts. When this is done, I return home to rest. I am most angrie when it comes to returning to churche in the evening, since I have forgotten my overgarments and arrive at churche very wet indeed. I drip through five droll hymns and then hurry home when the service is finished. I feel I have caught a most monstrous colde. Whilst warming my feet in hot water, I hitherto recount what it was like for the Saints who crossed to Cornwall on boats from Ireland and Wales. I think of this St Austell. It must have been sorely choppy and wet. For now, then, I am satisfied enough that I am of a different time when the conditions of our lives are of a higher standard.

I close for the night. Amen.

T.T.

OF PAPER

*'The Merry Myll now grinds and goes so brave
The World at will shall always paper have.'*
(Churchyard 1588)

YEARS ago man shaped clay into tablets in the Middle East, wrote characters or drawings upon them, and then baked them in order to preserve his efforts. To communicate his mythologies, his legends. And man the reader, the writer, has searched for the materials to communicate. A bright spark discovered that forests could provide the raw material for the paper industry, wood pulp.

But what of this? There are no trees on Hensbarrow. Well friends, after the wood, china clay is the most important raw material for the paper industry, and about eighty per cent of the clay mined is used in the manufacture of paper. Pieces of Hensbarrow in books and magazines, Shakespeare and Penthouse, documents and letters, fantasies and realities.

So that's why they dig still. That's where the clay goes. That's why paper feels so smooth. Smooth like the covers of glossy magazines, holiday brochures to Cornwall... Smooth. Sm-oo-th like the moth girl's skin. Smooth like the way the dozer shaved the side of the tip, sand crumbling down to the grass.

I was sketching down by Chutney Well at the head of the Gover Valley. Over Blackpool, a yellow dozer was excavating for a living. The sketch was good. I held it up. The tip angle was wrong. I went over it again with the charcoal. Better. More like it. The scene was almost idyllic. I say almost. The skylarks were chittering and Chutney was babbling. Halviggan tip almost became a romantic tor from this angle, but you could never get away from it. This was still Hensbarrow, but I tried at least. I put some diesel fumes in where the bulldozer's exhaust was. There...

It had not been a bad week in all, apart from the arrival of my great aunt from London. From her first steps into the cottage I knew she hated it. The clay and her just did not go well together. Chalk and cheese as it were.

I heard her moaning at my mother that it was the wrong sort of place for them to live. Wrong for the children, she had said. I told her at breakfast that I liked it here. Tom would have hated her. 'Two fingers to her,' I said to myself. They had all gone to

Polperro for the day. She would like that. Away from the dirty bit. I had come out sketching. It was Sunday.

Down St Mewan, I could hear the church bells ringing. From Greensplat Chapel, the Downsers were walking home. Tom had told me about Greensplat Chapel. Years ago, he told me, they used to have concerts up there. If the entertainment or preaching was good, the congregation stamped their feet and shouted, 'Purdy!' This was disapproved of by the chapels of Hensbarrow. A lovely word, purdy, like pretty and wordy rolled together. The chapelgoers passed me along the lane. They could not see me from the road but I watched them walk down the lane to where Blackberry Row was.

Two largeish houses hid behind Halviggan tip with cottage gardens. When I walked past them towards Higher Biscovillick, their drug-scented beauty rushed into me, so I walked with my nose high in the air. 'Purdy,' I wrote on the drawing pad next to the sketch. Purdy.

I then sat in a sandy grove of dandelion plants. I picked a few and shoved them into a frail for my sister's rabbit. The sky grew dark now. As the saying goes: 'Cornwall will stand a shower every day, and two for Sundays.' This was the first of the day. The shower was a heavy one, a crushing rain which seemed to flatten every living thing. I did up my anorak and waited under a gorse bush.

The rain came down. Streams of it running down the slope into the pit. I shoved the sketch book up the bottom of my anorak and watched the rain. It was ceaseless and cold. I could feel my anorak becoming damp. The pages of the sketch book would soon be wet as well. Tom would be up there in one of his sheds. 'Coming in dirty,' he would say. 'Tis coming in real dirty...'

As I laughed to myself, I heard the patter of running feet. Pattering, and sometimes a crunch when the feet hit some softer sand.

The steps rounded the corner. They were female. She had an umbrella and carried a pail, the handle clattering with each step. Then the wind blew her umbrella inside out and I saw her face. The moth girl.

I was about to help her when the wind blew the umbrella back to its correct shape. She was soaked. Her legs were splashed with clayey water. Her coat streaming, but at the well she bent over and filled the pail with water. She pushed her long hair back, then tipped out the water as if she was rinsing the bucket. This time, she stepped down on to a stone in the pool and filled the bucket with water from the spring. Chutney gargled with extra water from the heavy shower. It was still pouring.

She turned to face the bush that I was crouched in. The rain ran down her face like tears and dripped on to her jumper. She had overfilled the bucket. As she climbed out of the well, the water spilled on to her leg and she shivered. I felt she might cry. I stood up, knocking a quantity of yellow gorse flowers into my hair.

'In here,' I shouted.

Startled, she looked and almost dropped the bucket.

'In here,' I said again. I smiled. 'It's dry. Come out of the rain.'

After deliberating, she ran over to the gorse bush, leaving her umbrella and pail behind.

'Thanks,' she said quietly.

More gorse flowers fell from the arch we crouched beneath, and we stayed there, hearts beating like toy drums and limbs shivering like frightened rabbits. For a while we said nothing. I just watched her. Beads of rain skated over her blonde hair. Her jumper was soaked. I could see the curve of her breasts underneath it. Her jaw soft, slightly coloured.

'How long were you watching me?' she asked.

Off guard, I fumbled for a reply.

'Not long. About a minute. I'd only just climbed under the bush myself.'

'I must go in a minute.'

'Why? You can't. It's pouring.'

'No, I must get back, once it eases off.'

She stuck her hand out of the cover of the gorse bush. Drops still splashed on her upturned palm. She tried to make herself more comfortable but ended up catching her skirt on a thorn. With my help she managed to unhitch the material from the thorns.

'I saw you the other night, didn't I?' she said, tugging her skirt and showing her white legs.

'Where?'

'Up the top, top of Gunheath, on your bike.'

'Yes. I'd been to see someone in Carroncarrow.'

'Oh.'

Finally, she pulled her skirt, taking some of the thorns with it.

'You're from over Noppies aren't you?'

'Yes.'

She pulled out the thorns.

'You're from up Carroncarrow aren't you?' I asked.

'Yes.'

'Have you always lived there?'

'Yes... always.'

The rain was easing. My moment next to her was soon to end.

'I must get back...'

'What's the water for?' I asked.

'It's... it's for making... washing,' she said.

'But you can get water at the Greensplat spring.'

'I know, but it's fresher down here. Chutney's got the freshest water on Hensbarrow...'

She headed back to the well and washed out the bucket again. I loved the way she said Hensbarrow. It came out of her lips like a sunbeam, age old. Hynde Beorgh. She said it the way Tom said it. She filled the bucket again.

'I must go now,' she said breathlessly.

And before I could answer she was heading up the sandy road to Greensplat. I watched her disappear over the hill; a black dot beneath the white temple.

'Your name?' I asked, 'I still don't know who you are.'

Down in the valley, a rainbow had formed, but I could see only one end of it. I felt wet now. I wrung out my anorak and looked at the sketchpad. It was saturated; the leaves like papier mache. But for once it did not matter, so I flung the pad over the ferns and into flooded Halviggan pit. It floated on the surface of the lake. A message without a bottle. A picture without a frame.

In the evening, I went down to Nanpean, walking past Old Pound Chapel. Inside voices were singing: 'The ink is black. The paper is white. Together we'll learn to read and write, read and write.'

A mishmash of ideas in my mind now. The black and the white. The Quaker and the clay. The moth girl and the paper. Death and life. Night and day. The Devil and Christ. Evil and good... And I was trying hard to sort them out now, for I was falling, falling off Hensbarrow, spinning in the grey. I was scared because I had lost the safety net when childhood ended. But I was going to take the chance. So, let it be written. Let it be done. Like it used to be; tales from childhood.

Tales...

OF NURSERY RHYMES

'Jack and Jill went up the hill, to fetch a pail of water...'

'BEN,' called my mother. 'Stop reading Tessa those rhymes. I want you to get something for me...'

My sister frowned. For some reason she liked me to read rhymes to her. I always thought she liked me to speak childishly, but now I just thought she wanted the rhymes to help her escape. I spun the aeroplane mobile in her room and gave her some dolls to play with. Then I went down. Mrs Varcoe sat downstairs talking to, or rather at, my mother,

'I could see she was brave 'n chuff, Mrs Sexton. But I told her, her chield ain't wrapped up enough, not up here in this weather, what with the fog n' 'at.'

I could hear my mother making the occasional positive reinforcement. Mrs Varcoe was a hardened farmer's wife from down Old Pound. She was having her hair done. When I walked into the dining room, she had just been placed under the Dalek-like lid of the hair dryer, and she sat there in the middle of the room reading a glossy woman's magazine about fashion and things that would never touch Hensbarrow.

'Ben,' my mother said quickly, 'I'm not going to have time to go down to the shop today. Here's the list. There's a bag under the stairs. Nip down on your bike, will you?'

'Okay.'

'Don't wake your father mind, he's having a doze in the living room after his morning shift.'

'Okay.'

There was no fog today. I could see the snaking top of Blackpool tip. A gang of men up there in woollen donkey jackets, mending the conveyor spreader. A few children were playing at Old Pound crossroads, making the most of the last day of half term. As I came down off the downs I could see the Channel shimmering to the south and the lush rolling meadows that ran off the bottom of Hensbarrow towards the River Fal estuary. A relic of a more romantic industry – a tin mine – stood on the horizon. The main-line diesel was snorting through the vivid green of Coombe Valley. I saw Watt down in Foxhole.

'What Ben?' he said.

'A'right Watt.'

'What's on?'

'Shopping,' I said, showing him the bag.

'Mother and father a'right?'

'Yes.'

And as an afterthought:

'Tessa...?'

'She's okay,' I answered.

The village passed us by. I liked Watt. He was one of the old lot. An original. A bit older than Tom. Seen that much more. He was there when two tramps had been found guilty of begging in Foxhole and had been sent to prison for fourteen days. He would tell me lots of stories like that.

Another, from years ago, was about a labourer who lived up at Halviggan by the name of Trudgian. He came back blind drunk from the Grenville Arms in Nanpean one night, jealous about a lodger at his house, shot his wife, torched the cottage they lived in and ran across the downs. When the police finally caught up with him he killed himself.

And Watt had many more tales to tell, only there was not enough time now. Watt spoke: 'Still drawing, be 'ee?'

'Yeh, been doing a bit. Did a bit last week, down Halviggan.'

'You wanna' keep at 'un, boy.'

'Will do, Watt.'

'You want to be an artist do 'ee then?'

'I'd like to... yes...'

'Well boy... just so long as you get out of this place.'

'Why?'

'Well there bain't much to draw round here...'

I would have argued with him over that, but I did not have the time. Under my bed I had built up a large collection of sketches and paintings of the clay land. They had been even better this year with the painting equipment I had asked for when it was my birthday. I would think myself a professional some days, sitting in the heather with an easel and painting, on the whole, the tips. Those angles... and the contrasts. They made every painting surreal. Odd, the colours I used. Mainly whites, greys and blues. A touch of green and brown. Perhaps a purple. Nothing else though. This was my apprenticeship for art college... but hang on. That's not yet...

A clay lorry passed us.

'Brave bit of clay being shipped today,' said Watt.

A woman came down from the council houses, pushing a pram and leading a trail of children. They dodged Watt and myself.

'He's gone...' Watt whispered.

'Who?'

'Her husband.'

'Oh.'

A terrible gossip Watt. Sound as a rock though.

The village post office was quaint. Mr Scott kept the sweets in a long glass cabinet. Next to it stood a foot-worn, woodwormed chair which children could climb on to pick out their favourite liquorice, chocolate or sherbet fountains. It smelled good. People buying stamps. The Cornish talking. More stamps. Letters from the clayland. I bought some sticky peardrops.

Because the shopping weighed so heavy,'I had to push the bike up Watch Hill. I was sweating. It was close. 'Dogsdays' as the Downsers say. Half way up I rested, plopping down on the springy moss-thick hedge. I closed my eyes and dreamt. A car passed down the hill. They looked at me funny. I watched the car – a red Triumph Herald – go round the corner. Then I dreamt again. Sometimes it seemed that was all I ever did on Hensbarrow. Fantasise... but then that's the only thing you can do up there. And my daydream became a night time dream, a flighty fixation on a girl in black.

When I opened my eyes the sky was black. Blacker than thunder. And I had to cough. Smoke flexed overhead in evil clouds, making the air even more heady. I had heard about this.

It became less frightening when I climbed up on the hedge in the main path of the smoke. They were burning the gorse. The downs were alive – a sea of flame flowing along them, a great fire over the moor. Just over the hedge, knots of twisted gorse burnt to death. The farmer called back his dog. All I could hear was the snap of the fire and the bark of the sheepdog. The smoke rose higher, a hand of it dancing in an Egyptian manner over Blackpool. The seagulls, flustered, were heading back over the downs to the relative clay sanctuary of Dubbers. It was rich, like the best pipe tobacco.

I looked over at the old settlement at Beacon Hill. The burning seemed to me age old; and I was just a knot of gorse. The flames were like story tellers, weaving, dancing, showing... Out of a ditch first three, then four rabbits spurted across the road. On the hedge, my face became blurred as the flames leapt higher. We'll all burn one day, the preacher said, unless...

'You've been a while,' mother said when I returned home. 'I was hoping to make custard tonight for tea.'

'Sorry,' I apologised. 'I stayed on to watch the fire.'

'Fire?'

'Yeh. On Watch Hill. Burning the gorse bushes.'

We ate. My father was awake now, but dozey. Mother helped Tessa clear the table, and father and I washed the dishes. We had a stupid argument about the water not being hot enough. I went outside and fiddled around with a stick in the back yard. I could still smell the smoke. One of Tessa's dollies was lying in the yard; it had mud on it. I wiped off the worst of it, though really it needed to be washed. I opened the back door and placed it inside.

My parents were still arguing. I heard Tessa in the dining room, singing softly to herself. I could still smell Mrs Varcoe's perm lotion. I resolved to cycle up to Greensplat and catch a glimpse of the moth girl.

At Cocksbarrow crossroads I pulled over my bike and looked up to the top of Hensbarrow. The radio beacon was nearly finished, oscillating above the moor. Littlejohns tip was coming closer. Karslake was lighting up. Michael would have to stay in tonight.

I sat up there for three hours, most of it in the dark, waiting to see her. I cycled up and down the dead village several times, almost calling in to see Mary, but deciding not to; now was not the best time of the day to enter a witch's coven.

There was no sign of the moth girl, though, so I went home dejected. The thought of this girl, this woman, was with me every minute. I wanted to be near her, be with her. Feel her. Take her with me. I was being worn away by a jet of love, and my body was crumbling into a milky stream. The downs had become an Eden, and the monitors below were like fountains of love. And the Longstone... well, the Longstone's fantasies called to me over the heather and I turned to hear them.

The following day I tried again. But Tessa could not remember the rhymes. They were easy as well, and it was frustrating. She always said the first two lines fine: 'Mist on the hill brings water to the mill...' in a sort of English only I could understand, but that was all she could hold.

'Mist on the moor, brings sunshine to your door,' I said again, but she could not remember it. And I would like her to know that one. Let the sunshine in.

'Brighten up the chield's day,' as Mrs Varcoe had said.

Outside it was raining. How wonderful it must have been to see the hot moor when the first drops of rain fell. I could see it steaming in my mind. Hissing. I would like to paint that, but surely it was one of those cases when the reality was simply better than the art.

I resolved to return to Greensplat that very night, even though it was raining heavily outside. The pits would have enough trouble pumping water out tonight without turning the hoses on. It would be muddy down in the pit as well. Get a bulldozer to twist and clank over a crust of clay in the rain and it soon changes into a quagmire. And then it really could be the slough of despond down there on the night shift.

I had remembered that Tuesday was the night I had seen her cycling back to Greensplat, so I returned to the Cocksbarrow crossroads and waited. This time I took a thicker coat with me. I stared down Gunheath hill all evening, sheltering in the remains of Cocksbarrow Claywork dry. At about half past nine I saw a light at the bottom of the hill; a slow, small light. I felt sure it was her, but when the figure came closer it was too large for her... and it wore oilskins.

It was an afternoon shift worker going home. I waited longer, and the moon crept up above Gunheath tip. And it always felt strange to see the moon on Hensbarrow, because to the downsers Hensbarrow was the moon, craters and strange rock formations, dust, volcanoes and seas. From Hensbarrow the moon became the earth. Mare Tranquillitatis, and possibly over Littlejohns, Sinus Roris – the Bay of Dew. Everything higgledy-piggledy, wrong way up, inside out and upside down.

And that was when I saw her, a pale yellow figure, beauty in the confusion of Hensbarrow's universe.

She wore a hat so I could not see her face, but her stride and sway gave away her femininity. But she was pushing her bike. Last time she had ridden it up the hill. Again, her hair was wet, tied back this time, the pony tail bouncing as she walked. As she came closer I did not move. She passed me sitting in the dry, but I caught her eyelids flittering like tiny wings. Hummingbird eyes. She piped music to me and I followed her as she flew in and out of the light and shade, dancing on the moor. My moth girl...

Once on the road from Roche and the Barrow, she began to cycle again. I flung my bike down on the road and peddled after her like a madman, neither of us with any lights, but I could see her ahead.

'Wait,' I shouted, and I saw her back shiver. She turned around, but peddled faster. I had scared her.

'Please... Wait. Wait for me. I want to talk to you,' I yelled.

The road swung downhill through the village. She rounded the corner. A car came round the tight bend. The driver saw nothing until the last moment. I swerved to avoid him and the bike mounted the hedge. I could no longer see the moon, and everything went black.

'Jack and Jill went up the hill to fetch a pail of water. Jack fell down and broke his crown...'

And Jill came tumbling after. I was bloody and had been dazed by the fall.

'It's quite a nasty cut,' she said. 'We should have had lights...'

She was holding my hand.

'I would have stopped if I'd known it was you. I thought...'

'Thought what?'

'I don't know what I thought. It was dark.'

'I wanted to speak to you.'

Already my heart was thumping. It could thump some more.

'Yes..'

'I really like you, and I don't know what you're called. I think about you all the time...'

She was dumbstruck. I got up.

'I don't know what to say. I didn't... I mean I... Don't you know what I'm called?'

'No.'

'You'll have to guess. But first come with me. We'll have to do something about that cut. I don't think it needs stitches, but we must wash and dress it.'

I paused and looked back at the buckled wheel of my bike.

'Come on,' she said, 'Leave that here.'

And she took me by the hand, leading me away under the eyes of a Hensbarrow moon. I chose a dandelion this time. A love clock. I ripped half the petals away. She loved me. Some more. She loved me not. The last few. She loved me. I hoped.

My head hurt. The moth girl led me along the road in the dark, but in the moonlight I could see stains of blood on my shirt. We hardly spoke, but she held my hand so tight it felt as if our bloods were mingling. My other hand was grazed. It stung. A pleasant sort of pain, if there is one.

'In here,' I remembered her saying, and we followed the path towards Carroncarrow, brushing against the willow and gorse that bordered the path. I had been here before. Mary's cottage. And in the light of the window a figure watched us.

I smelt the rose-crammed garden, and its fragrance shut out the pain. A natural anaesthetic. She held me still, gripped me. I had gone soft. Like clay. She could have moulded me any way she wanted. Pushed me in any direction and I would have gone. Between the ivy and the primroses I was hers. My head hurt, but I was in love. You could see it in my eyes. Covered in moondust. The door opened. Mary stood there in a white dressing gown, a few locks of hair falling on to her shoulders. She looked afraid.

'Whatever's happened?' she asked.

'It's Ben, he's had an accident. See his head and his hand...'
'You'd better come in then me lover. We'd better get it seen to.'

I sat in an armchair that creaked when I moved. Mary fetched some bandages and some kind of herbal antiseptic from the back. In front of me sat the china doll. Rosy red cheeks. A baby face. Its eyes somehow winking. Around the room, Mary's watercolours swam. Drowning. I was drowning. Going under...

In a half-daze, Mary mended my head, not with vinegar and brown paper but with a brownish liquid which stank nevertheless. The bandage was itchy, but I could tell the wound had been cleansed and it was no longer bleeding. The moth girl watched, like the china doll. Mary came back in.

'Mother,' the moth girl said. 'Is he going to be all right?'

And I woke from my daze. I could hardly believe it.

'I didn't know Mary was your mother,' I mumbled.

'Mother told me you'd come here before,' said the moth girl.

They looked at each other. Mary's face was a little pained, moth girl's sad and hollow.

'Yes,' said moth girl, 'She is,' as though I had unearthed a secret. Opened up a wound. Dug further than I should have.

'We'll have to get you home,' Mary said, 'but God knows how.'

'I'm all right now,' I said. 'I can walk home by myself.'

'Only if you're sure now,' Mary said, taking up her Victorian bottles and little tin boxes of ointment. She went back into the kitchen. I turned to the girl. Her legs were crossed. Alive now. No longer a doll.

'Your name?' I asked.

A pause. She looked deep into me. I saw nothing except her cow-dark eyes.

'Clara,' she said in a whisper. And the moth fluttered across the room to me. She turned her face towards the fire and watched its glow. I had it. I had her name. Mary came back, wiping her hands.

'I'd better go,' I said.

'Yes, you'd better be off. Have you seen the time?'

I looked at the clock slung on the wall, slightly lop-sided. It was late, nearly quarter past eleven.

'Good night then.'

'Yes. Go safe now.'

'Night Clara... see you...'

She smiled and stood up to see me out. I walked down the path. At the gate I turned back and saw an hour-glass figure silhouetted in the light. It was late. I must go home. And the clock on the teak sideboard ticked slowly away from childhood.

OF LOVE

...which is a many splendoured thing.

WHICH is one of the great mythologies of the human race. It affects us all. Love is something we cry out for. Love is something within us. It is the heart that rules the mind. In literature, it is the 'Romeo, Romeo, Wherefore art thou Romeo?' On the fourteenth of February it is an anonymous card. It is kissing and cuddling. It is warmth. It is sharing. It is dreaming. It is discovering. It is finding.

But beware, for it is also the knife in the back. The assassination. The killer. That most bitter of pills.

Then, love was Hensbarrow. Love was Clara, and love was me. Love was clay. Love was the stones and the heather. Love was free. Now, love is... well; let's not say. Love is easier. Love is memories. But love has become a single thing. Love is sex. Love is soggy condoms. Love is AIDS.

Try praying that love is still dreaming. But enough, because love then was love. True love you might have called it. And this is when the mythology touched me and I reached out to touch the myth.

I don't recall asking Clara to go out with me. She just did. And when we became lovers we just did, as if we were the only creatures on Hensbarrow to feel it; the last mating pair on a clay ark. It was carried on the wind like musk or a scent, and we were drawn together.

We first started going out together in February, when the weather was still cold and the evenings dark. Clara went to school in St Austell to Poltair School, the old grammar school. I went to St Stephens, so we both lived for the evenings. We were nocturnal – creatures of the night – following the badgers. Only at weekends could we ever do something during the day.

She loved to watch me paint. We would climb up to the top of a tip, like Halviggan or Gunheath, and I would draw or paint the view.

'You should be a painter.' she said, 'I want you to be a painter. You could be famous. Exhibit all over the world. We can get away from here then.'

'Where?'
'Hensbarrow.'
'You want to get away? Leave Cornwall?'
'Yes. I hate it here,' she used to say, and the way she hated it felt as cold as the North Atlantic wind.

My parents adored Clara. She was the daughter they should have had. But Clara adored Tessa, and loved to help her. Whenever I told her that Clara was coming, Tessa's face would light up, and she would be well-behaved for the rest of the day. And Mary, well, she liked me I think. I was never sure what I thought of her. She always seemed distant. Perhaps it was the repelling of two like poles. Both artists. Both seers. Both lovers in the extreme, but I only realised this when I looked back on it.

Clara was smart. That had been Mary. Clara had what we might be called an unconventional childhood. She didn't go to a primary school. But with Mary's teaching, I felt she had learnt everything. The old ways. A kind of bond I could never quite understand, or break into. I felt it when I saw her at the carnival. Again, I had sensed it at Chutney Well. Regularly, we would walk down to Chutney to fetch pails of the water. Mary used them in her preparations.

'Tis the purest water, see Ben,' she said to me, 'and nothing else will do.'

Clara wore long dresses and cardigans. Dainty dolly shoes. She first told me that she loved me in return – I had told her almost from the outset that I loved her – in the relic of the pump house at Greensplat. We sat on the old concrete base for the twenty-inch pump. It had been removed only recently. Outside it was raining. We had gone inside for shelter. A few lovers had been in there before, so we knew we were not alone. On the base of the concrete mounting for the pump was a pile of rough sand. She took some stones and patterned them into a mosaic on the sand. 'I LOVE YOU' in tiny lumps of granite and clayey sand. Then she coloured and looked shyly away. To me again... then... the kiss. We returned to the pump house often just to be there, to hear the timbers creak, to imagine the pump working, to be alone. To be in love.

But I had kissed her before. The first was up on old Gunheath tip on a Saturday. You see on Hensbarrow there are no forests, no riverside walks. You make the best of a bad job. We made the best of it during a rain shower, the same sort of shower I had seen her getting wet from at Chutney Well. We sat underneath some lupin bushes; large bushes, lush and yellow, almost tropical. We had sat on the soft sand from which they grew. The wind rattled the seed cases.

The kiss was an enchantment, moist and sweet. Time stopped then. We stayed there long after the rain had stopped. I had kissed her. Kissed the moth girl. We were higher than Hensbarrow now, higher than Ten Men's Hill. Only when our lips were sore did we lie back and watch the grey sky pass overhead. There would be no cloud watching that day. There was no need to; for once, the dream had become the reality.

It was broken by Clara. She sat up and stripped a lupin prong of its flowers. Then another. Then she took a handful and pushed them down my shirt. I leapt up, grabbed several cream-flowered handfuls, and flung them at her. I missed, because the wind direction was wrong and they blew back to me.

'Catch me,' she shouted, and scrambled down over the soft sand with the agility of a mountaineer scree sliding. I caught up with her, my kicker boots full of sand as well. We emptied them, then went home, stopping at Carroncarrow pit to look at the water in there. It was no longer azure, but now the same colour as the rest of the moor, a dirty, muddy brown and green. But things like that did not matter any more. The tips had become dramatic mountains, the pits deserts, the lakes a Mediterranean coastline. Hensbarrow was innocent again.

Hensbarrow was Clara, and I loved it. The clay bonded us as lovers. The rubber band finally had sprung away from Southend, and its arrival was not a sting but a whip of pleasure. Clara was my Venus on an Olympian landscape, and I felt like a god.

We walked out to Roche to see the Longstone. It still attracted me as if a Dark Ages magnet. Clara had seen it before. She told me how she used to play there as a child. I did not tell Clara of the time Michael and I has sat there with our backs to stone, though I did think of it. The men and women of the old people's homes where the stone had been sited must have found it very strange as we waltzed around it, feeling it and loving every inch of it.

Clara knew its phallic connotations. She coloured when she thought about them. But we knew it was wrong there, without the heather and peat, without the lizards who used to bask beside it. Somewhere I could hear a ghost crying. It must have been there for a reason. But the clay people were keener on digging than eating the fruit of their past. Instead, in my mind, I transposed the stone and fantasised about making love to Clara up there. I watched her touch the stone. Dark stone. Old stone. Long stone.

'It's warm,' she said.
'I know.'
Walking back, I could not turn my mind away from the

thought of the two of us, plunging into the moor, writhing wondrously among the heather, peat and scurrying lizards.

Hensbarrow Ridge lies 1,032 feet above sea level. On it is a burial mound. From a distance it looks like a small hillock, below Gunheath tip. Closer, beneath the vearns and vegetation, you can see that once this place meant something – something holy – something valued. I valued it now. It brought back good memories. The barrow was late Neolithic. On it was erected a brass triangulation point. It would have been the highest point once. Before Cookworthy and all that jazz...

It was odd we found so much life up there, when essentially this mound was an ancient graveyard. Hensbarrow in the old language is 'hynde beorgh', meaning 'ten men's barrow'. Ten skeletons beneath us preserved in the peat. They never used to haunt us, though. Almost as if they liked to have us there. Ten men's eyes looking up from the moor. Spirit voyeurs. Mary used to say that we 'had gone courting up Hensbarrow'.

Actually, we used to go up there to snog. Find ourselves away from the rest of them. Normally lying down on the eastern edge of the barrow locked together. Afraid to let go. On top of the world. Higher than the tips, higher than the Shackletons.

And talk. Dreams. Ambitions. Fears. Loves. Hates. Hopes. Worries. Whispers. Nibbles on a cold ear in the Hensbarrow wind. The soft down of hair at the nape of her neck. She would hold my shoulders. Love her, right up over the real world, painting her naked body falling through space. And her teasing with a dry paintbrush, tickling... Up there, she would slip into her Downser drawl, and it sounded so perfect. Down the generations it came, her lips in an 'O' shape, pushing back her hair.

'Ben, my lover, give me a kiss.'

She sat on the triangulation point, her knees cupped against my side, and my hands feeling her breasts. I rubbed her nipples and tongued the inside of her mouth. Dry runs of sex. We imagined the ten men's eyes green with jealousy, and writhed in our ecstasy.

One Sunday afternoon, Clara wanted to see one of her friends down at Ruddlemoor, so we left the barrow and whizzed on our cycles down the steep Gunheath hill, under the old skip bridge and past the coal merchants.

At The Sawles Arms, we turned right and headed on the main road through the valley. They were knocking down a dry at the crossroads. Clara wanted to see her friend Helen about some school work. Her friend, Helen, lived in one of the council houses straddling the road. We were invited in and her mother gave us a Cornish high tea of saffron and Madeira cake.

'Slice of cake, Ben?' Helen's mother asked.
'No thank you,' I said, 'I'm...'
'Or Madeira, me dear...'
And we laughed at the joke, even though it was an old one.

Helen was a thin girl, very tall with dark hair parted in the centre. She wore it in plaits. She fancied Michael, it was rumoured. She went on to marry a laboratory technician from Treviscoe. I heard them giggling in the sitting room, supposedly discussing homework. I sat with her mother, watching Songs of Praise.

'We'd better go soon. It's getting dark, and we want to take the short cut back through Wheal Martyn,' I said.

Her mother fetched the girls.

'All done?' I asked when Clara came back in.

'Not really, but I can do it when I get back.'

'Ben... say hello to Michael for me...' said Helen.

'Okay,' I said, 'only for you mind!'

We thanked Helen's mother, then left for home. There was a useful short cut through Wheal Martyn china clay works. It was longer but it saved us pushing our bikes up Gunheath hill. Clara would never use it alone because it went through some woods and row upon row of rhododendrons. The atmosphere was sticky and sultry. We both sweated. I was hot. Then Clara shouted:

'Come and catch me!'

She cycled up the hill, her legs pushing the pedals of her bike round and round at a fantastic rate, as though her legs might fall off. I followed with all the intention of beating her. She rounded a bend out of my sight. I cycled on. As I came around the bend I heard Clara scream. Her bike was on the ground and her hands were waving in the air, like she was swatting some insects. As I got closer I saw a swarm of flies around her. She had frozen, her face filled with terror. The terror of a child. I grabbed her. The flies followed, irritating us both. She was frantic. So was I.

'Run as hard as you can!'

The flies dispersed, and headed back into the rhododendron plants.

'It's okay,' I said, my heart thumping, 'they've gone.'

Clara cried and grabbed me tightly. The flies had gone. She was trembling. When she relaxed I fetched our bikes, which had been flung down in the heat of the moment. We decided not to go back along the short cut, and so wound our way slowly up Gunheath. I talked to her. Small talk. Reassurances. I hate silences, pregnant pauses. But Clara had something else in mind. She placed her bike on the hedge, and ran down into Gunheath cedar tree woods. And there she showed me something special...

TOBIAS

30th October 1664.

ALL is well, and my first monthe as the Parishe Clerk hath given me much pleasure. Vpon the attempt to register all the recent births withine the Parishe, the Reverende Brewer and myself journeyed across the Moore, that the people call Hensbarrow, to a meagre place, name of Greens-plat, there to see a woman with new born child, and to register the birth. I have not observed suche a place as Hensbarrow before. I record here what I read today withine the Parochial History:
   'It is vpon a bleak elevation, surrounded with a direful stag of rocks visible above ground of various and tremendous shapes and sizes, affording shelter and pasture for little else beside sheep.'
   For this indeed was all I could observe. The name Hensbarrow, so folk do believe, means 'ten men's moore' in the Olde English, but I could see none of this. The moore hath little to offer. On oure journey back from Greens-plat the fog became wonderously thicke.
   I could not see the Reverende Brewer in front of me at one time, and became perplexed in the extreme at the conclusion I may well become lost. Fortunately the fog did ease and I spotted my guide once more.
   The Reverende then proceeded to what he says is the pagan stone. The stone is of ancient origine and stoode some twenty feet high. The Reverende, being of a nervous disposition, would not touche the stone, and when I reached to place my hand vpon it he was sorely afraid and bade me to come away. A Devil's stone he named it, but I could not see that it hath any diabolic qualities. What seemed to me more considerable was its enormity and lengthe.
   Some parishioners in Whitemoore do telle me that the stone ist in fact the staff of one Saint Austelle, so you do see that my Reverende is most wrong in his judgement. His staff was turned to stone by the Devil himself whilst on duties Christian.
   I do so worrie for the Reverende, for he sometimes hast twixt his ears an almighty space. Is it not likely that this Saintly man might have known the lamentable Saint Dennis of this Parishe? I would hope for this. Besides, I hath seen othere stones in West Cornwall

whiche might frighten the good Reverende even more. 'Hast thou seen the Men-an-tol?' I asks him. 'Nay,' says he, 'and neither would I like to, my boy.'

Today wast my twenty-first birthday. I do feel a real man now I am this age. When I returns to my cottage at Whitemoore, I do learn that my good mother hast managed to get a cake to my village. So I write here tonight, deare Lorde, in earthly paradise, eating saffron cake and pleased enough with my life so far in this worlde.

T.T.

OF THE GHOSTS

...of those who came, and now have gone...

IT was Tom's suggestion to take a picnic down to Gover. The day was a splendid one, and he was on rest days – his long weekend. Clara and I had gone to see him. He seemed better this time – more himself than when I had first taken her to see Tom. So we packed some food, all courtesy of Tom, and set off. Tom chatted nervously to Clara. I eavesdropped.

'So you like this 'ere young man then?' he asked in his drawl.

'He's okay,' Clara replied jokingly.

'Only okay! Well, my dear. He'd better be more than okay. I'm okay, but you wouldn't have me now, would 'ee?'

We sat in the middle of a field belonging to Higher Biscovillick Farm.

'Most of the old-timers have gone from down here,' Tom said, 'the real old Downsers what we call...'

Tom laid out the picnic. Clara helped with the plates. He had told me before about the Downsers. It was like an extinction. Class the Downsers with the Dodo. The Downsers had always had it hard. Just making a living off the downs was hard enough. Then, when someone discovered they had clay under their boots, life became even harder. So, as the clay people came on to the downs, the Downsers moved off.

'Clay is clay, see boy, and who were they to argue. You couldn't years ago.'

And Tom's friends had gone, the ones who lived at the top of Gover, at Higher and Lower Biscovillick, Penisker, and Goonamarth Farm; tucked away places in the folds of the valley, farming out an existence. He had friends in Blackberry Row, a set of houses, now a mere sketch of rubble behind Halviggan tip. Soon, they would all go. Beautiful houses.

Picture-book farms, caught in a web of clay. Sticky and sweet.

As we ate, Tom told us about the Gover path. It stretched right through the valley and into St Austell. The path used to be wide. Two men could walk abreast, travelling to mow a meadow or to go on the downs and dig. Now it was overgrown. The drys were also camouflaged and rusty cars and smashed televisions were the only things to be found between the creeping willow. I felt the ghosts of the clay workers. Clara seemed unconcerned.

See them all from Trenance Moor, from the railway line after St Austell; ghosts of Wheal Jacob, Biscovillet, Goonamarth and Carroncarrow. And Tom will tell you, clay ghosts are the most frightening of all because they are white even before they begin their haunting.

There are no more sand drags and mica drags, bluing houses and settling tanks. Nor the tools – the poll pick and the dubber, the swell jumper and the scrape. The buildings – the pan kiln and the linhay – are all gone now. Just clay covered shells. Memories of old men. Soon to be words on the wind, joining the ghosts of the men who spoke in the buildings and worked with the tools.

Tom lay facing the sky. I thought I could hear him thinking. I reached over, putting my weight on to Clara and kissed her.

After we had eaten, we packed the picnic holder and bounded down the field into the willow woods. Tom followed, already feeling a pain inside him. Clara and I tried to hear their voices back in time, but we heard nothing, or perhaps our hearing was not sensitive enough. Because of this, we just decided to run amongst the past, and so played kiss chase around the Linhay. Unknown to me at this point, Tom turned to face Trenance Moor with tears in his eyes. He and Mary had come here once, playing like Clara and I now.

Of course, I never guessed then that Clara was his daughter but I did notice Clara taking note of Tom's skywards gaze, and for a moment I was a stranger to both of them. Then Tom looked down, and I was Clara's lover again and she was no longer Tom's daughter.

And up on Great Longstone's tip a dumper grunted his approval.

THEY had agreed to meet like they used to in those earlier, happier days, the brief moments in clover they had together. But this time they met not because they wanted to, not because of any reconciliation attempt or hope to make things that good again, but simply because they had to, for the sake of two others.

The two silhouettes stood in the hay field above Higher Biscovillick Farm. She thought him scruffy, that he had neglected his appearance. He found her harder, harsher. In other ways, she still looked the same.

It had been so bitter; the final ending, like chewing a lemon for the rest of your life. Sharp and bitter. That's what it had been. Somewhere, Tom was still looking for sweetness. He opened.

'How are you, Mary?... after... well, after so long?'

'Very well,' she replied.

Once these formalities were exchanged, neither knew how to talk about the matter in hand. Eventually, it was Mary who began.

'I haven't told her. Ronnie's her father. But sometimes she hears people... she's not silly you know. The maid'll guess one day, if she hasn't already.'

'I never wanted it to be like this.'

'Tom, neither did I. Twas other folk who made us like this. We've got to do something about it now.'

'What?' Tom asked. 'What can we do?'

'Well. Ben, he's a good boy, but he's said to me, he's said that Clara looks like you. And my goodness, her eyes went wild, they did...'

'I've thought the same.' Tom said. 'But in the woods the other day, it was almost... almost...'

'Almost what?'

'Like she knew I was her father. Sort of instinctive like. And Ben ... well Ben, he's like a son to me.'

'I think it still might be best to let sleeping dogs lie. We don't want all the past to come out again. Most folk have forgot all about that now. And besides they pair are happy.'

'Aye... Maybe you're right maid.'

'We'll keep our eye on 'em, but I don't want us ruining their love, as other folk did to us.'

'Yes.' said Tom.

The silhouettes stood there, shivering in the field.

'I'd better go back, Tom.'

She began to walk away, then turned.

'Tom, I still think of you...'

Tom shivered again, and watched her open and shut the gate. His stomach went into a twist of pain and he howled his way home, crying like a child who has broken his favourite toy. Like a child who has no idea...

OF A BOMBSHELL DROPPED

'The Battle of the Falklands was a remarkable military operation, boldly planned, bravely executed and brilliantly accomplished. We owe an enormous debt to the British forces and the merchant marine.'

Margaret Thatcher after the Falklands victory.

'I'M going...' he said.
　'Going?'
　'Going to...'
　Then he dropped it. The bombshell.
　'Join the Army.'
　'You're not?'
　'Certainly am. I'm leaving next month.'
　'Where?'
　'Initial training is in Salisbury.'
　'You've passed all the tests then?'
　'Yeh... a doddle. No problem.'
　'Have to get your hair cut.'
　'Yeh. I know.'
　'What's your mother think?'
　'It's good. Thinks it'll make me a man.'
　'Be strange without you. You know... We've done a lot...'
　'Yeh.'

And so Michael left. I had known for a while he had thought about joining the forces. He was the type. He would do well. Besides, his house was going soon. The pit was marching up the garden path. The stones had already gone. His mother was moving to live with her sister for the time being in St Dennis. The clay company was supposed to be rehousing her. Michael had very little left when his grandfather died. He would have been proud of Michael. He served in the First World War. He had the medals to prove it.

They had all gone. The houses cried. Tears fell from the upstairs windows. Then the demolition began. That was the last time I saw Karslake; just a bed of rubble. The next time I peeped, and the clay monster had gulped it down without so much as a thank you.

For now, though, we chatted mate to mate.

'You've signed up then?'

'Yeh... It's gonna' be good.'

And it was good. Michael went to Beirut, Hong Kong, had a few years in Northern Ireland. Spent two years in Belize. He was in the Royal Engineers; was coming out with a decent pension and a trade. And it was good for twelve years until 1982, the year of the Falklands Conflict, the Antarctic comic opera, when Michael had his left leg and genitals blown off by an Argentinian landmine. As the politicians said, it was just 'a little local difficulty.'

TOBIAS

13th November 1664.

I hath hearde today of a most strange occurence vpon Hensbarrow last night that hath made me sore afraid, so muche so I do not know whether I might have good sleep tonight. I perchanced today to be riding o'er Hensbarrow, a typical day alack, raining to drown the cats and dogs as the saying is, when I spies one Henry Rickard, a shepherde. Henry Rickard is a Downser, that is a man who lives his 'saken life on that down. But he, being a Godfearing man, grabbed me – for he hath not seen a soul – nearly pulling me off my mount. I tells Rickard not to do this. But then, I looks in his eyes, and they were wide, very moon-like indeed, and he bode me a very strange tale.

   'A most frightening thing happen'd last night,' says he.
   'Steady thyself,' I says, for this man Rickard is shaking. He continued:
   'See yonder stones. The soft white ones...'
   'Aye,' says I. 'They are but clay rock, that is all.'
   'That be neither bee nor baw,' says he. He carries on.
   'I wast out in the rain last night, searching for a sheep I hath loste when vpon those stones, aye, in that very acre, vpon them fell a shower of bloode.'
   'Never,' says I.
   'Tis true enough,' he says. 'Look at yonder stones.'
   This shepherde then tells me the bloode fell in drops the size of sterling shillings.
   'Yon,' says I. 'You would put an ape in my hood, would you?'
   'No,' says he. 'Look at the stones.'
   So I dismounted and examined the stones. As I am sitting here, I could see crimson drops covering these stones. And one great shiver entered me, for I hath ne'er seen rain like this in my life. For, as well as this, around yonder stones on the heather and base of the moor were marks of bloode. Then he shows me his coat, which is also spotted crimson. Rickard do say twas the work of the Devil, and didst arche his back like that vile Spirit.
   Other showers hast fallen from yon sky. Men do talk that such events bring evil to us. The bloode be a prediction and the work of the Devil, gaining unsavoury revenge on the good Christian people

of this land and against the Saint who didst first do battle with him.

But I am uncertaine. I have not questioned my master about these stones for he, being a Clerick, is one worse than Rickard. But in my hearte I feel ill boding of this event. Legende tells us this is a warning. And as I write in this awful light I can only think of what plagues, wars, sickness and all the other bases of human life whiche will come. So tonight, whilst I relax on my bed, I shalt think of this.

I might look out of my window to see if the rain is now red. I have one more theorie as to the cause of yonder bloode marks. It is likely that old Rickard, for he is a poore, misguided soul, might have marked the stones himself with paint or daub or dye, but for the life of me he must be exceedingly good at daubing to have daubed all yonder rocks and the acre of the moor. Therefore, I am afraid again. The future bodes ill. Alack, I have muche work to contemplate in the morrow. Hallelujah anyway.

T.T.

PS: Twas odd. For two days later, not one, not two, but the whole of Rickard's flock wast struck down by some sicknesse. Within a week, all were dead. I shall pray tonight.

PART THREE

'Superstition brings bad luck.' –
Raymond Smullyan, 5000 BC, I.3.8

OF A MOON CHILD AND A HERMIT

...who both live a lonely life.

I WAS happy on Hensbarrow then. That's why I took the job. I felt no desire to do as Michael did. Besides, my life was there with Clara. I had been for the interview a few months earlier in the brand new concrete and glass headquarters of the china clay company.

I was taken on as a trainee. They said I should consider the accountancy side of things, but I wanted the material world. I wanted money. Besides, a few of my friends had been taken on and they said it was a doddle.

I had to go on day shifts until I was eighteen. Then shifts proper. I was based at Littlejohns – what irony there is in a name my friends; like Little John of Robin Hood fame. This pit was one of the largest in Western Europe – an enormous crater in the belly of the moor.

Back then, it was not quite so big. Now, it is not quite so little. My parents were disappointed. They had expected more of me. Mary was disappointed as well. She said I was foolish to drop art.

Only Clara supported me. She thought it was the right decision. It was a decision to make her happy. Tom said nothing. When I told him, he simply said:

'Well there tis boy. You must make the most of un.'

But I was proud. Proud as hell when they gave me an orange hard hat. It's like something special. Like being knighted. When you first wear your hat it's shiny, not a scratch on it, and you treasure it as if it's a crown. But friends, there are no kings or queens in the clay pit, only diggers; slaves to the soil. You should know that by now.

When I received the letter about the job I showed it to Michael. He was pleased for me. We decided to go out to celebrate our good fortune. The time was right. Michael was due to leave the next week for initial training, and I started with the company the following Monday.

On Saturday then, we went into St Austell.

They were all under age in The Cookworthy that night, but no-one said anything. Not in the jungle and jumble of people in the pub. Not amidst the noise of the fruit machines and the heavy thud of music. We had all huddled into a taxi. Michael paid on the way down. I was to pay on the way back. So, the St Austell ale flowed. There was a band on. A pot bellied singer called Wilf making an attempt at a Yardbirds number. We laughed at the guitarist's out-of-date beatnik hairstyle. A few girls prancing on the dance floor. They were older than us, around twenty-five.

I was getting drunk. My mouth had gone numb. Clara and I were slobbering over each other. Helen and Michael had begun to dance. An old man with a droopy fag who sold cabbages told me to 'get in there'. I wanted to tell him to get lost, but instead I grinned like a Cheshire cat.

I was happy, but it was as if these were the last moments of my youth. They were slipping out of my hands, sliding down the beer-soggy bar. Dripping out of the spirit dispensers. All numb, but not frozen. Time was melting the ice cubes. I watched Clara leave to go to the toilet in the cigarette mist. She was growing older. Something in her eyes.

'What's up with you?'

It was Michael, peering at me across the dance floor.

'Nothing.'

'Nothing?'

He twisted his head to one side as if to enquire what was wrong.

Then he spoke again.

'Come on. Get a few more down, and come up an' dance.'

So we did. We were last out of the pub. The barman looked at us suspiciously. We were singing. Clara and Helen were giggley. Once in the car park he shut the door on us. 'Good night,' was all he said.

'Up yours,' Michael bawled.

'Schhh...' said Clara.

At a phone box, we rang for a taxi. One arrived ten minutes later. The journey back sobered us. Helen's parents were away for the weekend, something to do with a great aunt being ill, so we stopped outside. I paid the taxi driver, overtipping him. Michael was singing. Helen held on to him, trying not to step on the cracks in the pavement, as if steering him away from destiny. Once inside, Helen made coffee and we ate some chocolate biscuits.

Clara and I sat exhausted on the sofa. After a while, I felt better, more alive again. In the meantime, Helen had taken Michael

down to the front room. We knew what that meant. We heard little giggles, inaudible conversation and banging.
'A nice way for him to leave,' I commented.
Clara just kissed me on the cheek as I caressed her leg. Then, she rubbed me between the legs, and I undid her blouse, uncupping her breasts and touching them gently. Outside it was raining. Inside it was warm. I was sleepy. I had it all... a job, a girl, a future.
I woke to the sound of the front room door being opened. About an hour had passed. It was Helen, her hair twisted, her clothes dishevelled. I opened my tired eyes and looked at her.
'Bleddy useless,' she said, 'He can't get it up.'
I smiled. She climbed the stairs to bed, and I pulled myself closer to Clara on the settee.

DO you know the phrase 'All good things must come to an end'? I felt that phrase seemed to walk hand in hand with growing older. I am thinking of another time... another slice of my life... Clara was attending technical college. She was taking business skill subjects, typing and shorthand, commerce and law.
I was in the pit. It was February. A cold morning. The time was seven o'clock, and I was heading down the rivulet criss-crossed pit road. The eager moon was still up. In the bottom of the pit hung a bed of white mist and a stinking loader was whining along the periphery road.
I was almost fully trained now. They were pleased with me. I had made a few mistakes; typical clay pit novice errors, like sanding up the gravel pumps, but Cap'n Varcoe wanted to keep me in his gang. I had a wage, and had just bought a new motorbike. Tonight I was seeing Clara. I was a miner. The rock was in me. I must have washed thousands of tons of clay by now and it never bothered me. After so long on the hose you become used to it. It becomes a body function. That morning I had been put on one of the bottom stopes, a flat and long stope that ran round to the right of the hose hut. And so to the hose again...
But I was changing. I had letters from Michael. He was doing well. He was the type. The misty mornings were taking their toll on me. Before, I never felt the damp, the wet, the mud, the numbness that enters the mind of mining every day.
Initially, I had liked the cribroom jokes, the rattle of the gravel pump, the swish of the hose; but increasingly they had become my enemies, and instead of taking out my frustrations on them, they had come out on my family, Tom and, most of all, Clara. The clay drudge was rotting my brain. I could not draw. I hadn't put pencil to paper the whole time I had worked there. I fought it

hard, but the clay dust was covering me. I was becoming a ghost of my former self. Buried.

'You shouldn't have to be up there mining clay. Shouldn't be up there on the hose...' my mother would say.

'Why not?'

'Because your father wanted better for you...'

I felt stuck in mud. A pig, as the saying goes, in muck. I could feel Hensbarrow slipping from me, the magic disappearing on the breeze. There seemed very little left. The stone, Karslake houses, Michael, dug out and gone. And inside me a voice was shouting: 'Rain on me.' A chip on my shoulder. A hatred of passing. The clock tick-tocking onwards. I only had one thing left; my soul mate, Clara, my crystal in the clay.

But a change was happening to me, and as the winter days became spring my fire began to burn brighter. I was breathing flames. And when I swung the hose round and a swash of milk came back, and trapped me by my boots, wedged in a quicksand of liquid clay, mica and sand, I could feel myself being pulled down. I felt as if I were going under. The wet clay soaked my feet and the drizzle ran down my neck. I was alone in this landscape that had nourished me.

Below the bench was fog. In the distance, just visible, were the lights of the conveyor. I felt as if I were floating in a nether world between life and death, a Cornish astral plane. It was time to make a decision. It was time to wash the clay away. A time for change. A bloody revolution...

Having lived so close to the ground for most of my life now – 'Earthbound', as Tom said – I often wondered what Hensbarrow looked like from far above. Perhaps from space, by a land satellite. Then you could see the whole unreal chain of cones on Hensbarrow where the earth had been turned inside out. To the rest of the world it looked rather insignificant, the mining area itself only twenty-five miles in circumference, but when you have lived up there, learnt their ways, made your life there, how it fails to be anything but significant I did not know.

When Neil Armstrong took that giant leap for mankind in 1969, and millions of television sets all over the world crackled with the first pictures of man on the moon, not many on Hensbarrow were impressed.

You see, these people, the clay people, the Downsers, they had always lived on their own moon. To see a man in a bulky spacesuit plant a flag in a white and grey dusty soil was, to be honest, nothing special, nothing out of the ordinary.

Tom had even done it. He had been to the moon. Sometimes he would take me. Right down the bottom of Blackpool pit. Open your eyes, and all you could see was a moonscape. Try it in darkness and it is even better. So who is this Neil Armstrong anyway?

And do you know the strangest thing of all was what Clara used to call me. I was a 'moon child' she used to say. Mary had used it first and Clara had picked up on it. They had been talking about birth signs and the Zodiac. Mary was a Pisces, and she believed in the power of astrology. Clara, a Virgo, followed her mother in her belief. They had asked me my star sign.

'I'm a Cancer,' I said.

'Cancer?' Clara asked.

'A moon child then...' Mary had said, almost as though I was not meant to hear.

And every time she called me by that name, it made me think of werewolfs and metamorphosis, but she always reassured me that it was because my moods changed with the cycle of the moon.

I could never see any difference, but Clara said she could tell the phases of the moon just by my mood. And so the moon and I became intellectual sparring partners.

While the rest of the world was discovering the moon for the first time, and Hensbarrow twiddled her thumbs, this moon child was ready to leave his moonscape. Clara had noticed it and, at first, she was glad. But later... well... let's not say... not yet...

A FEW weeks later, and I was alone, thinking of Landsat, space and time. Thinking of what was going to happen. Thinking whether I would ever go to the moon on holiday. I was thinking of nothing. I was perched on a granite block, part of a leper's house. Everyone in the clay world knew of it. It was a famous landmark that lay on the north side of Hensbarrow in the village of Roche.

The landmark consisted of tourmaline rocks, the biggest formation of which held the remains of a dwelling or chapel. The place was known as Roche Rock.

All kinds of legends had built up about it over the years. Some say a leper really did live there once, and that the villages had to pass up his food in a bucket. Others believe it was a monastery. Others say it was just a hermit's dwelling. The only hermit I could think of was Tom, and so I imagined a Dark Ages Tom Cundy.

Whatever reason, Roche Rock was magical. It was magical that day as I sat on the triangular gable above the arch-shaped window which looked so eerie at night. It had been magical when I had gone there years before with Tom and Michael. It would always be magical, and it was magical for many more people than me.

I liked all the legends about it – the tale about the magical rock containing water which flowed to the sea, but I liked the leper story best. It seemed to make it scary. Some of the leprosy still there in the cracks in the walls, or between the slabs in the floor.

The rock was one of the strangest formations about. Helman Tor, to the east, though sounding more diabolical, never conveyed the mysticism that this place had. The jointing was vertical as well, so that from the road the rocks looked like fingers and thumbs, knuckles and horns. The main rock sprouted out of the ground like a mushroom. The building itself is medieval. Time in its walls.

I could sit up there and escape the paralysing clay. It once had two levels to it, but only the gable end of the top level remained. Below that was the main living area with a door to the south east. A ladder with a beautiful smell of worn metal connected the two layers.

That day it was sunny. A few children from the village were dashing around in the vearns, having fights and climbing the rocks. It looked homely, comforting to see. But then, on a misty November morning, it could look like Hell itself as you went by, the mist low, as if suspending the black building. And when the crows sat up there from the trees in the village, they became ravens instantly, and fear oozed from the lichen on the granite.

So this was the rock, and I loved to act the hermit. I had many drawings of the rock, some in pencil or charcoal, others with pastels. The best was a painting from memory low down in the vearns, the only light coming through the arch window at the top. To the north and east the main road, the A30, the backbone of Cornwall and tourist highway. The road that took you out. The escape route.

Sometimes I felt I could see the rest of the world on the horizon, like when you re-enter the earth's atmosphere from space; the rock gave me such a power. To the south, the clay, blobs of white on a green and brown painting. All the other times I had been here there was only one way to go, and that was home. But now I turned my head and realised there was another choice. Another world.

THE bells in Roche church were ringing, peeling up over the downs. I bet even Woody could hear them. I climbed gingerly down the steps and then brushed through the vearns and on to the road. It was warm. The grasshoppers were singing. The Tarmac was sticky, there was the smell of my sweat.

I walked back towards the centre of the village, past the primary school and The Rock Inn. I turned south, my thoughts going back to Clara, and all I had in my mind was desire. That day I could barely wait to see the moon. I wanted to know what he looked like. But it was no good, for Hensbarrow was shrouded in a veil of cloud that night.

I was Harry Houdini. I was getting out. I was unpicking the locks. I had become claustrophobic. It had got too much. There was nothing left. I was going. Escaping. Packing up my lump of bread and cheese in a red and white knotted handkerchief and running away, bounding over the clay tips, reaching out for where the pavements were lined with gold. I was a bull in a china shop smashing through the porcelain.

But I was not. I couldn't. Not yet anyway. I had to decide my means of escape first. And when I dreamt, the tips seemed like tombs, barrows ready to bury the living in, and I could feel myself falling, falling from one of the quarry benches and yet never coming to a halt. Just hanging there in space. And the more I looked at the gang I worked with, the more convinced I became of them being brainwashed. The more I could feel the clay being a cancer. Something evil. And yet it was more than this; the clay seemed to be holding everyone back, reaching up out of the earth and grabbing people by the ankles, keeping them on Hensbarrow, never wanting to let them go. God-like it seemed to me, and it wanted to control peoples' minds.

And I began to see through it all; the innocence, the beauty, the azure pools, the yellow lupins, and the foxgloves. They were traps for the clay people. The clay was love, though. What more did people want? Folk should be grateful for what they have. And the only words I could hear were the words they used to describe Tessa – 'retarded', 'backward', 'handicapped'. This was Hensbarrow, and I felt there was no escape. I had been sucked in. Taken to it too easily.

On Tessa's eleventh birthday the doctor told her she might be finding some preliminary paralysis in her legs and back. I could see her frustration trying to climb the stairs, and I related her frustration to my own.

Often, it seemed like a cocoon, holding the perfect butterfly within. So much love, beauty, strength and power to be found here, but I never saw the cocoon open. All that which had gone before seemed just a fallacy. Nothing seemed white, clear-cut. Now it was a murky grey. Grey walls erupting out of the moor. Moving closer. Trying to crush me. Attempting suffocation. One face already under the sand.

The move away took a long time in planning, and in its completion. I took evening classes. This was the way out. Try to get a couple of A-levels and get into art college. I began to draw and paint again, the first time for nearly a year. Most of them were sketches of Clara.

Once I knew I was getting out I began to like the pit work more; an end to the tunnel. Besides it was summertime, and the pit is always better then.

Clara and I continued. We were close, but my plans upset her. She had a job now in St Austell, in a solicitor's office, and was progressing well. I had been accepted into an art college in London, on the condition that I achieved reasonably good A-level passes.

At first it was difficult, not to say frustrating. Working with the monitor all that time seemed to have taken some of the ability out of my hands. I had my doubts. But it came together. I tried more pottery and sculpture – easing back into the paintings. I tried to think art as well. Difficult when you are stuck in a clay pit for eight hours a day, but that struggle, that desire, taught me something else as well. Something that I would use at art college to gain recognition and respect. The art of escape had begun.

However, part of the structure I was building was about to crumble. The unbearable tension of just over a year exploded one night at Carroncarrow cottage.

'You've changed,' she said, staring at me with acid eyes.

I knew I had, but human nature told me to deny it.

'I haven't...'

'Then why are you going away?'

The crux.

'Because... I don't know. I can't live here forever. I've done all there is to do here. I've got to get away. Perhaps I'll come back again...'

'Once you've been away, you won't want to come back.'

My heart cried for her. I could see a rubber band forming.

'Going away. It changes people..'

'Not always.'

'Always.'

There was a moment of intense silence, Clara biting her nails, me just thinking. Then the confirmation. The denial of disinterest on my behalf.

'Okay. It does then... but I still love you.'

She hardly moved. We had discussed this before. The argument went past itself, going round in circles. Spirals and squares were forming. Awkward angles.

'I wish you hadn't changed.'

I was faltering,

'I haven't... really.'
It was still light outside.
'See, Up Country, everything's happening. Down here in Cornwall we're out on a limb, missing out. People think you're strange if you're an artist. You can't get anywhere...'
The tunnel was being filled in.
'Come with me then... come to London. We don't have to be married.'
'I can't Ben. My mother....'
The anger burst up inside her and flowed out in large teardrops. She sobbed. I listened. Each sob, her heart breaking. Then the crying turned to real anger. The truth.
'I hate you Ben. Hate you. I wish I'd never met you.'
She stood up, kicking over a chair. On the chair sat the china doll. I tried to save it but the doll toppled over, landing head first on the slate floor. The way the china cracked made both of us stand still. The very worst kind of crack. The room was silent. I lifted up the broken doll. Her rosy face was completely shattered. Now the ecstasy of anger. A release.
'Now see what you made me do,' she said coldly. 'Get out of here. Go home. I don't want to see you again.'
Her voice was controlled. Emotions quelled. It was out. Over and out.
'I'm sorry it's worked out this way,' I said. 'I really am...'
'Get out,' she said, nestling her doll against her breast.
I walked backwards out of the cottage. The door closed behind me. It was twilight. I walked down the path, sticking my two fingers up to the moon. The moon said nothing back, nor made any abusive gesture. I still loved her.
The next morning there was a postcard from Michael. I had been waiting for the postman to deliver his results. On the postcard was a rather gloomy picture of Stonehenge. On the back, words from Michael:
'Dear Ben, Hello mate. Thought you might like this postcard from Salisbury Plain. We are doing some exercises out here. Can't say what; it's all hush hush. I've been out a lot, been to a few clubs with the lads. Have met a girl called Sarah who I'm going out with on Friday. How is Helen? I still can't remember anything from that night! Suppose Karslake is all gone now? Still, don't really miss it now. Hope Littlejohns is all right. All the Georgie Best, Mike.'
There was also a letter from the health authority for my mother. It would be about my sister. Those sort of letters always were. Tessa had to go into hospital for a while. An operation on her spine. I was glad. Perhaps the operation would help her. She

was to go up to Plymouth in a few days time. I imagined her kicking and screaming in the ambulance. Men in uniforms scared her.

I was still thinking about Clara. I mentally carried her image everywhere I went. We had argued before but it had never been as bitter as this. I looked out of my bedroom window, up over the moor to Greensplat. I could see a trail of smoke from their cottage and imagined her in front of the fire, staring at the broken pieces of the china doll. Mary would know by now. I had not told my parents yet. Besides, I had half a hope still that the rift could be reconciled.

The next two days passed in a blur of sheer terror of waiting for my examination results. Those evenings and days I had put into the course. A ticket to getting out of there, the first step towards wrapping up the bread and cheese. They arrived on the Friday, a glorious sunny morning. The moment of truth as I opened the envelope. My heart flickering. Art 'A', history 'C'. Enough.

The college accepted me. Within the hour I had written to confirm that I would be taking up the course.

Tom was in the woodshed. He had great lengths of railway sleeper on a saw bench, attacking them with a well-greased bow saw. Sawdust was trapped in his bushy eyebrows and in his beard. He sawed regularly, in time with his breathing. There was a smell of creosote, pipe tobacco and soap. He knew I was watching him. I was waiting for Tom to turn around, but he continued sawing. Only when the heavy block of sleeper clattered to the floor did he stand up straight and speak.

'How's you?'

'Okay.'

I knew there was a slight nervousness in his voice. Tom knew me well, too well. He knew much about the human character. All the years of quiet skytip contemplation had allowed him to think about the rest of society.

'Whaf' 'ee been arguing with Clara 'ave 'ee?'

'How do you know?'

'I can tell boy.'

I was indignant. 'How?'

'Just can.'

Tom lifted the sleeper off the bench so that a new section could be sawed off. As he spoke he sawed. 'Going away soon, ben't 'ee?'

'Yes, I got my results yesterday...'

'Goin' to leave me up here are 'ee? Leave me, like I used to be. Old hermit like?' he joked.

'No. I'll be back.'

'Ess, 'ess. I know 'ee will Ben. Know you will.'
There was only the sound of sawing again. I felt a cue to exit this stage.
'See 'ee some more then,' I said in my adopted drawl.
'Ess. See 'ee some more,' he replied.
At the gate, I stopped. I was going to ask him. I returned to the shed. He was still in there. This time he had not noticed me.
'She's your's isn't she?'
Tom stopped sawing.
'Clara... your daughter.'
Tom stood motionless.
'And the photo... the photo on the sideboard. It's Mary isn't it? I could tell Clara was your daughter... the way you looked at one another down Gover. You're...'
Slowly, Tom turned around. He was old. I had just aged him a little more.
'Yes,' he said, 'You're right. Clara is my daughter.'
Tears fell down his face.
'Tis a heller you two 'ave split up. I was hoping...'
'How do you know?' I asked.
Tom looked me straight in the eye. The Downser's stare.
'She told me,' he said. 'She told me.'
I walked away, up past his sheds and wood and into the glaring sun, my eyes watering.

OF ART

...which is an imitation of life.

ART college, in many ways, passed as a dream, a kind of watercolour wash. Now, I can only remember fragments, scattered pieces of detail in the landscape...

'It's got a good structure Ben. Composition's nice as well...'

The voice of my tutor. An Australian. Hated mateship. Campaigned for Abo land rights. Loved whisky. Smelt of oranges. Wore a beard. Bushy sideburns greying slightly. Played the violin or, as he preferred to call it, the fiddle.

The picture was on the floor, propped against the wall. It had chipped the paint on the wall slightly, but the wall was so filthy it made little difference. It was a screen print of a London bus. It was upside down, a businessman falling through the roof. I had signed this one. It looked good. The way he wanted. On my bed, I squinted and framed it with his fingers. Yes, the composition was nice. The tutor had been right.

The room was mine. The landlord had the money. Bricknell he was called. Pricknell they called him because he was. He was a milkman who had a sideline in estate management. He would have been a dockland developer now. Came from a long line of milkmen, though.

My window looked out on a garden. It was not mine. Rubbish plants grew out of the mess. They looked reasonably pretty in the urban blandness. On the desk were a couple of brushes. One, my mother had bought me. There was a letter there from Michael as well, going on about some squaddie trick he had played on someone.

The lightbulb in the room had no shade on it, so the light was glaring. The ceiling was cracked around the wire so it resembled some kind of deep sea jellyfish with the bulb as its stinger. This was it; the Lightbulb Community. Ideas and inspiration – art college.

They liked my work. I tried hard. Sometimes, I would stay at the college late, then catch the last tube back to the house. Slithering in the earth again, but this time it was clean and modern, except for the tramps who used to mosey up to me and ask for a bit. I was 'out as well'. They understood.

I had been in London for some time. It was more than I had dreamed of. I liked the freedom. Liked the bright lights. Like as if Hensbarrow was a leviathan in my mind that I had culled. It was with me still, but its memory was being stamped on. I had London in my head, and it flowed down through my body to my feet, pushing out any remaining granite energy. People dressed differently. Mohicans and earrings had not even been seen on Hensbarrow. The students all wore them.

And on my bed I was thinking of Tom. I could smell his beard.

We had parted on bad terms. I left the woodshed with him shouting. I never thought I would do that. It must have been the Celt coming out in him. I could understand better now, though. He felt Clara and I should have been together. Sort of make him happy that.

But I had got on the train in St Austell. I remembered waving goodbye to my mother and father. I saw mother crying. I had pictured her as I went out of the clay land. Past Par Docks, where the white stuff tumbled down chutes into the deep hulls of West German freighters. And there was no turning back. It was crossing the Tamar, unlocking the cage that was Cornwall. Clickety clack. Clickety clack over Brunel's Bridge. She'd never fall down, that baby. Past the dockyard. Past Plymouth; Armada city and home of digger Cookworthy. I was returning to the earth from the moon, in a second class carriage on the way to Paddington, with a Maxpax black coffee. And things were getting lighter and easier to see as the dust blew away.

I remembered those sessions with my tutor, in the hot spring of that year...

'Justify it,' he said.

'I can't.'

'You should be able to. Every artist can...'

'Okay. It's my sister. She's a... She's a Down's Syndrome child. Sometimes, it's like we talk, but we used to talk better when we were younger. I used to read to her and she took it in, as if she understood. Now... well now it's like as if she hardly knows I'm there...'

'I can see now. See the face...'

'Yeh. I wanted to get that...'

'What about the lorry there? What's that?'

'I gave it to her. Just seemed right... a kind of image from childhood. Someone gave it to me but I don't need it any more, so I gave it to her. It's one of her favourite toys.'

'It's odd... But it's got something I really like.'

'Good.'

'Has it a title?'

'I thought... Broken Bubble.'

'Excellent. I want it in the exhibition, mind...'

Earlier on in my time there, I went out to get drunk regularly. To forget about art and wash it down with beer. In the morning, the living room stank, a staleness hiding under the sideboard; the remnants of a night out on the floor. I would be in the kitchen, washing the morning down with coffee, tuning into the breakfast show on the radio. I left the others in the flat sleeping. Then I shut the door and stood in the street – row upon row of tiny terraced houses, like a dream extension of Coronation Street. You couldn't cloud watch here; all the rooftops closed you in, and there was glass on the pavement. Smashing.

I was hung over for the practical. It was one o'clock in the afternoon. The tutor on the pottery course was demonstrating an alternative glazing technique. My eyelids were beginning to shut. The hangover was taking the day away from me. I wanted to sleep – the kind of dozy, cuddly, soft sort of sleep you crave for after night shift. The kind of sleep my father had still. But the tutor asked us to start painting later that afternoon.

I had no idea what to do. I had forgotten my sketches, so any real work seemed incomprehensible. In the end, I managed to draw for about half an hour. Not drawings really, though; more lines on a page. Black and white. Nothing really. Art for art's sake. No feeling.

Then the image came, crawling out of the hangover. It was the rubber band again. One pin in London. The other in Hensbarrow. I had lichen on my skin, the ghost of Cookworthy behind me, as if I could feel his breath...

Then there was the time art and reality actually did seem to mingle...

'I like it,' the tutor said, peering closer.

When he looked at paintings he held his spectacles on his forehead, as though they were clouding his real vision.

'In fact,' he went on, 'this is one of the superior pieces this year. Tell me about it.'

I looked at the work again. It stretched about ten foot across the wall.

'It's where I used to live. Like here, along the bottom, are five different places. That one's my house. That's a friend's place...'

'But they all see the same thing. That white triangle. So whichever room you are in you see it. Is that right?' he asked, lowering his glasses again.

'Yeh. The triangle is the clay.'

'The clay?'

The tutor's face was puzzled.

'China clay. They mine it down there. It sort of dominates everything.'

'And this? This tooth shaped area here?'

'That's the Longstone.'

'Longstone?'

'It's a standing stone... a really tall one. That's at this place. I used to... to go there once.'

'I really do like it, Ben. The colours are extraordinary... and the angles! I've never quite seen anything like it. I'm glad you did it large. I must be going now.'

I grabbed the coffee mug he had set upon a collapsed easel on the floor and wandered out of the studio humming to himself. I thought about the painting. It had taken two weeks from the original idea. I still had some of the foreground to complete.

Car lights filtered through into the studio as the November night pulled in. I was happy. I had arrived. In the half light I could almost see the Cornish mist rising up through the floorboards. Then I washed the brushes and cleaned up the palettes, which were in a state. Whites, greys, blacks, greens going down the sink. Last, the red palette. The tap ran, and I watched it drip blood into the sink.

As I walked home fireworks were being let off in the back gardens. Rockets lit up the sky like flak. I fished the front door key out of my pocket. My flatmates had just come down the stairs. I went up.

'Where're you going?'

'Upstairs.'

'You know what it is tonight don't you?'

'Yeh. Guy Fawkes.'

'Yeh.'

I climbed a few more steps.

'You're not coming out tonight then?'

'No. Not tonight.'

They had a last go.

'You can't stay in tonight...'

'I can,' I said, now climbing two steps at a time.

'Come on. We've been looking forward to tonight.'

'So have I,' I shouted from the landing. I needed sleep, and neither they, nor the fireworks, nor the memory of Clara were going to stop me. Waiting for sleep to call, I decided to name the painting 'The Dirty Bit' – the bit I had hung on to...

THE light that shone up from the arc lights in Gunheath Pit was slightly incongruous with the activities on Hensbarrow that night. The downs stepped back in time to let the pagan place become real again, but the present shone its torch on them as if to ensure nothing untoward was happening.

On top was a gathering – silhouetted forms twisting before the bright flames. The heat was incredible. No-one knew, but the fire could be seen as far away as Newquay. It was a second Spanish Armada. The beacon was alive once more. This time something homely, celebratory – not quite pagan; but November 5th.

The bonfire had been constructed day by day. Before lighting, it stood as large as the barrow itself. It was composed of the junk of the downs; vearns, tyres, old seats, carpets, throw aways of the age. The Downsers were justly proud. The fire burned wickedly. Even the tips close to the fire were turning orange – toasting their toes.

Clay children dared as close as they could to the flames, gingerly holding pieces of toast and potatoes on canes, trying to blacken them so they would taste real charcoal on their tongues. It's the pleasure, you see, of letting your eyebrows singe.

Reluctantly, Clara had gone here. Her mother had suggested she should go and meet some people of her own age. She sat on a sand trail leading down to the pit, clasping a cup of soup. Her ears were cold. She had cut her hair. The break had soured her. It was as if her wings had been clipped. Lost their dust...

Mary was scared for her daughter; scared because of her past. But she could feel no malice. She told me that later. I had done what was right. Escaped. Squeezed out of Cornwall's fist. Clara was still there, though, and in her eyes Mary saw a pain. A white hot poker piercing her heart.

They flung the Guy on. It tumbled down again. A few pieces of material alight now. Again, they threw him on. The Cornish burning the traitor. Then, in the queue, a hand. In this light the colour of clay. It was a hand Mary knew, and it was holding a coin. The same hand she had once held. The one who had touched her, felt her, loved her...

'A soup please.'
'Tom? I didn't think...'
'Well. T'in me really, but I thought I'd come up here to see...'
'To see?'
'See the bonfire, maid.'

Mary took the coin from his hand. Tom left it on the table. She saw its lines. The same. She gave him his change clumsily. Her fingers touched his. She wanted to feel what he was like after all this time. Not just a curiosity like the stroking of a cat, but a desire, like trading a secret. A code she wanted to decipher.

Tom smiled. In an instant it was over. He held his change, then picked up the soup, and the pheremones danced on their fingers.

'Thanks,' he said. 'See you...'

Tom brushed his way past several of the crowd. He was almost Guy Fawkes himself, what with his pointed beard, hat and worn jacket. Then he noticed Clara. He moved towards her and sat down. She was startled.

'Sorry...' Tom said.

'I didn't think you would be here for this,' she said.

'Neither did I really. I just...'

But his words were lost in the cheers of the crowd as the first fireworks went up.

Ooooooooow! Aaaaaaaah!

They were peacock feathers in the sky. Daisies in the night. They strained their necks upwards. White. Purple. Orange. Green. Drops of fire. Tom thought of the war. Clara of London. The fireworks of saying Goodbye.

Tom tried to talk, but was cut off each time by the explosion or the crowd.

'Wait till later,' Clara said.

More bangs and a Catherine wheel. Bang, bang, bang. Then silence. The moor was itself again.

'Have you heard from...?'

Tom could not finish the question, but she still answered.

'No.'

'Nothing?'

'No. Have you?'

'Fraid not.'

For a few seconds they watched some children with sparklers in front of them. Clara began again.

'Thank you for repairing my doll.'

'It was nothing, maid. She's a bit cracked though...'

'I don't mind.'

Tom became insecure.

'I'd better go. People'll think I'm chatting you up here maid...'

'They won't,' Clara laughed.

'Might do,' Tom said, and drank the last of his soup.

Soon, the silhouettes vanished into the dark. The night grew older. Down in Roche, Clara saw the crackles of the last remaining fireworks go off, rattling up over and beyond the rock. The bonfire was still burning. A few men kept it under control by brushing the remnants of fire into the middle. Black flakes of paper and cardboard were swept across the moor, then up over Gunheath Mountain, falling as black snow.

Her mother had gone home. She would be lighting the gas fire. It would have been silly to start a coal fire now. Besides, the heat from the fire could have kept her going for days.

However, when Clara got in Mary was not at home. She must have stayed up at one of her few friends, sorting out the soup and punch basins, scraping the barbecue grills of fat. There was nothing in the pantry to eat. No chocolate. So she sat down in the dark cottage. The silence was only interrupted by the flight of a Nimrod overhead. The pilot would have flown over the bonfire. A light in a training flight of boredom.

She had a flicker film in her head, like the cartoon characters she had drawn as a girl. Flick them through and they would move. She had images flickering in her head, becoming lower, like watching a candle going to sleep in its own wax. Flickering and dripping. There was the sound of her breath. The fireworks were a memory now – peacock feathers in the sky, rockets the colour of foxgloves, dripping purple fire... The film show was hemming her in. The dark sneaking up on her. She would go out. She would look for her mother. It would take her mind off things.

She grabbed her doll, carrying it around the waist like she did when she was younger. She walked up the hill again. All the lights were out in the cottages. The moor black as a chough. On the barrow itself, the fire was still burning. She could imagine the storytellers out there. The piskies in a ring... But hold on, she told herself, that was the Cornwall of the postcards, not Hensbarrow. Her glance was aimed elsewhere. She was drawn towards the burning mass. Flying again towards the light. Heart fluttering. She wanted to stand up there alone. State herself. Unafraid now.

The fire spat at her. It crackled. The long dead turned to dust. A pyre for Hensbarrow. Release of the old. She moved closer, kicking embers with her shoes. They became sooty and warm. She breathed in the stench of rubber. Then she spun round, lowering her left leg, and tossed the doll on the fire. The china smashed again. The doll's frock burned. Eyes no longer winking. Alone up there, she loved the fire. She could have stayed all night, but the toy's cremation had pleased her enough.

And the fire ate the dolly.

'Ee aye cherry o, the fire ate the dolly...'

It was almost twelve. It was cold now. Once away from the fire Clara shivered. She kept looking back to see if it was still burning. Yes. Still there.

Then, at Cocksbarrow, so named as to be a pun on Hensbarrow, were two figures, both furtive, like claywork foxes. She knew them. One had a bike, a woman's bike. The other, a tall and thin statuette. They parted, the one cycling away, but then he came back, wobbling slightly. When stationary, yet still on the bike, that figure leaned over and embraced the other. Then, the figure cycled briskly over the crossroads and on to the Whitemoor road.

'So...' Clara mouthed.

But when she got in her mother had the gas fire on and was embroidering a doily.

'What time do you call this?' her mother asked.

'The dream time...' Clara said sarcastically.

'Don't be silly. I just want to know where you've been. That's all...'

Clara felt she would leave her mother tonight, but not all the tale had been told. She would find out tomorrow. She went to bed with a knowing smile. Her mother followed, and turned the gas off. And for once, Mary dreamt of the Longstone.

In the morning, the village children came up and kicked around the embers. They looked for where the fireworks had been lit, and took a box of matches and relit bits that had not all burned. Under some hoops of wire a girl found the bottom half of a china doll, and she cried at the thought that it might have been hers.

'It was probably broken anyway,' said her older sister.

And then the following day, a low loader brought up a Caterpillar bulldozer on to this stretch of the moor to dig a new road into the pit. And in one bucket of sand, the fire place was covered. The black snow stopped blowing, and another piece of Hensbarrow fell from memory.

WHEN Mary asked Tom to walk her home that night the years slid away, like when the Downsers gathered around the fire.

The sight of each other had rekindled the old feelings, the feelings that had been buried, the emotion that had been carried away on the wind. It had begun with Tom standing the photograph up on the sideboard, It had developed when he saw his own body there as well. Mary had pushed it by the old look she gave him up at the bonfire. Now he was more certain.

He still had his doubts, though. She had been through a lot. Ronnie Parsons. A star he was. Tom could have killed him. He killed himself, though, through drink and fags. And always they thought Clara his daughter. He had heard them talking down Halviggan.

'Like her father to look at,' they would say. That's when it knotted Tom inside. He knew he dreamed of killing him. But he was old now. And what was the point now? Twenty years down the line. It was too late. He only had a few more years. Ten if he was lucky he thought.

'I'm not the same,' he told himself, scratching his beard and brushing his hair.

But Mary still had it. Still the maid he had been sweet on. She still had that look, and for her age she was marvellous. Must be those remedies she made. How could they ever call her a witch when she was the most beautiful woman on the Hensbarrow? And when she touched him it was as if their naked swimming in the Hose pools had been yesterday.

'I want to be with you Tom. My life has been pained. I know now. We should've then...'

'But...'

'I don't care,' Mary shouted, 'be with me...'

It would have been easier now. There is contraception. There is abortion. But then values were different. Keeping face was more important than love. Appearance was all.

'Now. From now on, it'll be different...'

Tom could hear the sound of an aircraft in the distance, but it was not a Shack, not now. Things had moved on. It was a Nimrod.

'I'd better go...'

'Yeh.'

Tom got on his bike. He began to move away. Then he circled back.

'Mary. I love you. I've thought of you every day since...'

'I know,' she said.

And on the way home across the black moor he told himself: 'You're never too old...'

'TOM Cundy is my father isn't he?' Clara asked.

Mary looked up. She was brushing the grate. Her daughter stood in her dressing gown. Her eyes were red. She looked tired. Mary could not speak. Like as if her tongue had been cut out.

'And you were with him last night?'

It was the inquisition.

'Yes,' Mary answered.

'Yes he is?'

Mary clarified what she had said.

'Yes I was with him last night. Did you see us? And yes, Tom is your father. It's...'

Clara did not move. She seemed to stop breathing. A statue in the doorway. Then she spoke.

'I knew it...'

'You did?'

'Yes.'

Clara was cold and computerised.

'For how long?' asked her mother.

'I don't know. Like I've always known it...'
They both sobbed.
'Clara. Come into the kitchen,' Mary said, wiping her hands with a floorcloth, and she put her arm around her daughter.
'We have to talk...'
And, in the kitchen, when Clara was sitting comfortably, Mary told her a story.

AFTER the story, the fairy tale ending. I had an invite, but decided not to attend.

The service itself was a small one at the register office in St Austell, followed by a reception in the White Hart Hotel. My parents went. My mother said Mary wore a pink dress with roses on it. Tom had even bought a new suit for the occasion, his buttonhole flower adding a touch of fragrance to a day Tom described as 'the best day in his life'.

No mention was made of any previous attachment, though at the head table Clara appeared embarrassed and uneasy, as if events around her were a crazy dream. A whitewash. On the wedding day I sat in bed reading yesterday's paper; my invitation lay on the desk:

Dear Ben, Mrs Mary Parsons requests the pleasure of your company at her forthcoming marriage to Mr Thomas R Cundy on December 3rd at 10am to be held at the Register Office, St Austell. R.S.V.P.

I still had it for a while, somewhere in the attic at Noppies among all the other things I had collected from weddings – doilies, napkins, horseshoes and place setting labels.

The wedding took place. But children, weddings are more than repeating the minister's words, more than thick icing and marzipan, more than good luck messages. More than hearty speeches. They are living together.

The metamorphosis for Tom and Mary was not easy. Over twenty years apart had left them with their own idiosyncrasies, their own way of doing things. Like Tom's beard. That was new to Mary. He had never had that. But they worked hard at it. This was no run of the mill, drop in the ocean marriage. This was a marriage that had taken a long while to come about. Both wanted a marriage made in heaven, but they knew that to achieve it would take a lot of effort.

Tom, it was agreed, should move up to Carroncarrow. So he trundled all his possessions over the moor in a cart – what he called a 'Dilly' – being himself to the last. And so he looked like some kind of travelling salesman from the early part of this century, carting his wares here and there. The whole process took about a week, by the time Tom had dropped a few shirts in some mica and entered the house.

When he was finally in he would keep remembering things he thought he might need, like a bradawl or his spare set of oilers, but Mary would calm him, and up there the night seemed for the first time in years to come without the dark. And in the room next door a woman listened to the muffled voices of a woman and a man she now felt she barely knew.

Neither changed outwardly when they married. They were just inwardly happy.

At first, Clara was very distant with Tom, and he with her, almost as if they did not really want to believe the other existed. But they did, and in time a bond grew, possibly a deeper one than between normal parents and children. So the three became for the first time a family, and the prickly barbs of the past were gradually eased out of their bodies. Squeezed out like a splinter.

IN THE April of the following year, when Clara was working and Tom was out in the garden sowing potatoes on one of his rest days, Mary stepped outside into the cool spring breeze. She felt Tom stop his work in the earth. Eyes on her, trowel in the soil. She felt a good shiver run up her. Nice to know he found her attractive.

She decided not to turn around, and continued hanging the wet clothes on the washing line. Towels dripped heavily on to the sandy path. Soap suds falling to the ground. She bent down further than normal to show her legs. A ritual. Then she turned around to smile at her husband.

His eyes were on her but he did not see her. A breeze of horror ran across Mary's face. He was lying in the cabbages awkwardly. This time the Dark had come. A scream over the moor. Footsteps up the path. From the vibration, the trowel toppled over in the loose earth.

God works in mysterious ways my friends. He grants us happiness, then takes it away from us. But it is not the people who go who are in pain, unless they take the elevator down – it is the people who are left. They feel the real pain. Life on a rack, s-t-r-e-t-c-h-i-n-g, feeling as I sometimes still do, the swish and swash of insanity...

TOBIAS

14th November 1664.

Tonight the Reverende Brewer didst visit me at my dwellynge and lyked not what he saw. For I, yea I, was lookynge out of my window at Susanna walkynge past my house when he, aye, the Reverende entered.

'Where is thy Latin?' says he. 'Hast thou completed today's duties?'

'That I have sire,' replies I.

The Reverende hast muche skille in panickynge. Earlier that daye I did telle him of the showere of bloode. He now says to me that the stones up on yonder downs must be destroyed, for they are the Devil's stones.

'Nay,' says I, 'for they are too large to e'er destroie.'

'The bloode bodes eville,' says he.

I feel like tellynge my master that if he ist so concerned he must take water and clothe up to the downs and wash the bloode off the stones himself. That I would fain see. But I said not this since my humour likes him not.

'We must do this withe all haste,' he says.

'Ny allyn ny,' I says in my native tongue to confuse my master.

'We cannot? What mean you by this?' says he.

'For one thynge sire, it is too darke now. And for another, bloode stains cannot be removed.'

'But the very Devil himself hath been at work on the moore.'

'Es sire,' says I, 'but you cannot change his worke now. What's done ist done. I knowe not what to thynk of this bloode showere. I am a poore Parishe Clerk and do not meddle with the minde of the Universe.'

At this the Reverende becomes annoyed in the extreme and paces up and down the roome knockynge my inke bottle over in his rage.

He is a fool, thinks I, but he does represent the parishioners and they are muche afraid of this showere, news of whiche hast spread far and wide over Cornwall.

They telle me they know of it in the capital at Launceston. A man who some know as a wise man says it bodes of many disasters. There hast been showeres before and there shallt be again. It is the way.

But this is an unreliable source. For now, I try to calme my master and leave the mattere of the rainfalle of bloode to men with greater minds than me to understande. For indeed this web is one I have great difficulty in untangling.

T.T.

OF DEATH

...which has, and always will be, the fear of the living.

I HAD always wondered what it would be like if Tom ever died, but it was only momentary and the thought was soon replaced by another happier one.

When the reality of the funeral came, it seemed worse because I had last seen Tom on bad terms. Tom would have forgiven me, but now my mind was full of 'if only' questions about our friendship. And all the good memories – the youthful ones – evaporated, and I was left with the image of the two of us arguing in his woodshed.

You could see his sheds from Greensplat chapel, many of them brim full of firewood for the next winter. He could have gone easily five winters without chopping another tree down, and now the wood lay there untouched on the moor.

There was a mainly male congregation lolling outside the chapel, chatting in lowered voices and sucking Polos. The wind was strong. Breathing the smell of moth-balled black suits and dreariness. Would he have wanted it this way? He was having it whatever.

Watt spoke to me, but even he seemed to consider me an outsider to this event, as if I shouldn't have been there, as if by going away I had broken a rule. Compared to the rest of the men, I looked very different in my smart suit and silk tie. They all wore their clay company gold watches and tie pins, but to me that looked beautiful, a sort of outward symbol of their unity.

Tom's old shift gang bore him into the chapel. It is then that the horror of a funeral hits you. That person whom previously you had touched, talked to and responded to was now encased in a cabinet of wood. Unnatural. Why can't we die without being boxed in? Death should be a release. He would have liked to have gone as an autumn leaf. Tom would have crawled into the bracken when he knew he was about to die, lay there and let death ease over him. Let the spirit go and the body rot.

Instead, we choose to case death in. But the service moved me. The minister asked the congregation to think in silence of one thing we remembered about Thomas Roysten Cundy, or Tom as he was known to his friends. And all I could think of was Tom catching me playing on the dumpers. Euclid dumpers that have gone. Now they have Aveling Barford fifty tonners. And now he was gone.

No-one cries at a Cornish funeral. It is a sign of weakness. You cry alone when the world isn't watching. Cry when you walk on the moor. I sat at the back.

'By rights,' Woody shouted, 'you should be sat up front.'

He was right. I should have been. I knew Tom better than any of the other mourners, except Mary and Clara. But they sat up the front, and it seemed incomprehensible to be near them now. If my pain was enough, Mary's must have been more. For twenty years they had not spoken, yet they loved one another deeply. And then within a year of their marriage, 'his soul was taken from us', the minister said solemnly.

In fact, Tom had suffered a severe heart attack. I did not really understand why, since he was not severely overweight and kept reasonably fit. Perhaps it was the pipe tobacco. Perhaps it was married life. That is what my father had joked about. Perhaps it was just one of those things. Mary had done all she could but by the time the ambulance arrived he was clay cold.

Above the pulpit, the organ creaked and the congregation sang the final hymn. The chief mourners filed out. I looked across the pews. Mary's face was white, tinged with a sickly green that betrayed her inner disbelief. Behind her came Clara, and everyone seemed to feel so sorry. The words, 'so sorry' seemed to rise like their breath's condensation on the chapel windows. She saw me but her face carried no hint of recognition, no sign that we were together once. This was almost worse than the funeral service itself.

They took Tom away in a black car. It was then that I had to turn and clutch my mother as if I were still a child.

The cremation service was only for the closest family. That meant Mary and Clara, who travelled with the dead Tom to Penmount Crematorium near Truro. I had a picture of Tom being guzzled by the flames, as if he were in some great fire. But I was too distant to hear his screams now.

I PLANNED to stay at home for a couple of days then return to London on Thursday. The very house itself seemed to feel the shock of Tom's death, as if it knew by Tom's going that it would not be long either, not long before it was turned to clay. Noppies was down there, out on the moor, perched on the edge of the quarry, but there was no light on. No smoke drifting before Halviggan tip. Nothing needed to be said in the household. All knew. Even Tessa. A moment of truth. A realisation. No more of my claywork druid. No more Tom.

But in the morning, there was more. I woke early, disturbed by the dumpers up on the western edge of Blackpool tip. Over the night, thick condensation had gathered on the windows of my bedroom, but where larger droplets had flowed down the panes of glass I could see movement out on the moor. In the early morning mist a woman stood dressed in black, Biblical almost, as if she were sowing seeds. But these seeds were grey dust. By the time I could wipe the window she was gone out of my sight. The ashes blew down into Blackpool. That morning I cried till tears fell like acid from my eyes.

'Bloody weather,' my father moaned as he came in from morning shift.

It was Thursday. Tom had been dead for a week. I was sitting in what they called the kitchen chair, an old dark chair that had been left in the cottage by the previous occupants, and which was placed in the corner of the room. I liked it because the back of it was made of strong smelling leather and the armpieces were shaped so that you could grip them. And that is what I felt I needed now, a grip.

Things were going on and around the cottage much the same as they had always done. My mother smelling of soap powder, baking in the kitchen; Tessa squatting on the sitting room floor trying to knit, my father moaning half-heartedly about the weather and how he could not do anything outside. But to me it all seemed wrong. How could they go on like this, as if their lives had not been touched.

I decided to go upstairs and pack my case. My funeral and wedding suit, a sombre charcoal grey thing, lay on the bedspread like a scorch mark. I folded it up and placed it over the top of my clean underwear and socks. I longed to paint, to exorcise my emotions, but found I could not.

By half-past four that night it was dark. My train left from St Austell at twenty-past five. I had booked a taxi to pick me up. Suddenly my thoughts went back to the driver who had talked to us on our first day on Hensbarrow. The air was heavy – 'dogsday' weather. A Hensbarrow thundercloud brewing. All day the weather had been on and off, and now it was finally deciding to play hell. I felt the clouds trundle in across the sky. A time when you feel the earth rotate. Watch the sky tumbling. Balls of cotton wool. I stood in the conservatory.

While waiting for the taxi I decided to water the geraniums, which had sucked up the last dribble of water in their bowls. I was using the teapot. There were several more to go when the taxi pulled down the lane. I shouted into the living room that I was about to leave. My mother came out to kiss me. Tessa as well, her's somehow more special. My father gave a nod. Outside it was beginning to rain.

The taxi driver lit a cigarette. The panes of glass in the conservatory rumbled as the first thunder belched. The Gods were angry. I dumped the teapot with my mother, and picked up the suitcase.

'Better go,' I said.

They watched from the conservatory as I crossed the yard, now running in streams of water. The taxi driver opened his door. It was raining hard now. A very cold rain. Chilling. I scrambled into the taxi.

'St Austell station?' the driver asked.

'Please.'

I slammed the door shut and the taxi pulled away. A few droplets of rain fell down my back. More dripped on to my lap. I lifted my hand up to brush my hair back. It was only then, in the half light of the taxi's interior, that I noticed my clothes were darkly spotted by the rain, and that in the mirror I could see red smears which ran down my face like American Indian warpaint and tasted of a pricked finger.

BEACON Hill was Hensbarrow's little brother. They bullied Foxhole and Carpalla, two linear villages that ran straight between the two of them. Well, that was not entirely true since between Foxhole village and Beacon Hill lay the old quarry of Mid-Cornwall pit, where the cows had fallen in a few years back, now well-seasoned with mica and mire and a wildlife sanctuary, a place where nature had managed to win back some of that which it had lost. Gorgeous stains were created on the mica as the plants took root then died, their colours and saps, phosphates and nitrogen compounds changing the colour of the clay, giving it purple and red tints. Clay highlighting.

Everyone knew Beacon Hill. Countless generations of clay children had run up and down its perfect lines, only to return as adults with their own children. It had a comfortable feel to it. The grass was still the same as when you first sat there years ago. In summer, footballs and bikes could be seen on its course; the few horses keeping their distance at the top, silhouetted when the sun fell like old druids. It had been a beacon once.

It was again in 1977 during the Queen's Silver Jubilee. That year the hill glowed. The embers are still there. But it has a more interesting history before the clay, before it became a nature sanctuary in the white wilderness. Once an ancient Celtic King lived there. He was called Pippin. His body is said to lie at the top, along with many treasures. They found him once, but only a few people knew where he lay and they would not tell. You could see an old line where a rampart had been built crowning the hill in the Dark Ages.

Now only ferns stood there, but you could see the mark from Watch Hill. At the back of the whale shaped crescent they had dug for clay. There were two smallish pits, both now flooded, but they were different. You did not notice they were man's work. They just fitted in perfectly, the bracken reflecting in their green waters, the lichen floating on the surface. There was a lovers' spot there, grove-like, a Garden of Eden.

Had the men whose limbs had hewn these holes known they had created a lovers' paradise they might have stayed. So many buttons had been undone here that the trees that overhung did not even bother to blush any more. Only the horses came to investigate if they heard lovers' voices, and that was rare. And so it stayed perfect.

Unlike Clara, whose life at present was the most imperfect she had experienced. She did not deserve this clay highlight, she felt. She had lost a lover and now a father. The world seemed to be slipping away before it had begun. She was twenty-two. She was lonely. She had come for a walk over the hill while her mother visited people in the village, putting on, as she said, a brave face.

Clara had hoped the hill would cheer her up. Compared to how she had felt before it had done the trick, simply being here. She sat on the edge of the smaller of the pools, pressing her wellie-booted feet into the black mud where the horses had come to drink. What saddened her was that she had very little left. She had given these two men her love and they had both gone. One dead, one might as well have been. She had lost her virginity. She was frightened of losing herself now. Clara needed a direction. She pictured her former lover at the funeral, and then remembered his absence at her mother's wedding. He was still on her mind, like as if she was pulling away the petals.

'He loves me.

He loves me not,

He loves me...'

'No, he doesn't,' she mouthed, 'or he would've come back...'

To the south, lay the Treviscoe and Trethosa clay tips; beyond that Melbur and Remfry, ominous triangles on a beautiful landscape. 'No 8' Salvage and Disposal Yard behind the Beacon, a cage of rusty boilers and peeling pipes, broken skips and chutes, time wasted valves and galvanised shutters.

For a second, she saw herself as a glamour model on an industrial debris modelling shoot, one leg set as a triangle, the other straight. Head back, slinky hair caressing the rust. The men adoring her. Only for a second though. She was beginning to see. She could see the rejection. See why he had gone. She could understand why she had stayed. All she knew now was that she must get out. Escape the paralysis... the rust. Shake her kaolin blues away and stop sweating.

Frustrated, Clara stood up and hid behind the willow tree. She needed it now. Pleasure. The kick. She hitched up her skirt and rubbed where it felt good. The willow swayed drowsily in the wind. She entered herself. The she let out a little moan that scared the horses away. Clara hoped King Pippin was not watching. And instead of the earth being turned upside down, in the best euphemistic tradition, it moved for her.

TOBIAS

15th November 1664.

Thynges of this life continue to perplexe me. The Reverende, aye, he who is unsatisfied of the presence of the bloode stained stones, is now vpon yonder moore with some thirty men destroieing the same stones. Methinks this an unwise move, since the stones are wonderously large and heavy. And for the lack of me, I cannot understand why he dost try to destroie suche work. For in mine eyes destroieing suche eville shalt only bring more eville. Alas, I do try and telle the Reverende this, but when I speaks in front of him and yonder high people of the village he dost ignore me and my wiles.

And so I become most worried of my position in this Parishe. The Reverende, for he is an olde man – I know tis morbid – but this is God's wille, he shall die soon. Perchance we may see another Reverende enter oure Parishe with more swaye towards me. I know that I am stille younge but I do complete my best for the good of the Parishe.

Though I do not record these events in the Parishe records, I write them here so generations who do follow may know of oure foolhardiness in dealing with suche oddities of Nature. I believe one day, man wilt be able to controlle his worlde more than we can now, and suche men as the Reverende may well be hung, drawn and quartered – and eighthed, by God!

The Reverende returned from the moore out of breath, and without destroieing yon stones. They are too large says he.

I know not what these events signifye – if they do signifye any matter at all. And now, I must leave my diarie and returne to less interesting matters. These are matters of Latin, which must be learnt by all Parishe Clerks. Alas, I care not much for them. I care more for yonder fellows in the square who do runne withe hoops and sticks and as well as this my chosen maid. Doubte continues to plague me as to whether I am committed enough to my chosen profession. I ende today with praise to my Lorde Almighty, and deare Lorde, I pray you give me guidance for the future.

T.T.

OF BLOOD

...which stories say is thicker than water and in this tale falls out of the sky... as it has always done... and always will do, if you believe in fairy tales.

'MR THOMAS Royston Cundy, Greensplat: The funeral of Mr Thomas Royston Cundy, aged 61, of Carroncarrow Cottage, Greensplat, was held at Greensplat Chapel, followed by cremation at Penmount, Truro. The Rev F Hicks officiated. Born in Whitemoor, Mr Cundy lived most of his life at Old Pound. Well known and highly respected, he was formerly employed by Cornish China Clays at Longstone's pit. Mr Cundy also served in North Africa during World War Two.

'Mourners were Mrs Mary Cundy, widow; Miss Clara Parsons, Mr Ted Collins, brother-in-law, Mr W Lobb, Mr and Mrs R Dowrick, Mr R Martin, Mr T Hoare, Mr P Litt, Mr B Sexton, Mr and Mrs A Sexton, and many other relatives, friends and neighbours. Unable to attend was Mr S Libby and Mr C Woodward. Funeral arrangements were by Mr R Martyn of Bugle.'

I was clutching Tom's obituary from the Cornish Guardian as if it were some chalice or cross to ward off evil. In fact, this was only a collection of words that my mother had sent on to me. And what was it? A life summed up in a few sentences. That obituary was not for Tom; it was for someone else. Not the Tom I knew. My druid. But the world needed order and the obituary was it. It also needed protection. I felt doom around the next corner – a black cloud about to engulf my world. I saw a monolith of terror ahead. I was sitting on the bed, recalling the train journey to London from Cornwall. Once in the carriage, I hurtled towards the toilet. In my hurry I did not shut the door properly so the light in the carriage would show that the loo was not engaged. I looked at my face in the mirror. A rough chin and a distinct red tinge.

'Water,' I said to myself, 'water.'

I sloshed water over my face until I felt clean. In the sink the water had a reddish colour, only slight, but enough. The liquid gargled down the plughole like acrylic paint. Above the sink I clicked on the fluorescent light and checked my jacket. There were spots, others on the collar of my shirt.

So, a shower of blood. Tom's words.

Or rather now, after more recent discoveries, 'a showere of bloode'. A blood that came when it rained heavily. A landscape seeking revenge for the havoc man had caused it. I did not know it at the time but there was a cloud of prophecy with me. The seventeenth century in my hand. I was clairvoyant. I had been shown. What now? I knew. Push it away with a ten foot barge pole. Give the thought concrete boots. Sink it down. Of knowing disasters, pretend you don't know. I sat doing this in the flat – pretending I did not know. Pretending Tom had never told me, and that I knew nothing of the Great Plague, the Great Fire of London and the Dutch and English War. I wanted to put them out of my head, but the heartbeat rises and the questions come.

What if this was just my shower of blood? A private prophecy. More frightening somehow. Better to share, share and share alike. I was confused and alone. The shower of blood dripped on me like the Chinese water torture, and I could feel myself being preserved in the clay, like the Terracotta Army. Left alone with my horror. That night, I prayed to God for the first time in a long while, and this time the prayer was not a mumbled chant but a plea for strength and guidance.

Nothing happened. Nothing at all, except a week later my final year exhibition started in the college gallery. I spent the week beaverishly working towards this exhibition. Mr Oz had ensured that many distinguished critics and a few famous artists would be there. I lined the whole gallery with white paper and sheets, so the traditional lines of the room were hidden. I displayed some of the paintings on the floor, others at odd angles on the walls. On one wall, I placed the long painting, 'The Dirty Bit'. And when it was ready I sat back and relaxed, letting the tide of criticism wash over.

Fortunately the reviews and comments were better than either I or the college had anticipated, and for once that week, while some American was giving me some bullshit about the piano creation, I forgot about Tom, the clay and the blood.

In the second week of the exhibition, the paintings and sculptures began to sell. People were picking up on them. I was getting known. Pictures at an exhibition being wrapped up and sold. For the first time in my life I had a taste of real money. On the Tuesday of that week I came back to the flat over a thousand pounds richer. Two clay casts I had made of two Chinese dragons had sold for fifty pounds each, and then the buyer felt them undervalued.

I was just glad of the money. My flatmates could hardly believe it. They never had the drive like me. Maybe it had been too easy for them – the public school education, the virtual assurance of a job with their father if the arty phase they were going through went out of the window. On Tuesday, we got in some decent food and ate well. I stopped off at Tesco's on the way home. As well as food, I bought some beer to celebrate my success. When I opened the front door there was a phone call. I picked up the phone mid-ring. The line crackled. A coinbox.

'Hello. Hello. Is Ben there?'
'Yeh. Speaking.'
I knew the voice. The Cornish oozing out.
'Hi Mike.'
'Are 'ee a'right then?' asked Mike, slipping into dialect.
'I'm fine. What's on?'
'Thought I'd give you a ring. I'm in Londonderry. Duty sergeant over here now.'
'Have you had much trouble?'
'Well, not me personally. There was a UDR guard shot over here last week.'
I nodded, not really knowing or understanding how my friend could pass over a shooting so quickly.
'Look. I've only got a bit of cash here. There was a reason for me ringing. Sarah and I are getting engaged next week. We're having a do...'
'Hey. That's terrific Mike. I'm really pleased for you both. Best of luck for the future.'
'Well I thought I'd better tell you, you old bugger. Things okay for you then?'
'Yeh. Good. I've sold some paintings this week... you know the exhibition. Look Mike, there's something I want to talk to you about sometime... about something Tom said...'
'I couldn't make the funeral you know...'
'It doesn't matter. Do you remember once he mentioned a shower of blood?'
There was silence at Mike's end. I knew he was thinking.
'Well, yes. Yes. I remember him saying something about it once when his wood was stolen...'
I was ready to tell Mike. I felt I could rely on him to respect my opinion and not laugh at my crazy idea.
'Something's happened...'
The pips were beginning to go.
'I'll ring again,' Mike said.
'Yes. As soon as you can.'
The voice went. A dull click. I was left frustrated. He would not ring again for a while.
We ate in silence that evening. I was in another place.

THE next morning, I was up early. I found myself waiting for the post now to see if there were any buyers' offers or contracts up for grabs. Today, there were three letters for me – one from a catalogue firm offering a free toaster if I took up their offer – another from the art college telling me I was still in possession of two overdue library books.

The one I opened first however was postmarked Plymouth. Inside was a legal document and a lengthy letter from solicitors acting for Mr Thomas Royston Cundy. Tom, it appeared, made out an extensive will at the time of his first heart attack. He had left his cottage and land to me. His money had gone to Mary and Clara. I could hardly believe it. The solicitors wished to see me as soon as possible, or at least for me to contact them to sort out a transfer of deeds. I determined to write that afternoon. A twinge of guilt snapped in me, and I felt as if really the place should not be mine. I meant more to Tom than I had thought. I thought of the toy truck in the yard at home, rusting away. Tom never let anything rust.

I dropped the letter on the fridge in the kitchen and went outside. The sunlight made me squint and this, coupled with the emotion I felt because of the letter, made me cry in a way I had not done since I was a small child.

But my life looked up considerably that week. The worry of the red rain had gone, and my rise both financially and artistically was progressing at a tremendous rate. Things continued spiralling upwards at another exhibition over the summer, when I spoke to a woman I noticed had visited the gallery every day.

On the Friday, I watched her carefully. She had long dark hair, cherry red lips and leaned back to look at the paintings. Then she would spin on her heels and suck the end of her spectacles. I guessed her to be about twenty-four. My attraction to her rebounded throughout the hall. With every picture she looked at, I was dying to explain what it was about, but I let her go. Watched her. Smelt her. Fantasised about her. And for the first time since Clara my feelings for another woman came alive again.

Today, though, I would speak to her. One by one, the other visitors made their way out. I stood looking at one of the paintings of London – not really thinking about it. She headed towards me in a waltz kind of movement. We spoke at the same time.

'Are these your paintings?' 'I'd love to paint you.'
We answered in conjunction also.
'Yes. Awful aren't they?' 'Would you?'
We laughed. Skating on broken ice now.
'So you're Ben Sexton are you? I really like your work. It's good

to meet you. I mean, I've been here to see your stuff most days this week...'

'Every day I think...'

She blushed.

Her accent was American, but there was something else in there, something nearer to home. The obvious question.

'Are you American?'

'Well, sort of. I was born in Wales, but we moved out to the States when I was about ten, so I guess I'm more American than Welsh really...'

'Do you live here?'

'Yeh, I do. A few blocks up the road. I write for a paper. I'm on a kind of journalist exchange. But really I should do my own stuff. Look... I really should be off now... I'll pop back next week.'

'Fine. Don't let me keep you,' I said.

'All right. See you then Ben,' and she laughed at the unintentional rhyme she had made.

'See you...'

'Chloe's my name. Chloe Evans. Bye now.'

With that she left, but out of the corner of my eye I watched her pass the windows of the gallery. I was hoping she would look back so I could see her face again, but she walked straight by without turning her head. The thought of her that day made me go home that weekend and, out of chicken wire and clay, make a sculpture I was pleased with. The object was tall and gangly, but I thought it somehow captured what I felt about femininity. I wanted to call it 'Chloe' but I told my friends it was just a female figure, as if I wanted to keep Chloe secret, at least for the time being. On Sunday evening I threw the last lump of clay on and moulded it. That night I went to bed with clay still on my hands. I was Prince Charming again, and this time I felt I had the glass slipper. All that had to be done was to ensure that it fitted.

That night, though my intentions to sleep were good, I had a nightmare. A nightmare that dug deep into me and reached far into the past. I still remember it clearly.

There was an enormous black hand, a hand that pulled out the image of Bill Brewer, the death I had seen as a child, and it waved this crushed body about my head. I was falling, and following me were huge lumps of granite. Finally, I fell into soft mica, but the granite was following... about to pulp me... crush every bone in my body... so that the blood and clay mingled making a pink colour. And when I was in a half awake state, I saw the air thick with dust. Somewhere Tessa screamed for me.

I was sweating. Sweating. No, it was nothing. Just a thing I had remembered. Something that had stuck. My first death. And there were to be others just around the corner...

THREE hundred miles away, another clay child woke with fear. Her parents rushed in to see what was wrong and the look in that child's eyes told them that this was no normal dream. But she could not tell them what it was. Physically could not. And so her parents hugged her until it was all right again. She shouted for Clara, but they could not understand her.
 I called this brotherly and sisterly love.
 Mutual dreaming.
 A parallel vision of the past and present.

MONDAY passed without Chloe entering the gallery, and by the end of the day the nails on my hands had been bitten down to white stumps and were nearing the white moons. But on the way home, a car pulled over. Someone asking for directions I thought at first. But no; it was Chloe.
 'Hey, need a lift?'
 I accepted. She drove an Escort. Inside, the car smelt of newsprint and of her French perfume. Somewhere I also smelt spirit duplicating fluid. We talked about what we had been doing.
 'I've thrown in my job,' she said.
 'You haven't?'
 'Well. I kinda saw it coming really. But I wanna leave, you know, write myself. I've got an idea for a novel.'
 The Cornish sensibility I had been so influenced by came out.
 'What'll you live on?'
 'I've got enough. I'll get through...'
 Chloe was crazy. She overtook cars on the inside, and had no second thoughts about sticking up two fingers to people on the road who annoyed her. She could laugh at herself. She dug me with her elbows. There was an obvious attraction. Opposite poles attract, and I was being drawn closer, the metal filings of my hair on end.
 'Do you wanna come back for something to eat? You can tell me about all your pictures...'
 Clara and Chloe were like chalk and cheese. Clara the old world woman whose eyes were set upon motherhood. Chloe was the modern woman whose eyes were set upon herself. Anyone who could keep up the pace could ride with her, and I wanted to. I never felt out of my depth, and I knew that even if I did Chloe would dive in and save me. There was no acknowledgement that we were having a relationship, almost as if we were scared to admit it, but there was a realisation that we had tumbled together in a nebulous of art, literature and sex.

Chloe was an enigma to me. She pulled me towards her from all directions. Often, it was strange, as if I should not have been there with this American woman. Incongruous somehow. Her flat itself was marvellous. I had been living with her now for just under six months. We slept together, though I had my own separate room where I worked on my paintings.

By this time, I had devastated the room. There were smudges of paint everywhere, blobs where the brush had slipped, stains on the floor where some spirit had been knocked over. But she said it looked like a real artist's studio, and that pleased her. Sometimes, she would come in and just watch me work. In the beginning it unnerved me, but then her power seemed to enter my body and the paintings became better. When she liked something she pinched my bum. If I felt good about the picture I would turn around and kiss her. If we had time we would make love, often in the studio. I painted her body once – then she mine. The we showered and watched the colour wash away until just the white of our skin was left. When we had finished, Chloe had gazed out of the window while I gazed at her. Outside it was raining. Inside the sun shone out from my paintings, and we lay there catching a tan.

At this time, all thoughts of Hensbarrow left me completely. In one sense, Chloe helped me forget the pain of Tom's death and the break-up with Clara. Besides, I felt my life was up there now, far away from that Dark Ages land. I could feel the Celtic layers of skin I had grown in Cornwall being stripped away. It was the pumicestone of London.

That autumn, Chloe flew back to the States. She asked me to go with her, but I had an exhibition in Swansea so it was impossible to go. Chloe was to be away for two weeks. She caught a British Airways flight from Heathrow. To her, the Atlantic seemed tiny; a run of the mill journey. Continent hopping.

Her parents were in the middle of a divorce. Both wanted to see her about signing some deeds with regard to their house. Their divorce had barely affected her. She saw it coming. And so I was left in the departure lounge while she boarded a flight to Washington DC. I watched her legs through the glass of the departure lounge, the same legs I had touched that morning in bed, now clad in black stockings. She looked good. The glass clouded. Love breath.

I was expecting delivery of a potter's wheel so once the plane had taken off I hurried back across London to the flat. It was a conscious decision to move in the ceramics and pottery direction. When I got in I flopped down on the settee with a can of coke and the Daily Mirror.

I read for a while then lay back, looking around her flat. Outside children were playing. There was the hum of London traffic. The room was tall with a grand ornate ceiling. The sofa was fawn coloured, a cigarette burn on its left arm. Most of the other furniture was cane. On one of the walls were a few classical prints. Above the fireplace some American film posters. On the coffee table, one of those adult toy cradles. I rocked the balls. She had a couple of pet terrapins which I sometimes watched. I heard the static crack.

There was a knock at the door. Hurriedly, I got up, spilling a drop of coke on my shirt. When I opened the door, I was still trying to wipe it off. A man stood there. He was burly with large sideburns and spoke with a Geordie accent.

'Mr. Sexton?'

I nodded.

'Got your wheel here.'

'Ah. Bring it in.'

I pointed to the studio room. The man and his younger companion man-handled the parts of the wheel into the room. It was heavy and the floorboards creaked.

'You an artist then?'

'Yes,' I replied, reorganising the furniture so that the wheel could fit in more easily.

'Are you famous?'

'Not really.'

'Can you sign here please?'

I took his pen and signed the pink strip of paper. He gave me a carbon copy. He walked out, then the man spoke again. He had remembered something else.

'You'll be wanting this as well squire...'

He passed me a hefty cardboard box that weighed down my arms. I knew what it was. The cardboard felt damp, as if there was something wet inside; something you did not want to touch.

As I unpacked the potter's wheel and constructed the unit it sat in, I was thinking about what had happened two weeks ago. Before Chloe had the chance to leave, the newspaper had sacked her. She had gone back again after they begged her earlier in the year but now she had stormed home crying, interrupting a peaceful lunch I was enjoying.

'They've sacked me,' she said.

'Why?'

'Oh, you know... do they need a reason? Not enough good stories I suppose.'

'Do you want some coffee?' I asked.

'They can keep their stinking newspaper. The editor can stick it right up his ass. No coffee thanks.'

It had been the same kind of weather that day, overcast, warm scratchy weather. Dogsday maybe.

I opened the box. I cut the thin aluminium riders that kept the box's shape. Inside was a grey mass encased in transparent plastic. Little areas of it stuck to the plastic. I cut open the packaging and dug in with my hands. It felt good. I played with the clay, not Cornish clay – it was too dark for that. Whatever, it suddenly felt as if Chloe's room and all her possessions had slipped away. I was falling backwards, the clay capturing my senses. I could feel the soul in it. I wetted the wheel and slapped the clay on to it. It squelched down like a hippo in mud. Dream time and real time merging.

When the phone rang I popped a small ball of clay I was working with into my pocket. The phone rang twice before I answered. The simplest of greetings.

'Hello.'

'Hi.'

Chloe across the ocean.

'You answered quickly.'

'I was beside the phone just as you rang. Did you have a good flight?'

'Yeh. Real smooth. I got in a couple of hours ago. Right now I'm at mom's, but tomorrow it's dad's so...'

'How is it? Between your parents...'

'So-so. You know...'

She wanted to keep me out of her family's domestic unhappiness. Her mother was embroiled in an affair. She changed the subject.

'So what have you been doing?'

'Well, the pottery wheel's arrived so...'

'Fantastic.'

'So, I've set it up, got it going. I've made something already.'

'What?'

'I can't say,' I said, squinting at the vase to see if the proportions were correct.

'When do you leave for Swansea?'

For a moment the line was unclear. Chloe asked the question again. This time I could hear her.

'Some time tomorrow morning.'

'Tomorrow morning?'

'Yes.'

I moved the phone to my left ear.

'It's strange to hear you from over there. It's not that long ago you were in London...'

'I know. It's kinda real strange to be talking to you.'
It was the satellite of love across two continents. It was also the unclear line. She said something about missing me. That was enough. It felt good to be missed by her.
'The line isn't very good is it?'
'No. Look, I'll ring you on Friday. Good luck with the exhibition. Love you...'
'Take care. Love you too...'
I kept the receiver to my ear until the line went dead. It was dark outside now. Not even the studio light was on. I sat on a corduroy beanbag in the corner of the room with a box of matches, burning them to smell the phosphorus, blowing them out just before they burnt my fingers. And on the wheel sat the vase, a swirling structure like the petals of a tulip. Not a tulip from Amsterdam but a tulip from clay. And for the first time in a while, light fell on to clay from the firesticks I was burning. And beauty shone back.

LOOKING back across the bay from the Mumbles I could see the dragons of the Port Talbot steel works pouring smoke and steam into the air, somehow not contrasting but fitting in with the bright blue sky that greeted me in Swansea. I had come down on the early train from Paddington. It was silly really. When the train went through Cardiff I kept trying to look out of the window, up to the green and grey valleys to see where Chloe was born. It was just the satisfaction of knowing where she came from, and knowing where she was now. The science of dislocation. The art of security.
Here was my first major exhibition outside London. The morning had been busy for me. Some of my paintings and sculptures were being exhibited in the Glyn Vivian Art Gallery under a theme of Contemporary London Artists. I was pleased that I had been chosen to exhibit. The exhibition was funded by the Swansea Museum Service and the city council, so there were many dignitaries to meet. The people I met were friendly and unpretentious, like the Cornish.
In the afternoon, I sat on the rickety Mumbles Pier. My view extended over the whole crescent-shaped bay. Far off, the brown and green hills above Port Talbot. Closer, the yellow cocklemen forking the sand. I was dreaming of visiting the twelve pubs in the Mumbles mile with Dylan Thomas. I searched for a handkerchief in order to knot the corners and put it on my head, to look the holidaymaker part.
In my pocket, my hand felt a soft ball. It was no longer shiny but was now covered with fluff from the lining. The ball of clay

was the same shape as the earth. I squeezed it with my fingers, touching the places I knew – Essex, London, Cornwall, Hensbarrow. I saw the continents of the world sketched on this tiny clay earth. I hardly realised it at the time but I was also feeling for China, feeling for the Falklands, feeling for...

Then the memory of the shower of blood flicked past, and I crushed the clay ball. I felt I ought to mould the clay into a mushroom cloud or some other symbol of destruction, but my fumbling in the tightness of the pocket prevented me.

I made the handkerchief hat and sat on the pier for an hour longer before heading off to catch the train back to London.

Chloe was glad to see me when she returned. Two weeks in the States seemed to have taken its toll on her. She looked tired when I met her at Heathrow. I gripped her hand tightly as we wound through the baggage and other passengers. When she felt no-one was looking she came close to me, put her hand in my pocket and nibbled my neck. It was her way.

Back in the flat I had a cold supper prepared for her. While she ate, I presented her with a clay figurine of herself. The piece was abstract but showed off the curves of her body. I had fired it in a friend's pottery kiln. She was pleased with it. Our legs locked together. She sat there crunching celery. The figurine stood on the dining table among the empty plates and salad dishes. When the washing-up was finished we relaxed on the sofa. Chloe took up the figurine and looked at it from every conceivable angle, closing first one eye, then the other. I played with her hair. And we touched one another the way toddlers do at play school. Just testing...

We talked as well. Chloe moved the conversation on to superstition and predictions. She said she had always known her parents would get divorced. She had known it as a child. She was convinced she saw it coming. A premonition.

'Do you believe in things like that?' Chloe asked carelessly, dangling the figure upside down.

'I don't know...'

But when the small hours came and we were still talking, I felt I should tell her. Tell her my story. And when I mentioned the shower of blood her eyes opened wide. She placed the statue on the coffee table and listened...

OF ARRIVAL, AND SOME TIPS

WHEN I rang to tell my mother that I was coming back to Cornwall for a few days break with Chloe she, as usual, panicked and wondered where on earth we were going to sleep.

The phone call home was a strange one, both of us having gone through the initial meetings a few years ago with Clara. The pain lived on. But as I told my mother, Chloe was my life now, or so I believed. My parents were good about such things. They believed people should make their own choices, and did not mind people living together, providing they were very committed to one another. I told her we were 'very'.

My thoughts were that this was a good time to visit Cornwall. Although Chloe had been home to the States, that did not really work as a holiday. She was also dying to see the places I had talked to her about. She wanted to find me, I believed, see where I was coming from. And the shower of blood drew her. Every day a new question about it, which would scare me.

In retrospect it is sometimes better to let sleeping dogs lie. Like legends...

I decided to drive down overnight so that we should arrive in Cornwall just as dawn was rising and the sun climbing from the east. She would see the colours on the tips that resembled gigantic white screens.

The journey was a long one. She slept for a long time. I heard the rattle of her slightly asthmatic breathing, the hum of the heater in the car. On Bodmin Moor – Jamaica Inn land – the mist was gathering in the dips. The cattle were lowing. Then we began to fall off the moor. On the shattering horizon stood Hensbarrow.

'Is that it?' she asked.

'That's it...'

See them from the A30, driving west on holiday, you people from up-country, you people the Cornish call 'Emmets', the dialect word for ants. You cannot miss them. Look left on your way down over Goss Moor to where Hensbarrow rises. You can see them now. The guide book refers to them as the 'Cornish Alps'. they are trying to kid you. Remember the guide book.

'Unlike the remains of most other industrial activity, they add to rather than detract from the beauty of the scenery.'

So from the A30 they do look like mountains. On a hot July day, when you are stuck behind some slow-moving caravan, you really can believe they are mountains, their peaks snow capped, their slopes whiter than white. A washing powder whiteness. At the bottom, thick pine forests ready for skiing through. And yes, for a moment, I was in Switzerland or France, about to take a cable car up to the north ridge.

But the fantasy collapses when you look again. They are not really mountains, just extended hillocks. The older ones do look rather pretty, half covered in vegetation, perfect triangles hiding the sun behind them. But there are the large slurs of white sand, landscaped level, vast stretches of waste overburden, sitting on top of Hensbarrow. See them; Gothers, Parkandillick, Hendra, Dorothy, Dubbers, Goonbarrow, Rocks, their trailing tips confusing the tourist. And those cable cars... well, actually, they are the beautiful conveyor belts.

THIS was not thought of by my father on a morning shift. Try a freezing cold morning in late November, fixing a broken conveyor belt up at Dorothy, perched on top of the tip, the wind snatching the few degrees of heat you have left in your body, and the rain coming in from the Atlantic.

On arrival, he finds the guidance rollers on the belt virtually worn through. His hands are so cold that the tools slip out of his grasp, falling to the hardened ground; lips chapped, the wind whizzing through the holes in your overalls. And then thinking, yes, it really is like being on top of a mountain. But this is not like the Alps, this is Everest. It is now too cold to work.

Every time the piece of plastic roller is inserted, he cannot hold the tiny bolts in position long enough for them to be tightened. He takes a break and gazes out over Goss Moor. But the cloud is low and the mist thick. It makes him feel dizzy to look out. He was Edmund Hilary. He was Sherpa Tensing. But where was he to go from here?

Perhaps to tell the story of selling Hensbarrow by the pound. After Aberfan, the tips changed shape. No-one wanted that to happen on Hensbarrow, not with the amount of waste being thrown up now. In that Welsh valley a school was crushed by a wave of black mineral waste. One hundred and thirteen killed. A generation dead. On Hensbarrow the mineral waste is white sand and rock.

Everyone saw the pictures. Everyone heeded the warning. Everyone dreamed the nightmare, and so the tips became flatter and longer, more stable, like huge white, squat Toblerones. Now, once they have finished tipping on them, they grass them over with creeping fescue and clover. Rabbits move in, and sheep keep the grass down. Only rarely do things go wrong.

Sometimes, if there is a rainstorm, the tip can wash away, but the company has a good safety record so the Downsers sleep well. Every time I drove over Watch Hill and saw the caterpillar tip of Blackpool I wondered. I saw the steps of tipping, the thousands of tonnes dumped every day by the enormous trucks. Where the hell was it all coming from?

The tips are the most important thing really. That is, you know the pits are there, but sometimes you cannot see them; like Littlejohns – hidden from public view. The tips show how well things are going. The more sand, the more clay. But the tips are more than that to clay people. Some romanticise them. Some write about them – the only mountains they will ever see. But the best sight, the very best sight of all, is the first glimpse of them travelling down the A30. Then they are diamonds shimmering on the horizon. That's when a lump comes to the clay miner's throat.

If you ever find yourself on Hensbarrow, go look at them. Go see Gunheath tip – the elephant tip with its lines and crevasses. Go see the humpback camel that is Longstone's, the whale that is Blackpool, the Loch Ness Monster that is Halviggan. Go see them all... touch them. They are sleeping animals. The Hensbarrow zoo of sleeping forms.

And when you've finished looking at them, and want to drown your sorrows – which you will – call into the White Pyramid or Cookworthy pubs. Pleasant views of old china clay workings...

You know about the Cornish being a race of diggers; they are also a race of climbers. They climb these tips of burrows with great agility and sit there watching. Never call these places 'Dirty Bits' for they are the Downser's Temples. Holy places. This land is sacred.

'BEN, tell me... What's it like at the top of a tip?'
'Like nothing on earth... thank God.'

Chloe and I later sat in Tregargus Woods – two piskies out of reach of human civilisation. The woods lay to the south of Hensbarrow, where the master Cookworthy discovered china clay. It seemed only right that we should come here.

Chloe seemed happy, relaxed. She was wearing dungarees and wellies. I was in my father's donkey jacket. In the pockets were chewing gum wrappers and some loose change. I lay the coat on the grass where we were to have our picnic. We were close to Tregargus Mill. On its south side was slung a large waterwheel which had not turned for many years. Ivy covered it and the slats were broken. Chloe tried to turn it, but it would not move.

I did not tell her that a man was killed here once under the weight of the massive grindstones. It would have ruined the picture for her, taken away the romance of the mill. I liked her to drift. She loved it down there, away from London and its bustle.

We had simple food with us, fruit, cheese and bread. It seemed to fit with the few flowers, the grass and the mill. In fact down there, the clay workings had nearly all grown over, even the great arches that housed some of the larger equipment.

So we ate and thought about what we had done that day. We had parked at the top of the valley below Goonvean tip. There, we had followed the river down, stopping to try a rope swing over the river, neither of us feeling it safe enough to swing out too far as the current was fast flowing and the water deep. Then I showed her where they mined uranium for Marie Curie, although I might have been wrong. But you know as time goes on fiction becomes truth. People will believe you if you make it credible enough.

Behind where we lay was a broken Morris Minor, ivy covered itself, but it somehow added something to the scene that made it more decadent, more lovely. I had come here with her. It made me justify my beginnings. Southend, now a mere memory and a once-a-year visit to my grandmother.

We were lazy and lulled into a sleep. Bees littered the air. Chloe's head was resting on my chest. I could hear her easy breathing, like she had all the time in the world.

She had a mind like a photographer's. Taking pictures. Snappy. She said she wanted to write a novel about them. We woke again slowly. Over an hour had passed. There was the thrill of waking up next to someone who loves you, a someone you feel at home with. Karma. Like John Lennon and Yoko Ono in their New York apartment; Chloe and I in a clayland wood, the place where it had all started. The first whitestuff out of the earth. Why the Longstone had been moved and the downs eaten away, why Karslake and Halviggan went, why there are holes there.

Chloe sat up. She brushed off the grass I had been piling on her stomach and laughed. Then her face turned serious. She brushed her hair back. Her earrings glistened.

'Ben,' she said. I noted a seriousness in her voice. I watched her tongue. It wetted her lips, then she laid it on her teeth.

'Oh hell. I don't know how to tell you this...'

I begged her to tell me. I wondered what it was going to be. Then it came,

'Look... I think I'm pregnant...'

OF COCOONMENT

...which is being inside a self-spun silky case, when we only know what emerges later, after transformation...

CLARA'S life after she split up from me had been a meaningless meander through a landscape and lifestyle she no longer understood. She had last seen me at Tom's funeral, and that was only a fleeting glance as she left the bleak chapel.

She was sitting in her state-of-the-art office in St Austell, a third floor room that looked out to the massive tower of the church in the centre of the town. Oh sure, her lifestyle had improved. She had a new car, all the clothes she wanted. She had even bought several new electrical appliances for her mother's house.

Now she sat at her desk, encased by mushroom painted walls, a moderately big wheel in her own soliciting world. It was embarrassing that morning. The slightly larger office next door to hers had been vacated by a retirement, and another member of staff was moving in there. His name was Chris Whitehurst. She had been out with him on a couple of dates. At first he had seemed everything she was looking for. He had the looks, the money, and he had put down a deposit on a house in Carlyon Bay, one of the classier parts of the town. But all this initial brightness had been overshadowed by his superficiliaty and lack of depth beyond the financial and soliciting world.

Outside in the corridor, he waved to her while carrying a small filing cabinet. She chose to ignore him and sipped her coffee. He still thought he had a chance with her. If he persisted she would tell him where to go.

But her frustration was no longer concerned with men. She felt numbed to the ways of things in Cornwall. The same get-out-of-bed buzz from her alarm clock, the same long face of her still-bereaved mother, the same Corn Flakes, the same journey to work, the same moans from Mr James, her boss. She was being gnawed inside by the sameness of it all.

In her coffee breaks, solace from the agony; she would think about new possibilities. She longed to let it all go; tell them where to stick the job. Tell them where to put their prospects.

She would throw it all in now, if only she had the guts. That trait came from her father. Clara wanted to drive a hippy Volkswagen around Europe like you see in those late '60s films. She imagined anything, anything that would lift her, for in the back of her mind she remembered another's words. 'Moth girl,' he had called her. And she was certain she would fly again.

Outside, a Nimrod roared over the town. She watched the dust-folded faces turn skywards. She saw the symbol of the clay company on the oily jeans of men coming out of Barclay's Bank. She saw the clay splattered hub caps and undersides of the cars which turned right at the newsagents. She felt her own heartbeat grow faster as if this was the cocoon. She stretched, as a momentary break from entombment, and spun the chair around. Chris was watching her legs. She glared at him, and he moved on. Then Clara smiled.

OF REMOVAL

...which often results in dislocation.

FOR both of us Cornwall seemed like another planet. I stood hunching my back over the small attic window that looked over the mess of. The Synagogue to the west. Below, the ring road. Beyond that, the tower blocks. I had a picture in my mind and was deciding the best way to paint it. From the ceiling descended a money spider, scaling down from a great height. Chloe watched me observing the spider. She was exercising, part of her antenatal programme. When she stretched her legs for the last time, she let out a deep breath. I faced her, smiled, then spoke.

'So... back to Cornwall then. You're sure?'

Chloe sat up. I noticed her bulging belly.

'Yes. I'm certain. I want to go there. It'll be good. Me, you and the little one.'

I moved across the flat, circling her and picking up a couple of pottery tools I had left on the coffee table.

'If we go we've got to find somewhere I can set up the pottery. Somewhere we can run the business from...'

'I know,' Chloe said. 'Somewhere I can write as well.'

Chloe felt me distant and unhelpful I think. She tried again; this time coming closer to my real doubts.

'It's Hensbarrow isn't it? You feel it's a step back right...'

I looked at her and blinked. She knew it to be the truth. She also knew it to be deeper. She knew my feelings about the clay. And the blood.

I wandered back into the studio room. I sat at the wheel and continued with my creation. Chloe took a cloth from the kitchen and wiped the clay off the coffee table. She saw her reflection in the window I had been looking out of. She felt fat, though there were still several months to go. She breathed in a bit and hoped that it would not be quite so noticeable in case anyone outside was looking. Then she went back to her typewriter.

In the other room she heard the turn of the wheel, the sound of water being flicked over the pot, like a countryside brook. She knew later she would feel the cold hands, the damp hands that she would warm.

Chloe's writing, though accomplished, came in great bursts,

and even though she was a confident reporter, her creative writing tended to be child-like. After typing half a side, she screwed up the page and threw it into the waste paper bin. She got up from her chair, picking up the material from the estate agents in Cornwall we had sent for.

In the studio I talked idly of the previous weekend. She swung over the lamp that lit her desk and focused her vision on a property that captured her; a converted mine on Hensbarrow. She got up and came into the studio room.

'Read this,' she said.

I mumbled the words as I read through the details. The property was at Wheal Jacob, just south of Greensplat. This was the one, I thought. I put any memories of Clara aside and then, like Chloe, felt the kick inside.

In bed that night, Chloe was looking at her belly. I was standing up, taking off my jeans. Across the road, there was a student party going on. Punk music filtered through the open top of the window. I shut it and got into bed.

Chloe had elected not to have a scan. She liked the wonder of not knowing. She touched her stomach, like the cat who had just eaten the cream. Because Chloe had decided she wanted as natural a birth as possible, I was worried, worried that the baby might be a Tessa, a baby with a chromosome problem, even though I knew the chances of that were slim.

I could not concentrate on my reading, so I snuggled beneath the duvet and closed my eyes. Chloe finished the chapter she was reading, then leaned over and switched the bedside light off. For a few moments we thrashed about to get comfortable. Then she moved towards me and put her warm hands where it felt good.

'Love me?' she said.

'With you like that?'

'It's good for me... and you,' Chloe said reassuringly.

And so we entwined our bodies. My hands changed from clay into caressing porcelain. After we had finished, we held on to one another tight, and fell asleep to the music of the Sex Pistols from the flat across the road. Anarchy in the UK.

A month later we arrived in Cornwall early in the morning. The white orb that was the moon was silently lowering in the sky and was finally blocked out by fleets of clouds which floated in over the moor. I had enough money to pay for the mine by selling Tom's cottage to the clay company. There was a rich vein of clay beneath it and they paid well for it, like most other properties on Hensbarrow.

Our flat went to a personnel manager from Marks and

Spencer. Deeds were exchanged, the money put down. Most of the furniture was already in 'the mine', as it came to be called. We had viewed the property a week after we received the details from the estate agent, staying at my parent's house, Most of our possessions went down a week earlier with a removal company.

Now, assortments of furniture and various boxes were scattered about the three layers of the mine. At the top of the building were the kitchen and bathroom; on the first floor two bedrooms; the ground floor had a living room and study. My work went into a large outside shed that had once housed some of the pumping equipment for the mine.

Though the previous owners had spent a great deal of money renovating the mine itself, the outer buildings were hardly touched, and there were still lengths of rusty pipe and valve heads in the shed.

Chloe located her work in the second bedroom. We slept well that night, curled up in an old Cornish mine – the way the mouse did in the Dutch Windmill.

In the morning we overslept. I rolled over and looked at the clock.

'Quarter to ten,' I grunted.

Chloe dragged her body out of the bed, pulling some of the bed clothes with her. She wrapped them around her and glanced out of the arch-shaped window that looked up on to the moor.

'It's like another planet isn't it?' she said. She did not expect me to answer, but I did.

'What?'

'The moor. Its shape. You know, there are places back home that are pretty weird but this beats it hands down.'

I listened, pulled the remaining bedclothes up around me and in doing so trying to block out the coldness of the moor.

'I like its silence,' she said, 'I can write here.'

Then Chloe put on her clothes and went up to the kitchen. I was left in a dreamy half awake state – the state of mind that allows your life to pass by in a few minutes, where you see flickering images of childhood, like the memory of taking home the foxgloves, like Mike and I up beside the Longstone and then fast-forwarding to the gallery where I met Chloe, and now a child in her belly and from that... the future. Then I woke properly, scratched my face and then looked around the house at the furniture we had to sort out.

'Hensbarrow Pottery', as it came to be known, took a good deal of investment and time to develop. There were bank loans to be signed for, more equipment bought, and a major advertising strategy to begin. There was also clay to be bought. This proved to be fairly easy, with a delivery coming every Monday afternoon which seemed to increase in size every week.

The sort of pottery I was aiming to produce catered for all markets. I based one design on the sort of pottery Tom used to keep in his kitchen. I called the range 'Traditional Hensbarrow'. It could have been Hong Kong for all I knew about Tom's pieces, but they seemed the exact shape and texture he might have wanted me to create.

The second range was more progressive, intended for richer customers on holiday. It took what I felt to be traditional lines but pushed them further.

The painting was also more detailed, many of the pieces being done in enamel. The actual firing itself proved a problem. Though art college had taught me some of the fundamentals, I needed technical assistance.

In the most this came from a man called Frank Kellow, a Cornishman who had tried to open his own pottery down in Mevagissey. He was thirty eight. The pottery had failed there, he felt, because he had produced the wrong sort of pottery, not enough day-to-day items. He was keen and had the technical skills. He commented favourably upon my skills as a potter. I also contacted a kiln maker from Ross-on-Wye, who stayed for several days and installed a traditional kiln for the pottery inside another of the outbuildings.

It was late May. We had only a few weeks to prepare for the summer and the rush of sun-creamed tourists. It was a race against time and we used every day as efficiently as possible. I sculpted the majority of pieces while Frank oversaw the firing. Glazing and painting tended to be done by anyone who was free. Often, when he was not working, my father came down to help with lifting jobs and cleaning out the kiln.

At night, I would retire with clay still under my fingernails. Only now had I doubts about the business, whether it had been a lucrative idea or not. I would fish into the past, remembering the conversations I had with Watt outside the post office. Listening to the tourists, I hoped this time they would come to 'the Dirty Bit', the bit I liked best, the bit I had returned to.

And somewhere inside there was a deep nagging of a prophecy. But to go to sleep I would only dream of sweet things, the happy faces of tourists returning with their piece of pottery, their piece of Hensbarrow. And so, like the Devil behind your left shoulder when you throw spilt salt at him, the prophetic thoughts left.

Fortunately, in the next month, the tourists arrived. I noticed that they came up to Hensbarrow to see the 'white mountains'. They actually treated it as part of their holiday, seeing perhaps the eighth wonder of the world; the 'pyramids of Hensbarrow'. And the pottery was a place to buy souvenirs of their visit.

Soon, I realised we could make the pottery itself an attraction. So instead of hiding the kiln I opened it up to the public and Frank, in his story-teller manner, handed down from the fishing quays of Mevagissey, told them secrets which they carried back home. He'd tell them a yarn he had learnt somewhere about the unscrupulous millers of Truro who, in 1814, mixed two hundred tons of china clay with their flour, making themselves a tidy profit, and making the people spread butter over clay bread; so that they ate the earth.

And so soon, the pottery began to make a tidy profit.

The unscrupulous times we live in my friends...

As the season changed into July, 'the Dirty Bit' became the interesting bit, and for one of the few times in my life I felt I was doing something worthwhile.

On the Friday of the first week in July, Chloe and I decided to go shopping. There were still masses of things we needed to buy for the baby, so we took the Land Rover to Plymouth.

It was a warm day. The sun seemed to bounce off every concrete surface in Plymouth. Traffic swam in the Armada haze. I had to walk slower because of Chloe's pregnancy. For the time being, her dreams of being a novelist had been thrown out of the window, yet she seemed satisfied to be having her own child.

I knew she wanted us to be happy, not like her parents. When thoughts like that entered her mind she grabbed my hand tight. After a morning's shopping we had purchased several baby items – a pram and a cot, things like nappies and talcum powder, a tiny plastic bath and a musical potty, small things like safety pins and several boxes of tissues. The larger items I took back to the Land Rover. Chloe waited for me in the square in the centre of New George Street. When I returned I saw her watching children in the way I had done, tumbling about on the grass.

'So this is the real Chloe then,' I said, 'All your motherly feelings are in there somewhere.'

Chloe looked at me, then she spoke, her voice relaxed and easy.

'Yes. I suppose they are... sort of deep down. Deep down we are still animals. For all our pretences, for all our artistry, we are only animals...'

'So?'

'So while I'm like this, the centuries disappear.'

For a moment she was wistful, thinking that her own thoughts were airy fairy nonsense. Then she got up from the bench.

'Where next?'

'We've got the shopping to do.'

We walked off together, me running rings around Chloe. Suddenly I wanted to marry her, make it proper. Show the world our love. But then, when we entered the supermarket, I knew that to do that might take away the magic of our togetherness. So I resolved just to do the shopping.

Inside the supermarket, we felt out of place. There seemed to be only three types of shoppers. Little old ladies (and they were little), buying tins of catfood, packets of tea, and chunks of dripping. Young mothers trailing around children, buying jellies, biscuits and frozen food, and assortments of men, from brickies to city businessmen, always a little distant, removed from the scene, and buying bottles of milk, cans of coke and cigarettes.

And then there was Chloe and I, buying the food we liked to eat; cheese, fruit, brown bread, the crisps I liked, the biscuits Chloe always had. But this time we thought of someone else, someone Chloe had carried since November and so we went to the baby food counter and bought a selection of condensed meals, and both of us joked about whether we could eat that sort of stuff. With the groceries bought, the two of us looked around Plymouth's concrete encased shops until it was time to leave, and we drove home in the pale sunlight that filtered through the dusty windows of the Land Rover from the west.

A BEAUTIFUL face scanned the moor. Not the rosebud beauty of a virgin's face but the face of a woman who has opened her petals and now feels the many times it has rained on her in her life, but somehow still keep that essence of wonder, like the Hollywood movie stars who never seem to fade. She was out picking flowers and heather in the still summer evening. She had taken off her shawl but her black figure contrasted deeply with the white of Carroncarrow tip behind her.

Though she could not see them, she could sense the tourists down in St Austell and Charlestown. A smell in the air, perhaps the suntan lotion carried on a breeze up through Gover. She picked 'Boots and Shoes' and a few stalks of other wild flowers she knew well for their medicinal value. She knew they would make a wonderfully sleepy summer pot pourri to place in the parlour.

She kept herself to herself after the funeral. That one moment in clover of their togetherness had gone. There were murmurs from the old folk that it was the witch in her, the way she kept the 'Old Ways' going. She climbed up to the top of Carroncarrow tip. Below the moor, several miles to the west, she could make out the earth satellite station at Goonhilly on the Lizard.

She knew them as the 'Dishes'. To the north she saw the space where Karslake houses used to sit. She pictured the Longstone there. She saw herself playing there as a child. And then the trek home through the vuzz, trying not to get her white socks dirty.

But she had other thoughts on her mind as well. She was increasingly worried about her daughter who was becoming estranged to her and her ways.

She had heard on the grapevine that Ben Sexton was back on the moor with a girl friend who was pregnant by all accounts. She felt grief for her daughter, of the things that could have been, and the things that should never have been.

And worst of all, from the tabletop of the downs, she saw the work that had begun around Tom's house. The hose was washing away his back garden. Old stalks of potatoes planted by him crumbled into the pit.

She felt her heart turning to stone no matter how hard she tried to stop it, and the rate of transformation increased when down Wheal Jacob she saw a Land Rover trundling along the road to the mine, and in it she could just make out the bearded figure of the boy, now the man, who she had once bathed in nettle water to make his warts fall away.

OF KAOLIN

...which is posh for china clay, or as chemists like Cookworthy write, Al2, 2Si O2, 2H2O, to show they have the elements of the earth under control.

THE initial batch of firing completed, it was with some satisfaction that I rested my back on the solid Cornish wall that supported the roof of the pottery and looked at this small but well run empire.

Bottles and drums of deflocculants stood on the shelves adjacent to the door. A blunger was towards the top end, used to mix up clay bodies from dry powders. Next to that was the pugmill, already clay splattered, used to mix the clay to an even consistency. Through a door to my left lay the fettling oven where the clay ware and pottery were cleaned prior to firing. In my hands I held some rough fly-ash, some of which was left over from carrying it from the firebox into the wood-fired kilns.

I mused over the pottery, the lifestyle I had created. The return to roots. Back to the clay. This time, clay on clay. The clay I was using here was not the clay I had pressed in my pocket in Swansea. This was china clay, the purest form of clay known to man. I had come here to work with that stuff. To use the material Tom, my father and myself had dug from the ground.

As far as pottery goes, china clays are extremely white firing and are very resistant to heat. They are also not very plastic. However, with additions they can, when fired, become translucent. In all white clay bodies they are the vital ingredient. I considered the substance.

It had the two vital qualities all potters desire. Firstly, to produce any object at all the clay has to be formable, and secondly to produce a durable object the clay has to be able to be fired at a point where it develops sufficient strength.

With the satisfaction of knowing my material inside out I put my hands together, making a kind of kneading motion. I had used all the clays in my time at art college; common clays, terracottas, ball clays, fire clays, but the medium I liked best, the one that gelled with my hands was china. Kaolin. The one I seemed to find spiritual enlivenment with. The clay where medium and maker seemed to become woven together.

It was where I felt the barriers fall. Such good plasticity. And an ability to retain form at the firing temperature that had been intended. These were the useful qualities of china clay; the tao of Kaolin.

I left the pottery, walking like a Chinese laundryman in little short steps. I almost skipped into the kiln where Frank was at work. I viewed the creations – seven stacks of pottery ready to be fired tomorrow. I watched Frank building up the wood stock as if he were creating a great funeral pyre.

And this was the odd thing; the sort of thing you never get used to, like the devil behind your left shoulder. For me now the clay meant something beyond the downs, past the pits, out from childhood and even remote from the splatters of blood I felt had once fallen. It was the way clay felt to touch. When you first touch it the surface is cold and soft. I can remember thinking I was touching a dead person. White skin of a corpse. The colour of bodies young doctors dissect in anatomy classes.

Clay somewhere equalled death. It was a strange notion handed down by my own enchantments. The way you found it in the earth. Pictures of rotting skulls. A saint's body. Pulping in time. Returning to earth.

Turning to clay.

Clay seemed to me to go with death, the way sunshine seemed to go with birth. Say clay. C-L-A-Y. Make the Y long. Each piece of clay a step nearer Doomsday. And now a peep-show of images; clay death masks, clay pipes, small ones with long stems, the sort the old miners used to smoke in photographs, white bones, ivory carved into a skeletal figure with a scythe, underground, the fall of earth on the lid of a mahogany coffin. Waiting for time, the many years that turn the man into clay; the same time that turns the land to sea, and the sea to land. For as the wise Chinese potters in Jiangxi province used to say as they perfected their intricate porcelain figures: 'Both king and slave become clay eventually'.

Frank and I came out of the kiln and headed for the mine, leaving the tao of Kaolin behind us; my thoughts full...

OF A CHILD

THERE were two other forward thinking males at the ante-natal classes we attended. One was a forty-year-old solicitor from Truro. The other was a man about the same age as myself who seemed to complete a variety of jobs, mainly on the seafront at St Mawes. The men did everything the women did.

At the front a young nurse with shapely legs, who had never had children, led in the movement. At first I could hardly keep a straight face. Then after the second class I began to take it more seriously. Chloe liked me to come with her. It seemed right.

'You okay?' she would whisper while controlling her breathing.

I told her I was all right. Right as rain.

The classes were held in Truro, in the hospital, though Chloe herself was due to go to Penrice Hospital in St Austell to have the baby.

On the way home, we were in the Land Rover passing along the stretch of road just before Blackwater. We were listening to Radio One. An alternative session on John Peel. From the A390, you could not see Hensbarrow in the dark, only the dazzling spot and arc lights that lit up Blackpool processing plant. From the dark road the lights looked homely enough. It was late, around quarter to twelve. Because most of the mothers were near to labour, and each had their own worries, the class had gone on later that night.

As we drove, Chloe said things like: 'Baby's kicking,' or 'baby's hungry,' as if we were already a threesome.

Back at the mine, Frank had been working late into the evening. He had left a note explaining what he had done with the new batch of teapots and where the custard creams had gone. We both laughed when we found the note under the front door.

Chloe was first to bed. She was tired. There were small bags under her eyes. I went to bed later, after I had checked what Frank had done outside. When I finally got to bed Chloe was asleep. I did not disturb her.

I was woken in the small hours by her. She was in pain and screaming, not screams of horror but labour-prompted screams of frustration. The bed was wet. Her rich waters had broken. She was in labour. I tried to make her comfortable. Neither of us had anticipated this. The baby was not due for another week. I made jokes about this and Chloe laughed, which took away some of the bone-tearing pain.

I would go for an ambulance. No. I would take her to hospital myself. No. She could not move now. I would ring for an ambulance. This was not an easy thing to do, since we hadn't yet got round to having a phone installed and the nearest telephone box was at Greensplat. I got into the Land Rover, stupidly looking up to the bedroom window to see if she was all right. I fumbled for the keys. They fell on to the floor.

More haste, less hurry. I found the keys again and rammed them into the ignition. I turned the starter. The engine coughed but would not start. I swore. I tried several times. Then I noticed I had left the radio on. She would not start now. The battery was flat. Tears of panic.

I sat hunched over the steering wheel. What was my next move? I resolved to tell Chloe what was happening but then, on climbing out of the Land Rover, I noticed a light on up at Carroncarrow. I kicked myself for not thinking of it before. I leapt over the gate of the mine and sprinted up the pot-holed track to the dark moor road. I had only my trousers and shoes on, and the still night air chilled my body.

'Mary,' I repeated over and over in my head, 'Mary Cundy.'

The moor was silent, apart from the sound of my heavy feet and a small hose working in Greensplat pit. I ran so fast my heart banged out of my ribcage. Sometimes I ran backwards, to look at the mine, but all I could see was the lit window of our bedroom. By the time I reached the black-painted gate of Carroncarrow Cottage, the one I had been so scared to enter as a boy, I was shouting, externalising the fear.

'Mary Cundy! Come out, wherever you are...'

It sounded like a nursery rhyme. The Three Little Pigs. I rammed my fists against the door, almost breaking it down. The ivy clinging to the cottage seemed to strangle me as I lay against the wall to rest, the leaves touching my Adam's apple. I shouted again; this time loud enough to wake the dead.

Voices could be heard inside muttering. Leaning against the door, I heard the bolts slide back one after the other. I virtually fell into the cottage. I was certain I was foaming at the mouth. Rabid with anxiety. Before me stood Clara. For a second the insanity disappeared. For a small second I seemed to be shouting for her. Then when I spoke, the worst put down.

'I don't want you. Where's your mother?'

'Coming,' came the voice of Mary, clunking down the creaking stairs into the parlour, her blonde hair slightly adrift.

'It'll be the baby me lover, will it?'

I told her the story. Mary listened.

'I know you can do... these things,' I said.

I had wanted to say 'deliver babies' but it did not seem the right way to say it in front of Mary; it was too modern. 'These things' seemed more appropriate to Mary's skill. She went out of the room and came back with a hessian sack, which clanked as she threw it over her shoulder.

In the meantime, Clara and I did not speak but merely glared at one another. We noticed what had changed in the time we had been parted. Clara, more modern, more upstanding. Opposite to the meek woman she once had been. Racing into another personality. It had hardened her. Clara noted me to be sadder, prematurely older, a slight balding at the back of my head.

Mary came as quickly as she could. She did not run, but walked in little skips that hurried her progress. When we were nearly there, I hurried on to see if Chloe was all right. I found her exasperated, near naked, straddling the bed.

I tried to slow down her breathing and asked her to take deeper breaths, like we had done at the classes. This was it. This was the human condition. The primitive. All the art and pottery that surrounded us had no place now. This was back to the egg. Back to the earth. Falling down the centuries. I wanted to slow my own breathing in line with Chloe's. I wiped away her sweat and made her sit in the 'correct position'. I held her hand tight and she grabbed me tight when she felt the contractions. She was screaming when Mary came into the room. Chloe managed to say:

'Who's this woman? Where's the ambulance?'

I did my best to explain.

'Stay calm now. Mary will help you. She's a midwife. She will make it easier. She'll help you.'

Chloe looked at Mary in horror when she saw the sack.

'No! No. No Ben. I don't want her here...'

Chloe heard the tools rattling in the sack. And this crow-like figure at the end of the bed was about to help her give birth to her child. Mary said something in the old language. It sounded like some kind of chant. Then, when Mary spoke and touched Chloe, the fear subsided.

'Relax now, me lover,' Mary said softly. 'I bain't going to hurt you...'

Chloe's eyes followed her around the room. The three of us were in this woman's hands. She looked at me, then spoke:

'Out you go. This bain't no place for men.'

The command was authoritative. I knew better than to argue with her, and although I felt I could have been useful, Mary did not think so. She did however ask me to fetch some hot water, soap, and some sheets or towels. Behind me, I heard Mary's croaky voice,

'Come on little chield. Where be 'ee?'

After I had given Mary her requirements, I went up to the kitchen and sat on a high-backed chair in the half dark. It was ten to three in the middle of the night. On the kitchen table sat a lump of clay. I leant over and picked it up and, while I waited, sometimes hearing bumps below, as in Swansea, I shaped the future in my hands.

Three agonising hours later, I heard crying from below. I ran downstairs, almost breaking the banister. Mary opened the door.

'Congratulations,' she said, and handed me a white towel parcel. Inside a red face peered up to me, arms and legs chunky and moving without co-ordination.

'It's a boy,' Chloe exclaimed, before I could ask.

I held the parcel as if it were the most delicate object in the whole world, which it was. I handled the baby as I handled porcelain pieces, as if it were a mortal sin to leave any fingerprints on it. Chloe was smiling. Tangles of sweat-soaked hair fell on to her face. She was exhausted. Mary was packing up her things. She had taken away the bloody sheets and was now washing her hands. A silly question.

'How was the birth?'

Chloe wanted to say painful, but she was overruled by Mary who said it had been quite straightforward, apart from the baby being a long time coming.

'I can't thank you enough... Mary,' Chloe said.

Mary was hard again. 'As long as the boy is all right,' she said. 'Let un suckle soon mind...'

I gave the baby to Chloe and followed Mary out. The dawn was just beginning to break.

'My job's done now,' she said, and she left, carried away on the morning breeze like some ethereal Mary Poppins.

It had not gone without notice in my mind that Mary, the mother of a woman I had once loved, had now helped to deliver the baby of another woman I loved. The irony for both of us was harsh and brutal, but necessary for mother and baby's life.

I decided not to tell the truth, for I knew the information would upset Chloe. I would make up some story. Inside, I watched with Chloe and our son as the morning steadily murmured across the downs. And the clayland and the rest of the world were suddenly joined as one.

THAT year passed in a dreamy wash of sunshine, tourists and

pots, nappies and rattles. My mother and father were overjoyed with the baby. In the autumn, Chloe's parents were coming to England to see their grandchild. The baby was named Anthony Lee Sexton. The Lee part came from Chloe's mother's family.

I had considered the vague notion of calling the baby after Tom, but that would be too damning. I thought of Clara on the hill, and could not do it, so we settled for Anthony, a name that held no connections for either party.

In fact, there had been some debate as to whether it should be William or Anthony. The final decision was made with the help of two mugs in the kitchen, under which we placed pieces of paper with the names. Chloe picked Anthony.

At weekends, Chloe and I left Frank to run the pottery to walk the two miles up through Greensplat to Hensbarrow. I usually pushed the pram, Chloe beside me, tucking in the blankets and ensuring Anthony was all right. We would stop half way up Greensplat hill to gaze out over the Channel, where the sea was as blue as the woollen booties my mother had made for Anthony.

A resort to my own childhood followed. The noises I made to interest Anthony, the moves with my hands, like some kind of Renaissance harlequin. Baby Anthony brought us closer together and renewed an interest in the clayland that had spawned me. The birth had promoted a rebirth, as if I were digging for my roots. Seeing where the seed was from.

Early in the new year, it was a Sunday, the first weekend in March, we walked up to Hensbarrow and sat on the beacon. Chloe fed Anthony on top of the mound as we looked down over Goss Moor and behind us into Gunheath Woods.

But the day was a warm one and by mid-afternoon great cumulus clouds were rising over the moor. The black of the clouds over the sandy grass of the moor gave to the horizon a distant line, sharp as a blade. I could feel Anthony sweating in the heat, the heady remnants of summer about to have the last laugh.

The sky rumbled while we walked back to the mine, Anthony crying as the clouds banged together. There was a charge in the air. Tiny grains of sand trickled off the tips. Lupins shook.

The rush to make it back to the mine was frantic. It had started to rain. Not drizzle rain, the rain Hensbarrow experiences nearly every day and twice on Sundays, but Dogsday rain, lumps of rain, lashings of water that had all day been sucked off the cloth of the earth.

You could smell the Tarmac, the first droplets slamming down, even the gorse plants buckling under the weight of water. It rained hard. Like a desert shower. It ran down last summer's gorges in the tips and collected in the new parts of the pits. It gouged into the loose sand and washed it out, carrying it along until it became fed up with the weight, then depositing it in damp snaky lines across the road.

When we got inside, Chloe and I dried off ourselves and Anthony. He was placid now and had become used to the thunder. Towards Old Pound, Chloe watched forks of lightning stutter down. They seemed very close. She wanted to lock the door. Shut the wolf out. Three little pigs in the house of bricks.

After Anthony had been fed we took him down into his still paint-smelling bedroom and placed him in his cot. A myriad of smiling faces looked down upon him from the Walt Disney wallpaper we had chosen.

We watched until he was asleep. Still the novelty of being a baby. On the ceiling was a farm animal mobile that spun when Chloe tapped it. Outside, the storm ranted and raged, but we were safe and sound.

Chloe and I went downstairs and flopped on the sofa. We were too tired to talk to one another. Each was happy enough with our own thoughts of the child. Occasionally, Chloe would jump to life when she thought she heard Anthony crying, but it was always the wind and rain.

We watched 'Songs of Praise', which was from Hereford, then the news and a film about the American Civil War that Chloe was interested in. In the warmth of the living room, we forgot about the rain outside. Both of us felt snug and smug.

After I had made some milky coffee, Chloe said she had better check how Anthony was. She took an elastic band from the mantelpiece and tied back her dark hair. I poured the coffee and fell into the sofa again. I watched her climb up the stairs. I waited for her to come down again, only half-listening to the television.

When she did, her face showed not the signs of a peacefully sleeping baby, but of tragedy, She screamed twice. Her jaw fell, the line of her face different, her footsteps heavy.

'Chloe. What is it?'
'He's dead,' she answered calmly.
'Who?'
'Anthony...'

I tore up the stairs into the bedroom, switched on the light and pulled the covers back. I touched my son. A chill entered my hand. I picked him up and listened. A half-crazed listen for a tiny heart at work, but I heard nothing except the rain tapping at the window and the cold stare of a hundred Disney characters.

Had I known then what I know now, I would have scoured the yard outside for red stains in the potholes...

OF ONE OF THOSE THINGS

HAPPY noises and jingles exuded from the radio on top of the fridge-freezer. While spooning sugar on my Corn Flakes I heard it was the first day of autumn. Chloe was in the bathroom taking a shower. She had forgotten to close the bathroom door and steam was escaping into the kitchen, producing condensation on the south facing window. I was rubbing sleep out of my eyes.

We had chatted late last night for the first time. It was an exorcism of our feelings. We both confessed what we felt and what Anthony's death meant to us. We both had difficulty accepting it, there was no denying that; someone had snatched away our moment of joy, our togetherness, our integrity. My thoughts ran back to what Frank had said.

'It was just one of those things...'

And we had tried to treat it like that, as one of those things. But this thing was our thing and we could not easily forget it. Having a child awakens many feelings in a person, and when that child disappears it is difficult to know what to do with them. They are there still, but without anything to focus on.

On one of the units in the kitchen, where we had kept the baby food, sat a stack of cards with messages like: 'Thinking of you at this sad time.' Under them lay the coroner's report, a high quality piece of paper, watermarked and with a seal. That made everything seem proper and I tried hard to put the memory of Anthony's body being removed from the cot and taken downstairs in a steel box.

Anthony was a cot death, whatever that was. The doctors did not know why it happened. He was a perfectly healthy normal baby. The coroner talked of possible asphyxiation and breathing difficulties, but these, as the report said, were only possibilities and not probabilities.

And so everyone knew that death had visited; it was how the life was taken that people wanted to know. Such a death makes people insecure, and that was how Chloe felt.

She demanded my love more than ever. She even felt worried about us 'living in sin', and felt that taking the baby away was some kind of revenge on us for breaking the Biblical rules.

But I could deal with this. I had taken it all apart, rebuilt it again, analysed all the reasons, all the possibilities. In the end I had come to the conclusion that it was just one of those things.

And that is what I had thought at the funeral. Anthony's body buried in the ground at Nanpean. We had buried some of his toys with him, or rather the toys we had wanted him to play with, in some vague recollection of Egyptian burials, so he could be happy in the after life. The two of us had cried for hours after. I never knew I had so many tears.

But I had dealt with all that. A darker thing niggled me. I was convinced a shower of blood had fallen on me, and that somehow Anthony's death was connected with this. History repeating itself. A parallel time zone. Less dramatic, but nonetheless a catastrophe for myself, my own personal disaster. It was a clay prophecy, and it was a prophecy that scared me.

I felt the blood pouring around my body. I could no longer bring a spoonful of sun-kissed Corn Flakes towards my mouth. I was dreaming of the crosses they daubed on people's houses in the Great Plague. Babies pickled in spots. 'Ring-a-ring of roses. Ring-a-ring of roses. Attishoo! Attishoo! We all fall down...'

I got up and ran down the two flights of stairs. But when I opened the front door and looked for a cross, it was just as normal. Then I kicked myself for being so stupid.

Chloe met me coming up the stairs. She had a towel wrapped around her head.

'What's up?'

I lied to her.

'One of the doors was blowing in the wind. I just shut it.'

Chloe started her breakfast and I finished off my Corn Flakes. She seemed okay now. Not so distant. Unlike the week after when she just sat in the living room like a stone statue, her eyes barely blinking. Only a slim recognition of me as anyone different from the other sympathetic listeners.

I had telephoned her parents, or rather her mother. She was distraught. She was due in England a week later to see her first grandchild. I could still hear her Welsh drawl.

'How did it happen exactly?'

There were other relatives in Wales to be contacted. I had done the ringing. I told friends from college. They were shocked and offered to do all they could. I was grateful, but never contacted them.

To start with, the death of Anthony brought us closer. We were more loving, more aware of the other person's feelings, and there was a mutual acceptance of responsibility.

What neither of us had expected was a disinterest in the physical side of our relationship. Sex died between us and frigidity hung in the mine like icicles. I could sense the problem, almost as though the white and greys of the landscape had entered us, making us virginal, sweeping through and brushing away our colour. The landscape was absorbing our physicality and we were crying out for love. And for me, the landscape that had offered me pagan love rites and freedom was now constricting, shrinking, taking away any virility. And now I wanted soothing of the wound in my heart. But all I could feel was salt being rubbed in.

At the breakfast table the conversation returned to trivialities. What each of us was doing. What time would she be back for dinner? Oh, and would she fetch some of those wooden joists from the timber people in St Austell? For weeks the conversation never rose above this intellectual level. The death was touched on but as quickly brushed over, as though we wanted the death to fade quicker than was possible.

That day, when Chloe returned to the mine from town, she found two large dustbin bags at the bottom of the stairs. I had been into Anthony's room and stripped off the wallpaper and the accessories in there. She peered around the door of the room to find me disassembling the cot.

'It had to be done sometime,' I said.

'Yes. I suppose so...'

'I think we'll burn it... No-one is going to want to buy it. We don't need it now...'

In this there was somewhere a reaffirmation for living, a glance towards the future. And Chloe carried my words with her up to the kitchen.

'Your joists are outside,' she shouted down to me, but I could barely hear her as I ripped apart the cot.

In the evening, Chloe cooked a meal. We sat upstairs in the kitchen eating the lasagne she had been making all afternoon. With it we drank some wine, a bottle left over from the previous Christmas. We were both impressed by its vintage. We giggled like under-age drinkers as the white wine splashed into the glass. With the alcohol, the darkness lifted. The two of us rose out of mourning as if riding on a magic carpet. Chloe spoke.

'What are you thinking?'

'Nothing,' I replied.

'Must be something...'

'I am thinking,' I announced, 'about what you are thinking.'

Chloe paused and tried to work out what I had said.

'Well, actually,' she said in her poshest English accent, 'I was

thinking why can't we climb one of the tips?'
'What now?'
'Yes. Right now.'
Chloe uncorked a second bottle of wine someone had given us. It was a rough home brew with some bits floating in the bottom. We rammed our boots on and went down the road to Halviggan tip. At the bottom was thick vegetation, and though the prickles stuck into us the alcohol numbed the pain. I pinched Chloe's bum and we both went scrambling up the tip, pulling out clumps of grass and laughing at each other's drunken steps.

Chloe was first up. She had chosen a more accessible route with fewer rain troughs. She sat at the crown of the tip like a bird of prey. I saw the bottle glistening in the moonlight. I came up behind her and covered her eyes with my hands.

'Guess who?'
'Don't know.'
'Go on. Guess.'
'A bogeyman,' she said laughing.
'No,' I replied with all seriousness, 'it's me.'
And we fell over laughing. I threw the first bottle into the thicket, but it did not smash. I kissed Chloe.

'Thank God I still love you,' I said.
She echoed my words. Our passion was interrupted by a hose being switched on in Blackpool pit. The lighting rig that lay beyond it lit up a section of the downs. I dropped the bottle on to a lump of quartz. I saw a space where Tom's house had once been. This time I could not cry.

'What's wrong?' Chloe asked.
'Nothing.'
The drunken night on top of Halviggan tip was just the kind of release Chloe and I needed. Chloe decided to begin to write again. It was a children's novel about a holiday in America. She was writing it in the study, working from early in the morning to late at night.

Frank and I worked in the pottery. We had made a profit over the summer and had paid back some of the bank loan. A new range was planned, as well as a new marketing strategy which could sell the pottery in other parts of Cornwall, in the bits that were not dirty, and in the rest of the country.

Not all was quite as it should have been however. As the months went on, and the summer of that year slipped gently into autumn, Chloe became increasingly estranged from me.

She demanded we had a telephone installed so that she could regularly phone her mother in the States. An agreement was made that in the New Year we should try for another baby. But somehow I could feel our relationship going under, like there was nothing more to say, no more to do.

One week, we hardly spoken to one another after an argument on the Sunday, It was the old problem. The accusations. The blame. Both of us said things we knew were untrue. Making up stories. We were pushing one another. Fighting on the edge, seeing how far we could go.

We argued over silly things. Things we had already decided hadn't been a factor in Anthony's death.

The 'Why did you put him to bed so early?' kind of points; the 'You chose that cot' kind of point. It was a war of attrition, an attempt to point the blame. Put the finger on one of us. And all the time memories of pushing a pram up to Hensbarrow strangled us like a garotte.

Chloe became fairy-like, tip-toeing everywhere, whereas before her strides had been powerful and sure. She bought some new clothes. She invited one of her friends down from London, and while they went out every day, travelling to Truro and Exeter, I worked in the pottery, while her novel stayed in her head.

But I cut into her as well. I told her what I thought of her. Told her she had changed for the worse. And sometimes – and I know I was guilty – my frustration erupted, but it was never a violent eruption, more a cold flow of emotion. I would slam the door and work outside, or walk down the valley and back again, taking my anger out on the creation of a pot, or stomping it away into the earth.

I talked to my parents about it. The kind of order they had in their lives, which I hated as an adolescent, now somehow soothing; the ritual of washing-up, the filling up of father's milk bottle before night shift, the way they bounced off one another verbally like fairground dodgems, knowing where to draw the line. It felt so good compared to the chaos of emotion at the mine. I could feel our relationship being strangled, and it was if we both were tightening the rasping wire.

It came to a head over a meal a week before Christmas. Fairy lights decorated the kitchen window. There was the smell of tangerines. The holy darkness of the downs. She was looking out of the window, tapping a bulb into position on the lights that were not working. The she turned and faced me. She spoke clearly and slowly.

'I hate this place.'

This was no surprise to me. She had talked like this before.

'I hate this place, hate the moor, hate the people. Most of all I hate the tips. Waking up every day to see the same bleak view. I'm fed up with it. The whole thing just pisses me off...'

This came quicker. A rush of words followed by the first tears. She was ruining the world view she felt, demolishing the plan. She had wanted to move here and now she felt nothing but coldness for it.

'It's what's happened isn't it?' I asked

'Yes,' she said, 'but it's more than that. It's like living here... You're so far from everything. I can't cope with it.'

'And me? What of me?'

'I don't know.'

'What do you mean?'

'I don't know... You've changed. I mean, we've both changed. I've changed.'

There was a helplessness in her voice, a sense of inevitability.

'We should have married...'

'Why?'

'It would have been different...'

There was a moment of silence, the awful crystal-shattering silence that comes in the middle of an intense argument. The silence of ruination.

'But...'

She cut me off.

'But what Ben?'

'It's no-one's fault. It's just the way things go. One of those things... I don't like it either, but...'

'Screw you,' she screamed, her breathing erratic, like when she was in labour. She swung her arm and knocked a pot to the floor. It fell with a heavy crack and splintered into hundreds of tiny fragments. Her frustration was being let out by physical anger. She said she had to go. She did not say she was going. She 'had to go', that is what she said, as if someone was controlling her. A force above us. She was a piece on a chessboard being moved from square to square.

She had threatened to go before, and I had begged her not to leave. Now the repelling from each other was too great. I let her pack. Sobs and swearing could be heard in the bedroom. I followed her about. She told me to stop looking at her so, indignantly, I went downstairs and turned on the television.

There was a report of a UDR man being killed in Ulster. A film crew had captured it. What a story. I turned over. On ITV was a comedy. I watched it with the sound down, listening to Chloe's exaggerated bangings about the house. More abuse. Abuse that should have been thrown at someone else.

We both knew we did not deserve to split up. Something instinctive. The last look of her from the sofa. My feet on the coffee table. Almost a reconciliation, but we had both grown hard.

The chill of the last year had frozen us simultaneously. I thought of Tregargus Woods. I thought of secret boxes being opened. But the thought was only a misapprehension. Another time. The now was a piercing glance across the drably lit living room, where the pit pump had once sucked up the wetness of the downs. Chloe's tears fell into the carpet, water soaking back down again.

She was carrying two suitcases. One was the tartan one I had bought for her in Harrods. It was a movie scene. To make it work again, I would go over to her and drape my arms around her, ask for forgiveness. But I did not move. I heard the front door slam and I imagined her carrying her cases down over Trenance Downs into St Austell, and then away from the clayland. She would not return.

In the morning the stoic Frank handed out his advice, but this time I did not want to hear. I wanted to forget, look forward to better times and...

OF MERRIE MAKING

I WAS merry – nearer to being smashed. The evening's drinking had taken its toll. Frank and I had gone out that night to The Cookworthy. I had spent the best part of £100. God only knew what Frank had got through, but now I felt good. Light headed. Numb to anything that the world could throw at me.

I paid the taxi driver and walked straight as a die to the front door. It was two days before Christmas Eve and this had been the potter's night out. I managed to get inside and fell to the floor next to the record player. I felt like playing The Beatles' 'Sergeant Pepper'. I found the record and lifted up the cover of the stereo system. I eased out the disc and placed it on the turntable. The needle clicked over and I listened, sitting guru-like on the floor. To my surprise I was not listening to The Beatles, but some classical album someone had replaced in the wrong sleeve.

I hummed along and gazed around the room. On the shelf above the television a picture of Chloe and I both in long coats in London, Chloe in a huge floppy hat that covered her face.

It was strange, but Hensbarrow had somehow been part of the '70s. It was something I had noticed. People had become conscious of change, of fashion, of trends. The previous decade had seen no real difference on the moor at all, as if the 1960s had never happened, and I felt that to be sad because part of that decade had been my childhood and it rang with innocence.

I saw brief glimpses of Tom and I rooting around in his sheds. But though the '70s had catapulted Hensbarrow forward, there had been talk of gloom in The Cookworthy. Redundancies at the clay company; too much clay. They were over-producing and there was no longer the demand. An American takeover was rumoured. Incentives for early retirement were being offered – six hundred jobs had to go.

The men in the pub were drowning their sorrows rather than getting in the mood for Christmas. My first thought was for my father. He only had a few years to go before retiring. I suspected he would take early retirement. A lot of the old timers would go, the ones who had been there first under the bowler-hatted Cap'ns, marking time in their own time.

With Christmas around the corner a lot of men went to their clay homes that night with long faces. It was their industry but their future, their children and the monster that was called the Recession was nibbling at them.

Punk had spread to Hensbarrow, I noticed that night – the music of the juke box, the anarchy slogans on the walls of the toilet, the painted leather jackets, the dangling safety pins. The Punk Cornishmen. That is a contradiction in terms but now, by the way they spread themselves over the bar, I knew that not to be the case. They were there, and the barriers were falling.

I could see it on the faces of the old timers; What was happening to their clayland? And when the girls walked in with their steel toe-caps on and their hair cropped short, I mind-read them. Where are the boys and maids now? And in that I knew something had been lost and something else had been found.

It was the 'Finders keepers, losers weepers' of life. But there was more. It was the voices at the bar. The way the young gave up their accents too willingly. How they accepted up-country words too easily. Got off on the slang. Couldn't give a toss. Their culture, their very selves being altered by the desire to fit in, their real selves crumbling to the floor like cigarette ash. And this was the sad thing, for no-one could stop the process. It was the permanency of change.

When I had considered all of this, and where my own life was going, the merryness began to fade and I side-stepped back into my real self. Real time again.

I got up off the floor and switched off the record. After the music and turmoil of thoughts the room was now strangely quiet. I climbed the stairs and drank several glasses of water in the kitchen to prevent a morning hangover.

The mine and moor were silent. A silence I had heard before. But it was not deja vu, it was the silence of childhood, the crystal silence of being alone with the Longstone. Then when I got into bed I smiled and thought of an earlier digger, or was it a Saint?

'WHY wouldn't they let the butterfly into the dance?'

'Go on. We don't know,' said my father.

'Because it was a moth ball!'

Groans ran around the table. I picked up the rubbish from the crackers and dropped it on to the fire, saving a purple paper hat for myself which ripped when I put it on my head.

My mother and father were happy to have me at home this Christmas. My mother had said earlier:

'We didn't expect you here this year...'
I restrained my sarcasm and just replied.
'Neither did I.'

But the atmosphere at the table was happy. Outside, it was a crisp winter day. While the meal was still cooking, Tessa took me for a walk to the bottom of the garden. I marked the slight oblique slant in her dark eyes and the strangeness and strength of her hand which led me down the mossy path.

'Look!' she said, and I gazed out over Blackpool pit. Noppies was gone now. And where Tom's garden had once been was a straight line of earth across to Greensplat. They were putting in a new road to replace the old Karslake road which would disappear in the New Year. But Tessa was not looking at this. She was pointing to the mine on the southern side of Greensplat.

'Your house!' she said.

'Yes,' I said, 'That's where I live. Looks a long way away doesn't it?'

'Yes.'

We went inside. Tessa's eyes focused on the Christmas tree lights. She would never lose that childhood sense of wonder, and I could never make up my mind if that was a good thing or not. But with Tessa's smiling face and the decorations, and the taste of my mother's plum pudding, for a moment I could believe that the white of the tips were snow, and Father Christmas was about to come down the chimney.

My father was on night shift that night.

'Only pumping out,' he said.

I stayed late, but could not concentrate on the television, or any of the games we played. I was angry because of the way my heartland was being destroyed and worried about Chloe. Other women also entered my mind that night, but I dared not mouth them. And the presents around the tree reminded me that one little soul had not lived to see this Christmas.

TOBIAS

14th December 1664.

Yuletide is near vpon us, yet I am no happier in my profession. I wilt leave if it continues as such. In the laste month of oure Lorde the Reverende has become wonderously foolish in all matters. I wonder now whether my Master's minde is entirely sounde, suche preposterous notions does he have. Says he that the next yeare wilt be a bad one unless other stones on the moore are removed, for he believes they againe art the stones of the Devil. He tells us, whilst we drink and eat at supper tonighte, that the harvest will be bad and that blacke clouds wilt descende o'er the Parishe of St Dennis.

The older he becomes, this man becomes madder. Of that, I am convinc'd. He weaves and jokes that the olde people of the moore who use enchantments and remedies are Pagan people at one with the Prince of Darkness.

'Horse leavings!' says I to him. 'And big lumps of it at that!'

The Reverende is not pleased with my attitude, and forthright says he will dismiss me if I continue in suche a manner.

I says to him: 'These people do no harme. We are but an olde land, older than that of Englande. We have more to offere and for that we shoulde be thankfulle.'

Unconvinced he is and so I finde myself unable to sustain my peace with the man. He is at greater sin than the people he chastises for turnip stealing at Gothers. I finde myselfe here beneath this fading lighte unsure of my ends here. Now I shall write to my mother asking her advice. Though this place pleases me and the people I like wonderously well, I finde myself thinking more of leaving the churche and working withe my handes. But na'more. I must forget suche worries and live on, for soon the Christ-mas approaches. Then there shalle be muche merrie-making and good thynges to eat. Praise to my Lorde.

T.T.

OF A BROKEN CHAIN

THE first tourists of the summer had camped themselves out on Charlestown beach, determined to catch some of the Cornish sunshine. They stayed into the early evening, until their pink skins began to fade, and then they crunched back along the pebbly beach, up the steps, under the tunnel and over the gates of the harbour.

Clara and Mary surveyed the scene from a bench above the beach. Naked tots ran into the sea and giggled. Old men with pipes and newspapers rested with their backs to the cliff face, and the fathers of the tots strolled down past the whitewashed and pink-painted cottages, their hands full of melting ice creams.

Somehow, down here, Mary felt intimidated by Clara, and for the first time she felt an old woman. It was the little things, the way her daughter asked her questions, the way she helped her up the steps. Whereas before they had been equals, there was now a subtle difference. Somehow Mary knew it was unavoidable. Her daughter was leaving her. She had been promoted and had been offered a better position in Exeter.

For Clara, it was the moment of escape, a chance that was welcomely grasped. She was leaving in the morning.

'How do you feel about tomorrow?' Mary asked.

'I'm excited. I'm not really nervous...' Clara replied, her gaze set on the Channel's horizon.

'And what about Chris?'

'What about him... It was okay for a while, but I don't think he's for me.

I'm not looking for someone like him. Anyway, at the moment I'm not really interested in men.'

Her mother could only remain silent. Clara's last words were cutting, almost as though they were aimed at her.

'It'll be a change. Just what I need in life...'

'What?'

'The new job. Moving to Exeter. It'll be good to live somewhere else.'

With these words, Mary could feel her daughter slipping away from her. The one remaining part of her life with Tom. Tears formed in her eyes, but she was brave enough not to cry. Life had hardened her well.

Clara's thoughts turned to me and the words we had exchanged over seven years before. Now she could put herself in my position. Then her thoughts turned to last year. The ordeal of the cot death for me. She could not wish on anyone the agony of their baby dying.

Sometimes, passing in her car down Trenance Road, she would half look into the pottery and see me in there, my long beard now greying slightly. Now the man; not the youth she had loved. She turned to her mother.

'It'll be okay,' she said. 'Don't worry.'

And she took hold of Mary's hand and led her down the steps. They walked back around the near side of the harbour, past the pink Pier House Hotel and the rusty harbour crane that never seemed to be used. Opposite were slung the iron chutes where the powdered clay used to run down into the hulks of ships. Now they were bent double like the legs of insects, but a whiteness still stained the iron. Years of rain had not flushed it all out. Never would either.

By the time the warm rays of heat had transformed to a sea breeze and the twilight was falling, Clara and Mary were travelling back in her new Vauxhall to the cottage at Carroncarrow. That night, Clara did not sleep the best. As for Mary, she could not sleep at all, once hopping out of bed to put socks on her strangely cold feet. If I had been there I would have said it was the old magic of Tom the mystic after her company. Mary thought it rather more his cold spirit haunting her.

Clara was up before dawn in order to drive to Exeter in time for an induction day at her new job. Later, she was to move into a flat she had found to rent for the time being. Up on Greater Longstone's tip, the police broadcasting tower was flashing.

Clara let the cat in and said goodbye to her mother. The car started first time, and as she drove over the downs, along the Roche road and out on to Goss Moor, she felt she was pulling a strong chain to breaking point. And then, when she turned around and could not see the Cornish Alps any more, she accelerated and a link broke.

A strange thing happened to the two women who had contact with me. There was a reversal, a topsy-turviness, an inside-out, a change around. A progression away from the woman I had first fallen in love with. They were no longer the same people who entered stage right. The clay had changed them. A swap had occurred.

In her cocoonment, the introvert, the shy flighty moth-girl that was Clara emerged from her larva stage as an extrovert, a stunning career girl who broke a thousand hearts with a silver pen in her crimson-lipsticked mouth.

The cream tights were gone, replaced by black stockings decorated with ribbons. A change in the eye, more cutting, harder, easy for her to control her tears. The break-up was over. She was ready to begin herself. The skin of her past shed off and cast away. Off came her long hair; now her style angular and punky.

She was aggressive. She knew what she wanted. Nothing would stop her. and she could feel the change. The transition was not a quick one. It was gradual and it took time for her to learn that she was changing. Beneath her was still that softness, the something special, yet now it was completely camouflaged. It would take a lifetime for that to break out again.

She shielded herself and walked a line that would never break her heart again. She even walked on the cracks in the pavement.

And it was the horror story; the two of them bound tightly in a metal chair. The electrode helmet on their heads with spaghetti wires. The flash of lightning, and then power. The swap of personality. And to both of them the mad professor with ze German accent was myself, though the force that had changed them was larger than that.

It was the clay, birth to death, and death to birth again. So as Clara became the woman she never thought she would be, Chloe did the same, and when she left me she did not build a larva to trap herself inside. Hers was an open cocoonment, a wander in the wilderness, a search for the self.

It was the sort of transformation that again was slow and painful, like the move we all make from youth to adulthood. Chloe dragged her heels in and hung on tight to the desert cactus, but the thorns soon became too sharp and so she began to loose her grip.

She dropped her feminist views, became a more conservative dresser, jumpers from Marks and Sparks, searched the easy way out, eased into chores, became more introverted, shutting up like a tight clam, forever dreading a prising open.

This allowed her to write her book because it was so internalised; her only outlet the black blood pouring down her arm and out of the pen. In her movements, when once she had walked confidently and assuredly, there was now a mellowing, a softer step, more graceful, incorporating the ballet dancing her parents had tried to ingrain into her as a child.

And she held her arms out as she walked, and instead of the sensual stare there was a slight fluttering of the eyelids. And beneath the foundation, the red cheeks, almost apple fresh. Her hair she grew longer, plaiting it Rapunzel-like, and she came down off her high heels. She was stepping on solid ground, and all her casualness had gone. She was on a helter-skelter ride into femininity.

So friends, mark this, as scientists say: 'That everything has an equal and opposite reaction.'

And if on this spinning globe in space, this pair had ever met, had a collision, there would not be a scowl or a pout, there would have been a mutual understanding, parallel lines running in opposite directions, and a look at their former selves, acted so desperately well by the other. Oscar winning roles.

TOBIAS

2nd April 1665.

Twixt duties today, the recording of the death of one Denzil Trudgeon – aged eighty-three by God – and the tidying of the books at the back of the church, I didst have opportunity to chance my skille at writing poetry. I slaved hard to write in the poetic fashion of mine age so that I may read suche lines to Susanna whilst we walk vpon the downs. It is some vague romantic notion I have. Alas, the lines are but laboured. Each time I do read them aloud they are most painful on the ear. They lack subtlety and wit. Accordingly, I do throw them away and seek not to waste any more paper. I do not telle Susanna I did try to write. She might thynk me odd. Therefore, I didst complete my duties early. The Reverende, having a malicious streak, dost give me more work to do. Because yon gravedigger Giles ist with the influenza, I, yea I, must begin to dig yon grave for the body of Denzil. I return home tonight earthy, sweaty and aching in the extreme. The Reverende is an Ass. I want to write this on a hymn book, but restrain myself.

Last night, I did have an almighty strange dream concern'd with the future and about what evil wast coming to the moore in relation to the bloodie shower. I am perplexed but do not let it bother me. I know that it ist the influence of the Reverende. Philosophers say that dreams are but muddles of oure awake thoughts, and not predictions or prophesies. I know that they are right. I swear I will not let suche dreams influence me.

Alack grim tidings come down the nation to this forsaken land. Oure Nation hast declared War on those Dutche devils in the New Worlde. This war, to me at least, seems much of a mistake; it being fought hard and long, only for commercial reasons. Also, of a strange illness affecting people, and that it dost spread quickly. I do worrie that suche an illness may travel to oure parts. For now, though, we have enough upon oure plates recovering from one exceeding hard winter. Several farmers upon the downs hath lost sheep and cattle. Oure Parish needs to work together, else we all shall perishe. I pray for this deare Lorde. Thy humble servant, Tobias. I close.

T.T.

PART FOUR

*'Knowing that Nature never did betray
The heart that loved her; tis her privilege
Through all the years of this our life, to lead
From joy to joy:'*

From Tintern Abbey by William Wordsworth, 1798.

OF TRAVEL

LIKE a bizarre blue and yellow snake, the train wound its way along the track that lay between the red cliffs and sea at Dawlish in Devon, so close to the water that it seemed the next Channel wave might engulf the flimsy carriages.

I sat neatly opposite Sarah. I was riding backwards. On a diagonal to me was Mike, his artificial leg out awkwardly under the table. It was Whitsun. I had been teaching art in Bristol, wading through the introduction of the GCSE syllabus. I was on half term and we had decided on a few days break in Cornwall. It had been their suggestion. A break. They had wanted me to come. Heaven only knew why, but I was there with them; perhaps a third voice, a kind of quasi-translator to fill in the silences.

I had been reading a thick newspaper left on the table. Intermittently, I took sips from a hot Maxpax coffee on the table. Sarah was dozing. Mike spoke softly:

'I remember I was going through here once, and I was asleep. And we went into a tunnel...'

I listened, unsure of what he was about to say next.

'...and the lights in the train...'

He pointed to the tubular lighting that buzzed above us.

'They went out. And I woke up in a tunnel, and for a moment it felt like I was blind. Only for a few seconds, but it really felt like I had lost my sight. Ever had that happen...?'

I said quietly that I had not. I said it must have been very strange. Mike agreed with me. Since the 'accident', as he liked to call it, Mike had been like this – desperate for conversation, a desire to know in himself that he was no different, that he was not a freak; something people turned away from, cast down their eyes. I told him there was no need. I told Mike to just be himself. For now I was tired, and could not be bothered to chat.

It might have been a mistake, for in the half-doze that followed I could see Mike's eyes peering out of the greasy window at the grey sea. The colour of the Falklands. Names that would never be forgotten. Headlines. Bluff Cove, Goose Green, San Carlos, Stanley, Mount Kent; names that just over a year ago he had never heard of. Now names that had been tattooed on his soul. I watched him.

I knew what he was thinking. A telepathy between us, the

same force that had been with us when we sat with our backs to the Longstone. I knew all the facts. The comedy of the war. The arrival of the scrap merchants on one of the earth's most Godforsaken spots. A Southern Hemisphere Hensbarrow.

Two months later, a thousand men had been killed and others like the man in the seat opposite me had been injured. And beneath all this was the politics of it all. Never The Falklands War; it was only a crisis wasn't it?

The train entered the busy estuary at Teignmouth and Mike's eyes fell back to the carriage. Then he watched a guard work his way up through the train. A man across the aisle lifted his eyes from a brick-shaped crime novel. I began to doze again. My thoughts mingling, a ticklish feeling inside my head. I was next woken from sleep with a voice over the Tannoy.

'This is your steward speaking. The buffet car, situated at the front of the train, serves a selection a hot and cold beverages, sandwiches and snacks. May I remind you that the buffet car will close after Plymouth.'

I decided not to wake Mike and Sarah to see if they wanted another coffee; they appeared to be quite content. Carefully, I stepped over Mike's leg into the aisle, fingering in my pocket to see how much money I had left. There was just over a pound. plenty enough for a coffee.

At the end of the carriage the automatic doors hissed open then closed again, while the train rounded a bend in the track. Through the filthy window, the lower slopes of Dartmoor could just be seen. I side-stepped the next door to let a man through with a trail of children, and hands full of coffees and teas. Then I padded through the second carriage. Train people on either side of me. Enigmas. Long coated students, the high hats of their personal stereos just audible, pensioners carrying brown bags holding flasks of tea, a nervous businessman, a girl with red glasses reading a book on psychology.

Then, in a single seat next to the door, with her back towards the front of the train, I saw the form of a woman. She was engrossed in a Word Search, sucking the end of her silver pen, chewing for words. She wore a patchwork jacket, her hair tied back with a black ribbon.

I felt dislocated to see her there. I could only picture Clara with her mother on the downs. The last time I had seen her was when I had rammed hard on her door the night Chloe was in labour.

In the second that it took to pass her, I attempted to acknowledge Clara, but she was filling in letters on the grid before her. I was just another passenger, another annoyance as the automatic doors opened. In the yellow-walled outer part of the carriage I tried to rationalise, but I wanted to step back into the carriage again to check if it was her.

Youth called, beckoned with foxgloves for fingers. I remembered things, all the things we had done flashed through my mind out there.

The way she had shown me something special... the recollection of her being like a moth. The way she came out at night. The way she carried herself.

But I stepped back into real time again and pictured her twisted face the night I had gone for for Mary's help. The links between the carriages rattled.

I listened to the clink of wheels over the points on the approach to Plymouth. At Marsh Mills there were a few clay wagons in a siding. The train was still travelling fast. I walked down the next carriage to the buffet. A race against time now before Plymouth. The dizziness of the rocking motion of the carriage.

I had a quick fantasy of a disaster. A train crashing. Loss of brakes. Crashing into Cornwall. Coming home.

Instead, I waited behind two elderly men for a coffee. The machine slurped out the black liquid into the plastic cup, and I picked up two sugars and a milk. I carried the coffee back up the train, holding it between forefinger and thumb. Flashes of the evening sun entered the carriage, making me squint as I walked.

I decided to walk past her without saying anything. It would save any embarrassment. Keep the lid on things. The door opened. The coffee was hot and it stung my hand to hold it. I grimaced. She was still there. This time the Word Search was lying on her lap. I saw the reflection of her face in the window. My pace quickened once inside. A woman looked at me as I caught her case with my left foot, but I had made it past her.

Then I felt a figure behind me stand up and I knew it to be her. She was leaving the carriage to go to the toilet. I could not resist turning around. My curiosity betrayed me, and she saw me in the middle of the carriage. I saw her mouth my name, the way her cheeks moved when she said the 'B', and in that small thing, the woman fell to the maid, the man into the boy. We were strangers who knew one another. Then she spoke.

'Outside...'

She beckoned. The door clicked twice. I found her standing next to the open window. This time, there was recognition. I saw in her the look of experience. I spoke first.

'Going home?' I asked as interested as I could.

'Yes. To see my mother...'

A chaos of language.

'Where did you get on?'

'Exeter. I'm working up there now. Gone up in the world... how about you? You sold the pottery then?'

'Long story... I'm in Bristol now,' I said. 'Teaching art and pottery would you believe?'

This was a cover-up on my behalf to explain my disenchantment and fear of the clayland. I had moved out again. I had needed to escape after the break-up with Chloe. The pottery had gone another summer, and now had a name for itself.

I had wanted to stay. Frank knew that. One more season and we would have been in the big time. But I was fed up with the pressure of running the business, and every day the mine and the pottery jarred my memory. Two important factors had gone, and nothing, I felt, could replace them. In the end I sold the business to Frank. Frank kept the name. I would visit him regularly when I was on the moor, though there was always an awkwardness, perhaps because of a time neither of us wanted to remember.

The last year had seen me complete a teacher training course in Bristol, supplementing what money I had left from my share of the pottery with some work in an up-market art shop in a modern shopping centre.

Then the Bristol post. The Bishop's High School. At least I had an order now, a regularity, a reality.

After I told her this, or a story like it, I changed the subject. 'How is your mother? I haven't seen her for a while. You know, I don't get back as much as I'd like to...'

She did not answer immediately. A slight delay... a frown on her face. 'Actually, she's not too good. I learnt this week she's got cancer so...'

Momentarily, I forgot the situation on board the train and thought back to my first encounter with Mary. I thought of warts and watercolours.

'She's wasting away,' Clara continued. 'It's in her lungs...'

'I see. Can't she make anything up? Her remedies?'

'Not this time. Not for cancer...'

I added the sugar and milk to my coffee. Clara seemed ill at ease.

'Are you by yourself?' she asked.

'Well. Not really. I'm travelling down with Mike and Sarah.'

'Oh... How is he? I haven't seen him since...'

'He's okay. He's coping with the disability well enough. It's the memories that get him...'

'Yes. It must be difficult.'

There was a pause while I took another mouthful of coffee, then she asked: 'So why are you going back to Cornwall?'

'Just a weekend break... you know, while the half-term is on. Get away from it all, as they say.'

We had been chatting while the train was waiting in Plymouth station to take off the buffet car. It now began to pull away over the viaduct which took the train over rows of terraced house and council flats. The two of us continued to chat. I had finished my coffee. The barriers were down now and both of us were afraid of losing our ground.

And somewhere in there, between the rattle of the carriages, between the years we had not seen each other, there was a twist, a zing of feeling between these strangers on a train who now seemed so far removed from the clayland. Somewhere, something was holding us back, a recall of the hurting perhaps. Recall of a whiter time, an innocence.

'I'd better get back... Mike and Sarah'll be wondering where I've got to...'

'Of course...' Clara said, gesturing to me with both hands to hurry back.

An escape route had been negotiated. The train creaked over Brunel's bridge. Below the choppy brown Tamar. Boats bobbing. Children waving. Clara felt the turmoil of her own thoughts. She picked up her Word Search once inside the carriage. She longed to say something more, something plausible, but it came out as simply:

'Be seeing you then...'

It sounded wrong. Too positive, but with a vagueness attached to it as well. I caught the tempo of this, and responded the same.

'Yes. Good to see you. I expect I'll be back up Hensbarrow sometime...'

I gave her a small silly wave, then continued up the blue carpeted aisle of the train.

SHE watched my form disappear through the automatic doors as if I might materialise somewhere else after stepping through there, like some character from Star Trek. The train wound into Saltash station. She watched the tourists' eyes. Cornwall, land of legend. She saw the children's sand castle eyes.

But Clara's journey was no holiday. The granite and clay beast that was Cornwall seemed to heckle her. It was sunny outside, but inside she was freezing like an icicle. She felt her heart stiffen some more. Sometime, somewhere she hoped this would end.

OF PASSING

...which all things must.

MARY was lamenting the Longstone. She did not really know why, but somehow, since the Longstone had gone from the moor, something had gone with it. As if there had been a spirit there, a talisman, a guardian of the Downsers, a saintly item taken away.

For she felt everything was slipping. Not only was Hensbarrow being turned upside down, now it was slipping away from her. She was losing her power, she felt. She could not find the flowers any more, as if they had been scared away.

Everywhere she looked there was sand, sand from Blackpool, Greensplat, Longstone's and Gunheath. She staggered down the road towards the overgrown ruins of Blackberry Row. From the ruins she saw a mirage of her marriage. All gone. Her lips dry when he kissed her. The tips of her fingers chapped. Her skin red. She saw the sun rising behind the tip, the two of them in the shadow of the pyramid, their faces as black as gorse, the corners of their mouths hanging down pointing to pit bottom.

She remembered the cruel neighbours. The reason why she stayed young looking, her preparations. Poor magician Tom, his ashes nesting on the downs. And then she saw herself following him into the mirage, ending the way a film does. Credits up on the screen.

It was the wrong day for lamenting. It was the wrong day to have cancer; a day so hot that the corrugated ashen tips themselves seemed to sweat. Tarmac blistering. Heat rising. Earth warming. Mary had reached Chutney Well.

She drank the water that was sacred to her, thanked God for it and pushed the taste of Hensbarrow around her mouth. The water was cool and delicious. Above was a children's painting sky, bluer than blue. Below, a hose lagoon that could have carried the Roman Navy. It was water that rang true, still and easy. Everywhere else was white, a whiteness that blinded the eyes, a light strong as the sun. Reflections of a star on the slopes of the tips and the cups of the pits.

Towards Great Longstone's sat the erect tower of a drilling unit. Men in sunglasses with bronzed bodies stood around the machinery, occasionally wiping sweat off their foreheads.

Mary saw the orange hard-helmets of the men controlling the borer, guiding the drill into the body of Hensbarrow; it was like some kind of absurd autopsy. She saw spurts of dust flung out into the air, heard the rattle of metal on rock.

She pictured the samples coming up; cylinders of rock-like, solid toilet roll-tubes to be laid in rough wood cases. They would then be taken back to the laboratory to be tested. Samples, sections of the moor, like the samples the doctors had taken from her. Samples of her lungs. Then the recognition of something unwanted. The growth inside. Cancer, the word you say almost as a whisper, like you can't believe it is there, like Father Christmas; born of fairy tales. Children beware...

Mary carried the bucket back up the lane. A clay company Land Rover passed her by. The driver put up his hand. Mary nodded. She rested half way up, feeling her lifeblood ticking away. She scanned the downs over to Noppies.

Dear friends, the clay company, known here as Mohammed, do not let the mountain come to them. They move mountains. Eight tonnes of raw material must be dug out to produce one single tonne of clay. That's where the earthmovers come in. Giant Dinky toys; scrapes, diggers, excavators, trucks, loaders with buckets like the jaws of hell, nutcracking the surface, munching the soil.

Mary could hear them, feel them rumbling along the sand roads. Whole tracts of the downs destroyed in a single hour; earthy smelling metal shovels biting into the downs, lifting hummock and heather away. Foxgloves toppling, animals screaming for cover from the attack. The machine's giant black wheels leaving a tread the width of a normal car.

They were all larger than life, the men who drove these creatures somehow out of scale. And for them it was just a day's work, a single shift. But Mary could see it all going, taking the spirit away. Boring into her. They say it is a long way from pick and shovel, digging with these beasties.

She knew that to be true – too true for her liking. As she blinked another fifty tonnes was carried away. Then she closed her eyes and imagined the Longstone crying at night. In the pit, the hole she could no longer see the bottom of, the hole she imagined might go straight through the centre of the earth to Australia, walls of clay were dissolving, being eaten away.

Above the noise, Mary managed to hear the song of a single skylark and this gave her renewed vigour to reach the top of the sand road and on to the new Tarmac road. She felt hot, her armpits wet, the bottom of her back warm. She felt light-headed. Unreal. A mirage. But this time a wash of pain exuded from her lungs and she gagged violently.

A rush of blood and sick entered her mouth, and she spewed it on to the verge. In her contortions, she kicked over the bucket of water and fell down on the verge. Trails of sick and phlegm strung down on to her dress. Then she heaved again. This time the pain was too much and she collapsed. Behind her, the drill continued its remorseless grinding. Above, the skylark sang as though nothing had happened.

MARY'S collapsed body was found by a clay employee on his way home to St Austell from morning shift. He was a driver of one of the bulldozers she had been watching. Initially, he thought her to be dead, but then he saw the slow rise and fall of her ribcage.

When she was admitted to hospital in Truro half an hour later, his hands were still greasy from the work he had done on the machine that morning, and he smeared one of the plastic surfaces. Mary had been talking to him throughout her ordeal, and by the time he got her there he felt some degree of friendship towards her. For some unearthly reason she kept chittering about the Longstone.

In his bones he could tell this was no ordinary woman. Time oozed from her. But all the while he sat there he wanted an explanation, a confirmation. Instead a male nurse came out and spoke.

'Mr Roberts?'

'Yes.'

'Mrs Cundy is in intensive care now. She has cancer, and she suffered a severe stoke today. She asked me to thank you. I'm sure her relatives will be in touch with you. We could do with more people like you around...'

And that night, Mr Roberts, a passing stranger, carried home the image of Mrs Cundy, and Hensbarrow gained another piece of mystery and another story.

WHEN the taxi dropped Clara at the end of the path leading to Carroncarrow cottage, she was tired after the train journey, and still perplexed after seeing Ben. Then, behind the rhododendron bushes she saw a white car. Two policemen were knocking on the door of the house. They were about to leave when they saw Clara's form in the twilight.

'It's my mother isn't it?' she shouted.

The policemen looked at one another. The approach they had been taught in training was shattered.

'Are you the daughter of Mrs Mary Cundy?'

'Yes.'

'I'm afraid your mother has been admitted to hospital after she collapsed whilst walking today...'

Clara listened. The other constable told her what had happened.

Inside the cottage it was pitch black as Clara fumbled for the light switch. She sat down in her favourite chair, hoping to gain some comfort from it. The policemen did their best to help, but ten minutes later she was alone in the house. All around were her mother's things, the silken embroidery left half-done, her wash paintings. Somehow, she knew they would never be finished.

She made herself a black coffee in an attempt to calm her nerves. The house was cold. The hot drink warmed her. When she had drunk most of it, she went out madly into the night and did not stop running until she reached a phone box. She rang directory enquiries and they found the hospital number. She rang to be told the news herself. Sometimes, we need to be hit a second time. Like the first is only a dream.

'Stable,' was the information that came back. A harshness in the nurse's words. Clara was seeking something more than 'stable'. The hospital advised her to visit in the morning. And yes, they did realise the circumstances but this was all they could do for now. There was a pause, then an adamant good night. The phone clicked.

Clara eased into the corner of the phone box, the floor clay dusty. There was now the sound of her own erratic breathing, a slight draught from a smashed window pane. Next to the phone box stood the chapel. And with the receiver still in her hand she called to God and prayed for her mother.

CLARA was travelling by rail again. She had chosen a forward looking seat on the Penzance train. She had decided to travel to Truro by train because it seemed quicker, a more urgent way to travel.

The train trickled out of the hillside mass of St Austell, first crossing the great viaduct that spans Carthew Valley. Her glance was greeted by the tower block of flats in the town, a monolith to the town planners of the '60s, and another awkward jar against the sky. Then, along Gover Valley, cutting through the north side to cross over at the top. She barely looked up the remainder of the valley where Biscovillick and Blackberry Row stood. Only the white masses of the downs did she see, but that was only because they were virtually impossible to ignore.

The train travelled on, Clara's mind running with thoughts about her mother. Flashes of childhood. Flashes of love. Then, as they passed by the smoking towers of Blackpool Mill, she resolved to keep her mind blank, shunting out what was to come. Shunting out like the clay wagons... Opposite, a man edged off his seat to talk with her.

'Mighty weird landscape isn't it?' he said.

His words did not register. He was a thin crew-cut American. Next to him sat his wife, her make-up so thick that it gave her the appearance of being a sad pierrot. He tried again.

'Mighty weird isn't it? The landscape?'

'Yes,' Clara replied, observing the man's wallet, thick with credit cards and £20 notes.

'It's the first time we've been to Cornwall.'

The Cornwall of what he had said came out wrong. Too long.

Corn-wa-ll. It was a tuppeny ha'penny place. He made it seem the size of Texas. Clara could have told him her story, but she thought it easier not to. So, she disguised her accent and replied with the innocence of a tourist.

'Mine too.'

At the back of her mind, Clara had a theory. Something she had seen on television, or picked up in a local newspaper. There had been other cases. Lung cancer, caused by radon gas. It was found in the belly of granite that had held her mother all her life. The gas was said to exist in areas of high granite concentration and could cause cancer if breathed in over a long period because it was radioactive.

It was in the waiting room of Trenance Hospital that she began to formulate this theory. Revenge of the earth. All the years of eating into the moor. Her mother now a victim of the moor's revenge. An innocent. Cancer washing through her. Chunks of her lungs destroyed. And for this moment she hated those who mined. Hated her roots. Hated the Cornish, the moles of the human race.

When, half an hour later, she was allowed into her mother's room she saw only a white body. The hair was still blonde, but matted on the hospital-stamped pillow. Several tubes entered her. She was surrounded by green-screen monitors, gently beeping. That was irony itself. Her mother, the homeopath, now in hospital, hemmed in with technology; the future keeping her alive.

Clara could barely kiss her. Though physically close on the bed, she seemed so far away from her. Then came the emotion, a draining of her fears.

'Mother... mother...'

'Clara me dear. I was worried about you...'

Underneath, she was the same.

'I know. I know. It's you we should be worried about.'

Her mother's face heaved a smile. Clara could feel her slipping away. A desperate grope for the right words. She could tell her mother was thinking.

'What is it?'

'It's all right maid... I feel Tom beside me. Calling me...'

'Tom?'

Clara could barely believe this. Mary nodded and turned in her bed. Her eyes were set on the window. A slight warmth entered the room from the morning sun.

'Go see the Longstone for me...'

Clara listened.

'I wanted to touch it once more... Feel the old stone... for me...'

'I will mother. Don't worry...'

After this, her mother's words became unintelligible, another language almost. Incantatory. A chanting rhythm. Something about books that she mumbled. Clara transposed herself. She saw before her now not her mother but something more; the last of an old way, a Downser dying...

Clara stayed a further hour with her mother, watching as the blip on the monitor became a steady small line. Medical staff came in and a doctor spoke to her.

'A hard battler your mother...'

'Yes.'

'There really isn't much you can do.'

'How long before...?'

'We really can't tell.'

The doctor brushed back his hair with his hand.

Clara turned. This time she was tearful. Too late now. Slipping. Desperately, Clara clutched Mary's hand to stop herself falling. It was white, cold and damp. A young nurse entered and escorted her outside. She hired a taxi to the station and travelled back to St Austell.

On Hensbarrow it was windy. It was quarter to five, the men of the moor were listening to the football results. Arsenal 1, West Ham 0... At Greensplat, she made a phone call. 'Mrs Mary Cundy died at ten minutes past four.' Clara walked back up to Carroncarrow, a scowl aimed at the chapel.

Legends...

SARAH was helping Mike into his wheelchair when I knocked on their door. The hotel had been helpful, giving Mike the only ground floor room. It was Sunday morning. A smell of bacon and toast eased into the bedroom from the dining room across the corridor.

A few residents congregated in the conservatory looking out over the wide estuary that was Carrick Roads. Towards St Anthony Head sat an oil rig platform, Eiffel-like.

First, small talk.

'Think they'll ever find any off Cornwall?' said Mike, pointing to the structure.

'What?'

'Oil.'

'I don't know. They say there is. Perhaps when the North Sea runs out... Make Falmouth a boom town anyway.'

Mike looked at the folder of documents I was carrying. He was curious. 'What's that?'

'Something we need to talk about... I found something out in Truro. Look... What are you doing today?'

Sarah entered the conversation.

'Just going to have a quiet day really. Mike and I might go round the waterfront...'

'Well. Can I borrow the car?'

They had hired a car for the weekend.

'Sure. What's on?'

'Well later, I want to drive back home...'

'To Hensbarrow?'

'Yes.'

'But I thought you didn't want to go back there this time,' Mike said.

I paused.

'Yes. I know,' I finally said. 'But things have changed.'

I cleared a small table in the room and carried it over to Mike and Sarah. Then I tipped out the documents on to the table, my hands racing over them.

'These are photo-copies from histories of Cornwall. William Kay, Tonkin and Gilbert, and then this diary of this fellow, Tobias Trebilcock. They talk about a shower of blood on claystone on Hensbarrow in 1664...'

'So...?'

'Don't you remember Mike? Tom told us. Remember... when he came back from hospital. His wood was stolen. You were there.'

Mike thought. Sarah's face was puzzled.

'Yes,' Mike said, 'I remember something about it... but only very vaguely.'

'See this blood shower... it shaped peoples' lives back then and has done from then until now. Like a sort of prophecy. When it rains red, it's a warning of something bad. The moor having its revenge on the people who live on it. We betrayed nature. Look, see here...'

I laid the Trebilcock diary fragments I had found in front of Mike.

'The Dutch and English Wars, the Great Fire of London and the Plague. All just after 1664...'

'But that's because it was 666, the year of the Devil, the number of the Beast,' said Sarah.

'True,' I said. 'But see, it was predicted. That's the thing. And the same thing that predicted those things also predicted the things that have happened in our lives...'

'Like what?' Mike asked.

By now, I was wandering around the room. Spit flew from my mouth as I hastened to get the idea out.

'The cot death...'

Sarah and Mike's faces lowered.

'It rained on me one night. After Tom's funeral. I know it...'

'You sure?' Mike said laughingly.

'Damn right I'm sure. All right then... you... your leg. It must have been the same thing.'

'No. That was in the Falklands.'

'True... but it could have rained on you before...'

'It's creepy Mike,' Sarah said.

Mike was still sceptical. I continued.

'Like as if it's Hensbarrow having its revenge. The clay getting its own back...'

'But the first recorded shower, that was in 1664... They started mining clay in 1746...'

'Yes,' I said, 'but the thing is, there must have been earlier diggers.'

I thought aloud.

'The Phoenicians. Some say they streamed for tin at Carclaze. They could have dug clay as well. There must have been diggers in the Middle Ages... and even before that...'

'The Longstone?' Mike said.

'Of course. Yes. That was set there by an earlier digger...'

Suddenly, the history became the reality. There was a silence in the hotel room. The Longstone was an experience common to us all. We had all touched it. Touched history.

I sat at the window. Mike and Sarah could only see me in silhouette and though I hardly knew it my form must have resembled John Opie's drawing of the ageing Cookworthy. Privately, we all thought of the blood. Time stood still. A brake on a spinning globe.

There was a jumble of ideas in my mind. My eyes saw Tom, a clay childhood, Clara, Mary the witch. Remembrances. Thoughts of a time past. The cows stuck in the mica. The blast. Black raven-like Shackletons. Working the hose. Smashed plates in the pottery. A dead son. Chloe gone. A tiny part of me, dead. And now, I knew it was the moment to make a history of a time to come.

'Pry wyn. Pry wyn,' I mouthed, 'I've got to get up there...'

'Pry Wyn?' Sarah asked.

'The old tongue,' I said. 'In the Middle Ages, that's what the Cornish called it...'

'What?'

'White clay,' I said softly. 'Tom told me.'

IT TOOK me a little over three quarters of an hour to reach the clayland. On the way there I drove badly, erratically, breaking speed limits. Though the car, a Ford Escort, was new and well designed, I had crunched the gears often and let the car stall pulling out of Truro.

I smelt badly as well, my armpits soaked with sweat, crotch warm, my trousers damp. I was shaking slightly. A cold shiver came over me as the car rose to the top of Watch Hill. I looked over the same hedge I had as a boy, only now, where the gorse had blazed, it was yellow with flowers. A few sheep grazed between the bushes, greasy wool trails on the olive coloured thorns.

I knew I was behaving stupidly, but now that I had made the discovery something demanded that I should be on this moor. The granite magnet pulled me from afar, reeling me in; a small fish struggling on the sand.

By the time I arrived at Longstone's clay works, the toytown red body of the car was splattered with clay. I was wearing sandals, hardly the shoes to wear around the claywork.

Looking back towards Old Pound, I saw the pink wash of my parents' cottage. I imagined Tessa beside the fire, her eyes resting on the reds and oranges. She loved the rich colours.

I finally stopped where I should not have been. I was trespassing on clay company property. I stopped the car and got out and left the radio on. Jimmy Savile was going through some oldie records; 1966 was the year. I strived for orientation. Janey Gummow's house was where? And Karslake houses?

I tried desperately to recollect. The land had changed so much. There were sad patches of heather between the white sand. I was running now, through the muddy tracks of scrapes and loaders, through diesel-coloured puddles. Imagination taking over. Trying to recall. Recalling a time before I even came to Hensbarrow. Take away the tips. Take away the holes. Make a wish for the clay not to be there.

Now I was skipping, kicking the occasional stone, shouting, swearing at the land. Above, the barely visible trail of a Nimrod, a pencil line in the blue sky.

Madness overran me, the cork bursting out of the bottle. Angry champagne spilling out. I jumped some more. The car was now a good way behind me. I failed to notice a Land Rover turning the corner of the sand road on its way up from Littlejohns. I was getting closer to the edge of the pit. Heather creeping down, regaining what it had lost.

I stopped there, my eyes streaming, the wind oozing the tears out. I had no intention of jumping. I just wanted to say something. Stand above it. Become the master and not the slave.

Five minutes passed. Eventually my anger faded. Pain gone. My feet were wet and sandy. There, on the edge of the pit, a few feet from me, was a small clump of foxgloves. I ripped one up, its root system enormous. Then, from behind, was a voice'.

'All right there?'

I turned around, gesturing half-heartedly with a foxglove sword. When I saw my absurd position I dropped the plant. The voice was a clay company Cap'n. Around his shoulder was slung a walkie talkie radio which crackled in the afternoon air.

'I was just looking...' I said, my voice reverting to childhood.

'No problem boy,' said the Cap'n. 'Only, by rights, you shun' be up here.

Is that your car back there?'

'Yes.'

'I'll give 'ee a lift back to 'un.'

I climbed into the Land Rover. We crossed the sand road quickly. The radio was still on. The reception worse.

'Frightened me back there boy...'

I got back into the car.

'Sorry,' was all I could manage.

The Cap'n drove off, the beacon on top of the Land Rover flashing idly, as if in recognition of my confusion.

IT IS common knowledge that if one asks a mountaineer exactly why he or she climbs something, like Everest or K2, the answer is most likely to be 'because it's there'. The Cornish climb tips for the same reason, because they are there.

On Longstone's tip, very near the place Tom had fallen a few years ago, stood a figure. In silhouette, it was clear to see she was a female. She had watched the arrival of the red Escort, and the strange motion of the man who had driven it, with a great deal of interest. His was a form she knew, a form she had felt. When the Land Rover had gone, the car did not move. The driver merely sat there, as if in some state of recovery. She began to climb down the tip. Some of the sand was still wet and loose.

The going was easy, unlike most of the other tips, corrugated by weathering and thick with vegetation. To save time reaching the car she walked around one of the settling pools. White bubbles gurgled below her feet as her steel toe-capped boots caught on the duckboards. She had no idea why this man was up here, just a feeling of excitement. A knowing.

But she was also scared. The running and the skipping, the strange contortions of his limbs. Was this the same man?

Beside the old Cap'n's office she frightened some playful rabbits. She jumped over their droppings, then brushed through some heather. The car was not far now. Absurd almost; such a deep red on the white road. The driver's head was back, his side door still open. She could hear music, a dull thud reverberating from inside the car.

She wanted to check her appearance. Were her eyes still red? Her cheeks still ruddy? She felt she had tried to grab its spirit again. Her mouth opened to call his name, but she decided not to. Thirty seconds more and she was with him.

'WHAT are you doing up here? I thought you didn't want to come back...'

I opened my eyes, not a quick jump to life as she had expected, but a meandering flow back to normality.

'Clara?' I said, rubbing my eyes.

'I saw you...'

'Oh.'

I was embarrassed. She hung on to the door.

'I've got some sad news...'

'Your mother?'

'Yesterday,' she said first, then more exacting. 'Ten past four...'

'I'm really sorry Clara.'

My heart froze. My mind on another age. Being time detective. A helter-skelter on a historical spiral. Now Mary as well. I wanted to say more. I turned to face Clara. She tried to discover what I was thinking, but I was asking the questions.

'Did you mother ever speak of a shower of blood? Ever mention it?... Any time... Can you remember?'

'Why?'

'Because it has happened to me... to Mike as well maybe. Your mother... She wasn't meant to die like that. We're caught up... and I know this sounds strange... on a bitter land. A land which takes lives...'

'I don't understand,' said Clara.

'Look... get in. Can we go back to Carroncarrow for now? Later, I want to go back to the Longstone...'

'That's strange,' she said, 'I need to go there as well. Something my mother said. She wanted to feel the stone before she died. Now I'll go myself...'

My thoughts began to re-awaken again. Back in control.

'What time did your mother die?'

'Ten minutes past four, or so the hospital said. Why?'

I said there was no reason, but there was. It was precisely the same time I had discovered the document in the museum about the shower of blood. My own hands were now weapons of death, as if I had gone to Mary and strangled her myself. As if I had opened a story that should never have been read.

It was a chance in a million, I told myself. Coincidence? Then why did my heart race. The downs were becoming unreal. A dream time, but this time a nightmare, a raging nightmare thundering in like the Atlantic clouds.

'Pry Wyn,' I uttered, repeating it over and over again so that to Clara it sounded like a diabolical spell. I started the car and pulled away. The car bounced over the cattle grid at the top of Old Pound, then raced along the new piece of road past Blackpool.

'What's that mean?' Clara asked. 'I know that's what Tom called his house.'

'Everyone knows what that means up here Clara. You've known it from the day you were born, longer than I have,' I said.

'Clay?' she said.

'You got it.'

A few minutes later we arrived at Carroncarrow, my saint-like sandals squelching because of the sladdys I had run through on the downs. Clara opened the door. It was the first time I had been there for several years, yet the smell was the same. The taste of berries. The slight smell of the coal bunker from outside in the back-kitchen. The doll no longer on the chair.

'Tea?' Clara asked.

'No thanks. Sit down...'

When Clara came back into the parlour, I began.

'I've something to tell you Clara; something so strange I barely believe it myself...'

But this was not the story of a young warrior and a beautiful princess. This story was altogether different...

'So we'll go to the Longstone now...' I said, once I had told her. She looked at me from across the room. Her body was cold. There was no fire. The look she gave me was no ordinary look; her eyes pierced my skin, flicked my senses. The same feelings, the same as on the train, same as when we were both caught in the rain. I thought of childish rhymes as I waited for her to speak. 'Ring-a-ring-a-roses' and 'London's burning'.

'No,' she said.

'No? Why not?'

'Because I want to go there in the dark. In the night, as it should be. When they went there...'

'Who?'

She did not answer. Out on the downs the wind blew. Every stalk of heather rippled. Clara came over, her perfume touching me.

'Pry Wyn,' she said, her mouth in an 'O', her finger touching her lips, demanding me to be silent. I brushed a hair from my beard away from my lips. Then strongly, as if her life depended on it, she kissed me, her lips draining all the love she could. A love that had been grassed over. The velvety moles were up, and now both of us could see the earth again.

IN THE moonlight of the small hours, the Longstone had a shade of purple about it. Already, dew was gathering on the lawn of the old people's houses. A Morris van passed along the road, but appeared to take little notice of us.

'Come,' said Clara, and we crept on to the green.

'Some stone,' she whispered half-sillily, half because she was scared. We crossed over the flower bed and leaned against the stone, me with my back to it, Clara astride the acute slope. When our skin actually touched the stone, we recoiled back from it.

'It's warm,' I said.

'Like a body.'

Time entered us. Mind and time becoming one. Some cold kind of explanation desired. My mind back to Tobias. My past... my possible past.

'St Austell's staff. It's a protector. It's with us, only it might not be protecting us now that it's off the downs... Should never have moved it. We shouldn't have played with time.'

Then out of the black of one of the bungalows shone a torch. 'Oi! What's your game? That's nothing to do with you...'

The bright beam drew closer. It was the warden of the bungalows. Clara and I touched the stone once more, then sprinted across the wet grass to the car. In our minds we knew that much had been lost. Surely now, something on this hell-hole of a land could be found.

TOBIAS.

17th April 1665.

Good hearte, I am sorely worried as to the fate of oure nation. Muche talke have I hearde from Sellers, Musicians and Preachers and the like of a monstrous plague whiche has engulfed oure capital. Not having been there myselfe I knowe not what to expect, though by worde of mouth, and tis by this I learne most, Plague leaves children and adults bespeckled, shortly after falling into Death. There ist talke of over halfe the population being affected in this mannere. The stories as to this Plague's origine vary to a considerable degree. I knowe not what to believe. One Sire tolde me that Rats, aye, rodent creatures, broughte the Plague aboard shippes from the Continent, places suche as France and those devils the Dutche, against whom oure War still continues. I am now especially vigilante in destroying these creatures whence I see them. These plagues travell so swiftly. One needs only to looke in the Bible, and my Reverende is quicke to point this out to bothe me and his congregation. I worrie each time a newe pimple appearest vpom my chin. I keep my distance from travellers, though in general they are fewe around the moore. Indeed, I didst hear one rumour of the Plague being present in the nearby Parishes of Tregony and Veryan. Yon outbreake there, I am tolde, wast caused by an infect'd handkerchief, dropp'd by one foolish traveller.

To this ende I thinke back to last yeare and the showere of bloode that didst fall, and my good Reverende's words. I beginne to wondere whether he hadst some morsel of wisdome withinne his skulle. His talke of the bloode showere being a warning dost beginne to make sense, though why I believe it to be so I do not knowe. I had thoughts – and silly thoughts I knowe – that this place might resenteth us Christianising it and mining it, and that the pagan and nat'rel should be left.

Or failing this, it almost doth seem to me a displaced piece of history from the era of that usurper scoundrel Cromwell. Thank heaven he ist dead. I cannot praise those who did take a king's position. Thank the Lorde, King Charles hast regained the throne. I barely can remember the Civil War, but methinks, as do many other noble Cornish, that we should back oure good King.

Alack, I have greate fears about this Plague. Tis a curse of some kinde – cruelle and most eville. Tales come to me in Innes that those who have the Plague have crosses daubed on the doores of their houses. I hope no paint comes to this house by Heaven.

Tonight, I do pray for those souls already withe the sicknesse, and for those already departed. Further, I do pray for all Physicks to findst a quicke cure for this vile Plague whiche grips us wholly. I close.

T.T.

OF THE PAST

...which stories say, was a different place. True or false?

'...I hath heard today of a most strange occurrence vpon Hensbarrow last night, that hath made me sore afraid, so muche so I do not know whether I might have good sleep tonight....

'...For as well as this, around yonder stones on the heather and base of the Moor were marks of bloode. Then, he shows me his back, which is also spotted crimson. Rickard, he says, tis the work of the Devil, and arches his back like that vile spirit...'

I sat in the armchair, re-reading sections of the diary. I was alone. Strange this one. The interconnections; the way none of us are separate from anyone else. It was scary. Real fear. Perhaps people had invented the shower of blood to justify those events. Deep digging. Far too deep. Inventing stories.

But no, not Tobias. He rang true. What I found difficult was why here? That question was unanswered but I did discover other predictions later. And anyway, what could they have done about it, those seventeenth century Downsers. How were they to know of the disasters to hit London and the English nation. They thought it would more likely happen to them in their own land. No, that would come three hundred or so years later on Hensbarrow. But hang on; What of Mike and the Argies? Yes, him as well.

Now for once, I recalled facts. I ignored the fiction, the stories, the legends, and took instead ingrained knowledge from school. Bread and butter history. In April 1665, a terrible plague, even worse than the epidemic of 1625 broke out in the congested slums around St Giles in London.

Facts now – things pushed into my head by my history teacher, the drooping mustached face of Mr Kingdom. The dead numbered over one hundred thousand, a fifth of the population. The plague raged throughout one of the hottest and driest summers people could remember, and people deserted the city for the country.

I imagined boney families striking out in all directions. Then the houses, marked with red crosses, as I had once incredulously imagined my own. Pest houses – what a name! They were primitive isolation hospitals for the plague ridden. I thought of stomach-heaving Baroque churchyards. Hundreds of corpses buried in the same grave. A Renaissance holocaust. Ladders in the mud. Rough wooden coffins if you were lucky. Splinters in the hands of those who were left. And the black clad Puritans said it was the Devil's revenge for the misguided lives people had been living. And when I thought of this, it played on my mind like a mental funeral march. I even tried analysing my own sins.

No sooner was London rid of the plague then it suffered another catastrophe; the Great Fire of 1666. I remembered the time – one o'clock in the early morning of Sunday 2nd September, in a baker's shop in Pudding Lane. The summer had again been hot and so the timber-built houses were dry. The flames soon spread to neighbouring houses. I saw them burning, the sheds and the warehouses along the waterfront – merchandise going up in smoke, the eastern wind strong, fanning the flames.

And the other bit I could remember, the fire did not cross the river to Southwark because there was a gap on London Bridge where houses had been burned down in a previous fire, and the flames were unable to cross the gap.

I was at the same time, pleased and saddened by this good O-level memory.

There was something earlier than this as well, to go along with the 'Ring-a-ring-a-roses...' My primary school in Southend. Twentieth century little voices joying in seventeenth century agony.

'London's burning, London's burning.
Fetch the engine, fetch the engine.
Fire, fire.
Pour on water. Pour on water...'

And I had a thirst for knowledge and could not quench the bloody flame. The fire was snapping down the centuries, calamity spiralling through, and I could feel it falling on to me. Black on to white; the way ink pours from a pen. Reality on to art. There was no escaping it any more. I could smell the smeech in the air.

OF BOOKS

...which are but words on pages, stories, and nothing more, right?

I WAS ready to slide into her. She wanted me to enter her body.

There were a few more touches, a finger running down my back; the feel of my hands cupping her breasts. No longer a boy and maid, now man and woman. She sat on top. She felt my chest. I watched her breasts wobble. Then a wet warmth. Synchronisation. Now we were warm and colourful.

From our lips came pleasant murmurings that no-one else could hear.

The dawn had come. Dull light fell across the bed and touched some of the pictures on the mottled end wall. There was a sweet smell of pot pourri, and for me the smell of a woman's bedroom. I now had little to say to Clara, not for want of saying it but merely because she had taken me so beautifully into a love again, so much so I had lost all speech. I was made mute by her.

She herself had spoken little of her mother's death. She now lay still, my hand draped over her back. Her oval-shaped head lay in a cradle formed by my chest and arm. I decided not to disturb her. But I was now awake and alive, and so decided to watch every second of the dawn and listen to every pat of rain on the roof above. I was listening and watching time.

The cottage was oddly comforting, the furniture all old. A porcelain basin and jug were still kept under the pine dresser. It could have appeared as a designer room in some up-market catalogue for Laura Ashley.

Mary had not intended it to be that way. It had been her home. Nothing more. The sheets felt stiff still, but I felt enormously protected under the white of them. It was a screen blocking things out, sifting only what I wanted.

In my mind I went over the last few hours. The melodramatic chase off the Longstone. 'Silly bugger,' I mouthed, thinking of the warden. I thought of the drive back to Carroncarrow in the rain, the rushed phone call to the hotel in Falmouth to let Mike and Sarah know what I was doing. And then the love we had both wanted.

But still, within me, there was something else. The reason my hand was only draped across Clara's back, why I kept scratching my neck, why sweat sat in the line of my back.

I was restless. It was not the rain that scared me. It rained too often for any red rain to be my concern. No, it was me back on the clay again.

It felt as if someone was watching me. I listened for over an hour in the same position. Clara woke when the rain began to stop.

'You're so hot. Really sweaty,' she said.

When the dawn turned into morning, I jumped out, tickling Clara, and then ran naked down the stairs.

'I'll go for a bath and cool down,' I shouted.

'You need one,' she said, throwing my shirt at me.

Clara put on her undies and went to look out of the window. A black shape loomed in the sky. She watched it circle Blackpool before she called to me.

'Up here. Up here a minute. Come on...'

'What is it?'

'Come and see. You'll like it...'

Still Adam-naked, I ran up the stairs, two steps at a time, and pressed myself against her.

'What?' I said deadpan.

'Over there,' she said, wiping her breath from the window.

I looked.

'It's a Shack...'

'I know.'

'What's that doing up here?'

'Don't know.'

'It must be for some display or something. Not at St Mawgan, though. Theirs is in August...'

'Why do you like them?' she asked.

'I don't particularly...'

'You don't?'

'Just brings back something,' I said. 'Me and your father talking. Ol' Shack he used to say.'

I mimicked Tom's accent. We watched the Shackleton until it disappeared over the brow of Hensbarrow. Then Clara followed me downstairs and we shared a bath, covering our bodies in soap bubbles.

In the afternoon the two of us went walking, just as we used to, across the downs. It culminated in a fern fight on the lower slopes of Halviggan tip. But our joy together was broken when just before tea the funeral director arrived to check the arrangements for the morning. We were walking up the drive when Clara saw the black car in front of the cottage. She dropped the yellow 'Boots and Shoes' flowers she had been collecting, then walked solemnly towards him. I did not bother to pick them up.

In the event, Mary's funeral was short and sweet, not because there was nothing to say but because that was how she had wanted it. Clara and I heard whispers in the small congregation about us being together, and also whether her mother was 'fit n' proper' for a Methodist funeral because it was so rare that she went to chapel.

They knew Mary's was an older religion, not a heathen one, but certainly one that did not need the pretensions of a chapel. I could never quite understand this, since Methodist chapels are among the most basic places of worship in the world. But as Clara said: 'It just wouldn't be right for her...'

At the funeral, the old harangues came up again; the acid comments about her looks, Cornish tittle-tattle. The ruination of twenty years of two people's lives; two lives that should never have been split. Never have been blasted apart. There was a hum of cutting voices in which I could recognise my sister's slightly out of pitch with everyone else's. A tone lower as well.

When the coffin was brought in, I found it hard to resist crying. Clara was already tearful. I was trying to work out why so many had come to Tom's funeral, and yet so few to his wife's. Perhaps they did not know about it.

Perhaps they did not know Mary the way I did. I touched the place where the warts had been. I looked at my digital watch. It beeped one-thirty. I could not see anyone from the claywork, apart from my father.

I looked around during the wistful singing of the first hymn. The preacher, who had cut himself shaving, asked the congregation to pray and they did. While facing down, I tried to comfort Clara. Her sobs were loud now. Her joy had all gone.

For Mary it was over. There were a few euphemisms outside the chapel; the Cornish covering up their fears. Mysticism oozing out of their lips.

'Well... She's gone on,' and 'she bain't got to worry 'bout anything any more, and that's a blessing.'

Pearls of wisdom I thought as Clara and I got into the hearse. It took us down over the moor, down the valley and on to the Truro road. In Truro, she would be burnt and join Tom. I knew Clara would come back, close her eyes and empty her ashes over the moor, just as her mother had done. The Downser way. In slow motion, I imagined the grey particles falling delicately through the mist, then gently through the heather, and finally on to the peat. That's where the clay starts brothers and sisters...

I watched the sad face of my sister as the hearse pulled away. The sparkle gone from her eyes. She, too, no longer innocent.

THE day after, my father was late home because of an incident at work. It happens to all hosemen at least once – a 'runner', that's what they call it. He had been on morning shift. He had swapped over as normal for the last hour on the hose. He never really saw the need to have a radio or any distraction in the hose hut.

He was a perfectionist when washing the clay face. He rounded every rock, like Tom. He cannoned every particle. It had been raining all shift, a sticky heavy rain. Every ten seconds or so he had to wipe the windscreen. In these circumstances he should have foreseen what was about to happen; water building up behind, and in the stope of clay, until the clay could no longer support it.

The result is a mass slide of material. He had been working on a fairly high stope on the bottom of Littlejohn's pit. It is an awful feeling when it comes. A runner – an unstoppable bulk of clay and water.

This one covered the hose and touched the hose hut.

When the clay runs like that, it is scary. You feel you will be washed away as well. My father needed help with this runner. He would need a loader and a gang to dig out the monitor. Outside the hut, the mass was still flowing, oozing down the pit. He stepped out, nuggets of soft clay entering his boots. Walking through liquid white chocolate.

Further down, he waved to the pumpman to ring for the Cap'n. It was still raining. He took off his hat. Still, he could not see him. He imagined him reading the Mayfair and Knave mags in there. Then, down one of the sand roads, came the Cap'n's Land Rover. Seeing the Cap'n, the pumpman came to life and knocked back the pump so that it would not run out of water. The Land Rover trundled across the rock striations. Soon it was with my father. The runner had stopped.

'W'as on Art?' said the Cap'n.

'Hell of a runner.'

'Ee is be buggered...'

'I've never seen anything like it...' said Arthur.

The Cap'n tilted his pit helmet, then fumbled on the dashboard of the Land Rover for his walkie-talkie. Under the Pools coupons and a couple of hose nozzles, he found it, and called for assistance.

'L4 here. Request excavator help at S1. Large runner. Over.'

He heard the radio crackle back.

'Can 'ee hang on here this afternoon Art? We'll have to get the mine manager out here to look at this. He'll want to see you about what happened. Dunnee worry mind. Tin your fault.

Believe you need a change of boots there as well boy...'

But it was not his boots my father was worried about. He felt as though the Devil sat on his left shoulder, and in mock superstition he threw sand behind him. When he had done this, momentarily he thought he may have been blasphemous to act in such a superstition way. The thought however was soon air. Then he began to whistle and walked over to the pressure valve to turn the hose off. The water stopped flowing, and then the clay stopped crumbling.

A brilliantine rainbow was stretching across Gover Valley as I drove down through Trenance Downs. One end began in the housing estate on the opposite side of the valley, then the colours turned northwards, so the other end appeared to fall into the old Halviggan pit. I wondered if I would find any gold there. Probably not, I thought, since the village had long since been decimated.

But the clay industry is not all about decimation. It is an industry conducted with an enormous public spirit. The workforce are part of one massive family, where everyone knows everyone else. Indeed, it would be a severe challenge for any industry to find a more co-operative work force. One could not really go very far with the company by joining as a pit worker, but the money made up for that. And in these times a job for life is a rare thing. And that was what these people were offered; jobs for life.

To the outsider, it would take some time to come to know the codes and values of the industry. They are not to be learned in a day. They go deep. It is these men who, over the years, have learnt the values and come to respect the job they do.

I was considering this as I steered the car around the bends at the bottom of the hill. I knew most of the clay miner's ways. Tom had taught me those...

BACK in the village of Trewoon, several blue and white china clay lorries were rumbling long the A3058, dropping fine particles of clay on to the road. Dust covered the roadside dandelions. And if you were stuck behind one – in a hurry – you thought: 'Why the hell are these things allowed to drive along here?' But that, my friends, is the way of the clay world. Like it or lump it.

The journey into St Austell was being made because we needed groceries. I parked in the oily floored multi-storey car park in Trinity Street and went into Tesco's to buy the things we needed. I took a trolley and wheeled it into the store.

Clara was at the cottage, rummaging through her mother's things, trying to sort out what she wanted to keep. She wanted to do this sooner rather than later. To begin with, Clara sorted out exactly what she wanted of her mother's.

Some of it might go for jumble sales, but after some time at the task she became frustrated with her own ineptitude and her mother's vast hoardings of junk. Her mother's room smelt ill, the furniture dying, clothes rotting. She sat at the dressing table. At first, she tipped the mirror away because she was afraid of seeing her eyes, bloodshot and tear stained. Then she flipped it back and looked at her reflection, as if it were someone else's.

'Mother, mother,' she said softly.

Some of the things she decided to burn. These she put outside, next to the outhouse. There was an old lamp, some damp carpets, a broken easel, one of her cardigans. There was one coat she would never throw away because it brought back memories. Clara took a break from the work and looked towards St Austell, the Saint's town. The air was warmer now, and the rain in the valley had stopped. She could only see a quarter chunk of the rainbow.

After the sunshine had warmed her, she went inside again. This time, she would have a look at the cupboard under the stairs.

She knew what to expect, the small brass key tied to a piece of rust-stained string. This was the key that opened a second cupboard in the well of the main cupboard. She bent over and placed the key in its hole. When she turned it the door opened.

Inside were Mary's books. This was what she had spoken about in hospital – only what Mary had said about them Clara had found unintelligible. She had always known them as 'Mother's books'.

She lifted them out carefully, one by one, and flicked through a few pages, her mother's handwriting jagged and interesting; t's that were never quite crossed, r's with extra loops. They were books containing details of Mary's homeopathic medicines. In reality, they were recipe books; menus from the Dark Ages.

'Clubmoss (Lycopodium clavatum),' she read, 'if cut on the third day of the moon, is good for eye diseases.' Elsewhere, details of Camomile and Scabious or the 'Devil's Bit'. There were many more as well. In some of them were small pressed flowers and leaves, showing exactly the plant pieces to be used. They were beautifully illustrated as well.

In the twelfth book was a collection of pen and ink maps of the downs, detailing where each plant could be found, along with the best week in the best month to pick them.

She scanned the latter entries. They were sad. Her mother had noted changes in the climate, made notes of things like the eruption of Mount St Helens and condemned the use of aerosols which, she said, were changing the weather. 'Things are not as they used to be,' she had written in capitals.

Clara looked on the shelves in the cupboard. There were tiny blue and green glass bottles of herbs, leaves and roots, minute mushroom pieces, mouldy festering things that appeared to serve no useful purpose, but undoubtedly did. There were many more in the kitchen. Then, under a tin of spoons and palates, was another, slightly newer book.

The hand inside was different. This time, it was closer to her own. These were the things Tom knew. Mary had got him to write them down. Ley lines stretching across the moor, ancient pathways, sites, scattered stones on the barrow. At the end, all he knew about the clay.

His was a tiny hand, and she had difficulty in reading it. It was a book of the old ways, Tom's signature at the end. The power she held in her hands made her shudder, shiver at the enormity of it all.

The key on the wall was not only the key to that small cupboard, but also the answer to many of man's mysteries; the mythologies of time. The disbelief that her mother and father had the power to solve them...

The doorbell rang. Clara put the book on the shelf and shut the cupboard. She recognised my mother's thin figure at the door. Behind her stood Tessa. She opened the front door.

'Clara. Hello,' said Pat. 'Ben not in?'

'No. He's gone into town...'

'Oh...'

She paused for a second.

'Can I help?'

'Yes,' she replied. 'It's a delicate matter...'

She brushed Tessa's coat as she talked. A clayey streak ran down one of the arms.

'About Chloe.'

'Oh.'

'This letter arrived this morning for Ben. It's from America, so we think it's from her... I'm sorry, I was hoping to catch him alone, but there's no use beating about the bush... you know what happened anyway.'

Clara did not mind, but she was interested in what the letter was about. She placed it on the sideboard.

'I'll give it to him... Don't worry...'

'Thanks. Sorting out are you?'

'Yes, but there's so much stuff. I'm going to have to burn it.'

They gazed about the house. There were a lot of things to be burnt.

'What about the paintings?' asked Pat.

'I'll keep those,' Clara replied, 'I can't throw them away. Besides, I like most of them...'

'Well. Shall we give you a hand to get the fire going. I think we can do that between the three of us, don't you?'

'That'd be helpful if you've got time,' said Clara. 'We'll begin in the cupboard.'

Carefully, Clara moved the books out from under the stairs and put them on the Formica-topped wooden table in the kitchen. She admired their dust-free covers, and the way they were bound. They had a medieval appearance – the paper creamy, thick and rich, possibly hand made. Tempting to write on.

'There's some paraffin in the outhouse.'

'Okay. We're moving the stuff to the back of the garden... That bare bit of earth. Is that all right?'

'Fine. Yes. That's lovely,' said Clara, knowing she should be helping. The books had never interested her this much. Her mother had told her about them when she was a child. It was once when she was fetching some water from Chutney. Then they got back and she showed her. They were diamonds in a bed of granite.

MY car would be heard coming up the drive, coming to a halt on the gravel outside. She would give time for the car to rock into the right place in the potholes where both of us parked, then listen for the door shutting. Clara ran to open the front door. I was digging in the hatchback of the car. I brought out several bags of food and one large cardboard box of groceries.

'Hi ya,' I said.

Clara moved forward, her words babbling like Chutney Well.

'Ben... I've found mother's books. All the books she kept of all the medicines. Where to find the plants. Everything. Tom's written some stuff as well. All he knows... I'd forgotten they were there, what they meant...'

I dropped the shopping.

'Show me,' I said.

We went back into the cottage.

'They're in the back-kitchen,' she said.

'Mother's here is she?'

'Yes. She's doing the fire with Tessa.'

Clara entered the back-kitchen, but the books had gone. Immediately, she looked to the top of the garden. Tessa was tottering up the path with the books. She had the first in her right hand ready to throw on to the fire. The flames crackled. Smoke bellowed up over the tip.

'No!' Clara screamed, 'not the books! We want them!'

My mother looked astonished. Tessa was already at the fire. Precariously, she dangled the first book over the flames, watching them lick the cover. Then mother understood. She took the book from Tessa and moved her away from the fire. One was singed but still readable.

'Clara say everything burned,' cried Tessa.

'I know my love... don't worry.'

The stack of books toppled over on to the damp grass. Clara ran up the path and held me. We comforted the confused Tessa and took the books inside.

OF A DEPRESSION

...which may be caused by: 1 a lowering of atmospheric pressure; 2 low spirits.

TOWARDS the west, grey rain could be seen coming down in sheets, thunderous, the sky reddish with pain, while on the open body of the downs a siren reverberated as Tessa and my mother walked back across to Noppies on the new road.

The Tarmac was still clean, hardly yet ingrained with any white dust at all. My mother was walking quickly, pulling her dawdling daughter, who was picking hard-heads and launching them into the air. The few birds on the moor had also risen into the air and were flying southwards.

The siren was intensifying. There would be a blast soon. Every time she heard that noise, she thought of the man who had been killed; killed for the sake of stone in that first week they had moved down here. When the blast came, she stopped momentarily and heeded the cloud of dust that blossomed in one of the stopes of the pit.

Then they walked on. This road was a new way for her, a new way of seeing the moor. Usually she kept to the tracks, the way the saints had walked, but as the sand piles grew larger the tracks became invisible. That was the world she lived in, and she was forced to accept it.

Back at Carroncarrow, she could see the black smoke of the fire they had built. She could still lick the smoke that lined the inside of her mouth. Beside her, Tessa was singing. Not normal singing, but an atonal chant, semi-holy.

Sometimes, she wanted to hit her daughter, even though she was now a young woman, or leave her with someone else. But this was not one of those times. Tessa's incorrect face looked at her mother. She sang with her daughter. This time not a humour to make Tessa feel she was part of everything, now a true joy. Something only the saints knew of.

And when they arrived back home, Tessa made a cup of tea for both of them, without any assistance.

Mother and daughter's peace was interrupted by the arrival of my father. The back door opened and a clay covered, damp smelling figure stood before them. Beyond the door, my father's bike stood on the floor, not carefully placed as normal between the wall of the kitchen and the outhouse, but a scattered metal frame on the yard.

His leggings, normally tightly rolled with a large elastic band, were now strewn over the path. It was only now she realised he was several hours late from work. She spilt some of the tea from her mug.

'Had a runner,' he said slowly.

She did not know what to say.

'Bleddy mess. Fed up with it up there.'

'It's no good being like that...' said my mother.

'Have you got any clean clothes?'

'In the airing cupboard, where they've always been...'

She had heard the term runner before. He would come home from one of the shifts and tell her about them. This time it seemed more serious.

'Have they got it cleaned up yet?' she asked.

'Got a loader coming up there...'

She thought back to the caterpillar loader that had bounced past them along the new road.

'We saw it... walking back.'

'Been over Carroncarrow have you?' he asked, reaching into the airing cupboard and stepping out of his boiler suit at the same time.

'Yeh.'

'How's Clara?'

'Okay. They've been sorting out...'

'Oh?'

'Found some old books of Tom and Mary's...'

'Books?'

'They reckon they are important.'

Arthur sat down in the kitchen wearing only his underwear. His wife poured him a cup of tea. He spoke.

'I've had enough of it. Going to take early retirement. Today was the last straw. Bleddy clay crowd. Sometimes I think...'

'Think what?'

'Sometimes I think we should never have come down here. I don't want to be like Tom.' His voice was soft and childlike. 'And end up living the rest of me life here. Five more years and we'll be going. We'll have to go anyway. There's clay under us. They'll make us an offer we can't refuse...'

That night, my father went to bed wanting to smash every china object in the house, and my mother felt the chill of Cookworthy fall over them. In the morning, he went into St Austell to see a doctor, who diagnosed mild depression.

After my mother and Tessa left, Clara picked up the letter she had left on the sideboard. She walked slowly into the kitchen, and gave me the envelope. She said nothing, then wandered back into the passage and up the stairs. Half way up she shouted.

'Your mother thinks it's from Chloe. It's from America. Read it in private. I'll be upstairs...'

'I shouldn't. She shouldn't have written to me...'

'Come on,' she said. 'She was the mother of your son.'

I looked at the envelope. It felt light. The writing was Chloe's. Of that I was sure. I tore it open awkwardly, so that it would not be easy to keep the letter in the envelope. She had used blue writing paper. I recognised her hand. A kiss at the bottom.

325, 86th Avenue
Eastern Side
New York
USA

12th February

Dear Ben,

Hi. Hope you are okay. I know this letter is probably a blast from the past, but I figured I should write, maybe to stop you from guessing. When I left, I went back to the States. After everything, it seemed the best idea. I'd like you to know that I really enjoyed the time we had together. I only wished things had gone differently. Anyway enough of that...

Right now, I'm in New York to promote my novel which has just been published here. I'm coming over to the UK next week, with my publisher for some promotion. Perhaps we could meet for lunch or something, though I don't really know where you are. That's why I wrote to your folks. I'm flying into Heathrow on Saturday and I'll be staying at the Holiday Inn, Strathclyde Street, London. (Tel 987 6616)

Give me a call if you want to meet up.
Chloe
xxx

My initial reaction to was to screw the letter up. I'd show her. But I resisted. I called up the stairs to Clara.

'She's coming over. She wants me to meet her.'

Clara peered over the banister.

'Here, have a look.'

I took the letter up to Clara. She read it carefully, without any emotion, or if she did feel anything then her face chose not to show it.

'What does she want?' Clara asked.

'I don't know. I don't want to know really.'

Then came the real question from Clara.

'Are you going to meet her?'

'No.'

'Promise?' asked Clara, a first hint of jealousy in her voice.

'Promise,' I said. 'I'm burning it.'

I stomped down the stairs and went outside. I was ready to throw the letter and the envelope on to the fire. Let them burn, I told myself. But I found I could not and so, as I walked up the path, I tore out the hotel number. The rest of the letter went red, then black, then turned to dust. I had never broken a promise before, but this time my curiosity told me I might have to. But one thing I knew for certain, I was not going to leave Clara. This time she would be my bride.

And outside that day many aged and wonderful things went up in smoke, and the sad thing was that no-one shed any tears.

OF A HAPPY EVER AFTER

...which comes to most good stories.

IT WAS early evening when I carried out the heavy, wooden-cased clock that had sat on Mary's teak sideboard for what seemed like eternity.

Clara had no qualms about it going. I felt the intricate carving on the case, observing that it had been made in Plymouth, probably top of the range in its time, around the early part of the present century. Outside, it was still ticking, the hands moving minutely. Nearer the fire, the ticks seem to increase, and the mechanism rattled.

Then it was over. The clock fell on to the fire, its thick glass face shattered. Only the noise now of sticky flames. I gave the fire a half-hearted poke around its periphery with a galvanised pole, then went inside again.

Clara was sitting cross legged, lotus-like, in the parlour. A veneer drawer taken from a cabinet lay in the passage. Piled in it were countless photographs of her mother, Ronnie Parsons and herself. I slumped beside her on a chair and looked at the smiling faces.

The photographs were grey. No romance here. No brown stained Victorian style cameos. Instead, pictures of people standing next to dry stone faceless walls. In the bleak distance, white cones, upside-down cornets.

There was a more recent one of Clara at Helen's wedding. She cringed at the dress she wore, which was well and truly out of fashion now.

'I'll keep these, I think,' she said, screwing up her face.

'Yes. You want to keep those...'

Clara gathered up the photographs and placed them delicately back into the drawer.

'Tea'll be ready in a second...'

I carried the weighty drawer into the cold passage and rocked it into the grooves of the cabinet. Then I carefully pushed forward and closed the drawer. It shut grindingly.

A smell of potatoes and vegetables swam around the cottage.
'It's only stew,' Clara commented as she stirred the saucepan's brown contents.

I moved to the door and watched the reds of the fire light up the garden and the lower slopes of the tips. I stood silent. Clara busied herself in the oniony kitchen.

'You're worried about something aren't you?' she asked.

I leant against the dern of the door.

'The blood,' I said. 'there's got to be more...'

'No. Surely not. Isn't the Longstone our sort of protector?'

I told her my theory.

'Yeh, that's true. It's holy, like a chalice...'

We both laughed for a release. The conversation seemed absurd. Bogeymen. The big bad wolf. Stone Age fears.

'The clay here,' she said. 'It means something. Something more... but I can't explain anything any more.'

'Neither can I,' I said, 'and it scares me...'

'But we have my mother's books now... And Tom's.'

Neither of us had looked at the books after the incident in the afternoon. The time needed to be right.

'Clara,' I said, 'they worry me even more...'

We looked at each other. Moth girl and moon child. Children of the clay.

We ate, but the food was tasteless. Other things were on our plate. Worries about the land that had shaped us. The sculpturing seemed out of control. Crafting our own lives now appeared impossible. Moulded. Fingered. Spun. Turned. Thrown...

We stopped wondering about the game of blindman's buff we were a part of later in the evening, when we heaved the books into the living room and turned through them. History spun out from them like tiny webs, adhering to our imaginations.

'We've got to copy them,' I said. 'The knowledge in here is priceless.'

'You really think so...'

'No-one will have ever seen anything like this. It is true knowledge. Knowledge handed down orally...'

'From who?'

'Who knows? People on the moor. This, look...'

I pointed to a method of preparation for healing a deep cut on the index finger.

'These are hundreds, maybe thousands of years old. I don't know. From the Druids maybe...'

But there were not only herbal remedies in the books. There was more than old homeopathy. There was information of global significance. Universal significance even; the phases of the moon and the resultant changes on the earth. Ley lines. The stones of the moor. The language of legends. The saints. Travellers. Sellers. Story-tellers. Preachers. Mystics.

I read with amazement what Mary had written about the stone circles that had been destroyed by the clay industry. She had noted that one of the stones had been cut up in the seventeenth century and had been used for stone-walling on the moor. I wondered whether it could have been Saint Austell's hat. There were entries about crystals; the powers and properties of the different types that could be found on Hensbarrow. Details of the heathers that grew on the moor. Old philosophies. Some possibly from the Phoenicians.

All of this was beautifully written and illustrated. The words spun around us in the plain parlour, knitting a web of glory, origins, powers, beliefs, good, evil, truth, childhood, religion. Each page brought a new revelation, new information, a new inquisition; new challenges to old beliefs. The text was absorbing, Clara barely believing her mother could have written so much.

Tom's work, though smaller, contained an equal quantity of information. He explained how he felt he had somehow lost his way. He had forgotten many things, and hated himself for it. The books, as they went on, seemed to be almost written for us. There were words and comments that only we could understand. Some of Clara's went back to the depths of childhood. The books reached towards us, and we pulled them in.

While we were reading, the back door was open. Clara felt a slight chill as the night wore on. Before that we had not noticed the cold at all. Some time had elapsed. It was strange. It was late now; past midnight. She got up off the floor on to the settee and lifted her feet on to the soft cushions. She saw me standing in the doorway, my figure must have resembled a match burning, the light of the last embers at the top of the garden a halo around my head. I shut the door and came back in.

'The fire's okay. Still burning that old carpet a bit...'

Though half term was in February, it had not snowed this year. Sarah and Mike had returned home after the weekend on the train. I had kept the hire car. And to think, I had not wanted to stay long down here.

The house had an atmosphere of late springtime about it. It might have been the raised dust in the air, or the warmer temperatures of the night. Or it might have been the information we had read that night. A new beginning. A new understanding. A way forward... by going backwards. It was time for bed now.

'Come on sleepy eyes. Time to climb the wooden hill...'

Clara placed the twelfth book she was reading on to the stack in the centre of the room. Her initial thoughts of guilt about us sleeping together in her mother's house had now subsided. We were birds of a feather, and now we rested together.

Outside, the night was still. Soon Clara was asleep, no longer needing to dream. I was more restless. I had judged coming to bed wrong. I was overtired and now the starchy sheets had become hot and creased. Frustrated, I threw the pillows out in order to cool off and tried lying on my arm. Then, when my arm got pins and needles, I turned again. Clara woke. I had many things on my mind. The most important thing now, a shaping of my own future. But when Clara asked in a half-awake voice.

'It's about Chloe isn't it? The letter...'

It seemed only right to say yes. That somehow strangely comforted her, and she launched into sleep again. I turned towards Clara again, but it was not the last time I turned that night.

I woke in the morning with a haze of interweaving ideas strewn around my mind; in that state in which you feel light and breezy, almost transcendental; between the conscious and the unconscious.

Then, there is the stretch and the yawn... and then reality dawns. Clara had gone. The pillow still had the dent of where her head had lain. I stretched over and looked at the alarm clock. Twelve-thirty it read. It was never that time. It was not. I checked my own watch. It told me it was an hour earlier. Clara was one of those people who chose to have an early lie on by allowing themselves an hour to wake up, and still get up on time.

My breath smelt awful. I could feel tartar on my teeth. Naked, I went downstairs to the bathroom and started to clean them. The toothpaste was new and oozed out of the tube easily. Then, on the kitchen table, I saw a note.

'Left you to lie on. Gone for a walk up Roche rock. Can you cover over where the fire was. There's rubbish blowing around the garden. Clara. XXX'

I read the note aloud, through my teeth. A few blobs of toothpaste landed on the table, which I wiped with the back of my hand.

Once refreshed, I dressed in my favourite Levi's and a bleached stained smock. Underneath, I had put on a thick itchy jumper. I took a pair of gloves with me. The morning, though sunny, seemed colder than usual. I pulled on my boots and went out into the garden.

The wind blew strips of black burnt material around the moor. I took a shovel and covered over the black heap with earth, the earth on the moor itself, peaty, almost the same colour. Black on black. When the earth ran out I shovelled on some old moss-covered coarse sand that Mary had been waiting to use for a rainy day. This was the rainy day.

The night's restlessness had made me sure. I would have to ask Clara. I wanted to. I knew that soon half-term would be over and I would be travelling back to teach again. I did not feel frantic. After covering the ashes, I calmly took my sketch book and pencils and placed them on the passenger seat of the hire car. Old habits die hard.

The car was costing me a fortune, but that no longer seemed to matter. I wanted to catch her at the rock. It would not have been the same anywhere else. There was something about that place, as if our names had been carved on the stone that made the cell of St Gonand, while we had been away.

The car started first time. I looked southwards. St Austell Bay was a murky grey. There was a trawler near Blackhead, some larger clay vessels out to sea. Even so, the expanse settled me.

On top of the downs the sun was shining through the gaps between the girders of the beacon light, so that the sun appeared criss-crossed and unnatural. The yellow grass of the downs rippled in the wind.

A Land Rover on a clay mission followed me down to Higher Trezaise, where I turned off on to the Roche road. At Roche, the sun became eclipsed by the tourmaline mound that was the rock.

I parked the car next to the ancient stile and locked it. I thought of stories; the wise confessor who lived here, the chapel itself dedicated to the Arcangel St Michael. So many stories, made up because man cannot understand. There were childish thoughts in my mind. Thoughts of train sets and footballs, vearn and lupin fights. That was finished now. Then the lorry Tom had given me, that heavy red painted toy truck.

Now it was in Bristol in my house up there, on a shelf above the television; not passed on to my son. I was singing as well – a mumble of nursery rhymes in a deep unnatural adult voice.

The warm weather had given the bracken an early flourish for the time of year. It was thick, though I knew someone else had got through by the crushed stalks in the peat, and the small heel marks in the black ground. I scanned the rock's profile with the efficiency of a soldier planning an attack.

I had to search her out. It was a hunt for love. This time, I told myself, the something special would be kept forever. I could not see any movement inside the eerie chapel itself, and so decided to explore the smaller of the two main masses. I heaved myself up over several layers of the lichen-strewn rock that was good to feel.

At the top of the largest toothy mass, I could see across into the chapel. There was nothing there, or on the mass on which I now stood. Climbing down again, the sun dazzled me. When I jumped the last few feet at the bottom, I dropped my sketch pad. One of the drawings got dirty inside, but that did not matter. Art, the imitation of reality, was furthest from my mind now. I demanded the real thing.

The chapel called me. I ran up the incline and climbed efficiently up the same ladder I had climbed a hundred times. I knew every crack in the floor of the cell. I was no longer frightened of the leprosy. Now I was calling her name, a siren of my anxiety.

I viewed the rough ground again. She must be up here. I climbed into the chapel itself, becoming king of the castle. There were names carved into the stone. Liz 4 Shaun. Somebody loves somebody else. Beyond the chapel was a small plateau of rock. My heart ticking like Mary's old clock, only the ticks were beats, faster and louder in my head.

'You made it then moon child...?' came a teasing voice.

I stood still, not turning around.

'I'm glad you came. It's so lovely. I've been asleep. Was it you shouting?'

I turned. Life ahead stood before me.

'Marry me,' I said softly. Her face was puzzled.

'Sorry?'

'Marry me, Clara. Please...'

I said it desperately, my voice demanding an instant reply. My features pleaded. There were seconds of anticipation. There was no running backwards. The space on which we stood was small. There could not possibly be an avoidance. I hoped not.

'When?' she asked.

My arms motioned. 'Whenever. Soon. When you like.'

The proposal was not romantic. On my behalf, it was a reaching out, a last grasp. Clara knew it, but it did not dissuade her. She flitted past me and climbed down the iron ladder. I stood very still, trying to control my breathing. My face contorted. She looked up when she reached the bottom. She was skipping.

'All right,' she said quietly, almost so I could not hear, and climbed down the next ladder.

I barely believed it. 'You will?'

I followed. In the cell, the wind dropped. Her face looked over the top of the ladder.

'It's what I've always wanted you know...'

'I know,' I said.

'Follow me then...'

I held the ladder and climbed down with her.

'Come on,' she said, 'It's a wonderful day.'

Clara led me down to a clearing in the ferns. Clara's emotion became explicit. She pushed me down to the ground so that firstly I sat. Then she kissed me. The time for something special. Gradually, I went down with Clara astride of me. Down, down, and in. It was more beautiful than when the morning mist gathered in the sladdy bottoms of the moor, and much more beautiful than the finest porcelain will ever be.

Compared to life, my friends, art is but a single sand grain in many millions, a drop in the ocean...

OF TELEPATHY

...which is the communication of impressions from mind to mind without use of the senses.

THE hiatus of the half term had refreshed me. This time the Cornwall I had gone back to had changed. The dirty bit had become the good bit, the bit I wanted to hang on to now, and never let go. A marriage date had been considered for Easter, and it was this I had in mind when I arrived back at the small terraced house I rented in Bristol late on Friday evening.

Tucked in my wallet, though, was a telephone number whose digits led to the past; a voice at the end from a while back. Some good times. Some bad times. An awfulness when I thought of my son's grave. A piece of him missing.

But I would phone, not to dig up the past or start anything new, but just to see. You know how it is... Curiosity – the thing that killed the cat.

She had been a part of my life. I had made a child with her. I had started a business I wished now I had never ended. I had discovered a lot with her. She made me less vulnerable. Made me tougher. And I had given her a lot as well. Inspiration, I hoped. Love, not always. Ambition, yes, I had given her that.

I tried to recall her smell, the taste of her lips, the feel inside. Somewhere, hers and Clara's mingling, and I hated that. I told myself there was nothing I felt for her now. She had left me, left me to sort out the business and the mortgage, most of the divorce details, though her parents had contacted me and had agreed to help.

Since then, nothing. Nothing until now, and that was what puzzled me. But then, she was not even close now. She was on the other side of the world. And tonight I could forget about her and go to bed with sweet dreams of Clara.

I stayed late in bed in the morning, rising just before noon. I shaved – the beard had gone over half term – and spent the rest of the afternoon in the craftshop at the back of the house working on some sculptures in plaster of paris for the school play.

I determined to try the hotel number in London at four o'clock. That would allow plenty of time for her to arrive and unpack.

Four o'clock came, and the receiver had not been lifted. I had mislaid the number. I searched all over the house, including the workshop. Eventually, I found the scrap in a pair of trousers I had put in the basket for washing.

Once composed, I dialled the number. I heard the relays clicking, the micro-processors singing. Guilt entered me. I was scared Clara might burst in and find me talking to Chloe. A reception voice answered. The hotel. She had arrived. They would put me through. There was a ten seconds delay, which seemed longer, then her voice, the same voice that had once magnetised me.

'Hello. Chloe Evans speaking...'

'Hi Chloe. It's Ben. I got your letter...'

'Oh fantastic!'

Her surprise was genuine. She was glad to hear from me. It had been a long time. The flight went well, though they had been delayed at New York by some kind of security problem. And, yes, it was good to be in England. I was pleased.

'Where are you calling from?'

'I'm in Bristol. I'm teaching here now...'

'What, art?'

'Yes... you got it.'

'Hey, for a moment I thought you were going to say astrophysics...'

'No. Afraid not...' I replied. I heard her giggles. I saw her dark hair being pushed back by her slender hands.

'Your book's good news. I knew you could do it. Is it big in the States?'

'Yeh. It's sold a few copies you know. Hang on a second. Kurt is speaking to me...'

I hung on, my mind wondering who Kurt was, wondering whether I should put the phone down. She was back.

'Kurt's my publisher. He says we're down in Bristol on Monday for a promotion in the afternoon. That's great. We've got to meet for lunch.'

'Lunch it'll have to be. I'm teaching all day Monday.'

'Okay. That's fine. Where shall we meet?'

'At the entrance to the art gallery and museum, at the top of the hill where the university is. I'll meet you at twelve. The school's just up the road... You got all that?'

'Sure. No problem. Be seeing you on Monday.'

'Monday it is then.'

'Bye now Ben...'

I clicked the phone down. Contact had been made. She was just the same, the same woman I had once loved, the woman I had once held. Sucked. Caressed. Kissed. Touched. The woman

Clara and Mary hated. The one Tom never saw. The one who did not belong. The one who had got out. Escaped its clutches, escaped the very paralysis I myself feared I would catch.

She was coming to see me, and a nervousness crept through my body, a paralysing force. In the early part of the evening I found I could work no more, and spent the rest of the weekend laid embryo-like before the television, concerned not about the elephant's trunk that was Cornwall, but about a woman from America, a New World female.

NOT surprisingly, my teaching on the Monday morning was haphazard and ineffective. I almost lost my temper in two of my classes, and sent one boy to see his head of year for acting the fool in a pottery class. The lunch would ease this. Now, I wanted to get it over. Tell her the truth.

When we saw one another, no words were needed. There was an instant recognition and a look of pleasure. Digging up a lost loved one. The pain had gone from both of us now. The memory was there as well. So much was clear from the avoidance of that subject matter. Chloe had barely aged; a few lines around the mouth, but nothing else.

I did however note a change in her personality. She seemed now to lack that confidence, the get up and go that had caused her to leave me, though her legs were still strong and young. Her face stayed wanton. In me, she said, she marked an ease, a turning off of pressure, some portent of satisfaction.

Quite what, she did not know though. And for a minute we just smiled, communicating elsewhere, letting the primitive take over, feeling the pheromones, holding hands the way we used to. Mentally making love. She kissed me. A while ago, with that kiss, I would have been ready to go to bed with her. Now, it felt sweet, a sort of 'thank you very much' kiss. A chocolate box kiss.

'Can we leave lunch?' Chloe asked. 'I want to talk more than eat...'

'Yes. If you want to...'

'Let's just get a snack.'

We crossed the road and bought two cheese rolls in a baker's. I suggested we sat on the steps of the university. Once we had crossed the road and sat, I began.

'So, your book. What's it called?'

'Grafton Street,' she replied. 'It's about my time in London and New York... kind of fictionalised and made more interesting... Here, take a copy. No charge!' She handed me a hardback edition of the book from her bag. It was wonderfully bound, with an arty photograph of Chloe on the back.

'You've kept your name then? You didn't want a pseudonym?'
'No. I didn't want to let that go...'
At our feet pigeons and brave starlings ate the crumbs from the rolls; desperate for food, begging an existence.
'You with anyone?' I asked.
Chloe finished the mouthful she was eating.
'No. I haven't got anybody at the moment.'
I did not want to probe further, but Chloe wanted me to.
'You know, when I left you I went back to London for a while. I met a guy there but it didn't work out. He was a real loser. You know, there's been people in the States, but...'
'...Not really for you.'
'Yeh. You're right. None of them were for me...'
There was a pause – a relief in the talk. Both figures faced forwards. Something passed. As if I knew. Intuition maybe...
'Did you meet me... so we could maybe get together again?'
Chloe turned her head sideways. She did not need to answer. The clues had already been laid. Crumbs dropped.
'Yeh. I thought...'
'I know.'
Then Chloe looked in her own crystal ball. Mind read. Picked up the Tarot cards.
'You're with someone,' she said.
'Yes.'
'Ah well...'
I touched her.
'Look Chloe. I still fancy you. But I'm marrying Clara...'
'I knew it,' was all Chloe said.
She finished her cheese roll. I looked at her.
'It's just we had a lot going once. A lot of real fun...' she pleaded. The tears were ready to roll.
I listened.
'I'd do anything to have you again...'
Her face was not now the confident woman novelist I thought I knew. It was a face desperate for love. A crying for me to take her. Hold her. Make it real. Give her back the innocence. Make her a maid. The whiteness. Clay colour.
'I can't Chloe. Not any more. My commitment's with Clara. I've got happiness with her.'
Chloe held back the tears. They would come later, back in the hotel in London. One last try she thought.
'I know I left you in Cornwall. That was wrong. I was silly. I know I got the book done and I'm rich, but I ain't got anything... anybody.'
She watched my face. It had not changed. She knew. I wanted

her out. She was the jigsaw piece that did not fit. She was from another box. Another puzzle. Another time. We had become muddled.

For a while we sat in silence, mind reading one another, knowing our exact thoughts. Then Chloe's expression changed. She gave an acceptance, a realisation that things were too great for her to untangle, and she was not going to let it upset her. She had realised it before we had met. Writing the novel had taught her that. Her sex oozed back, and she looked into my eyes.

'Come with me.'

'Why?'

'Come on. I want to show you something. I know you'll like it. I did. It brought back some good memories...'

She did not need to say bad memories. That was already understood. I felt her hand around mine, the same hand that used to...

'At least let me have half an hour alone with you.'

I followed her into the art gallery. She led me up to the third level. A few students passed us. Reminders of another time.

In one of the exhibition halls was a Sir Carel Weight Royal Academy exhibition. A 1951 painting; me not even a twinkle in my father's eye – well possibly. The painting was on the end wall. Bold strokes. Oil on canvas. 20 x 24. Private collection. 'Kaolin Mines'. Nothing needed to be said. Our lives flowed in and out of one another. She let go my hand.

'I came in here this morning,' she said. 'This is where I came in... It's also where I go... get out.'

Outside, and it was time for me to return to work. There was an understanding now; a sadness as well, one that Chloe would feel more than me. The goodbyes were simple, short things. False signals.

'Hey. Stay happy, mind...'

'I'll read the book.'

'You're in it,' she said.

Then we both wandered away, thinking of what might have been.

I said I felt too ill to teach that afternoon – which I was – and went home to read the novel until dawn ate the crumbs of the night, and the flocking starlings of Temple Meads railway station left for work.

TOBIAS

9th September 1666.

Vpon my soule, I do not knowe what wille hit oure nation next. Nor do I knowe whenst this hated hot weather willt cease. Some three days ago, I have learnt that one terrible and ferocious fire did engulf muche of London town. Worde has passed down the countrie to us on this forsaken moore. I do praye muche for those burnte to Death. It seems that one eville is no longer enough for this lande. First, oure bloodie war with the Dutche. Second, this greate plague whiche hast ransacked oure countrie. And nowe, but this, one ferocious fire at whiche no matter how many pails of water were throwne, the fire would not be put out. They do saye it started in one Pudding Lane, at a Baker's shoppe. Believe this if thou wilt. I believe twere some prankster.

The Reverende disagrees with me muche, as usual. When I did telle him of this storie, and once he had heard the tale himself, he didst howl with an almighty roar: 'The Devil's doing. Tis his yeare see. Six hundred and sixty six...' And the parishioners, they did shake and quiver with feare. Knowing my good sire as I do, on other occasions I would have no difficultie in laughing betwixt my teeth at this. But nowe, thynges do scare me. More and more I become afraid to walke on the moore alone, especially at the site of the bloodie stones. By my troth, I sense eville at work, and necessarily one great eville. I pray suche catastrophes may never be repeated. And surely men wille come with powers who may ende suche abominable thynges as Plagues, Wars and Fires. An ende must come I feel.

The Reverende, aye, he who stands righte nowe spouting in the fielde, talks much of Damnation and of the Ende of the Worlde. The events vpon the moore, says he, are but signals given by the Devil. In particular, he talks of London for, says he, that is a sinful place, full of, alas, bawds, thieves and all manner of eville people. Yet still he speaks of the showere of bloode. This, says he, is a sign for the people of Hensbarrow Moore to mend their wayes, or the fires of Hell wilt come. I sit awestruck in my study listening to his outpourings, normally consid'red by me to be but horse leavings, and bad horse leavings at that.

I do thynk now that he may have some sense.

They do say the Fire has done a good thyng. What goest the saying? – 'Each cloud has a silver lining.' Folk do telle me that suche a great Fire willt kill many of the rats and creatures carrying the sicknesse. As well as this, and I know it a tragedy, some of those people fallen to the sicknesse willt burn. By this, I mean those who are not stronge enough to walke or runne. In that then, perchance the Plague may ende.

By God, I hope in future times men may not suffer suche pains as this generation, for sorely it saddens me so to see so many agonies and paralysis of the Will. Holy terror, I finde myselfe thynkynge like yonder Reverende. There may be hope for your servant Tobias yet, deare Lorde.

I close praying that you do destroy the Devil deare Lorde, and guide us so that suche misfortunes may never touch man nor beast again. For certain, oure Worlde is one...

T.T.

OF A CRACKED MIRROR

AT the motorway services, Sarah had bought a large extravagantly-wrapped Easter egg, and remnants of the delicious chocolate shell were still being eaten as we turned off Goss Moor and climbed on to Hensbarrow.

This time it was a happy homecoming, to marry the woman I felt truly I had always loved. And Sarah and Mike were happy as well. Mike had recently undergone an operation to improve his walking.

Seventeenth century diaries had been forgotten, and the shower of blood seemed as far away as the South Atlantic. At last, something was graspable, tangible; no longer swimming out of depth.

Our wedding tomorrow. And, best of all, Clara pregnant. A future. It was Good Friday, the first day of the Easter holiday. Mike had taken time off work. He was currently on a government retraining programme, working on computers at an engineering firm in Bath. I had finished my job at the Bristol school. Luckily, I had found a position at a school in Truro teaching art and pottery, which started in April, after Easter.

Our fast car bounced up over the downs, all of us ignoring the mass of Littlejohn's tip, its shadow now stretching across to the barrow itself.

Neither Mike nor I thought of the day we had come up to Cocksbarrow to look for remains of the old Spitfire. That was somewhere else, sealed away; not to be thought of again. But I did think of the day I had waited for Clara at Cocksbarrow crossroads.

I remembered every detail, each strand of blonde hair blowing across her face, and then the crash when we cycled down into Greensplat. All that somehow seemed closer, only yesterday, like as if time had stopped and nothing else had happened. But when I saw my own haggard face in the wing mirror and Mike's leg, I knew it not to be the case. Things had happened. Things could not be changed back.

On the Gunheath side, a pipe-laying team were having an

afternoon cup of tea. I recognised some of the faces, but did not wave. There was a nervousness within me, as if I wanted our marriage to be a secret. That nothing would ruin it. History would not be repeated, I told myself. No red rain here.

Clara was already at Carroncarrow. She would be clearing out inside the old railway carriage at the side. I had been down several weekends to help in the cottage's conversion and modernisation. The railway carriage would be gone soon. The mottled wall had been knocked out between the dairy and the back-kitchen. New kitchen units had arrived, and were ready to be fitted.

It was a gloriously hot day. Not a single cloud passed over the moor. The sea shone a navy blue. The forecast was for another swelter tomorrow. I could already feel it becoming close, though I put this down to nerves and anticipation of tomorrow.

The wedding was at eleven at St Austell Register Office, the same place Tom had married Mary. A reception had been booked at the Carlyon Bay Hotel, with a disco arranged for the evening.

'What's it like to be back again then Mike?' I asked eagerly.

'Just the same. Doesn't change does it?' came the deadpan answer.

From the back seat Sarah spoke: 'You're sure it's okay to stay at your mother's, Ben?'

'Yes. They're expecting us. I said about half past two, so we're on time...'

'What... then you're going to see Clara later?'

'Yes. With you. Make sure everything's all right, if you know what I mean.'

At the bottom of Greensplat, I turned right and accelerated along the new road. Five minutes later we were inside the cottage at Noppies. It had been a while since my parents had seen Michael and Sarah, so the greetings were long and well meant.

My father was on afternoons for the weekend, but had taken the shifts off in order to attend the wedding. In a few months, he was going to retire. Taking the money. His was one of the six hundred jobs to be lost. He was only fifty-nine, but we all felt it was the right move. Leave him time to enjoy something of his life.

My mother and father had booked a holiday in Italy for the summer, somewhere they had always wanted to go. So the talk was of Rome and amphitheatres, of a visit Sarah's friends had made to Florence and Venice. Cornetto jokes.

My mother asked who wanted a cup of tea, as we were thirsty from the journey and the talking. When she counted up who wanted what, I noticed Tessa was missing. In the kitchen, I asked mother where she was.

'I don't know,' she replied. 'She's been awful strange these last couple of days. Hyperactive... I think she's excited. I told her about the wedding. Her back's getting worse you know. She's probably outside. Down the garden...'

I slipped out of the back door and looked for my sister. Unusually, she was silent, sitting on the stone wall at the bottom of the garden. Every time I saw her I felt sad. I felt lucky as well for she loved me so much. Having said that, I hoped our child would not be like Tessa. I hoped for perfection. I dared not think about my feelings if there was not. When she saw me, she gave me a toothy smile that in anyone else would have looked artificial.

'Look,' she said eventually, and pointed a podgy finger over to Carroncarrow.

'I know. My house... where Clara and I are going to live,' I said, and smiled back to her.

But in return, her mouth dropped and she shook her head. Her pupils dilated. I ignored this. It was normal, only more indecipherable than usual.

'Come on. Let's have some tea...'

Tessa walked before me, marching like a Grenadier guard. Inside, initially she spoke to everyone and drank her tea, but for the rest of the time sat in silence, blinking rarely and apparently listening intently.

'So we'll pick you up around seven,' said my father. 'Got plenty of cash on you?'

Before the wedding we were going on a kind of joint stag and hen party – a hag party in The Cookworthy. My parents were coming as well. Mrs Grose was coming up to look after Tessa for the evening.

I left home just as the early evening news was about to begin on BBC-1. I got into the car and drove across to Carroncarrow. In the drive, where normally nothing could be found, there were now littered stock piles of sand and cement, concrete blocks, new wood and lengths of piping. Near the flower bed squatted a skip, full of old plaster and pieces of wood. Clara came out wearing a pair of old dungarees. There was dust and plaster on her face.

'Hi. You made it then?' she said after kissing me.

'Yeh, I wasn't going to let you down...'

'Have you been around already today?'

'No...'

'That's good. I've only been back a while. I went into town this afternoon to get a few things...'

'Well. You seem to have been doing a lot here as well. You're still on for tonight?'

Clara's face looked strained.

'Actually, I've been sitting down for half an hour. I haven't been feeling too good.'
'Where?' I asked.
'My stomach. It's a bit like morning sickness. Nothing to worry about...'
'You sure?'
'Yes... Look. I don't really want to go to this thing tonight feeling like this. I won't enjoy it, and I'll only dampen everyone else's spirits...'
I didn't know what to say.
'You go... enjoy yourself with the others. I really don't feel up to it,' she continued.
'Are you nervous about tomorrow?' I asked.
'Yes, but that's got nothing to do with this.'
'It won't be the same without you there...' I said, moving closer to her and holding both her hands. She looked into my eyes. I spoke.
'I can't wait until tomorrow,' I said in a child-like voice.
Clara kissed me, a long lingering deep kiss, and pressed her full belly into my body.
'Neither can I,' she said.
We kissed again. Then I went back to trivialities.
'Do you think it could be the weather? It's getting warmer as well. Really thundery...'
'Might be,' she replied, 'I'll leave the front door open. Get some air in here...'
I sat on the window sill of the living room. Clara sat opposite on a sheet covered settee. Our minds were churning, spinning.
Finally, together. Moon child and moth girl. But there was no need to say anything any more. Our look told it all.

MY father put the windscreen wipers on to double speed as we drove into St Austell. In just an hour, thundery clouds had formed in the early evening sky out of the haze of the dogsday afternoon. The rain was not cold. It fell with an almost frightening warmth, a reminding warmth that it was there.
I was in the back seat with Sarah and my mother. Occasionally, drops of rain hit my face, coming through the window my father had opened slightly to stop the car from misting up. Mike sat up front, wiping the inside of the windscreen with a duster.
Initially, everyone had been sad that Clara was unable to come, and had tried to persuade her to change her mind. By seven o'clock, I had been unsure whether to leave her since she felt worse than earlier on. However, it was Clara who insisted I go out. But I marked the anger she felt at not being able to come.

But now, everyone seemed determined to enjoy themselves, and if not putting Clara at the back of my mind, I at least sidestepped her, for there were bound to be a lot of people at the pub and the pressure was on me not to let them down.

My fear now was that it would develop into an extremely childish stag night and I would find myself left naked and blind drunk wandering about the town. Because of these concerns, the rain did not bother me.

Inside the pub, we hung up our coats and were greeted by cheering. There were many faces I knew inside, and by the end of the evening I would have spoken some twaddle to them all, my speech becoming absurder as the night blasted on. I made an announcement about Clara – that she wasn't coming. This was greeted by cheers, which at first annoyed me; then I saw the funny side of it. Mike ordered a pint, and the partying began.

And in this temple to Cookworthy and what he started, the partying went on all evening, until last orders were rung. Then the glasses were collected and the ladies and gents were asked to make their way home.

Outside the rain fell, but this time not an ordinary rain but a rain so torrential that the streets of St Austell were flooded and the debris and flotsam of the drains floated along. So heavy that the water rose in the town centre and flooded Tesco's. So heavy that the water in the white river in Gover Valley burst its banks. So heavy that the sponge that was Hensbarrow could not take any more.

And up in the pits the hoses were switched off and the pumps put on ten to suck it out. And the Cap'ns bit their nails. And the bosses gnashed their teeth over the lost profits.

And in places, the white streams oddly became stained a crimson colour...

Or could it have been that this night, the spirit of St. Austell was crying because the Devil was weaving a storm, and Tessa ran downstairs when the rain eyed her, for she knew. And Mrs Grose chased after her around the house until Tessa, like a playful kitten, opened the door and ran out into the downpour, out into the night. And she may have been wrong, but Mrs Grose was sure she heard her bawling. 'Stop! Stop!'

CLARA lay in bed, having mentally completed her bottom drawer, and still not feeling A1, yet in a half-dreaming and half-conscious state, wishing tonight was our wedding night and she could feel the warmth of her moon child. Her skin was goosebumpy, her breathing slow.

She had been sick earlier on, the sort of sick, she felt, was probably caused by pregnancy. Now, she was more relaxed, and had eased into the whiteness of her bed, feeling a pillow form that she imagined was me, and our bed stretched out over the moor so she could reach over and pick the heather. She felt good. She felt warm.

CLARA did not know it, but in the next thirty seconds she would dream no more, for above the cottage the vessel that was Carroncarrow sand tip could hold no more of the reddish water that could not be seen in the black night.

Already, huge wash fans had appeared at the bottom of the slope, one of them rushing over into the back garden, taking the hedge with it. The sand and rock no longer capable of retaining the moisture, the tip now a wash of sand. Root systems were ripped apart, plants carried in the wet sand bulk. The tip was on the move.

Tessa saw it. Like a lightning bolt, only across the ground. First the centre slumped down. Tessa heard it. 'Plop,' it said. Two lonely sides were left. Then they collapsed inwards. Millions of grains of sand losing their identities.

Friendships broken. Crumbling. Falling. Snaking. Ploughing. The tip collapsed, tonnes and tonnes of sand creeping on to the cottage. Years of Hensbarrow's waste travelling.

The tip buckled the cottage walls as if they were paper. It burst in through the upstairs window. Sand rained on Clara. She woke. But that was her last breath, for the outer wall collapsed, taking the upstairs floor with it. The bed slid down, landing in a pulp of rock, quartz and water.

There was a hand raised above the quicksand, a tragic lady of the lake, but no sword came, only more sand. And like candles on a birthday cake, her life was blown out.

IT was the chance in the million. The impossible. But it had happened. And above where the grate used to be a cracked mirror hung, a mirror Clara had bought earlier that day with some wedding present money; a mirror that had not even seen the reflection of her distraught future husband.

It made national and international news. Reporters were on the scene before dawn had broken, beaming Hensbarrow across the world, showing up the clayland. Across to America, China, down to the Falklands.

Words were used such as 'devastation' and 'landslide'. Cameras were erected on scaffolding. Journalists waited for members of the family and representatives of the clay company to arrive. It was still raining, but the tip had stopped sliding. Excess water now flowed through the sand and into a gorse-clad pit at the bottom of Greensplat.

When first light came, the flashing lights were switched off and the earthmoving equipment was brought in. Fifty tonne trucks – the ones which had dumped it there in the first place – crushed hedges and cracked Tarmac. Steel loaders bit into the sandy lava that had pushed away Carroncarrow. Yellow jacketed clay workers and sad faced firemen did their best to tackle the ultimate clayland nightmare, but it was like searching for a needle in a haystack, like counting the grains.

Each time they dug, more sand caved in. A task to rot the mind. Bulldozers were brought in as well, making the mass more stable.

From the air, a helicopter spun over the site, a film crew aboard. They filmed the sand delta fanning over the moor. How only one person was killed God only knew.

And in the morning news bulletin: 'And now back to St Austell in Cornwall, scene of a major landslide during the night. Martin Russell reports...'

A director of the clay company surveyed the devastation. What was his opinion? Is anyone to blame? He fought off the questions bravely, telling reporters of their one hundred per cent safety record, which was correct until now.

He explained the technicalities of tipping, and how this tip was an older design which was being levelled out. But even the greedy reporters could see this was not his fault. Not anyone's fault. Freak weather conditions had done it.

When they could not get at the truth, they made up their stories to take back to London. They interviewed locals, and used the right language. There would be an enquiry. The company promised to re-examine tipping procedures. It might mean the end of operations on Hensbarrow. The rainfall might be too high.

Questions buzzed on the moor. It was 'Aberfan Revisited', 'The Sandy Tomb', 'The White Pyramid Disaster', according to the tabloids. It was Andy Warhol's 'Everyone is famous for fifteen seconds.' It was media overkill, and Clara was dead.

And on the tip, no-one except me would notice that the clayey soil had a pinkish tinge... and smelt of a pricked finger.

THE party returning from the William Cookworthy had discovered the disaster in the worst way possible. Though the night was wet, in the car we were singing. My father sang as well, even though he had not been drinking in order to drive home. The Friday had turned into Saturday, for we had stopped for some chips on the way home. The windows were wound down, me singing.

'I'm getting married in the morning... Ding dong the bells are going to shine...'

Our spirits were high as the car rose up Gunheath hill; life for me seeming to go up and up. But at the top we were met by a dripping policeman who informed us that the Greensplat road was closed. The car became cold.

'What's the problem, officer?' my father had asked.

The policeman wiped his beard before answering in a formal tone. 'Afraid there has been a tip slide. Quite a disaster really. The rain...'

I strained out of the car and in the night, red lights could be seen. Somewhere, the downs had changed. At first, it was distant, the thing that happens to everyone else. The 'Thank God it wasn't them', but then the more clues the policeman gave, the more the reality began to sink in through the windows of the car, sobering us.

Before the policeman said it, I knew. I could do nothing. I was wedged between my mother and Sarah in the stuffy car.

'It's at Carroncarrow isn't it?' I asked the policeman. And before he could answer – 'The cottage?'

'Yes it, is sir,' the policeman replied, amazed at this man's knowledge.

'Clara,' I said, and the policeman's face crumbled. This man before him was cold and collected. I let my head rest on the rear parcel shelf and I closed my eyes. I thought of everything and nothing. Internally, I felt my organs collapse.

In the rain I heard the policeman's radio croak above my family's attempts at consolations. Then, the sick came over me. The nausea that one instantly recognises. The butterflies, those butterflies that twist and fight inside. We could go no further this way now. It felt like the end of the road. And in the morning, I knew that no confetti would fly...

THE disaster was inescapable. Over Saint Austell's land, it was everywhere. At Noppies an atmosphere of disbelief pervaded, a sense of this not being real. But when my parents stood at the window and looked across, they saw the grey mass that used to be Carroncarrow tip sprawled over the moor like a beached jellyfish, like the ones we used to find on Charlestown beach. Hordes of people went up on to the moor over the weekend to see it. Now the police had closed all roads that crossed the downs.

They found Clara's body on Saturday morning. My father carried out the identification. I was too distraught. It would be like a grotesque parody of burying someone in the yellow sand at the seaside.

My mother probably thought back to her own childhood when her father had buried her on holiday in Great Yarmouth. Only now, she thought about Clara not being able to breathe, the suffocating way she had died. I had seen it all before, though, as if in a premonition. I thought of the cow and her unborn child, who had died in the mica.

An enormous amount of compensation was offered by the clay company. A man arrived at Noppies one Sunday. I did not speak to him. My father talked with the representative for most of the afternoon. But there would be no problem. Compensation would be paid. The company was forced to take responsibility. Short of God, there was no-one else to blame. This was definitely a case of there being more to life than money but, as my father said: 'It helped.'

I blocked it out. I dealt with it differently this time. Not the continual breakdown and reassembly of events, as when Anthony died. Now, there was no acknowledgement of it even happening, at least to my family. I felt it best to stamp on my thoughts. Catch them before they grew out of control.

But try though I did, they came back, reproducing in the night; not only the death of Clara, the woman I had loved for so long, but also of our child. It was worse because of that. Two lives in there. I had not been up to the scene. I could not, and so was forced to imagine what it was like. I was being treated for shock.

For much of the time, I just lay on my bed recalling childhood, stepping back into innocence, remembering things Tom had said to me. Old philosophies. Old words. Times of boys and maids. But now, I was the man and the only way of dealing with it was to let the adult phrases ring out beneath the tears.

I was externalising it, throwing out the hurt, flinging it at the world. Everything was narrowing, coming closer I felt, drawing inwards. Somewhere, I wanted to get off this roundabout that pained me. I was clinging to the handle, spinning, my foot was dragging on the floor, going round and round, scuffing leather on new shoes. New shoes for a wedding.

Then, there was Tessa singing happily in the next bedroom. She knew. She had known on Friday. The innocence. Her sixth sense. Like why only children have tooth fairies. Why children can speak to ghosts. Primitive. A force to move mountains. She had felt something. I pictured her chubby finger pointing up to Carroncarrow. I should have known. One day, I would ask her. When she was old and wise...

I was lying with my feet up on the pillows, upside down on the bed. I wore only my underpants and a T-shirt. Normally, it would have been cold up there, but my blood was still boiling and I needed no warmth.

Soon, I would have to go to the toilet. Let the body carry on again. Forget about the spirit. Twisting, I scratched my groin and spun around on the bed to look at some of the paintings and sketches on the walls.

Standing on a shelf above my head, some of my favourite pieces of pottery, now gaudy figurines in blues and greens, turquoise couples, occasional pots that had worked and could never be repeated; none of them with eyes but all staring at me.

I reached up for one of the pieces. It was a ballerina study I had done at college. The form now so fragile, so remote, so pretentious. So much art. I hated it. Still here, when the real had gone. I envisaged a future archaeologist finding it on the moor still perfectly preserved. I imagined them finding Clara's bones.

I broke the ballerina in two, not a violent aggressive break but a delicate snap, like the sound of a twig when a foot trod on it. But the snap felt good, and instead of being destructive I felt constructive. I got up, switched off the light and went downstairs.

Under the arc lights the cleaning up continued. Sand and stone being carried away. Corpuscles too, red and white. Remnants of the cottage as well now. Pieces of furniture. Ornaments. Crockery. Tools for the conversion. Paintings. Shards of glass from a mirror. Pieces of paper... were what I thought about as once more I climbed the stairs.

The books! In my anxiety about the future, I had forgotten about the past. Precious gems buried in the sand. The Cornish had entered me. I knew I had to dig. Get them out. Save them. They might still be there. The last time I had seen them was under the table in the living room.

A future flowed back into me; not my future, but a future for others. Something special up there; buried. I had to get at them before they were turned to clay as well and became nothing. They would be there, I told myself as I pulled on my now smoky and sweaty trousers from the suit I had worn to The Cookworthy. That did not matter now. I flung the coppers out of my pocket and they rolled around the floor.

I went downstairs, briefly stopping to see the mournful faces in the living room. I said nothing, then ran out to the car, grabbing a shovel on my way.

A light drizzle still fell and a fog hung low down the dip at Blackpool. I drove carefully, but quickly. I knew that access to the area would be difficult. A few reporters were still there, warming their hands on cups of soup and black coffee from a caravan, but most had moved on, gone to the next headline, to greener pastures.

I was no longer confused. I knew what I wanted. I knew what was necessary. Mourning could come later. It could kill me, but I did not care. Clara would have agreed with me. I tried to imagine the place as it was. A mound covered it. A new creation. On the horizon, there was a gap where the tip should have been, half of it washed away. A policeman stopped me: 'I'm afraid that area is restricted, sir.'

I glared at him. Authority was stopping history.

'It's my house. Where I was going to live...'

The policeman was experienced: 'Sir, I cannot grant access to that area while the earthmoving equipment is there.'

I looked over the hedge and saw the scrapes and loaders munching the sand.

'Look.' I got angry. 'It's my house. I'm Ben Sexton... I was supposed to be marrying Clara Parsons.' I was surprised at my ability to be unemotional now about her name. The situation demanded it.

'I want to rescue some things... private things... before it all goes...'

Authority relaxed. The policeman warned me to be careful. I ran into the area, slushing through the mud and up to where I thought the cottage was.

'Who's that?' one of the reporters asked.

Off guard, the policeman told him it was Mr Sexton. No other cue was needed. They overran the officer and entered the area.

In the meantime, I made my way to the shell of the house. For a second, I tasted death, smelt the clay. Saw the bloody water the way Tobias had told it. I went into the parlour. Much of the sand had gone now, as had most of the furniture.

I searched where I thought the books were. A loader passed me, with tyres higher than a man. When it had passed by, the journalists descended on me with flashing cameras and questions. I shied away from the photographers and answered as best I could. The police were there. My mind was on history. There was aggression, the grasp for the scoop. The lover. The broken man. The one piece of the story that was still missing. The human angle.

Among the violent feet, I caught sight of a sheet of paper in the mud. It was no longer readable, but the paper was thick and creamy. Even in the mud it was good to touch. I ran closer to the snaky glacier that the loaders ate into. A driver stopped what he was doing, realising I wanted something.

'What is it?' he asked.

'Books,' I said. 'Books under the table...'

'It's all gone chief. Taken away a few buckets ago. There wasn't much of it left.'

'Where?' Where has it all gone?'

'Down Blackpool way. They're back-filling down there. Look...' They were still in pursuit.

I turned and tripped, my face landing in the wet clayey sand. I was shaken. There was blood before me. I imagined it was from my nose by the way it felt, but then I stood up. No, the nose was fine. Nothing broken. Nothing cut. No, the bloody liquid oozed in the sand the way mica used to. It seemed to soak out of the sand and trickled towards the pit.

So, they spoke the truth. Tom and Tobias. The land having its revenge, and not caring who it swept away... the same as that mining scavenger who did not care what part of the moor's carcass he stripped away. Hensbarrow protects those who love her.

Maybe, just maybe, that's why I survived...

I needed no other cue. Dodging the reporters and police I returned to the car and drove to where the fifty tonners were back-filling. The drivers honked at me for getting in the way of the giants, entering their territory. A wrong move and the car would have been pulped.

I came to a halt where the ground was fresh. Two dumpers screeched a warning of their reversing. Once out of the car, I stood between them and watched greasy hydraulics lift their earthy buckets. Grains of sand fell over the edge. Beneath lay muddy water. Then a few more rocks fell. Ten more degrees and the mass tumbled out. Tonnes of waste rock and sand. Which ones had killed Clara?

'What do ee want?' came a voice.

A half-shaven driver chewing a sandwich came towards me.

'My furniture... and some books...'

'That's all gone boy. Went down half an hour ago. Buried up to the nines now... and there's no bugger going down there... not in a month of Sundays... A deep pit that one.'

Tears formed in my eyes at this man's simple words. But he did not know what lay down there. No-one did. Down there lay secrets, turning to clay. Down there lay past and future, fruit that no-one no longer wished to taste.

The buckets of the dumpers hissed down and the man left me alone. I tried to recall what was in the books, the secrets they held. I could try telling people, but I would be dismissed as a crank.

The books had the facts, the evidence, the truth. And now I only had stories for the telling.

TOBIAS

29th October 1666.

Blackened London town ist to be rebuilt. In that smouldering city, they do say chaos ist all, and that looters and all kinds of vagabonds do wander the streets, pillaging the remains of the fire. And, believe this as well, that some four and eighty churches, including Saint Paul's, did burn. This indeed is most terrible. Figures arrive here of thirteen thousand houses destroied in four days. Perhaps, dwellers there willt now build their houses of stone instead of plaster and timber.

The Reverende dost not believe there will be any other tragedies to affect oure nation. Each of the three sixes of the yeare have affected us. First the War, then the Plague, then the Fire. Brewer dost say to me that the Fire comes last, as in his notion of the pit of Hell.

In the last yeare yon Reverende has aged enormously. He now talks by slapping his chest to give himself breath. He lives in the next room to me, reading from the Bible before sleeping. I continue here with my diary.

I pray the negotiations for Peace shalt begin with the Dutche, for oure Nation willt soon be poore and without Allies. With luck, we shalt retain New York and New Jersey.

Good Susanna ist, she dost telle me, withe child. I plan one hasty wedding before any sign of the child dost show. I dare not telle the Reverende. He willt die soon, knowing that I have become a good servant to the church, whilst leading a Christian life. I am no longer as certain on how the worlde's future may evolve. The events of the past two yeares have soured me completely. Fortunately, I finde muche solace in the company of my family. I contemplate vpon returning westwards to take up a higher position. The mining industry does increase down there, and places of worship do sprout up continually.

I must confess, these days, by what I have hearde, that I have more time for superstition and stories that men do telle others. I worrie for the people of this land. They have no future. The ground is but of little use at all. It perplexes me more that this land hast the Devil's presence o'er it. I assume this, since he did win 'gainst the Saint. Only one holy relic remains. For certain, that must stay upon the downs, if the land is not to be totally at Evil's mercy. The land hast a power.

I close tonight praying for the future and of those souls who come to live on this land. I pray for the Hensbarrow children. May they continue to walk 'mongst the heather, lie in the sladdys and take notice of oure ill-consider'd ways. They will have more sense deare Lorde... than the fools of oure Age...

T.T.

OF RE-ENTRY

HOME, they say, is where the heart is. I sat in my father's former armchair in the cottage, eating my breakfast, trying to track down the pieces of my shattered heart.

And, dare I say it, my mind. Sure, large chunks could be found here, but there were other smaller pieces scattered everywhere. I had the emotional glue, I had the time and the patience I never had before, when repairing cracked porcelain.

Finding the pieces was the problem. There seemed to be so many. Simply thousands of fragments. I had tried before but now the task seemed impossible. I was the warrior on Hensbarrow counting the grains of sand. I was the Hensbarrow hermit, a reincarnation of the fellow on Roche rock. I was tied to the black crucifix of the Shackleton, and gorse wound its way around my head.

Outside, I could hear the creaking of the 'For Sale' sign in the Hensbarrow wind. The sign had just been shoved in the rough grass at the front of the cottage and was insecure. People had come yesterday to view the house. A chap who worked at Blackpool refiner. He wanted another bedroom, though. Said he would have to spend a lot 'doing it up'. I cared, but did not wish to think about it. It would go to the clay company in the end.

Maybe I knew no-one would want to buy the cottage. It was close to the edge now. It would go the same way as Noppies, crumbling like Weetabix in my bowl.

My mother, father and sister had gone away. They had gone away from the dirty bit. My grandmother had left them her house in her will back in Southend. It was the right move. My father had taken early retirement. He had done it; got out. Found the key and opened the cage.

They stayed until I was more myself again. Comforted me. Said the right things. But there was a limit. And there was no need. I was all right now, or that's what people said to me. Or else they said: 'Got over it...' or sometimes they said nothing at all. And when there was no-one else to talk to often that made things worse. Chewing tasteless cud.

Of course, there was no denying that things had shaken me forcibly. Life... a continuous pneumatic drill. The pain a monotonous noise heard every day. The things that could have been, but the ground was old now and had been trod over before. And what was the use of crying over spilt milk. I had to bring the cow down again. Milk everything for what it was worth...

At least I was home. I had done it, I told myself, gone away and tasted things, felt things. And for now that was good enough. It was like the live landing of the Space Shuttle on the television that morning. The crew coming home after looping the earth, drifting over Hensbarrow. Feeling the warmth of re-entry, the black tiles a protection against the heat. A sweat beneath the crews' underarms.

Then, in the blue, the first sight of her. A white blob in the Arizona cloudless sky. Up go the Northrop fighters to guide her in. And the Shuttle breathes a sigh of relief when she lands.

I knew Chloe would be watching this. She was always fascinated by space, and some of her enthusiasm had rubbed off on me. Man probing into the blackness, reaching for contact, asking questions, pleading answers, playing with fire. New frontiers. New stories. Discovering. Challenging. Digging. These feelings upon re-entry. Greater than that, being down to earth. Earthbound. Rooting... And yes, curiosity did kill the cat eventually.

These days, I did not try to think. I just did. I found it better that way. More manageable. That's why I washed up the breakfast dishes with the radio at full volume. Used nice things to keep evil things out. But when I did think it was always about lost opportunities. The incredible way it all happened.

Last night I had read Chloe's novel again. Pointless really; I knew almost every word. I just wanted to feel the pages, scan the paragraphs as though she were next to me. Some kind of runners-up prize in a quiz show. A consolation. If only I had responded better to her in Bristol she would have kept in touch.

After Clara, we could have got together again, sculpted a rebirth. But that idea had to be aborted. She was a big wheel now in the States. A best-seller. She would have left any Celtic memories behind. The plastic surgery would come next. And so, this was the snakes and ladders of life. Some were climbing up the rungs, others were slipping down the reptiles' backs. Back to the egg.

And there was a jealousy. Not for love. Not for a future, but for a child. I would see them, the children of the moor. The eight year olds, those the same age as the Anthony who never quite was, who might have played with him the way Mike and I did. I saw them touch the gate posts, leap over the stone hedges. Maybe some of them the rock from Saint Austell's hat. Hear them laughing, crying, shouting, believing, the same way I used to.

I wanted to give them the tin plate lorry Tom had given me. But they had other things now. Computers, televisions, laser guns and rockets. They would not need the lorry. They would not know what to do with it. They had no room for play. Babies born the adult...

And I felt inadequate because I could not tell them stories when they passed by the cottage. Not like Tom. He was special, he oozed of mysticism. I was different somehow. I was beginning to understand it all, but I had no real knowledge, not like in the books. Not like the earlier diggers.

Time was passing. Soon, I would have to go to afternoon shift. I'd started with the company again. It was quick changeovers as well. Home at nine to get up at four. And then not being able to sleep, so you ended up dog-tired.

It was just under a year since Clara had died. Her body was buried over at Nanpean churchyard. Green sparkling crystals covering her cold body. When I visited her I changed the flowers. I took the vessel over to the trough that was always full of leaves, under the dark bushes, wash it out and scoop in fresh water, so cold I wanted to drink it. But I never did. It was water for the dead.

And now I could weigh it up, look up to Goverseth refining plant, back up to Longstone's pit, over the recently re-surfaced road where I had walked in the carnival. Where I had first seen her. But I always told myself that moths were delicate things. Their lives were short. They were born, they made love, then they died. And this helped her soul to re-enter me.

After arranging the flowers on Clara's grave, I walked back down the red sand path to Anthony's small grave. I never stayed there long. I couldn't.

I never started the Truro teaching job. There had been a another job advertised in Bodmin for a pottery teacher. Someone with experience. I could have walked into it. But I did not want the pressure, pressure greater than the hose this time...

I was back in the pit again. The gang found it ironic. I was the one with the education, the artist now back in Cornwall working with them. I realised I was lucky to return to the industry. Jobs were scarcer now. The work computerised. Button pressing, digitised. Holes bigger than before. Holes in people's hearts as well as the earth.

So, I was back digging. Digging the material I used to work with. Cookworthy's genius. The stuff that when glazed and painted and formed into art sold for thousands. The stuff I could shape no more. I had lost all desire to create anything artificial. I no longer had a need to mimic. Now I demanded reality. The day before I started I shaved off the beard I grew after Clara's death. Had my hair tidied.

I was thinner too. Dents in my cheeks. Ribs showing where once a stronger chest had been. And yet I had been eating as normal, even after Clara had died. But it felt good. Cutting down on the cholesterol, getting rid of the rich Cornish food the holiday-makers loved. Out with the pasties and out with the cream teas.

Change had occurred, and yet it had passed me. The tips I knew as a boy were grassed over now. You could not slide down them. And there I was, in the monitor hut, the start of one dream and the end of another. Something had pulled me back here. It was the fantasy destroyed. It was the rest of my life. It was returning to earth. It was my death. It was the way I stared at the rockface, the way my tongue lay motionless on my teeth, the way a numbness entered my legs. It was a paralysis and a destiny, the same way a moth flies into a flame.

LONDON'S orbital and often chaotic ring road, the M25, is perhaps better known now than a seaside resort in Essex. And so to the left of Junction 29 on the M25 lies Southend-on-Sea, where a lone young woman absurdly played on a beach with a bucket and spade watched by her parents.

The father was asleep, soaking in some of the spring sunshine. His head rested on his sheepskin coat. He had fallen asleep listening to the sports round-up on the radio. He felt safe and secure, though only a few feet away waves washed in over the dull sand and pebbles.

Next to him sat his wife. Outwardly, she looked happy, but if one looked closer there was a pensiveness in her eyes, a realisation of the fragility of existence. But then, appearances are deceiving... aren't they...?

On the beach, a few other families were making the most of the first of the warm weather. There was still a coldness in the air, but it made little difference to the children who splashed in the sea, the boys and maids with buckets and spades.

A dog was barking, a cutting growl, while chasing a football across the shore. They had been eating ice creams a few minutes ago, and a few crumbs of the cornet had fallen on to the woman's stomach and legs. She did not stand to remove them, knowing her figure was not what it used to be; a world away.

In the sunshine it was difficult to think of anything but good things. Like when the young woman had made the tea without any help. She was now digging in the sand.

Her mother could see how deformed her back had become as she grew older. There was a visit to the hospital next week, which her mother always dreaded and her daughter detested.

The father, woken by the dog barking, kept his eyes shut, only allowing small filters of sunlight to steal through the tiny gap in his eyelids. He was wondering if they could sell the cottage down there, the place he had worked hard to keep going for much of his life.

But he knew the reality. Unless a buyer came quickly the clay company would buy it at a reduced rate and drill bore holes. After that, another Downser's dwelling erased. Extinction.

Earlier in the day he had been sorting out things they had brought up from Cornwall. He had stopped when he discovered his son's pictures, all bound and covered. He had uncovered them. He did not understand them, nor the sculptures and pots. The garage was full of pieces of art. He remembered what his son had said when they had left.

'Take them away. They're of no use to me. They're imitations... that's all.'

The man looked at them again, and felt proud. He felt a sense of guilt as well. He remembered his initial disinterest in his son going to art college. Then it seemed so alien. When his son made money out of it of course, he changed his mind. But it had all gone wrong from there. His son in Cornwall now.

Then he rose out of these thoughts and propped himself against the concrete base of the promenade. The mother was with a young woman near the water's edge. He watched them. There was an amazement in her expression. A return of wonder. She was looking closely at the beach where the woman, by now identifiable as her daughter, had been playing.

'Come down here,' she cried to him. 'Come here!'

There was an urgency in the tone of her voice.

The man stood up by sliding against the promenade, narrowly missing hitting his head on the overhang. He tip-toed across the pebbles and beach debris to the softer, darker sand where Tessa and Pat sat.

'See this...' she said.

He looked at the creation beneath his feet. In the sand, the daughter had created a three dimensional map. It was instantly recognisable. Tiny grains of sand fell down the scaled down tips. It was the something else Tessa had – her sixth sense – a greater intelligence. Taking things in that did not seem to matter. The map was to scale, and full of intricate detail. An exact model of Hensbarrow. The clayland. The daughter smiled as her father gazed in amazement. Then she became bored and jumped in and

out of the waves. Words were coming out like they did so often from her, in an unpunctuated monotonal mass. But they caught two words before the map was washed away by the swish-swash of the Thames estuary waves. The old language.
'Pry Wyn,' she was shouting, and it could be heard all along the beach. She stopped when the last of the miniature tips had been washed into the sea, and her parents calmed her down.

THE stork had passed by, or someone had searched under the gooseberry bush. These are the mythologies of birth my friends. The cover-up for children, and how they are made. Don't tell them about the pain and the agony, the blood and the afterbirth. That's only for adults. X-certificate stuff. And don't tell them on Hensbarrow the Shack passes by, or someone searches under a gorse bush. No, don't dare tell them that, for it might be a lie... or a myth, like Saint Austell and the Devil, or the shower of blood. And no-one says anything about medicine and hospitals, but it had done the trick. Mike's operations. Micro-surgery, where the landmine had hit.

And now Sarah held a baby tight against her. Her baby. What they had always wanted. This had not been a birth under a gooseberry or gorse bush. It was a maturing woman's birth, not a Mary with her hessian sack birth. It was a clinical precision birth, a green masked, oxygen-assisted whiter than white birth.

It was what they wanted. No chances taken.

And so the birth was very perfect. So walking down the steps of the hospital, with Mike struggling yet succeeding in keeping up with his wife, this baby did not cry. It just smiled and smelt of innocence. And for longer than a minute, maybe two, Mike forgot.

Suddenly the Falklands were no more. He could understand now. Forget, and look forward. He had a daughter whose hand was as big as his greasy, once trigger clicking and mine-detecting index finger. Contact had been achieved.

When his daughter opened her eyes inside the taxi home from the hospital, he cried. Not the same kind of crying he had felt when his mother clipped him round the ear for forgetting the vuzz for the fire but a crying that told everyone he could still be someone. But when they got home, and when they placed the baby in the cradle at the bottom of their bed; when he thought deeper, he knew it to be a crying for Ben, of something he might never have.

They were in Bath, now encased in culture. The sandstone buildings. The black iron railings. The 'Who will buy my sweet red roses?' crescents.

The baby shops full of designer clothes. The normality. This child would grow up different to Mike. It would know nothing of the old ways.

That's the way they wanted it. No stories. And when the maid, the cheild, Victoria Emily, cried in the night, or was sick, neither Mike nor Sarah wanted to use homeopathy.

Besides medical science is wonderful now, you know.

Good to know if one needs to be ridded...

OF A MADNESS

...In this newe Year yon bloodie white stones have been smashed, muche to the Reverende's pleasure. When news of this arrives, his condition does improve. It is likely that some of the stones shalt be kept as evidence of this shower, though I know not where. I says to him that fellows shalt listen more to oure elders and betters now. I supplie him with books and sticks of sugar to keep his spirits up. He, for a change, is grateful and consid'rate. The Longstone stays, though I have a notion alas that soon it will be removed...

I NOW knew that the force I had been fighting with was stronger than I ever could be. Its only match might have been found in the books. There was to be no bartering or reconciliation. It was not possible. I could see what had happened but I could not understand it.

Had I been a microcosm caught in the spiral of history? That is what I felt like. A rotten history I had stumbled upon. A land I had not even been born in. Now just a dot on the landscape, a full stop on a sheet of white paper. A moon child falling back to earth. I felt it was the primitive playing with me, sucking the edges, toying with a life.

I had been for treatment. I had tried putting it down to coincidence, but found I could not. Recent events had swayed me too far. I knew I was losing my hold, slipping so the monitor would splash back stones in the spray. I could hear them cracking on my eggshell helmet. But the clay was still being dug. That was the important thing. And the dirty bit stayed the same while they still dug. It seemed the clay would always be dug whatever.

...More so, I believe we are through this time of darkness. Peace has been made with the Dutche scoundrels over the Newe Worlde, though they do say that oure Nation is bankrupt and hast not two coins to rub together. This matters little though, since the Dutche, I am told, have not any items to rub together!

The Plague dies now. In fact, I canst not recall any newe outbreaks in oure Countie...

AND I had secrets; You-tell-me-yours-and-I'll-tell-you-mine secrets. But not just secrets. More than that. Powerful secrets.

But I dared not mouth them. They would think me a fool, a simpleton.

So I never spoke about them, and the rotting books that lay in a back-filled pit stayed there, alongside the waste that had killed my ripe bride.

When it rained I did not care. I just got on with it. Put on my oilers and forgot about the Reverende. Pretended I was Tobias and ignored superstition. So I would not mind walking under ladders or not touching wood, or not throwing spilt salt behind my left shoulder. And I did not mind not knowing the truth. I had no feeling for order. No quest for peace. I was the upside-down and the topsy-turvy. I was the clouds and the carnival. I had no need of stories...

... 'Tis most strange; fellows do arrive upon the Moore with tools and items to dig. I hears last week that they find small tin deposits twixt Karslake and Carroncarrow. To win the ore alack, they must first dig through layers of useless clay whiche they do fling in small heaps about the Workings. This is an ill consider'd pursuit. I am certain it will not last..

AND one Sunday it was I who was up at dawn to drive to Roche. I had stopped at Harmony Close. There was a desire in me, a desire to shift the blame. It was his fault – Saint Austell's; the Holy man. I did not know the reason. I just knew it was the fault of the Saint. Had he not been strong enough against the Devil? Could he not beat the clay and live on? At least I could desecrate his memorial, the Longstone; no longer a menhir, now the staff of Saint Austell. The protector had failed me.

In my car I had cans of spray paint. I put two in my pockets and held the other two in my hands. Then I shut the boot, using my elbow. I sprayed in a frenzy, shouting, screaming, doing tiss-tosses across the grass, spraying my face and clothes. And once close to the stone, I eyed it like an artist about to begin my creation, a canvas on which to let go.

Run riot. And so I did, spraying curses at Saint Austell. Language on the stone. Defacement. Looping the stone and spraying. Spraying paint like the monitor did water, but the stone was not falling.

And by and by, the lights in Harmony Close were switched on, and in the early morning arrived the white car with the blue flashing light that told the artist it was time to go. And so the graffiti stayed, and I got away.

But they were following. I was clipping edges. I had lost my wing mirror. They were close behind. Another car had been called for and was travelling up the Cocksbarrow road. I saw it, and spun off on to the sandtrack. I got out and ran. It was clayey, but I had lost the knack, and it could be shaped no more.

I was running across the moor away from them. I wanted to smell the foxgloves, taste the urts, cloud watch again. Watch the Shackletons. Hear stories of warriors and princesses. But they were following. Those who would take me away. Away from the clay.

I took handfuls of it, smearing it over my face, then plastered my clothes with it. Then I lay down in the heather, and felt the earth spinning. They could not have me now, I told myself, and squelched my hands together.

It was sunny, and it would not rain. The skylarks were singing.

Then I saw the figures above me, black menhirs of agony, their shadows forcing me down.

I closed my eyes, feeling a white, cold grit under my eyelids. The shadows moved closer, digging deeper. Now at last the dream time could begin again.

After the clay...

THE END